SINFUL EVER AFTER

A Sinful Serenade Sequel

CRYSTAL KASWELL

Also by Crystal Kaswell

Sinful Serenade
Sing Your Heart Out - Miles
Strum Your Heart Out - Drew
Rock Your Heart Out - Tom
Play Your Heart Out - Pete
Sinful Ever After – series sequel

Dangerous Noise
Dangerous Kiss - Ethan
Dangerous Crush – Kit
Dangerous Rock – Joel
Dangerous Fling – Mal
Dangerous Encore - series sequel

Inked Hearts
Tempting - Brendon
Playing - Walker
Pretend You're Mine - Ryan
Hating You, Loving You - Dean - coming summer 2018
Breaking the Rules - Hunter - coming fall 2018

Author's Note

Dear readers, thank you for sticking with the Sinful Serenade series though the last four books. I love these guys to pieces. I hope you love them as much as I do :)

Sinful Ever After is a sequel to the first four books in the Sinful Serenade series and it should be read after book four (Pete's book, *Play Your Heart Out*). It is the last Sinful Serenade book, but don't dismay. It's not the last of the Sinful Guys! Miles, Drew, Tom, and Pete will be appearing in spin-off series Dangerous Noise. The first book, featuring guitarist Ethan and his heroine Violet, is available now!

Get *Dangerous Kiss* here.

For every boy or girl who ever stepped on stage and sang, strum, rocked, or played his heart out.

SING FOREVER

Chapter One

MEGARA

That can't be him. It must be a mirage. There's no way Miles is standing in front of the bio building, his hands in the pockets of his leather jacket, his lips curled into a smile.

I must be imagining things.

He's supposed to be in Tokyo. Or was it Osaka? It's hard to remember your boyfriend's schedule when he's a globe-jetting rock star.

His blue eyes fix on me.

That's him.

That's really him.

"You survived your first semester of medical school." Miles slides his arms around me.

His arms are heaven. I grab onto his waist as tightly as I would if I were on the back of his bike. Miles is here. My boyfriend is here. We have the next four weeks to be together before I'm due back for Spring semester.

His hand curls around my cheek. "I missed you."

"I missed you more."

He presses his lips to mine.

He tastes so fucking good.

I dig my hands into his leather jacket. It's too slick for me to get a grip, so I tug at his soft t-shirt. He's here. He's not in Asia. He's at UCI Medical School, with his arms around me, with his lips against mine.

I slide my hands under his t-shirt and soak in the warmth of his skin. "You're supposed to be in Japan. Didn't you have a show?"

"In Osaka." He pulls me closer. "Encore was fourteen hours ago."

"You flew straight here?"

He slides his hand around my neck. His voice is light, teasing. "You catch on fast."

I flip him off. It only makes my smile wider. At the moment, it doesn't feel like I'm ever going to stop smiling. "Give me a break. I've only slept ten hours in the last week."

He smiles back. "Good thing I'm planning on spending the next two weeks in bed."

I nod and look up at him. I'm nearly six feet tall, but Miles is still two inches taller. "I can't believe you're here."

I haven't seen him in a month. Twenty-nine days, to be exact. His band, Sinful Serenade, has been on an international tour. This was the first tour where neither one of us could visit.

It's the longest we've been apart.

It's been awful.

Miles spends four or five months a year on the road. I should be used to it by now, but I'm not. Every time he's away, I miss him more than the time before. Every time, he feels farther away.

Every time, the separation is sweeter.

I missed him so much.

My knees falter as I sink into his body. I'm too tired to move. But it's okay. He's got me.

He pulls me closer. His lips hover over my ear. "How is it that none of your classmates recognize me?"

I nestle into his chest. "Do you want me to scream 'Oh My God, are you really Miles Webb? I love that one song you do, *No Way in Hell*.'" I offer my best schoolgirl giggle. "Is it really about falling in love?"

"I want you to scream." He sucks on my earlobe. "But only the Miles part, and only once we're alone." His hands go to mine. "You have any energy left?"

"Enough for a proper reunion."

He laughs. "I'm not sure you do." He squeezes me one more time then he steps back. He nods *follow me*.

I take a shaky step. Miles has a point. I can barely walk. I'm not sure I have the energy to fuck his brains out the way I want to.

His expression is a mix of amusement and concern. "I'm taking you somewhere. We can go to bed after that."

"Which kind of to bed?"

Miles laughs. His piercing blue eyes shine in the sunlight. "The kind where you come until you can't take it anymore."

෧෧

I ASPIRE TO MAKE CONVERSATION, BUT MY LIDS ARE HEAVY. I close my eyes, rest my head against the window, and drift in and out of sleep.

Miles squeezes my hand. "You're exhausted, aren't you?"

I nod.

"Was thinking about taking you to a hotel in Beverly Hills and fucking you against the wall."

"You were not. You're teasing."

"I was *thinking* about it." He smiles. "Wasn't a plan yet, but it occupied a lot of space in my thoughts."

"It's been twenty-nine days."

"I've been counting."

"I think you're as responsible for my hand cramps as finals are."

He laughs. "For once, I beat school."

"Miles, it's been twenty-nine days."

"It has."

"And we aren't having sex right now."

"Better change that soon." He squeezes my hand.

I squeeze back. He rubs the space between my thumb and my pointer finger with his thumb. It's sweet, intimate. He's really here. We're really in the same space together.

And I'm really exhausted.

My hands go to the zipper of my hoodie. I have a surprise for him, but I'm terrified to reveal it. This is serious, forever, the next level of commitment.

It's been a year, but we haven't talked much about forever. A while back, he asked about getting married. I said I wanted to wait until I was done with my first year of medical school, and that was it. We haven't talked about anything since.

We haven't even discussed getting a place together. I stay with my parents during the week—they live twenty minutes from campus—and with Miles on the weekends. His place is nearly two hours from school, depending on the traffic.

The zipper is cool against my skin. I pull it down an inch, but I can't will myself to pull it down any more.

Soon. I need to do it the first chance I get. Before the sex. I don't want him getting derailed when we finally get out of our clothes.

It's been way too long.

Miles changes lanes and exits the freeway. He pulls onto a familiar street. We've been here before. Together.

Oh.

There's a cemetery on our left—the cemetery where his uncle is buried.

It's a strange choice for a celebration, but it's perfect.

Miles parks and helps me out of the car. He slides one arm around my waist.

His eyes go to the ground. Is he actually bashful? I'm not sure I've ever seen him bashful before.

"You don't have to explain," I say.

"Sure you don't want a celebration with champagne on the beach?" He leads me through the wrought iron gates.

"Neither one of us drinks."

"Sparkling apple cider."

"I don't like sparkling apple cider."

"What if I'm licking it off your tits?"

"Then you're the one drinking it."

He laughs and squeezes my hand.

The shining sun casts a glow over the vivid green grass. The world is alive today. Except for the mild chill in the air, there are no signs of winter here. The sky is bright blue and free of clouds. The air is somewhere between crisp and warm.

I follow Miles to his uncle's grave. *Damon Webb. Father. Uncle. Friend.*

Miles's eyes fix on mine. "You remember what I said about Damon?"

"How he'd sit you down and tell you to stop running from your feelings?"

"Yeah. I always have a lot of time to think when we're on the road. That's how it started, me taking drugs. I needed a way to shut out my thoughts." He runs his fingers through my hair.

"I know." I lean into his touch. "Everyone runs sometimes."

"You don't. You never did."

"Yes, I did. Just I used school instead of drugs." I stare into his clear blue eyes. I don't want to run from my feelings either. I'm scared of the constant separation, but I love Miles more than anything. I want forever with him.

I want him to see the evidence of our forever.

Here goes nothing. I press my lips together. "I have to show you something."

"Let me go first." He presses his palm into my lower back. "Okay?"

I nod.

"This tour, it felt like we were traveling twenty hours a day. I had a lot of time to myself. Mostly, I thought about you. About us having a life together. About how much brighter my life is than it was before I met you. Used to be the only thing that soothed me was writing a song or stepping on stage. But you..." He stares back at me. "I know I promised to wait until you finished your first year of med school, but I have to do this now. I have to do it here." Miles lowers himself onto his knee.

He... he's really doing this.

He pulls a ring box from his jeans and flips it open. "Megara Smart, will you marry me?"

Chapter Two

MILES

Meg's brown eyes go wide. Her fingers go to her soft, pink lips. She stares at me like she's in shock.

Usually, I know how to work an audience, but right now, I'm too nervous to have a clue. The sound of my heartbeat is drowning out my thoughts.

Is that *oh my God, yes?* or *oh hell, no?* I know she loves me, but she's young. School comes first. It should. I love how ambitious she is.

None of that makes waiting easier. I've done a lot in my life, had just about everything a guy could want. Nothing—not platinum albums, or Grammies, or ten thousand fans screaming my name—compares to Meg.

Her eyes soften. Surprise fades to joy. Her lip corners turn upward. "You're asking in front of your uncle."

I swallow hard. Fuck. I can't remember the last time I was speechless. A nod is all I can manage.

"That's sweet." Her smile spreads to her ears.

"He would have loved you."

"Really?"

9

"Really." He would have adored her. Especially the way she gives me shit. And the way she doesn't take my shit. And those gorgeous brown eyes of hers. That vibrant smile. The way she laughs with her entire body.

"Why?" she asks.

Where the hell do I start? "You make me better. Stronger."

"You have it backward. You make *me* better. You make *me* stronger."

My smile widens. Still, my stomach and chest are floating. Fucking nerves. Stage fright has nothing on marriage proposals.

"You're supposed to answer," I tease. "But I am willing to kneel here all afternoon."

"You can't kneel here all afternoon. I need you on your knees later."

I melt. I'm asking her to marry me, and she's replying with a sex joke.

She's perfect.

Her voice drops to a whisper. "Yes. Of course."

She's smiling. Her brown eyes are bright.

She's not just happy. She's ecstatic.

My entire body goes light. I slide the ring onto her finger.

"Is this really happening?" She stares at the ring. Her eyes fill with wonder then they're back on me. "It's huge."

"We both know you can take huge."

She laughs as she traces the outline of the stone.

I want to feel every ounce of her joy. I wrap my arms around her and pull her into a deep kiss.

"Miles," she murmurs. "Your uncle will see."

Her hands go to my hair. She pulls me closer. Her lips part to make way for my tongue.

I know her body, know how to make her needy. I drag my

fingertips up her thigh until she's groaning into my mouth. She arches her body into mine, spurring me on.

She sighs as she pulls back. "Not in front of Damon."

"Why not?"

"Miles!" She squeals. "I don't want him to think I'm a tramp."

"He wasn't 85, Princess." I call her by her *Star Wars* nickname. Last Halloween, she dressed as Princess Leia. I knew she would, so I dressed as Han Solo. I've been calling her Princess ever since. It used to annoy her, but now it makes her smile. "He didn't think anybody was a tramp."

She flips me off playfully then looks at the tombstone. "I love your nephew—"

"He adopted me."

She nods. "I love your son more than anything. I'm sorry we couldn't meet. I'll try to take good care of him."

I push myself to my feet and slide my arms around her.

Relief floods my limbs. I fucking missed her.

Meg presses her lips against mine with a hungry kiss. We have a lot of time to make up for, but she's clearly exhausted. I can't fuck her the way she deserves to be fucked. Hell, it's not just what she wants. I haven't gone twenty-nine days without sex since I started having sex.

I need to be deep inside her. I need her nails raking across my back, her limbs shaking as she comes.

I need her coming again and again.

My lips press together. I fucking miss the taste of her. Especially the way her thighs press against my cheeks as she comes on my tongue.

Now to find a spot private enough that I can peel her jeans to her feet, slide between her legs, and lick her until she's screaming my name.

"I have to show you something," she murmurs. Her fingers dig into my shoulders.

She's close to falling asleep in my arms. This will have to wait until we're in a proper bed. I'm not about to go easy on her. Not for anything.

"Miles." Her fingers find the bare skin of my chest. She pulls my t-shirt aside and traces the lines of my tattoo.

Her lips part with a sigh of desire. A lot of women have ogled me, but none do it the way Meg does, with this mix of need, lust, love, and appreciation.

No one knows me the way she does. Damon is the only other person who ever saw me, all of me.

She takes a half-step backward.

Her eyes fill with vulnerability. Even now, after a year, it's rare that she has her guard this low.

Slowly, she pulls the zipper of her hoodie to her waist. Her hands go to her chest, covering her cleavage.

Huh? Meg isn't shy about her breasts. She knows how much I appreciate them. In fact, there's no one in the parking lot. I should take her there and suck on her nipples until she's purring my name.

Her eyes turn down. Her cheeks flush.

She's nervous.

"I... I did this last weekend." Her cheeks turn even more red. "Damn. This is scary. How do you strip on stage every night?"

"I know my strong suit."

She smiles, but it's quickly replaced by a nervous look. Slowly, she peels one hand off her chest. The other goes to the strap of her tank top and pulls it aside.

My exhale sucks up every drop of breath in my body.

There's ink on her chest. Three little words: *Be Brave, Love.*

The song I wrote for her, to tell her I loved her.

The song she begged me not to write.

A mirror of the tattoo I got for my uncle. Same place on her chest. Same font.

"I don't know that I've ever seen you speechless." Her voice lifts until it's confident. "I should get more tattoos."

My hand goes to her skin. I trace the lines with my fingers. My words are on her body. This connection between us is on her body.

It's forever.

The ink curves over the swell of her breast. It's outside her bra. It will be on display whenever she wears something low-cut.

I'll see it every time I get her naked.

I need her naked immediately.

"Let's go." I slide my hands to her waist. Again, I pull her body into mine. "I need to be inside you."

She laughs. "I'm holding the cards."

"You're always holding the cards."

She shakes her head. "No. I'm not. But right now, I have you exactly where I want you." She slides her hand over the neckline of my t-shirt. "It's intoxicating. Is this why you're obnoxious twenty-four seven?"

Blood is quickly fleeing my brain. Her hands on my skin do nothing to help the situation.

We're teasing. God knows, I love teasing her. "You don't find me charming?"

"You are charming." She smiles. "You're charming, and you're at my mercy."

"I'll rip off your clothes right here."

"Not in front of your uncle!"

"In the car."

"Let me see yours again." She tugs at my t-shirt.

I pull the garment low enough that she can see every tattoo on my chest. Her fingers go to her name—*Megara*—in thick black letters, then they're on the quote on my other pec. *Be Brave, Live.*

"People are going to think you're the world's biggest Sinful Serenade fan," I tease.

"I am." She looks up at me. "There's no one in the world who appreciates your mouth more than I do."

Damn, she's reveling in having the upper hand. Can't complain. She looks just as adorable drunk with power as she does blushing.

This is going to be a miserable drive. But it will be worth it. My place is forty minutes without traffic. Drew and Kara's place is closer. Twenty minutes. But it's only useful if they're out.

Damn, it's hard to concentrate with all my blood rushing to my cock. I could swear Drew said something about flying straight to San Francisco to visit with her family. But maybe that was Pete flying to New York to see Jess's family.

Meg laughs with glee. "You're at my mercy."

I stare into her brown eyes. "Was it the marriage proposal that gave it away?"

She bites her lip. "That helped."

Okay. Need enough blood in my brain to think of where I'm going to rip off her panties.

I take her hand and change the subject. "You get that ink by yourself?"

She smiles. "You won't believe me."

"Try me."

"Mom came with me."

"Susan went with you?"

"You have to call her Mom if we're getting married. She'll die of happiness. She adores you. She thinks you're a gentleman." Meg bites her lip. Her eyes bore into mine. "Do you like it?"

"I fucking love it." I plant a hard kiss on her lips. I'm

tempted to pin her to the car right here. I need to show her how much I love the tattoo. How much I love every inch of her. "Now get in the car so I can have my way with you."

THREE MINUTES ON THE ROAD, AND I GIVE UP ON GETTING to a house. Any house.

I need Meg naked immediately. I need her screaming my name as she comes.

I pull into the nearest hotel. It's a budget chain. Not as high class as the night of our engagement deserves, but I can't say I give a fuck about the setting at the moment.

Meg clears her throat. She's attempting confident and aloof, but with the way she's pressing her knees together and biting her lip, I know she's as desperate as I am.

Fuck, I bet she's wet.

She's always fucking wet.

It takes much too long to check in. Meg perks up as we take the stairs to our room. Her hand slides under my leather jacket then under my t-shirt.

Damn, I love the way her hand feels against my skin.

I unlock the door and push it open. Might as well make a gesture. I scoop her into my arms and carry her over the threshold.

She laughs with glee. "Miles! If you break my back, I'm not marrying you."

"Fair enough." I kick the door closed and set her on the bed.

"You know I'm keeping my name," she says.

I smile. "You know I'm about to rip off your jeans and panties and lick you until you're screaming *my* name."

Her lips part with a sigh of pleasure. She still attempts to stay in control. "I did know that."

"Good. Unbutton your jeans." I sit between her legs and take off her socks and shoes.

She relaxes into the bed, squeezing her toes and arching her back.

Fuck, I almost forgot how responsive she is. It's been a while, but there's no excuse for forgetting anything about the woman I love.

I roll her jeans to her knees. "You should keep your name."

"Really?"

"Yeah. It will mean the world to your mom."

"Oh." She shifts her legs to help me. "Carry on then."

"Take off the top and the bra."

She does. I pull her jeans to her ankles.

I soak in the sight of her body—her long legs, the gentle curves of her hips, waist, and chest. She thinks she's too gawky, too flat-chested, but every inch of her is perfect.

Especially those breasts. They're a perfect handful and they're responsive as hell.

It's still there.

Be Brave, Love.

I can't wait any longer. I pin her to the bed. My hips sink into hers. She squirms, arching her back and rubbing her crotch against mine.

"Too many clothes," she murmurs.

"Fair." I pull my t-shirt over my head and toss it aside.

I kiss her hard. I never got jazzed about kissing before. But with her, I crave the intimacy of her lips against mine.

She groans into my mouth as she squirms. My focus shifts lower. My cock will get what it wants soon.

First, my mouth gets what it wants.

I kiss my way down her neck. Then I'm at her chest. I take one of her nipples into my mouth and suck gently.

"Miles," she groans. Her hands go to my hair. She tugs at

it as she rocks her hips against me. "Stop teasing. It's been twenty-nine days."

I suck harder until her groans get low and desperate. When I'm convinced she can't take it anymore, I do the same to her other nipple.

My hand slides down her torso. It finds her panties and pushes them aside.

I place my palm against her.

Fuck. She's wet.

I trace the lines of her tattoo with my tongue then kiss my way down her stomach.

She squirms with anticipation. Her sighs get louder. Her hands go the comforter. She squeezes it so tightly her knuckles go white.

"Miles," she breathes. "Please."

The need in her voice sends the last available hint of blood to my cock.

I pull her panties to her feet. Under normal circumstances, I'd tease her a little longer. Right now, I need her taste on my tongue and her moans in my ears.

I press my lips against her inner thigh. She gasps, her back arching.

I kiss my way up her thigh.

She smells fucking good. I pin her legs to the bed. She sighs, impatient and needy.

She's exactly where I want her.

Slowly, I slide my tongue over her clit. She tastes like home. And she's already filling the room with her groans, already digging her fingers into the back of my head, already bucking against my lips.

Fuck, I love being between her legs. Best place in the whole fucking world.

I lick her up and down, taking my time tasting and teasing every inch.

Her knees fight my hands. Her hips buck. Her groans fill the room.

My fingers dig into her soft skin as I make my way back to her clit. I play with my speed and pressure until her thighs are shaking with pleasure.

I hold her in place so I can work my magic. She bucks against me, moving her cunt against my lips like I'm her personal sex toy. She tugs at my hair as she groans my name again and again.

My tongue works harder, faster. I lick her until her knees are pressed against my ears. Until she's screaming my name.

There.

Her hands dig into my shoulders as she comes. She shakes, all the muscles in her body tensing. Then everything goes slack. Her legs fall open. Her back relaxes as she collapses into the bed. One arm falls at her side. The other stays on me.

Her touch is soft as she drags her fingertips to the back of my neck.

She looks down at me with pleading eyes.

She doesn't have to ask. I need to be inside her. I need her soft folds enveloping my cock.

I shimmy out of my jeans and boxers and reposition our bodies so I'm on top of her.

She tattooed her body for me.

She's going to be my wife.

The intimacy of it overwhelms me.

My hands go to her hips. I pull her body onto mine. My cock strains against her cunt. Already, she feels fucking good.

I need to watch the pleasure spread over her expression as I fill her.

I need our eyes locked as our bodies join.

For a moment, I take in the gorgeous mix of desire and

satisfaction in her expression. Her cheeks are flushed. Her lips are pursed.

Her hands slide around my neck. They settle on the back of my head. She pulls me into a deep kiss. Need and affection pour from her lips to mine.

I dig my fingertips into her hips as I slide inside her. One delicious inch at a time, I fill her.

Damn, she feels good. Wet, warm, silky smooth.

I lower my body onto hers, pulling her closer as I thrust deeper. Meg keeps her hands pressed against the back of my head. She pulls me into another kiss. It's still deep. Still hungry.

Thoughts slip away. I'm only aware of the sensations in my body. Her soft lips. Her aggressive tongue. Her hips shifting to push me deeper.

My body takes over. It needs more. Needs harder. Needs every inch of her.

She rocks her hips as I thrust into her. We're working together to bring our bodies closer. To bring each other to orgasm.

"Mhmm," I groan. My nails dig into her skin.

She breaks free of our kiss to groan. Her eyes fix on mine for a moment then her lids press together.

Her lips part with a sigh. She's almost there. I know how to get her there.

I guide her hips so I can drive deeper. She groans.

Then it's her hands on my chest. Her nails digging into my skin. Her hips arching.

She groans. "Miles."

Her thighs squeeze against my hips.

And she's there. Her cunt pulses around my cock, pulling me closer, inviting me deeper.

I shift my hips to drive into her.

Fuck. She feels good.

My lips go to her neck. Her shoulder. I sink my teeth into her skin as an orgasm takes over.

With my next thrust, I come. She groans. One hand goes to my ass, holding me close as I fill her.

I linger inside her for a moment. Then I shift onto my side and pull her body into mine.

"Promise we'll never be apart that long again," she murmurs.

"I can't promise that." I pull her closer. "But I will do whatever it takes to make this work."

Chapter Three

L ying in a hotel room with Miles is nearly as familiar as cuddling on his couch. How many nights have we spent pressed together in a hotel bed?

At the moment, I'm too tired to do the math. I nestle into his chest and let the steady rhythm of his heartbeat lull me to sleep.

When I wake, the sun is setting and Miles is sitting in the armchair in the corner with a paperback in his hands. A *Star Wars* novel. One that came out two days ago.

"Don't spoil it," I plead.

He smiles, that smile that means *Meg, you're adorable.* "I couldn't." He pats his lap. "Wanted to get Nobu for dinner, but traffic will be insane."

"We're on Sepulveda. Traffic to anywhere will be insane."

Miles is wearing only boxers. I'm still wearing nothing. I slide into his lap, reveling in the sensation of our skin connecting.

He's here. I'm here.

It's overwhelming how much I need his body next to mine.

I press my forehead into his. "You leave in two weeks."

"Then you come with me for two weeks."

I like that part. Not as much what comes after. "Then four months on the road?"

"Two months, two weeks off, another two months on."

"Just a U.S. tour this time?"

He looks up at me with those clear blue eyes. His fingers curl over my chest, tracing the lines of my tattoo. "Be Brave, Love."

I nod.

"What is it you're thinking?"

I bite my lip. I don't like the direction my thoughts are heading, but I don't want to run from them. "You're on the road the next five months. I'll be finishing my first year of medical school. When are we going to find the time to plan a wedding? To even have a wedding?"

"What if we do it in Vegas?" He stares at me, his eyes as deep with affection as the ocean. "We can leave tonight and get married first thing tomorrow."

"Just us?"

"Your parents will want to see it."

I nod. "Our friends will want to see it. And I want them there."

"Even Tom?"

"Especially Tom."

"Thought you hated him."

"I did for a while." I run my fingers through his hair. "But I know he meant well telling me to get lost. He'd never admit it, but he loves you. And I know he'll kick your ass if you start using again."

"You think Tom could kick my ass?"

"If you were high, you wouldn't see it coming."

He laughs and presses his lips to mine.

Damn, his kiss is intoxicating. I don't collect my senses until it breaks.

"You still worry about me relapsing?" he asks.

I nod. Miles has done well for years, but there's no way I'll ever stop worrying about him relapsing. I still have nightmares about Rosie's overdose.

I nod. "Yes. I trust you, but—"

"I know. It's okay to worry, Princess. I worry about you burying yourself under the weight of your coursework."

A fair concern. I stare into his blue eyes. "Is it a good idea, you going to Las Vegas?"

His expression softens. "As long as you aren't planning a runaway bride move."

I trace the lines of his tattoo. *Be brave, live.* I'm braver with him. I live more when I'm with him. I have no doubt I want to marry Miles, no doubt I want to be with him forever.

But I'm not as sure about planning a wedding in under two weeks.

"I've been thinking." He runs his fingertips over my shoulder. "What if we toured during the summer and kept it short the rest of the year? You could come with me."

That would be amazing. I look into his eyes. "Could you really make that work?"

"It's possible." He runs his fingertips over my chin. "The band can slow down. We've talked about it."

"There's no way Tom has talked about slowing down."

"He has a wife now." His voice softens. "Things are different than when we started. Our priorities are different."

I shake my head. "You need the stage, Miles. You're at home there."

"Yeah, but I'm at home with you too. I'll still have the stage, just less of it and more time with you. Wouldn't you want that?"

"Of course." I'd love to have Miles around more. I'd love

to have him home every night. But not if it means he's giving up his passion. "I can't be the thing standing between you and your dreams."

"You aren't." He presses his lips to mine. His fingers go to my engagement ring. "Let's go to Vegas. Let's get married now."

"Why?"

"Because you want to marry me."

"But why now? Why not in a year?"

"Why in a year?"

As Miles would say, fair enough. Why not now? Why in a year?

"You like depraved rock stars," he says.

I smile. "I do."

"See, you're already halfway there."

I laugh. I want to be there. I want to throw away all my concerns.

"I think you want a depraved rock star husband right away."

He's right. I do. I want forever with Miles, and I want it right away. Why not now?

Now is good.

I press my fingertips into the spot where his neck meets his collarbone.

He shudders with pleasure. His hands go to my lower back. He pulls me closer.

"Promise you won't think about quitting Sinful Serenade." I muster all the confidence I have. "Promise, and I'll go to Vegas with you and get married now."

"Then no question." He leans closer. "I promise."

THE NEXT MORNING, WE CALL MY PARENTS OVER BREAKFAST

—they're surprised, but supportive—and drive straight to Vegas.

The city is breathtaking in a strange, money-worshiping, party-worshiping kind of way. Even in the afternoon, the neon lights stand out against the blue sky. One side of the freeway is miles of desert. The other is an oasis of depraved, adult fun.

There's no specific theme to our hotel. It seems the concept is luxury. Our suite is adorned in shades of mauve and silver. It's sleek, modern, and a little showy.

Miles sits on the bed, his legs spread. It's inviting. I want to mount my husband-to-be.

Damn, this is moving fast.

I linger in the thought of Miles as my husband—a long honeymoon on the beach, us buying a house so we can really live together, him surprising me at school, me surprising him for a weekend on tour.

We'll have a good life together.

There are obstacles, but we'll figure them out, one at a time.

He pushes himself to his feet and stretches his arms overhead. Then his eyes are on mine, this look that says *let's go*. "Ready to start looking at venues?"

No. But I want to marry him, and there isn't much time for everything.

I nod. "Ready as I'll ever be."

❧

OUR FIRST STOP IS A DRIVE-THROUGH CHAPEL. FOR A MERE two hundred dollars, we can get married in a drive-through. It's only an extra hundred dollars to have Elvis officiate the ceremony.

I watch in horror as another couple ties the knot. They're

sitting on the top of a bright red convertible. Her dress and lipstick are the exact red of the car. He's in a sports jacket and jeans.

When the officiant says I do, they lean in for a sloppy, drunken kiss.

My stomach twists.

This is all wrong.

"It's different," Miles says.

I shake my head. My lips barely part for my objection. "No way in hell."

"My old favorite song." He runs his fingertips over my t-shirt, tracing the spot where my new tattoo is. "I have a new favorite."

"No, Miles. I'm not getting married in a drive-through."

"You want something classier?"

"Is there something less classy?"

He laughs. "Fair point."

I take a deep breath. The sun is bright in the sky. We're near the Stratosphere tower. I'm sure they do weddings at the top, but that isn't right either.

I don't want a church wedding.

I don't want a drive-through or a hotel deck either.

Nothing feels right. They all feel like places Rosie would hate.

"I don't know what I want." I dig my fingertips into my jeans. "I've never thought about it. We haven't even been engaged twenty-four hours."

"You don't want a drive-through."

I nod.

"You didn't like the little white chapel."

Again, I nod.

"That's two things we've eliminated. We'll find something today or tomorrow."

"Today or tomorrow?" That's fast. Really fast.

Miles's voice is steady. Calm. "That a problem?"

"No, I guess not." My voice is the opposite of steady. I turn to face him. There's all this certainty in his piercing blue eyes. I don't feel any of that.

It isn't right that I don't feel any of that.

"Trust me. I'll find the perfect place for Your Worship." He presses his lips to my forehead.

"I'm *Your Worship* now?"

"You don't want me on my knees?"

I laugh. A full blown belly laugh. It eases the tension brewing in my shoulders. Miles makes me happy. Miles brings me joy.

We can do this.

We have to be able to do this.

Chapter Four

MEGARA

We can't do this.

None of the twelve places we visit are right. The hotel garden isn't right. The church of Elvis isn't right. The poolside altar isn't right.

The last stop, a tiny chapel downtown, is the worst yet. The walls are a garish mix of orange and neon green. The woman manning the counter is wearing last night's makeup. Her clown red hair is in a frizzy perm straight out of an 80s movie.

She looks at us with faint irritation as she takes a drag of her cigarette. "We have ten spots today. Each spot is fifteen minutes. For an extra two hundred dollars, you can add fifteen minutes of photography." She recites the words without a hint of passion. "Samples of our photography packages are available on the wall behind you."

I turn so I can take in these so-called photography packages. They're as tacky as the interior of the chapel. It's not beautiful or special. These weddings look like accidents.

I close my eyes and sink into his touch. Something is

missing. I can't picture us here. I can't picture us at the top of the Stratosphere, in the hotel ballroom, in the garden.

Miles takes a slow, steady breath. "We'll find something. Trust me."

I look up at him. That same certainty is in his eyes. I do trust him. But– "I've had enough for today."

He nods and pulls me closer. "Kara and Drew are flying in. We're meeting them tomorrow morning. She can help you with your dress. I'll take care of the rest."

"You're going to find a wedding venue?"

"You doubt me?"

No, but– "This is sudden."

"Trust me. I've got it."

He leans down to kiss me.

His lips are soft. He tastes good.

Slowly, my senses shift back into focus. Warmth floods my body. Then desire. My hands go to his messy hair. My back arches. My crotch presses against his.

I do trust him.

I want him.

I love him.

Hell, I need him. I need him like I need oxygen.

◈◈◈

AFTER A LONG EVENING MAKING UP FOR LOST TIME, I TAKE a shower, change into my new hot pink *Las Vegas* pajamas, and collapse in bed.

For sleep, this time.

This still feels like a dream. Starting at my nail, I trace the ring finger of my left hand. Chapped skin, hard bones, the bump of the knuckle, and my engagement ring.

Marriage is as forever as it gets.

I want that with him.

I want everything with him.

He slides his arms around me and presses his lips to my forehead. His voice is nervous. "You still excited?"

I nod. "And scared."

"That's normal."

"You're scared?"

"I miss you when I'm away. It hurts." He runs his fingers through my wet hair. "Used to be, I thought it was easier, never getting invested in anything enough to hurt."

"Me too."

"It's not. Better to have seven months a year of joy and five where I miss you enough it hurts to breathe."

"Really?"

He nods. "I'd rather it be ten months with you and two away, but I can make this work. If you want me around more, all you have to do is ask."

I trace the tattoos on his chest and shoulders. Each is another piece of his heart. A fierce dragon scaring off anyone who tries to get too close. A rose covered in thorns, enticing, beautiful and guarded. Spread wings, ready to fly away from everything that hurts.

And those words.

Be Brave, Live.

Megara.

His chest heaves with his inhale and falls with his exhale. His eyes are closed.

He's asleep.

I *do* want more of him. I want 365 days of him. But I'm never going to ask for that. He needs the stage. I need medicine.

We just have to figure out how to balance the two.

Somehow.

For the better part of an hour, I try to sleep. Around three A.M., I give up and go to the main room. The lights of The Strip flow in through the window. Even at three A.M., the city is bright and vivid. Even at three A.M., the streets are lined with cars and with people walking from casino to casino. Most are in winter coats. A few are in cocktail dresses, no doubt buzzed enough the cold temperature doesn't bother them.

What would Rosie do if she were here?

Get wasted.

But if she were sober? If she'd survived the overdose and clawed her way through recovery the way Miles did?

After she gave up on telling me to put school first, she'd find a gaudy venue, pick out an ornate dress, and spend our parents' money like it was going out of style.

There would probably be a horrifying bachelorette party with male strippers and penis-shaped straws.

I close my eyes and remember her room. It was loud, like her. Bright colors, ornate lights, flashy vanity mirror.

Perfect for a Vegas wedding.

God, I wish she were here. It still hurts that she doesn't exist in the world.

Miles is the only thing that makes it hurt less.

The energy in the room shifts. He's up.

He comes closer. No words, but I can hear his breath and his footsteps.

Then he's behind me.

Miles slides his arms around my waist. He pulls my body into his.

The world makes sense when we're pressed together.

Can I go another two months without those arms around me?

I'm not sure I can.

His lips brush my earlobe. "You look fuckable when you're all pensive."

"Do I?" I arch my back to rub my ass against his crotch. I'd like to be thinking nothing. He can help with that.

Miles chuckles. "Princess, it's impolite to use your fiancée for his body."

"Is that right?"

He nods. "You keep going off someplace. Rosie?"

I nod. "She'd love a Vegas wedding."

"Damon too. He had a soft spot for whirlwind romances." Miles presses his lips against my neck. His hands slide around my waist, pulling me closer. "You've got an anchor tied to your ankle."

"Since when do you speak in metaphors?"

"It's something new I'm trying."

"For your lyrics?"

"For everything."

"I thought you were letting Pete take over writing Sinful Serenade's lyrics," I tease.

"I'll have to punish you if you don't show me respect."

"Okay. Let's go now."

"It's not a punishment if you ask for it." He slides his hands to my hips. "You know I'm happy to fuck you any time, any place."

"And yet my clothes are on."

He presses his lips to my neck. "Remember our deal?"

"What deal?"

"No secrets, no lies."

"The deal we made when we were fuck buddies?" I laugh. "Another part of it was no falling in love. That didn't work so well."

"You can't blame me for that." He presses his cheek against mine. "I didn't realize how adorable you were when you blushed."

"Yes, you did."

He laughs. "I didn't realize how much I needed you."

"How much?"

"We're like puzzle pieces. You fit into me. I fit into you."

I turn back to Miles and stare into his eyes. "I don't know if I can do it."

"Get married?"

"I want to. I want to be with you forever. But... I don't know if I can survive your tour schedule. It's selfish, but I want you in my bed every night. I want your arms around me when I get home from work."

He runs his fingertips over my shoulders. "It's not selfish to want it. I want that too. But you know what I want more?"

"What?"

"I want you happy. And you won't be happy if you give up medical school."

"You won't be happy if you give up the band." I slide my hand over his. "We're at an impasse."

"No. We have a problem that we can figure out together."

"What if we can't?"

"We can."

"Let me guess. You just know?"

"Yeah." He pulls me closer. "Our first performance is in fifteen days. That gives us fourteen days for a wedding and a honeymoon. Or fourteen days to hang out in Vegas."

"And have lots of hot sex?"

"You think I could go anywhere without having sex with you?"

"Maybe I need to be reminded." I rise to my tiptoes and press my lips to his.

Miles groans as he kisses me. We had sex just this afternoon, but there's still so much time to make up for.

I pull my t-shirt over my head.

His eyes go to my chest. Then to my new tattoo. His pupils dilate as he nods.

I push my pajama bottoms off my hips. "Let's start with right here. Then we can move to the bed."

He does away with his boxers. "Princess, I love the way you think."

Chapter Five

MEGARA

Miles and I sit at a cozy corner table at the Starbucks three blocks east of Las Vegas Boulevard, sipping our drinks and soaking in the silence.

My eyelids press together. I can see bits and pieces of a wedding. I can see the two of us at an altar. It's not as pristine as the one in the hotel chapel. It's bright and brilliant, overflowing with red roses or maybe purple orchids.

His eyes sparkle. My hands are on his. There are wedding rings, simple silver bands. There are words falling from our lips.

A shriek of glee pulls me from my thoughts.

"You're getting married!" Kara squeals. Her friendly voice echoes around the room.

She bounces toward me. Her long, dark hair bounces with her. Her makeup highlights her brown eyes and her round lips. Her navy wrap dress shows off her enviable curves.

Drew, her fiancée, Miles's closest friend and the guitarist of Sinful Serenade, is a few paces behind her. He wears his exhaustion all over his handsome face. There's something else in his dark eyes— he's wrecked with worry. More than usual.

She throws her arms around me. "I'm so excited. Do you have a venue? Do you have a day?"

Drew makes the *cut it out* expression.

"We don't have anything," I admit.

"Don't worry, Princess. I'll take care of it." Miles presses his lips to my forehead. "Go get beautiful with your friend."

"Get beautiful?" Kara puts her hand on her hip, feigning indignation. "She's gorgeous right now. And so am I. Not as gorgeous as my poor, jetlagged baby." She blows Drew a kiss. "And he's not even wearing eyeliner yet."

Drew shakes his head. "Every day since Tom's wedding."

"It's hot, baby." She pulls him into a close hug. Then she's on her tiptoes, and he's leaning down to kiss her. Even in her wedge shoes, she's at least six inches shorter than Drew.

Drew groans with pleasure. He's crazy about her, but he's not the PDA type. Well, not with us watching. I've heard plenty of stories about public sex.

After she pulls away, she looks into his eyes. It's a plea, a secret one.

"It's Pete's fault," Drew complains. "Jess swoons over him in eyeliner, so now he wears it every day."

Miles chuckles. "Steele's got game. Can't fault him for that."

Drew turns to Kara. "Will you—"

"No." She cuts him off. "Don't say anything. To anyone. Please."

"About what?" I ask.

"It's nothing. A surprise... for after your wedding." She bites her lip, not quite believing her words. "I have a dozen shops bookmarked. We're getting home late. So don't wait up, boys."

"My parents are coming in. They want to meet us for dinner," I say.

"Okay, okay. Most of these places close by eight. I permit you to meet Dr. and Dr. Smart for dinner at nine." She turns to Miles. "You, arrange dinner. And no excuses about how you were too busy writing love songs or getting new tattoos or something."

Miles chuckles. "Sure thing, Kara. Good to see you again. How did you like, uh..." He runs his hand through his hair, trying to recall the city of Kara's trip.

"Shanghai. It was different." She turns to Drew with an encouraging smile. "Throw a depraved bachelor party. Put Tom's to shame."

"A depraved party that ends in time for him to get to dinner at nine?" Drew asks.

"You're in Vegas. I'm sure you can squeeze lots of depravity into the next ten hours." She laughs. "I believe in you."

THE BRIDAL SHOP IS HUGE AND IT'S PINK. EVERY INCH OF space is pastel pink—the floor, the walls, the frames around the mirrors, the couches, the register.

There must be a thousand dresses. A few hundred are close enough to my size—they do rush alterations here—that they make viable options.

There are several hundred dresses to choose from.

And I haven't got a clue about my venue. About the time of day. If I'm inside or outside.

My heartbeat picks up. It's hard to breathe.

Where do I start? I've never thought about a wedding. Not the dress, the venue, the cake, the flowers. It's never crossed my mind.

Now, I'm attempting to arrange everything in a span of 48 hours. Seventy-two max.

It's overwhelming.

"Relax, sweetie," Kara says. "I've got this."

"But..."

"Do you have any idea what you want?"

"Not boring but not tacky either."

"Ah, I've got it. Sit down." She nods to the pink couch in the dressing area. "Allow me."

"Okay."

I collapse on the squishy couch. I'm still working at a sleep deficit, and this is a hell of a comfortable seat. I let my eyes close and take a half-nap.

Twenty minutes later, Kara is ready to go. She hangs the dresses in one of the stalls and taps me on the shoulder.

I focus on my reflection as I step into the dressing room. Is that really me, in a boutique, trying on a gown? Frizzy dark hair, brown eyes, and gawky figure—yep, it's me.

I'm really doing this.

After I strip to my panties and hook a logline bra, Kara helps me into a gown. It's heavy white satin, so white it catches all the light in the store.

There's something flattering about the sheath dress—it makes me look statuesque and classy—but its utter lack of adornment is boring. It's barely fancier than a maxi dress I'd wear to the beach.

She adjusts the bust and waist. "Too simple?"

I nod in agreement.

"I have just the pick." She helps me out of my dress and my bra, and into a fluffy ball gown.

I'm swimming in taffeta. The ball gown makes Cinderella look under-dressed. The ruffled skirt takes up most of the dressing room. The bodice is adorned with rhinestones. They catch the fluorescent lights.

"It is loud," I say.

She laughs. "When in Vegas..."

"Sparkle like the stars."

"You do sparkle." She steps backward and takes a long look at me. "You hate it, don't you?"

I nod.

"I have an idea."

Despite the horror that is this dress, I trust her.

She helps me into another half-dozen dresses. None are right, but we start to narrow in on what I want—ivory, not white, a ball gown or a princess dress with a touch of adornment.

We must be at dress ten. I'm about ready to fall asleep on that pink couch. It feels like it's been hours.

Kara looks me over. "You want to break for lunch, or do you want to try two more?"

"One more."

"I'll make it count." She looks at the dresses left on the rack and picks one. "Here we go."

It's pretty. It has a light sparkle, a full skirt, and a gorgeous, rich ivory color. It's almost cream. Not that I know the difference.

Kara undoes the corset back, and I step into the dress. She takes her time lacing the back.

Her voice gets bright. "I think this might be the one."

My chest feels light. Is it really possible I'm in my wedding dress? The thought is equal parts exciting and terrifying. "Really?"

"Really." She takes my hand. "Let's look in the main room."

The dress is a few inches too long. I'll have to wear heels. As it is, I'm barefoot.

I stumble all the way to the mirrors in the center of the room.

My exhale is a mix of relief and excitement.

The dress is straight out of a dream and it fits like a glove. Between the sweetheart neckline, the v-waistline, and the full tulle skirt, it's the perfect princess dress.

I really do look like a princess.

A tear forms in my eye. I go to wipe it away. No good. There's another. Another.

Blinking does nothing to stop the happy tears from forming.

"It's perfect," I whisper.

She chokes back a tear. "Oh God. Now I'm crying. You look beautiful. That's it, Meg. That's the dress."

My eyelids press together. I can see myself at the altar in this dress. I can see the look of delight in Miles's eyes as I walk down the aisle. I can feel his fingertips on my chest, tracing my tattoo.

Your Worship, you really look like a Princess.

I love you.

I know.

Don't Star Wars *me at a time like this.*

He smiles so hard that he can barely get out his I love you too.

My gaze goes to my reflection.

The sweetheart neckline is low enough to show off my fresh ink.

The reflection of the words is backward in the mirror. Still, I read them over and over.

Be Brave, Love.

I want to be brave. I want to run to my feelings instead of running from them.

Chapter Six

MILES

U nder normal circumstances, Drew isn't exactly what I'd call "a barrel of laughs," but he's in an especially off mood today.

I send him to get suits so I can tour venues on my own. None are quite right. But one gives me an idea.

It takes a few hours searching online, but I find the perfect venue. I can see her there, can see us there.

I book it for the day after tomorrow.

Fuck, maybe I am rushing, but I can't help it. I need a better explanation than *I want the world to know she's mine* if I want to convince Meg's parents this is a good idea.

She won't do it without their blessing.

Fuck, I won't do it without their blessing. We don't have much family between the two of us—mostly, it's her parents and the guys in the band.

I make dinner reservations and rack my brain for parent-friendly charm.

My fingers dance over my cell screen. I know the dress is a big deal. I don't want to rush her.

But, fuck, I need to check in.

Miles: Any pictures for me?

Meg: You're always a bad boy.

Miles: You love it.

Meg: Maybe. It's bad luck to see the wedding dress before the big day.

Miles: You found something?

Meg: Maybe...

My phone buzzes with a new picture message. Meg isn't wearing the dress. She's isn't wearing anything.

My blood rushes to my cock. My eyes fix on the tattoo curving over her breast.

Be Brave, Love.

I'm going to get hard every time I sing that song for the rest of my life. Not that I'm complaining.

Meg: Not what you were expecting?

Miles: Better.

Meg: I did get a dress. And it's beautiful. You'll love it.

Miles: Princess, it only matters if you love it.

Meg: I do. Did you pick a restaurant?

Miles: We have reservations at nine.

Meg: I'll be there at eight. In a new dress. Without underwear. I'm sure I don't have to spell it out for you.

Damn. I can see her sleepy grin. Already, I want her in my arms. I always want her in my arms.

I text her the details for dinner. I almost text her a promise that we can do this on her timeline, but that doesn't belong in a text. It should be whispered in her ears between kisses.

It wouldn't exactly be a problem if that led to one of my hands on that tattoo, the other between her legs, stroking her to orgasm.

Fuck, that thing will be the death of me.

֍

THE RESTAURANT IS AN UPSCALE STEAKHOUSE OVERLOOKING the hotel's pool and garden, far enough away from the casino floor that the classical music flowing through the speakers is louder than the beeps and bops of slot machines.

Meg is already here, sitting in a booth by the bar. It's the perfect booth for this. It has a high back and it faces the wall. It's just enough privacy that I can get my hands under that skirt and test the veracity of her claim.

Her eyes light up as she spots me. She slides out of the booth and meets me halfway. I wrap my arms around her and pull her close.

She smells good.

Her long hair is pulled back. Haven't got a fucking clue what the style is called, but I can tell it's some sort of wedding run through. It's elegant.

She's wearing makeup too. She's bare-faced most of the time. I can't say I care much either way. If I had to pick, I like her in last night's smudged makeup, her long hair a frizzy mess. That's the way she looks after the nights where I make her come until she can't take it anymore.

My cock stirs at the thought. I tell it to calm down—this is strictly for her—and run my fingers over her cheek.

"You look gorgeous." I slide my hand over the curve of her hip. Somehow, the purple wrap dress is sexy and elegant at the same time. What is that shade of purple called? It's gorgeous on her. Brings out the flecks of honey in her eyes.

The desire in her eyes.

"Thanks." She buries her face in my chest. "If I never see another makeup brush or bobby pin, it will be too soon. I liked the makeup artist. She said she's available anytime in the next few days, but I got the feeling that she does a lot of last-minute weddings. I'll have to call her as soon as we have a date and time."

"We do."

"What?" She looks up at me, her brows arching with surprise. "Miles, when did we... what did you do?"

"I booked a place for the night after tomorrow."

Her eyes go wide. Her jaw drops straight to the ground. "What if I hate it?"

"Then we'll find a new place. But you won't." I pull her closer. She smells good—a little like hairspray, but still good. "It's perfect."

She nods, her fingers curling into my button-up shirt. "Fuck. I'm going to get makeup on your white shirt." She pulls back and stares into my eyes. "Why do you look so good cleaned up?"

"You like a bad boy in a nice package."

"You're more like a sweet guy in a bad boy package."

"Sweet guy who gets you off in a booth before you meet your parents for dinner?"

Her cheeks flush. Her teeth sink into her lip. She's right where I want her.

And fuck, how I want my hands under that dress.

But we need to get conversation out of the way first.

I stare back into her brown eyes. "You nervous about your parents?"

She nods. "What if they don't approve?"

Then we're fucked. "They will." They have to.

She slides into the booth.

My gaze goes to her legs as she tugs the skirt up her thighs. My hand needs on them immediately. "Need to make this fast in case your parents are early."

She nods and leans closer. "Beat your old record."

"Haven't been timing it."

"Can't have been more than three minutes."

I smile. She knows exactly how to bait me.

Her fingers curl around my forearm. Her head rests on my

shoulder. This wedding stuff is exhausting. It's weighing on her.

She needs a break.

I need her eyes rolling back with pleasure. Need to see her floating so I know this heaviness is temporary.

Not that I need an excuse to get her off. Fuck, getting her off is the only thing I love more than the stage.

I stroke her thigh until the server stops at our table to take our order. For now, it's drinks. Iced tea for her. The same for me.

By the time he's back with our beverages, Meg is panting. Her lips purse with a needy sigh. That sigh is music. It screams, *I'm yours. You can do whatever you want with me.*

Her eyes meet mine. The plead for release.

Maybe I will break my old record.

I do live to break records.

I press my lips to Meg's. Her tongue darts into my mouth. It's aggressive. Needy.

She sighs into my mouth as I slide my hand up her thigh. Her knees part. Her body turns a few inches toward mine. If I move, she'll be flashing anyone who walks by.

She's open, vulnerable.

It's fucking hot.

I kiss her back. My cock is at full attention. It doesn't have any intention of waiting, but I've dealt with blue balls before.

Meg doesn't waste time. Her hand goes right for my crotch. She rubs me over my slacks. Fuck. My eyes close. My lips part with a sigh. These things are thinner and slicker than my jeans. The friction is intense enough to get me off.

That's not how I want to meet her parents.

I grab her wrist and bring her hand to my waist. She takes the hint, digging her fingers into my shirt. There's enough heat in the touch that I'm half-worried she'll set the cotton thing on fire.

My tongue slides over hers as my fingers find her folds. I slip one finger inside her.

She groans into my mouth, tugging at my shirt. Fuck, do I want her. It takes every ounce of self-control I have not to unzip and bring her hand to my cock.

My thumb curls over her clit as I slip another finger inside her.

She moans into my mouth. Tugs my shirt untucked. Then her hands are on my skin.

She brings her mouth to my ear. "Please, Miles. I want to get you off."

"Not here." I rub her harder.

Harder.

She barely manages to muffle a groan. Her brown eyes fill with pleasure. They stay locked to mine.

"In the bathroom," she breathes. "I want to suck you off."

Fuck. My cock is already hard as granite. Not gonna say no to that.

I nod. My lips find her ear and I suck hard on the lobe. "If you keep your voice down."

Her groan is half agony, half pleasure. Still, she nods. Her posture relaxes. Her expression fills with bliss.

No more heaviness.

Only desire. Need. Affection.

I check to make sure the coast is clear, then I go for the kill. My fingers thrust into her. My thumb rubs her.

My lips meet hers. She groans into my mouth. She's almost there. Her thighs press together. Then the knees.

Her back arches. She breaks free of the kiss, brings her mouth to my ears, and whisper-moans my name.

Then she's there, sinking her teeth into her lip as pleasure spreads over her face. With the next motion of my hand, she comes.

I watch the orgasm spread over her face. I'll never get tired of that. It's the most beautiful thing I've ever seen.

It takes a minute for her to settle. She crosses her legs. Her lips curl into a smile as she nods to the single-stall bathroom in the corner of the restaurant.

"My turn," she whispers.

I'm not about to deny my future wife what she wants.

Chapter Seven

MILES

Meg is the first out of the bathroom. I take a minute to clean up and collect my senses, but I'm still nearly incoherent.

I wash my hands a few more times for good measure.

The damn things are shaking.

This is as bad as the proposal. I've never given a fuck what anyone thought of me before. I don't know how to deal with how badly I need her parents' approval.

I wipe my hands and adjust my shirt and slacks. The business casual look isn't as bad as I figured it would be. Between the graduations, the engagement parties, and the weddings, a collared shirt and slacks are getting to be a habit.

No time to waste. I take a steady breath and step out of the bathroom. Meg is standing in front of the restaurant, her cheeks still flushed, her updo coming undone, talking to her parents.

They don't seem to notice how just-fucked she looks.

Meg smiles and nods to the table. We meet there.

Her cheeks are still red. "Miles made us reservations. We already got a table, but we thought we'd meet you in front.

We only ordered drinks. Iced tea. You know he doesn't drink, and I don't really—"

"Sure, sweetheart." Susan, Meg's mom, turns to me. "Miles. It's always nice to see you. Even if it's because you've whisked my daughter to Sin City for some illicit rendezvous." She hugs me hello.

"Nothing illicit about a wedding, Dr. Smart," I say.

She smiles the way she does every time I call her Dr. Smart.

"Just Susan. You can call me Mom if you want. But I understand if you don't. I know your mother—" She presses her lips together. "I know the situation isn't ideal."

I nod and turn to Meg's dad, Douglass. "And you too, Sir." Damn, it's usually easy for me to impress people. I've seen a lot of Meg's parents but I'm failing my usual smooth and seamless thing. Douglass is a man of few words. And a diehard Angels fan. "Hell a season the Angels had, huh?"

Douglass lights up with a smile. He jumps into a long explanation of the season and the playoffs. Meg squeezes my hand, nodding as she pretends to follow along. Susan does the same, only she squeezes her husband's hand.

"Sweetie, why don't we sit down? I'm famished," Susan says.

Douglass nods. He gets the *enough sports* message and takes his seat. The rest of us follow.

My wife-to-be hides behind her menu. Her eyes scan the page. Then her fingers are circling the salmon entree.

My lips curl into a smile. "Why do you pretend you'll order something besides salmon?"

"I might," she insists. "I'm still deciding."

"What will you order?" I ask.

"Uh..." Her eyes go to the menu. "Well, the pasta sounds good."

"The lemon garlic salmon pasta?" I ask.

Susan jumps in. "I love salmon too, honey. Don't worry. Your father used to torment me about it. Eventually, he accepted that I know what I like."

"You need variety," Douglass says.

"Sometimes. Sometimes, you need the thing you know you like. Something to comfort you." Susan smiles. "Besides, there's plenty of variety with salmon. Baked, broiled, poached, grilled. On salad, pasta, rice, with vegetables or mashed potatoes."

Meg clears her throat. "I like other fish too. Mahi Mahi. And ono. And tuna, any kind of tuna." She turns to me. "Fish is healthy."

"Whatever you want, Princess." I rub her palm with my thumb.

Susan cocks a brow. "Princess?"

Meg shoots me a *what have you done* look.

"Like Princess Leia," I say.

Susan's expression relaxes. "Oh, that's perfect. You know, Meg went as Princess Leia for Halloween five years in a row."

I smile like Susan doesn't tell me this every time I see her. It's sweet the way her eyes light up when she talks about Meg as a little girl.

"Of course, Rosie hated Princess Leia." Susan laughs. "She hated *Star Wars*, but she still went as Luke Skywalker one year. She went around with this little—what's it called?"

"Lightsaber," Meg says.

"That's it." Susan drifts into a memory. "She hit everyone with it. We had two dozen parents call us that night, insisting Rosie never be allowed another sword."

"I don't remember that." Meg's brow furrows with concentration.

"She was a stubborn girl. Almost as much as Meg is." Susan looks from Meg to me. "You're very handsome, Miles, and from the sound of things, quite wealthy-"

"Mom!" Meg covers her face with her hands. "Is it always about money?"

"Sweetheart, let me finish." Susan folds her hands. Her expression gets serious. "It's not about money. Douglass and I can take care of Meg forever. And I have no doubt that Meg will get through school and become a doctor. I know you won't stand in her way, Miles."

"I'll die before I let her quit medicine," I say.

Susan's lips purse. "You're as stubborn as she is, but... I learned the hard way that you can't always protect the people you love." She blinks back a tear. "You can't make good decisions for them."

Meg bites her lip. She looks to me then to her mom. Her expression twists with uncertainty. My fiancée isn't exactly a people person.

"I understand your meaning. Meg deserves to make her own choices, free of what you or I want for her," I say.

"I'm right here," Meg says. "I know you guys mean well, but please don't talk about me like I'm out of the room."

Susan turns to Meg. "Of course, sweetheart. But you're my baby girl. I'll always be protective of you. It's a lot for a mother to see her little girl get engaged—with plans to get married a few days later." She turns to me. "Tell me I was dreaming when you said you're doing this the day after tomorrow."

I study Susan's expression. I'm not sure she's convinced. Must be a better way to do it. We want the same thing— what's best for Meg. Just have to honest.

Fuck. That's not my strong suit. I can snap my fingers and conjure up a charming smile. But Susan will see through that. I need to lay my cards on the table here.

I make eye contact with Susan. "I have a venue booked for that evening, but it's up to Meg to make the call. She can live with the two of you forever, if that's what she wants."

Meg gasps in horror. "No offense," she mumbles.

Susan looks from Meg to me. "Douglass and I were together three years before we got engaged."

Douglass nods. "We were engaged for a year and a half."

I study Susan's expression. There's apprehension in her honey eyes, but there's a willingness too.

She wants to be on board with this.

"We won't do anything without your blessing," I say.

Susan smiles. She gets that dreamy, falling into a memory look on her face. "You know, when you first showed up last Thanksgiving, I could tell Meg thought you would scare me."

"Was it the tattoos or the motorcycle?" I ask.

Susan laughs. "I'm still horrified about the motorcycle. Do you have any idea how many organs we get from motor-cycle accidents?" She shakes her head. "Will you give up the motorcycle if I ask?"

"If that's the only way you'll offer your blessing," I say.

Meg turns to me. She raises a brow. "Really?"

I nod. "I have all the excitement I need with you, Princess."

"And you have enough money to buy another dangerously fast car." Meg laughs. "You don't fool me. I know you crave speed."

I stare into Meg's bright brown eyes. "I'd give it up for you. I'd give up anything for you."

"Miles." Her fingers curl around my hands. "Don't talk like that."

"I'm a man of my word. I won't think about leaving the band. But you always come first." Fuck. My cheeks are burn-ing. I don't do affection in front of other people. Not even in front of my fiancée's parents.

I can do it when I'm in control. But here, I'm fucking powerless. If I don't convince Susan, this is off. And God knows how Meg will react to that.

Life is good now. Hard sometimes, but good. It can't change. Not again.

I can feel Meg's eyes on me. Hell, I can hear her sighing. My eyes meet hers. She might as well be screaming, *Oh my God, you're adorable.*

Damn, this must be how she feels all the time.

No wonder she used to get all pissy when I called her adorable.

This is awful.

Susan lets out a friendly laugh. "You're such a sweet young man, Miles. I know you don't want anyone to think that about you, but it's true."

Dammit, I can't control this. I'm still blushing.

Meg pulls out her cellphone and takes a picture. "No one will believe this happened."

I fold my arms. I'm usually on the other side of this kind of poking. The only way to make it stop is to pretend it doesn't bother you.

Deep breath. I keep cool.

Meg laughs. Susan too.

Douglass looks at me with solidarity.

Susan pulls a small box from her purse and sets it on the table. "I'm not going to tell either of you how to live your lives. This is fast, but sometimes, you know something is right." She wipes a tear from her cheek. "Megara, sweetheart, I'm so proud of you for completing your first semester of medical school. If you want to marry this man, I'm happy for you. I'll be happier if you wait, but I'm happy now." She wipes another tear from her eye. "I'm going to be a crying mess."

"Mom." Meg squeezes her mother's hand. "I love you. Thank you." She looks at her father. "You too, Dad. We still... it's not final yet, but if it is, will you walk me down the aisle?"

Douglass starts crying, full-on bawling. It's the most emotion I've ever seen from him.

"Of course." He nods.

Susan pulls the lid off the box. There are two rings inside. Both are platinum. "Your friend, Thomas."

Meg sticks her tongue out. "Thomas? You mean Tom?"

Susan nods.

"Thomas makes him sound so... polite."

"He was very polite," Susan says. "He seems like a nice young man."

Meg bursts into laughter. "Mom, he..." She shakes her head. Her eyes meet mine. "Can you believe this?"

"The man can have a cock piercing and be perfectly polite," I say.

Susan laughs. Douglass has that *oh fuck, ow* look of sympathy pain.

Meg hides behind her palms. That's better.

Susan shakes her head. "You two seem happy. That makes me happy. And Tom really did seem nice. He was gushing about his wife. His wedding sounded nice." She lets out a dreamy sigh. "Hawaii on the beach. You sure you don't want to do that? Maybe... in five years?"

Meg squeezes my hand. "We want to do it soon."

Susan pushes the rings forward, giving us a better view. "He gave me your ring sizes. These were made in the same style as your father's and mine were." She wipes back another tear. "They're our present to you, if you'd like to use them. We won't be hurt if you decide you'd rather choose your own rings."

"Do you have a best man, son?" Douglass asks.

Fuck, that's a decision that will ruffle some feathers.

"You should have the guys share it," Meg says, "or give it to Tom."

"He's married," I say.

"So?" Meg shoots me an incredulous look. "Since when do you care about tradition?"

"I guess I'll ask Drew, Tom, and Pete to share it." I look at Susan. "Compromise."

"Why don't you hold onto it for us, Dad?" Meg asks. "Until the guys get here."

He nods.

Meg squeezes my hand. Her parents are really on board.

We can fucking do this.

Chapter Eight

MILES

Meg's parents spend most of dinner reminiscing about Meg's and Rosie's childhoods. We don't leave until the restaurant is about to close.

I slide my arm around Meg's waist to help her stay upright. She rubs her eyes as she yawns. She must have spent the last month studying. She's exhausted.

I kiss her cheek. "Meet me at the hotel. I'm going to walk your parents home."

She looks from her parents to me and offers a sleepy nod. She rises to her tiptoes to whisper in my ear. "If you stay out too late, I won't have the energy to fuck you when you get back."

Her cheeks flush a soft shade of pink.

Damn. I hate to miss out on Meg screaming my name, but making sure her parents are on board is important.

I kiss her goodbye, and we separate.

Susan and Douglass are staying at the Bellagio, the hotel famous for its fountain shows. It's only a few hotels away. They spend the walk lost in the same memories that captured them during dinner. I listen with rapt attention. Meg has always been an adorable little nerd. Turns out she had a phase in elementary school where she collected dinosaurs. Her room was flush with them. Her parents were convinced she would end up a paleontologist.

They were relieved when she moved on to dolls, and even more relieved when she started performing surgery on the dolls.

The fountains are roaring when we arrive. They dance to Elton John's *Your Song*.

Susan's eyes go wide. She grabs onto the concrete railing.

"I'll meet you up in the room." Douglass plants a chaste kiss on her cheek and makes his way to the hotel entrance.

There's no chemistry between them. No passion. It's clear Meg's parents support each other, but there's a distance too.

That must have a lot to do with why Meg is scared. Not that my parents are a better example. If anything, my parents make hers look like models of everlasting romance.

Susan pulls her arms over her chest. She rubs her triceps, but she's still shivering.

I shift my leather jacket off my shoulders and offer it to her. It's a cold night, but I don't mind the bite of the chill.

She waves it away. "No, thank you. The cold is nice." She makes eye contact. Her lips curl into a smile then her attention goes back to the fountains. "You love Megara a lot, don't you?"

"I do."

"I know you'll take care of her. But, Miles, if you get in the way of her studying medicine, I'll do everything in my power to get you out of her life."

I fight my desire to laugh. Susan has no idea how badly I want the world for Meg. "I won't."

Her voice softens. "Not on purpose. But I know what happens when you're in love. I've been there. I can count on one hand the female classmates who stayed in medical school after they got married. They told themselves they'd go back, but they never did. They moved to the suburbs and switched to raising a family." Her eyes meet mine. "That can be a fulfilling priority. God knows, I love Megara, and I... Rosie... it brought me a wealth of joy, raising children, but Meg-"

"She won't be happy if she gives up medicine. I know that." The fountains flash with a burst of white light. "You had kids, and you're quite the surgeon now. Must be possible to make it work."

"It is. It's hard, but it's worth it." Susan presses her lips together. "I was much older when I got pregnant with Rosie. Well out of medical school."

"I can't believe that."

She laughs. "You must have done well when you were single. You're a charmer."

I nod.

"You don't have to charm me. I see the way my daughter lights up around you. I know you bring joy into her life." She watches as the fountain show ends and the lights turn off. Her eyes stay on the pool of dark water. "I'm sure some of those women were happier raising a family instead of practicing medicine. Is that what you want?"

I press my palm against the concrete. I can't say I've given family much thought. Fuck knows, I don't want to follow in my parents' footsteps and fuck some poor kid up. Better to opt out of the whole thing. Not sure whether I ever want kids. Meg isn't sure either. It's not something we dwell on.

Susan is a woman with her shit together. I need a better answer than *fuck if I know*.

I turn toward her, keeping my expression neutral. "We're waiting to see how it feels to really have a life together."

Her brow knots with confusion. "What do you have now?"

"She lives with you."

"You're saying she's moving out after the wedding? I didn't agree to that." She smiles, teasing.

"I'm still working out the details," I admit.

Susan's eyes fill with affection. "You two can stay with me and Douglass if you'd like."

"Forever?"

"And then some."

"And when we wake you up with our loud sex?" I tease.

"I sleep with ear plugs."

I laugh. "And Meg's dad?"

"He'll get over it." She smiles. "I'm glad you're so passionate about her."

"You're glad I love fucking your daughter twenty-four seven?"

Susan doesn't blush. She doesn't even blink. "I'm older, Miles. I'm not dead. Douglass and I have an active sex life. It's not what it was when we were your age. And since Rosie died, we're still not all the way back to normal. But yes, I am glad you love having sex— well, I assume the two of you engage in oral and vaginal sex. Perhaps anal sex as well."

I laugh. "You want to know if Meg and I have anal sex?"

"I don't need the details, but I'm glad you two have an active sex life. Sex is good for you. It produces dopamine. It's good for back pain and stress relief." She turns toward me. Her expression shifts, more serious. "But that passion doesn't last unless you make a point of keeping it alive. Studies show that the rush of excitement that comes with new love fades after about two years. If you want to keep it alive, you need to do new things together, to make a point of holding hands and scheduling dates. Novelty keeps the Dopamine rush alive."

"You telling me to sexually experiment with your daughter?"

Susan is dead serious. "If that's what the two of you want."

This time, I can't hold in my laugh. My hand goes to my stomach. My knees buckle from the weight of my belly laugh.

She chuckles. "I'm a gynecologist. There's nothing you can say about sex that will surprise me."

"And recommendations?" I raise a brow.

"I'm not Dr. Ruth. I don't specialize in sexual pleasure. But I can point you to a few great resources if you'd like." Her smile spreads. "I'm glad it matters to you."

"You're glad your daughter's sexual pleasure matters to me?"

"Of course." Her brows screw. "I know most parents are afraid of their children having sex, but I've been married for nearly thirty years. I know that you need to make an effort."

"Thanks, Dr. Smart. Susan." I look into her light brown eyes. "Can I ask you something personal?"

She nods.

"You and Douglass... are you still happy?"

"Yes." Her eyes go to the dark water. "We've had our rough patches. I almost left a few times. After Rosie died, I thought that was it. A part of me died. A part of him too. We couldn't connect. I couldn't look at him. All I saw was her absence." She swallows hard. "Stressors are hard on a marriage. The loss of a child is one of the biggest ones."

"Why did you stay?"

"He's my best friend." She takes a slow breath. "He holds me up when I need him." She presses away from the railing. "It's hard on a marriage when two ambitious people put their careers first. It's good that you'll understand each other's priorities, but, Miles, you have to promise me you won't let inertia take over. You have to promise you'll always make her a priority."

"I will."

Susan hugs me goodbye. She steps backward. "I should get to bed. Take care of her for me."

I'M SURE THIS ISN'T WHAT SUSAN MEANT BY *TAKE CARE OF my daughter*, but I doubt she'd object.

I find what I want quickly. It's not the most conventional wedding present, but I know Meg will love it.

"Excuse me." The voice that asks is shy. Barely a whisper. "Aren't you Miles Webb?"

Ah, a female fan in a sex toy shop. Two years ago, this night would have gone a different way.

I turn to face my fan. She's a pretty girl, and she's dressed to party—high heels, tight skirt, enough makeup to drown her features.

Two years ago, I'd have leaned in and whispered *yes, but baby, you can call me Miles*. Two years ago, I'd have gotten her panties to her knees by the time we were out the door.

I don't miss that guy. I don't even like that guy.

She's looking at me like she hopes I'm that guy. I'm not sure what to think. If she really is a fan, she should know I'm taken. My tattoo was big news. Women everywhere wept over the *Smoking Hot Vocalist, Miles Webb, Off the Market* headlines.

My temper flares. It's been a long time since I've hit anyone. Most of the time, I'm steady as a rock.

No wonder I denied the existence of love for so long. It breaks down your walls. Makes you vulnerable.

"Sorry, I'm not familiar with that name." I nod a goodbye and make my way to the register.

I can feel her gaze on me. There's a *No Cameras* sign posted on the wall. There are about twenty *No Cameras* signs posted on the walls. She doesn't look like the rule-breaking type. As far as I can tell, it took every ounce of courage for her to talk to me.

It's been a long time since I've hit anyone. Don't want to start again.

I finish my purchase, step outside, and text Meg than I'm inbound. Usually, she replies right away. Nothing tonight.

Nothing when I'm back at the hotel.

Damn, the elevator is taking forever. I need to break out this gift and use it with her.

Finally, the damn thing arrives. I step into the elevator and lean against the mirrored wall. All the walls are mirrored. Gives me ideas. Fucking amazing ideas.

It takes the elevator an eternity to reach our floor. I walk quickly. My key is in my pocket. There. The door flashes green as it unlocks. I step inside.

The lights are off. Even in the bathroom.

Meg is lying on the bed, naked and fast asleep.

This isn't how I expected the night to end, but fuck, does she look cute in her sleep.

I've already got a plan figured out. I spend an hour squaring away the details, then I brush my teeth, strip to my boxers, and slide into bed behind her.

Her body stirs. She mumbles my name, nestles into my chest, and falls back to sleep.

Chapter Nine

MEGARA

I t's heaven waking up in Miles's arms.

Math is difficult at this time of the morning, but mine suggests I have another twenty-seven days in the same bed as him.

Most people don't get twenty-seven great days in a year. Some people don't get twenty-seven great days in their life.

I'm lucky, but still, I want more.

I get up, brush my teeth, and rifle though my attire options. Thankfully, Mom brought me a suitcase of clothes. I dress in jeans, a t-shirt, and a cozy cashmere sweater.

Miles rises and goes through his morning routine. He slides his arms around me and pulls me onto the couch with him. "That sweater is entrapment."

"Is that right?"

"Mhmm." He presses his lips to mine. "Can't do anything but hug you."

"Why is that a problem?"

"Because we have someplace to be." He releases me and brings his arms to the bed. "Our tour of the venue is in an hour."

"You should have woken me."

"You look too cute sleeping." He brushes my hair behind my ears. "I made reservations for dinner tonight. Private room at a Japanese place. It's not technically a rehearsal dinner-"

"You're that sure I'll love the venue?"

He nods.

"What if I don't like it?"

"Then we'll find another venue."

"And the money for the deposit?"

Miles laughs. "Princess, we're getting married. This is the one time where you don't think about trivialities."

"Money is a triviality?"

He nods.

"How rich are you?" I know Miles is wealthy. The several-million-dollar beach house purchases give away how well Tom and Pete are doing. And Miles makes more than any of the other guys in the band. He's the only one with a side gig.

He's the only one who inherited a fortune.

"Convince me to tell you," he teases.

"Don't we have someplace to be?"

"Damn. Guess you'll have to wait."

"Miles! Tell me! Please."

"What's in it for me?" He tugs at my sweater.

I press my palms together. "My eternal devotion."

"Hmmm." His eyes pass over me. His tongue slides over his lips. "Can you sweeten the deal?"

I flip him off playfully.

He smiles. "About thirty million. Give or take."

He's effortlessly casual about it. *I'm worth thirty million dollars. No big deal.*

We'll be worth thirty million dollars.

I'm willing to say goodbye to fifteen million dollars in the event you tire of me.

A long time ago, we agreed that he'd pay for anything we do together. I've never felt compelled to challenge the rule. Since I quit my job as an ER scribe last May, I've been without income. I spend all my savings on textbooks and the caffeine necessary to get through the day.

But thirty million dollars...

"Breathe, Princess." He rubs my shoulders. "It's good news."

"Do you want a prenup?" That's what wealthy people do, isn't it?

"You planning on divorcing me?"

"Of course not."

"Then no."

"What if something happens?"

"If I let our relationship get to point where you want to take me to the cleaners, I don't deserve a cent of that thirty million dollars." He slides his hand around my neck, cupping the back of my head. "I've had a lot of money for a long time. It never made me happy."

"But-"

"You make me happy, Meg. Happier than any amount of money."

"But thirty million dollars."

He laughs.

"This is important." I look up at him. "I'd never take advantage."

"I know." He drags his fingertip over my chest like he's doodling on my skin. "I wouldn't either."

"Huh?"

"Of how badly you want me." He pulls my sweater aside so he can trace the lines of my tattoo. "If you aren't one hundred percent after the tour of the venue, we'll cancel and we'll fly to the Caribbean early."

"We're going to the Caribbean?"

He nods. "For our honeymoon. Unless spending the week on the beach doesn't work for you."

"No. It works." It sounds amazing. Exactly the break I need. I meet his gaze. "You're really ready to get married tomorrow?"

"I've been ready since the day I got this." He pulls his t-shirt down to show off his *Megara* tattoo. "That's more permanent than a ring or a piece of paper."

His blue eyes shine with certainty. I run my fingers over his tattoo. It makes me as happy as it did the first time I saw it.

I need him as much as I did that night.

I love Miles more every day.

That's what matters.

"I don't want to disappoint you." I lean closer. "If I don't like it."

"You won't."

"You promise?"

He nods. "Whatever you decide, we have the rest of our lives together."

ॐ

THERE'S A LIMO WAITING FOR US.

"Your chariot." Miles presses his palm against my lower back as he helps me inside. His smile is ear to ear.

Even after a year together, it's not like him to wear his heart on his sleeve. Not this nakedly.

"I don't know how to handle you being this openly affectionate." I scoot next to him on the bench seat. "Say something sarcastic. I have to be sure you're my Miles Webb."

"Whose Miles Webb do you think I am?"

"That's a start."

"I don't mind you ordering me around, but it's not going

to end with us using our mouths for conversation." His voice shifts, half cocky, half sincere.

That's the Miles I know. "Better." Nerves dance in my stomach as the limo pulls away from the hotel. We're going to our wedding venue. I have to make the call on whether or not we're getting married there tomorrow night.

No pressure.

Teasing with Miles feels normal. Like it's not three days after my first semester of med school, two weeks before he leaves for another four months, God knows how many minutes before I decide when we make this official.

I shift onto his lap. "How should I order you around?"

"Oh, you want me to demonstrate?"

I nod.

He tugs at the neckline of my t-shirt. "Get rid of this."

"Why?"

"You'll like what happens after."

I like it already. I pull my t-shirt over my head and watch as his eyes go wide with desire. "We've never had sex in a limo."

"Better change that." He unhooks my bra and slides it off my shoulders. "You still look nervous."

"I am."

He smiles. "You trust me."

"Miles, you're supposed to be rocking my world with passion. No conversations about the future of our relationship."

"How should I be using my mouth?"

I turn my head, offering my neck to him. His hands go to my hips. He pulls me closer as he presses his lips against my skin. It's a flutter of a kiss. The softness sends heat racing through my body.

My thoughts have been running in circles for the last two days.

I need this break. I need to stop thinking and feel.

There's no patience in my movements. I tug his t-shirt over his head. Then my hands are on the hard muscles of his chest. His lips are on my neck. He kisses harder. Lower. His lips trail over my shoulders. My collarbone. My chest.

He kisses every inch of my new tattoo. "Fuck, this is the sexiest thing I've ever seen."

"Show me."

His eyes connect with mine. "Gonna be fast."

"Good." I shift onto my knees so I can unzip my jeans and slide them off my hips.

Miles takes over. He pulls my jeans off my feet. Then it's his jeans at his knees. His boxers.

Damn, he looks as yummy as ever sitting there, waiting for me to mount him.

I plant my knees outside his thighs, bringing my body onto his. No more thinking. Right now, I want to feel how much my body needs his. How much my heart needs his.

He presses his palm against my sex. "Fuck. You're wet."

I nod.

His hands go to my ass. He watches my expression as he pulls my body onto his. His cock strains against me. Then he's inside me, stretching me, filling me.

My hands go to his shoulders. I stare back at him. *This* is where I belong. If only we could skip the rest of the world. No work, no friends, no family, no ceremonies of any kind.

Nothing but our bodies joining again and again.

I lean down to press my lips to his. He tastes good. Like toothpaste and like Miles. His tongue is as hungry as mine is. He kisses me like he's never kissed me before.

My love for him overwhelms me. I feel so fucking whole when we're joined like this.

We belong together.

We'll figure the rest out.

I rock my hips to meet his movements, pushing him deeper. My thoughts fade away as he thrusts into me.

He moves deeper. Harder.

Pleasure collects in my core. I squeeze his shoulders and break the kiss so he can work me properly. His mouth goes to my chest. His tongue flicks against my nipple, sending pangs of pleasure through my torso. Again. Again. Again.

My sex clenches. I'm getting there. But I want more.

I bring my mouth to his ear. "Rub me."

He groans with pleasure at the command. His hand goes right to my thigh. He rubs my clit with his thumb.

Fuck. That feels good. He always takes care of me. Here. And everywhere else.

He kisses his way up my chest and neck. Then his lips are on mine. The kiss is equal parts tender and hot.

Affection pours between us. We're already pressed together, but still, I want him closer. Deeper. I press my palms against his back and pull him closer.

I spread my knees wider so he can go deeper.

"Mhmmm." Miles groans. His fingers dig into the flesh of my ass. He holds my body against his as he drives deeper. Harder.

Pleasure overwhelms me. Almost.

I spread a little wider. Shift a little closer.

His mouth goes to my chest. He sucks hard. His groans vibrate against my skin. It's like this is the only way he can contain himself.

I surrender to the sensation of our bodies joining. He has all of me. I have all of him.

That's what matters.

The tension inside me builds to a fever pitch. With his next thrust, I tumble into an orgasm.

"Miles," I groan. Pleasure spills through my limbs, all the way to my fingers and toes.

My sex pulses around him, pulling him closer.

He's almost there. I can feel it in the fast movements of his hips, in the way his chest and stomach muscles tense.

He sucks hard on my nipple. Then it's teeth. He bites just hard enough it feels amazing.

I tug at his hair so I can manage the sensation.

With his next thrust, an orgasm overtakes him. He groans against my skin. He digs his nails into my hips. He thrusts into me, his cock pulsing as he fills me.

We stay pressed together until we arrive.

We're here. At the venue.

It has to be perfect. I don't want to wait.

I want to marry him as soon as possible.

Chapter Ten

MEGARA

My eyes go wide. It's perfect.

The courtyard is bathed in bright sunlight. Ribbons of chiffon flow from the altar in the center out to the edges of the room.

Right now, everything is decorated with white and pink. White chiffon, white ribbons, soft pink rose petals.

But it can be purple.

It's going to be purple for our ceremony.

The coordinator, Candy, shows us pictures of other ceremonies they've performed. There are dozens of different color schemes, dozens of styles. Some are busier, louder. Some are simpler.

One is perfect.

The aisle is decked with red rose petals. It's lined with potted roses. The altar is overflowing with red roses. It's so full it looks like it's going to collapse on the happy couple.

It's beautiful.

Like a fairytale.

Miles pulls me into a close hug. I slide my hands under his

leather jacket so I can pull him closer. I'm used to the smell of that jacket. It smells like him. Like home.

I blink back a tear. Damn. Look at me. Getting emotional over roses and bows.

"Would you like to see the reception site?" The friendly coordinator asks.

Miles rubs my shoulders over my coat. "I think she needs a minute."

"It's beautiful. You should be crying."

"Princess, I thought I didn't cry."

"You *don't* cry."

"You want me to cry?" He smiles. "That's cruel."

"Miles." I stare into his piercing blue eyes. "I love you. It's perfect."

He leans in to kiss me. It's chaste for him.

Fuck that. I rise to my tiptoes so I can press my lips to his. I slide my tongue into his mouth. My body is no longer satiated from our limo sex. I need him again.

Now.

I need him every night. Forever.

My heartbeat picks up. I let my thoughts drift away as I follow Candy to the reception site. It's just as beautiful, just as straight out of a fairytale.

The grand ballroom is painted in shades of ivory and silver. And it's decorated with that same rich, red motif. Roses are everywhere. Crimson bows and touches are everywhere.

Candy laughs. "The ceremony this afternoon has a clear theme."

"My fiancée wants everything purple." Miles squeezes me. "The brightest purple you have."

I squeeze Miles's hand. "You really want purple?"

"Of course." He presses his lips to my forehead.

He has everything figured out. He's perfect.

"Any changes you'd like?" Candy asks.

I shake my head.

Miles laughs. "I think that's a no."

They exchange goodbyes. I'm too in a daze to notice what it is they're saying. The decorations will be purple tomorrow.

Rosie will be here. A little piece of her will be here.

Miles waits until Candy is gone. He pulls his cellphone from his jeans and turns to me. "I want to show you something."

"Is it your cock? I'd like to see that again." He unlocks his cell screen, taps it a few times, and hands the phone to me.

"Is it a picture of your cock? That would be quite the curveball."

His smile spreads ear to ear. "Princess, I don't delete my old photos. I'm sure there are plenty of pictures if that's what you're after."

"Good."

His expression gets serious. "Look at the screen."

I do. It's an itinerary. Flights. One from Phoenix to Orange County. Then, two days later, from Orange County to Denver. A week later, a flight from Seattle to Orange County. Then from Orange County to Chicago.

It goes like that for five months.

There are a dozen round trips. We'll never be more than ten days apart.

I look up at Miles. There's all this affection in his clear blue eyes. "You're going to spend your entire tour on airplanes."

"Only the breaks."

"This is too much."

"No. It's just enough." He rubs my shoulders. "If you get spare time, I'll fly you out. But if not, that's okay. Your life doesn't have to change. You don't have to give up anything you want, Meg. Including us together as often as possible."

I do the math. This will give us forty days together. With the break, that's almost two out of the next five months.

I can do that. But- "You want to stay with my parents? Half these dates are during the week." It's no problem staying at the Malibu mansion on the weekends, but, with traffic, it's two hours from school.

The same smile spreads over his face. "About that."

"About that?"

"Go to the next email."

I do. It's a confirmation for a lease. The address is in Newport Beach.

It's an apartment for us.

There's even a message about Miles wanting to add my name to the lease.

"There are pictures," he says.

There are. It's smaller than the place in Malibu—it's hard to compete with a mansion— but there's plenty of room in the modern condo. There are two bedrooms, a wide main room, a balcony and a shared pool.

And you can see the beach from the windows.

"Fifteen minutes to UCI. Half an hour in traffic." He drags his fingertips over my neck. "It's ours through May. After, we can renew or we can find a more permanent place."

"You want to live in Orange County?"

"I want to live where you are, Meg."

"What if I do my residency in Arizona?"

"Then I'm in Arizona." He slides his hand to the back of my neck. "I talked to Tom. He wants to slow down too. More time off during tours. Fewer private gigs. We might not make as much money, but-"

"You're already worth thirty million."

He laughs. "Yeah. Only eight or nine for the other guys, but that's plenty."

"I can't believe you're bragging at a time like this."

He smiles. His forehead connects with mine for a moment. Then he pulls back enough to stare into my eyes. "I'm not saying it will be easy. I'm sure there will be days where you get home and wish I were there. I'm sure there will be nights on the road where I need you like I need oxygen. But we'll figure it out. Any time you need me, call. I'll find a way to be there."

"What if you need me?"

"I'll find a way for us to be together." His eyes fill with affection. "You're going to be a great doctor one day. I'll always have music. That will change with the times, but it will always be in my heart. Right next to you."

"But I'm the only one here." I drag my fingertips over his chest, over the tattoo of my name.

"Yeah. You're the only one here." He leans down to press his lips to mine.

When the kiss breaks, I stare back at him. "Okay. Now, I believe you promised to show me your cock."

He laughs. "Princess, you know I always give you what you want."

He whisks me back to the limo.

And we make excellent use of our free afternoon.

Chapter Eleven

MILES

We barely make it out of the limo in time to pick up our marriage license. Damn. We're late. I check the clock when we stop at our hotel room to change. Again, I'm in slacks and a button-up shirt. Meg wears a knee-length ivory dress and silver wedges that give her an inch on me.

The woman lives in flats. I'm almost never looking up at her.

Well, not when we're dressed.

What the hell time is it anyway? I check the clock again. As hot as she looks with the dress hugging her chest and waist, this has to wait until after dinner.

The Japanese restaurant is packed to the brim. I lead Meg through the fray, straight to the reserved room in back.

It's through sliding screen doors. They're white and tan, a stark contrast to the dim room and its black accents.

Despite its lack of windows, the private room is bright. Paper lanterns hang from the ceiling. There must be a few dozen in shades of red, pink, and blue.

The room is full of friends. I'm sure I'll be sick of the

three of them by the end of the tour, but I'm happy to see them now.

Tom, Drew, and Pete—they're my family. They get on my nerves, get in my space, and piss me off because they love me.

Everyone is seated at a long table. Tom's wife—fuck, I'm still not used to that—Willow is next to him in the back. Her magenta dress matches her magenta hair. Behind them are Pete and his fiancée, Jess. She lifts her head from his shoulder to nod a hello to me. She smiles at Meg.

Kara and Drew are on the other side of the table, next to Meg's parents. She jumps out of her seat to hug us hello, first me then Meg.

Kara whispers loudly enough I can hear. "Is this really happening?"

Meg nods.

Kara squeezes her tighter.

Drew is next. He offers Meg a quick hug. We make eye contact, a look that says, *I'm happy for you, but I don't desire the proximity of your body.* We shake hands.

The Steele brothers are wearing their usual trouble-making smiles. Tom brushes a hand through his sandy blond waves. The other hand is curled around a wrapped present.

He thrusts it into Meg's hands. "Don't open it in front of your parents."

"Oh." She looks at the purple wrapping then looks up at Tom. "Is it a sex toy?"

Tom laughs. Pete chuckles.

"I should kick your ass for that." I address both of them.

"Wait until you see what it is. You'll like it." Tom gives Meg a tight hug. He shoots me the same look Drew did.

"Oh, don't be a pussy about it." Meg pushes us into a hug.

It's quick. A second. Then Pete takes his turn.

He whispers something in Meg's ear. Her cheeks turn red. Damn. Knowing the dark-haired bassist, I'm sure he said something positively filthy. I should kick his ass for that, but Meg looks fucking adorable blushing. And she's eyeing me like she's already thinking about what we'll do when we get back to the hotel room.

Pete hugs me without any of Tom's shyness.

"You dirty talking my girl?" I ask.

He chuckles. "Offering some advice for later."

"Advice about pleasing a man?"

He chuckles, shakes his head, and pats me on the back. "Can't believe you're doing this."

"You got engaged after three months."

Pete shrugs as he pulls back. "Don't have commitment issues."

"That cuts me, Steele."

I glance at his fiancée. Jess plays with her long blond hair. Nervous or... no, she's antsy. She's got the look of a woman who wants to be alone with her man.

I can respect that. I did drag the two of them away from their bedroom. I catch her gaze and nod hello. She waves and smiles back.

Tom busts between us. "When do we get to see the new tattoo?"

"Do I ask your wife to whip out her tits so I can gawk at her tattoo?" I come back.

That earns me a laugh from Tom and a glare from Drew.

Willow gets up from her seat. She hugs Meg and me then settles next to Tom. "Is my husband bothering you?"

"My wife is so rude." Tom shakes his head with mock outrage. "I'm going to have to take her back to the hotel and punish her."

Willow blushes. She turns to us. "I'm happy for you guys. You're such a lovely, tall couple."

Tom laughs.

"What?" She pouts. "They're really tall. Both of them are taller than you are."

"You're emasculating me, kid." Tom squeezes her.

"Right," she says.

"You should remind me of my virility right now." Tom smiles.

Willow shakes her head, endeared. Then she motions to Meg. "I was thinking." She leans in to whisper in Meg's ear.

Meg blushes. "Oh. I don't know that we'll have time."

"We can do it tonight," Willow says. "I'll send Tom away."

Tom shakes his head with mock incredulity.

"Aren't you having a bachelor party?" Willow asks.

"Do you want one?" Tom looks to me, his brow screwing with confusion.

Don't drink. Don't gamble. Don't have any interest in lap dances from strippers. Makes bachelor party options pretty slim.

I shake my head.

"Miles has seen enough tits to last a lifetime," Tom teases. He looks at Meg and motions to the present in her hands. "Use that well."

Again, Meg blushes. She manages to hold Tom's eye contact. "Did Miles really talk to you about slowing down?"

Tom nods.

"Do you hate me for that?" she asks.

"Fuck no. He's making me look accommodating, for once. Miles asks to slow down. I reluctantly agree. I get to spend more afternoons pinning my wife to the wall. Besides, it's not just Miles. Drew–"

Willow clears her throat.

"Nevermind about that. I get more time to fuck my wife." Tom rubs his nose against Willow's. "That's what matters."

Meg's expression screws with confusion. "Tom, you want to slow down?"

Tom runs his hand through his hair. "No, I... I just think it's important for Miles to keep you around. I'm not going to be the one watching him like a hawk every time there's alcohol nearby." Tom laughs. He looks at me. "I swear I'm not trying to scare her off."

"Uh-huh." Willow rises to her tiptoes to whisper in his ear. She turns to us. "Congrats again. You really are a beautiful, tall couple. And I'm looking forward to tonight, Meg. Don't eat or drink too much. You want your agility." She winks.

Meg giggles.

"What's tonight?" I ask.

"A surprise," Meg says.

"Fuck, he's slow. Even I put those pieces together," Tom says.

"Honey." Willow slides her arm around Tom's waist. "If you delay me, I won't have time for you tonight."

"Fuck that." Tom nods goodbye and pulls Willow back to the table.

Jess is up next. She hugs Meg hello and doesn't quite whisper in her ear, "I told you he'd ask."

"But an hour after finals?" Meg asks.

Jess nods. "You should hear how he talks about you when you aren't around. He's gaga for you." She turns to me. "I hope I'm not speaking out of turn. You guys are going to be so happy." She rises to her tiptoes to hug me.

After hellos and congratulations with Meg's parents, we settle into our spots at the table. It's just in time for appetizers—miso soup, edamame, and mixed greens.

Meg squeezes my hand. She leans in to whisper, "I've been thinking... Sinful Serenade is your family. And they're mine too."

"Yeah?" I stare into her brown eyes.

"Yeah. I love that you got us a place in Newport. I love

that we'll be by my family all week. But maybe we can be by your family all weekend? In Malibu, or we can find a place that's closer to everyone. Fuck, we can take turns staying with Tom and Pete, if that's what you want."

"Taking turns with the Steele brothers?"

She cocks a brow.

"Don't tell me you've considered it."

"Maybe..." She tries to hold a poker face, but it's not happening. "Okay, I haven't considered anyone but you."

I whisper in her ear, "Why is it so hot that we're getting married tomorrow?"

"Wedding night sex?" she offers.

Yeah, ripping a gown off her chest sounds fucking amazing. I lick my lips as I nod.

"We should wait until after the wedding." She pulls back enough to look me in the eyes. "I don't like it either, but we should. It will be better."

Chapter Twelve

MEGARA

After dinner, Willow and I swing by my hotel room for supplies, then we go straight to her room. We ban the boys for the rest of the night. They can't interrupt our boudoir photo session. Though they do try. Our phones buzz with *Are you ready?* messages from our perspective lovers all evening.

Under normal circumstances, Willow is a little shy. But when she steps behind the camera, she's authoritative and in control. I feel silly posing on a hotel bed—she assures me she and Tom have yet to fuck in it—in my new lingerie, but her encouragement helps me loosen up and get into it.

It's well past midnight when we finish. I dress, return to my hotel room, and collapse next to my sleeping fiancée. Even rock gods need their rest.

In the morning, I wake before him, pack a small bag for our wedding night, complete with the Steele brothers' totally embarrassing present of crotchless panties and a matching open-front bra—white lace, of course—and meet Kara for breakfast and caffeine.

She beams when she sees me at the coffee shop. "I'm so excited for you."

But her cheeks are a little green.

"Are you okay?" I ask.

"No, but it's nothing you need to worry about. We'll talk when you get back from the honeymoon."

"You sure?"

"Positive." She hands me a cup of green tea. "No coffee. That much caffeine will send your nerves into overdrive." She checks her watch. "We have an hour until the shop opens. Everything will go fast after that. You ready to be a bride?"

I nod.

I really am.

◌◌◌

NERVES FLUTTER IN MY BELLY, BUT I FORCE MYSELF TO EAT my lunch, a perfectly bland vegetable and hummus sandwich. The bread is wonderful at soaking up my anxiety.

My hairstyle takes ages. My makeup takes longer. Then, all of a sudden, there's no more time to wait.

We're due at the ceremony site in half an hour.

This is happening in half an hour.

I'm marrying Miles.

My heart is thudding against my chest. Every inch of my body is light, but the nervous energy is good. It's like the adrenaline before stepping onto a roller coaster.

I'm scared but I'm excited.

Kara helps me into my dress. She cinches the corset back so tightly that I can barely breathe. It's uncomfortable, but it's gorgeous. The snug bodice pushes up my chest and creates the illusion of curves.

The hair stylist attaches one more pin to the tiara.

Now, I really am a princess.

Kara squeezes my hand as she leads me into the limo. My skirt is huge enough I need an entire bench to myself.

The other girls joke about something, but their words fly through my ears.

I'm getting married.

This is really happening.

Is it really medically safe for my heart to be beating this fast? Unlikely. I take deep breaths and play with my engagement ring in an attempt to calm down.

Willow scoots next to me. Gently, she places her hand over my left ring finger. "You're supposed to wear the engagement ring on your right hand during the ceremony. So the wedding ring is closer to your heart."

I nod. She got married two months ago. She's been through this. My eyelids press together as I recall Willow's wedding in Hawaii. She looked so calm, like she was floating down the aisle in her breezy chiffon dress and pink wedges.

How the fuck did she look so calm? I think my heart is going to explode. And I'm overheating. It feels like I'm sweating off my makeup.

I check my reflection. It's okay. I look nervous, yes, but my makeup and hair are still perfect. I still look like a bride.

In fact, I look about as beautiful as I ever have.

The limo slows to a stop. The driver shouts something. It must be meaningful, because the other girls are moving.

I switch my ring to my right hand.

"Good luck," Willow whispers in my ear. She smiles and exits the limo.

The orange light of sunset floods the dark interior as she pushes the door open.

"You look beautiful, Meg. Miles is going to melt." Jess blows me a kiss as she slides out of the limo.

Then it's me and Kara.

She sits on the bench seat opposite mine and looks me

dead in the eyes. "If you're not ready, I'll make them wait. Even if it takes all evening."

I take a deep breath. My heart is racing at the speed of light. Mostly, it's excitement. "I'm ready."

She squeals. "Okay. I swear, I won't cry until the *I do*." She squeezes my hand. For a moment, her gaze goes outside the limo. Then it's back on me. "Your dad is here to walk you down the aisle."

"Oh."

"Are you that ready?" Her voice is still steady, reassuring.

I nod. I am that ready. I think.

"Good luck." She slides out of the car.

Then it's my turn.

I take a deep breath and slide out of the limo. Dad is standing on the sidewalk in a sleek black suit and a purple tie. He offers me his arm.

I take it.

Candy, the bubbly coordinator, is here. Her bright blue shift dress draws my eye.

She presses her hand to her earpiece. "Okay, they're ready for you." She turns to us. "Whenever you're ready."

Dad turns to me. "You ready, sweetheart?"

I nod. "I know it's been fast."

He smiles. "I knew I wanted to marry your mother on our third date. Sometimes, you just know."

He takes a step forward. I step with him. My feet are actually moving. It's hard to believe. There's certainly no evidence of it with this monster of a skirt, but I can feel them under my crinoline.

We walk through the reception site, through the open doors adorned with orchids.

Then we're there. We're at the ceremony site. There are a dozen people in the seats—the friends and family who were able to make it last minute. The aisle is covered in purple petals. My gaze follows them all the way to the just as purple altar.

For a split second, I register the presence of my friends—Drew, Tom, Pete, Kara, Willow, Jess—then all of my attention goes to Miles. His blue eyes are sparking. His lips are curled into the widest smile in the history of the world.

I've never seen him this happy. I've certainly never seen him this earnest and breathless.

The wedding march plays.

This is it.

Slowly, I move one foot in front of the other. I'm walking down the aisle. I'm walking to my groom.

Then I'm there. Dad crosses in front of me. He sits next to Mom.

I take my place across from Miles.

There's an officiant at the podium. He's saying something, an introduction about the beauty of marriage and commitment.

I hear none of it.

In this moment, my entire world is the certainty in Miles's eyes.

In this moment, I'm as certain as he is.

He takes my hands and holds tightly.

"The bride and groom have opted to write their own vows." The officiant turns to Miles. "Miles, why don't you go first?"

Miles's eyes go to the officiant, then they're on me. He presses his lips together. He's nervous.

My effortless cool, rock star husband-to-be can get on stage in front of ten thousand people without batting an eye.

But he's nervous for this.

My heart sings.

He moves a few inches closer. "When I met you, I was adamant about not being interested in a relationship."

There are chuckles in the room.

Miles continues. "Back then, I didn't believe love could do anything but destroy you. I only saw the ache that came from losing someone. I couldn't see the elation that came from handing someone your heart, from trusting them not to break it." He takes a nervous breath and squeezes my hand. "I didn't want to fall in love with you, Meg, but I'm glad I did. I trust you with my heart. I trust you with every piece of me. You make me complete, and I'm going to spend my life making sure you feel like a princess. I'm going to spend every day trying to make you as happy as you make me. Whatever happens, whenever you need me, I'm there. I'm yours."

My cheeks flush. My knees knock together. I can barely breathe. It's sweet and romantic and raw. His words are usually more polished and clean. Not this. This is straight from his heart.

"Meg." The officiant nods to me.

I take a deep breath. I tried to memorize these things. I hope I did.

"My heart was broken when I met you. I was sure that nothing would ever repair the damage. I certainly didn't think a tattooed player would put my heart back together."

There's laughter and a few *awws*.

I stare into Miles's piercing blue eyes. "You reminded me how to laugh. You reminded me that I could feel good. That I could feel pleasure."

My blush spreads to my cheeks as everyone in the room laughs at once.

I continue. "You taped my heart back together, Miles. Every time I'm afraid I'm going to fall, you're there to hold me up. I'm not sure what life will bring for either of us, but I promise to stay by your side, holding your hand, for the entire journey. I promise to make sure you feel loved. And, of course, I promise I'll keep you humble."

The officiant looks to the groomsmen. "The rings."

Someone hands them over. I think it's Drew, but it's hard to say with the way Miles is staring at me.

The officiant turns to Miles. "Miles Webb, do you take this woman to be your wife?"

Miles looks at me. One hand goes to the palm of my left hand. The other slides the ring onto my ring finger. "I do."

The officiant hands me Miles's wedding band. "Megara Smart, do you take this man to be your husband?"

I slide the ring onto Miles's left ring finger. "I do."

"Then, by the power invested in me by the glorious state of Nevada, I now pronounce you husband and wife. You may kiss," he says.

Miles leans in and presses his lips to mine. His hands go to my hips. His tongue slides into my mouth. I don't care that our friends and family are watching.

I kiss him like the ship is going down.

It *is* our first kiss as a married couple.

I need to make it count.

Chapter Thirteen

MEGARA

The reception is a blur of congratulations, dancing, and cake. It's beautiful and romantic. Hell, it's downright magical.

We don't stumble into our limo until midnight. We have another four days in Vegas before we fly to the Caribbean.

I'm not planning on seeing much more of the city.

Miles sits on the bench seat next to me and takes my hand. I study the way my silver wedding band looks on my hand as it intertwines with his.

Miles turns my palm to look at the back of my hand. "Your engagement ring."

I hold out my right hand. "The wedding ring is supposed to be closer to my heart."

Slowly, he takes the engagement ring and slides it onto my left hand. The softness of the gesture melts my heart.

He drags his fingertips over the back of my hand and over my wrist. He says nothing, just meets my gaze with those gorgeous blue eyes of his.

I lean in to press my lips to his. The kiss is soft. He tastes like chocolate and sugar, like the cake that compromised the majority of my dinner.

Can't say that I'm hungry. Not for food.

I'm kissing my husband.

Damn, I wonder how long it takes for the novelty of that to wear off. It's not happening tonight. I'm sure of that.

I do my best to slide into Miles's lap. The dress makes it difficult. On my third try, I get halfway there. My legs hang off his knees. Our bodies form a forty-five-degree angle.

My hands go to his collar. He looks so nice in his suit and tie. I hate to ruin such fine attire, but I've had enough of him wearing clothes. I need him naked.

I fumble over the knot of the tie. Fuck, this is difficult. I have to break the kiss to focus on it.

Miles takes my hands and places them on his shoulders. "We'll be at the hotel in two minutes."

"Too long." I press my lips into his.

He tugs at my dress with the same need. He's just as ineffective.

I laugh as he mutters a curse.

Between the long-line bra and the steel-boned bodice, I can't feel anything that happens over the dress. I thrust my chest into his hands so he can run his fingers over my bare skin.

His hand settles on my tattoo.

He draws the words on my skin.

Be Brave, Love.

I am. I really am.

I'm breathless and needy when the limo stops. I push off Miles and collect my dress. He adjusts his tie and repositions his slacks. It does little to hide the erection that's straining against the fabric.

My husband's erection.

It's so romantic.

The trip out of the limo and through the lobby feels like an eternity. Everyone who passes offers their congratulations. I must say three dozen *thank yous* before we finally get to the elevator.

Miles pulls a keycard from his slacks. "We have a corner suite."

I nod, only vaguely interested in anything other than the bed in our hotel room.

He pulls me into the elevator and slides our key into the slot.

The carriage takes the floor info from the key. Its doors shut, and it rises.

We're alone.

"The suite has a Jacuzzi." He slides his hands around my waist and pins me to the elevator wall. "Two couches. Two beds. A balcony." He presses his lips to my neck. "Four days is barely enough time to mark every inch of the room."

"Oh." That sounds much more appealing. It's not nearly as interesting as his lips on my skin or the weight of his body sinking into mine. Between the corset sucking the life out of me and the heat pooling between my legs, I'm struggling to form a response. "We're married."

Miles doesn't mock me. If anything, he looks even more excited than I am.

He nods, his lips curling into a smile. "Yeah, we are. Never fucked a wife before."

"You sure? You've fucked a lot of women."

He laughs, then kisses me. "Never fucked *my* wife before." He looks me up and down. "Fuck, you look amazing in that dress."

"Really?"

He nods. "Like a princess."

"That makes you my prince."

"Princess, nobody would mistake me for a prince."

I shake my head. "You are my prince, Miles. You saved me."

He presses his forehead to mine. "I know. You saved me too."

Again, Miles tugs at my dress. Again, he fails. He reaches around for the corset back, breaking the kiss to watch his work in the mirror.

His lips find my neck. He plants kisses over my skin, settling on the spot where my ear meets the back of my head. "These mirrors are giving me ideas."

Me too. And I love the ideas. I open my mouth to express my enthusiasm, but the only thing I can articulate is a groan.

It gets the point across.

By the time the elevator arrives at our floor, Miles has my corset half-unlaced. It's not enough for the dress to slip. It's only enough that it makes it possible to breathe.

He leads me to the suite in the corner, unlocks the door, and kicks it open. Just like on the afternoon of our engagement, he leans down, scoops me into his arms, and carries me across the threshold.

I cling to his chest until he sets me down. The room is amazing. It's the size of the first floor of his mansion. There's a bedroom, a living area and a full-blown kitchen. Fuck. It might be bigger than our new apartment.

We have a new apartment.

We really have a life together now.

We're married.

Before I can think, his lips find mine.

I kiss him back. My tongue slides into his mouth. My hands curl into his hair. My back arches. I try to press my hips to his, but with the layers of tulle, I can't feel a thing.

"Turn around," he mumbles into my neck.

I do.

Miles runs his fingertips off my shoulders. Slowly, he pulls out the pins holding up my hair. Bit by bit, the wavy strands fall over my back and shoulders. I sigh with relief. That was a tight updo.

He brushes my hair out of the way. His hand settles on the back of my dress. He undoes the lace-up back as he plants kisses on my neck. It must take five minutes before the dress is loose enough he can slide it to my hips.

I step out of it and turn around to face him.

My husband.

He's mine forever.

As usual, he's patient and I'm panting. But I can't say I mind.

Fuck patience. I want him immediately. I undo the hooks of my longline and toss it aside. I slide my crinoline off my hips.

I'm in nothing but lacy white boy shorts, my shiny silver flats, and my rings, and Miles is looking at me like I'm just as beautiful as I was in my gown.

His hands go to my hips. He drops to his knees to slide my panties to my ankles and help me out of my shoes. Then he's spreading my legs wider.

He kisses his way up my thigh. He's hungrier than usual, less patient. He plants his face between my legs and licks me up and down.

My husband is eating me out.

I dig my hand into his hair. The other goes to the wall behind me to help me keep my balance. Anticipation has me shaking. I can barely stand up straight.

The man is damn good at this. Pleasure builds in my core as he works me. Within moments, I'm at the edge.

I squeeze my thighs against his cheeks to contain the pleasure welling up inside me.

Fuck.

Almost.

There.

All that tension knots tighter and tighter then it releases. I scream his name as I come. Pleasure spills to my fingers and toes.

"Miles," I groan. I tug at his hair for good measure.

Miles pushes himself up. In one swift movement, he scoops me into his arms. He carries me to the bed and lays me flat on my back.

"Clothes off," I breathe.

He smiles. "Your wish is my command."

I watch as he strips. The tie and blazer go first then shoes and socks. He takes his time with the buttons of his shirt, with his belt, with his slacks.

Then it's just Miles and his black boxers.

I push myself to the edge of the bed. This is the first time I'm going to see my husband naked. It needs to be special.

I bring my hands to his hips, push his boxers to his ankles, and lean in to take his cock into my mouth.

He tastes good, and he's so fucking hard. I flick my tongue against his head a few times to tease him. Once he's groaning with the agony of anticipation, I take him deeper and suck hard.

Miles tugs at my hair. "Get on your back. I'm coming inside you."

All the heat in my body pools between my legs. Hell yes.

I lie back and spread my legs. Miles climbs onto the bed. He slides his hands under my ass, positioning my body so his cock strains against me.

My husband is about the enter me.

It's romantic and hot at the same time.

His fingers curl into the flesh of my ass as he slides into me. He does it slowly, one inch at a time. I soak in every second of it.

It's our first time having sex as a married couple.

It's fucking amazing.

He keeps one hand on my ass, using it to guide my movements as he thrusts into me. We move a little faster. A little harder.

His piercing blue eyes really are at their most beautiful when they're filled with pleasure.

I need more of his affection. I need every ounce of his affection. I slide my hands to the back of his head and pull him into a deep kiss.

We stay locked like that, my tongue in his mouth, his cock inside me.

Pleasure overtakes me. The tension in my core knots tighter and tighter, then it unwinds in one hell of an orgasm. I squeeze my thighs against his hips, groaning into his mouth as I come.

With a few more thrusts, he's there. His torso shakes. His fingers dig into my skin. I can feel his groans vibrating over my neck and chest.

I can feel his cock pulsing as he comes.

Our lips stay locked as we collapse onto our sides. He pulls me closer. It feels so good kissing him, kissing my husband, that it takes minutes for us to come up for air.

He pulls back. His eyes meet mine. "You want to get the couch or the Jacuzzi next?"

"The couch."

"In that case, I have your wedding gift." He shifts away to pull something from the beside drawer.

I've seen this before. It's a couple's vibrator.

Heat rushes through my body. I'm on my way to being ready to go again.

"It's a romantic choice," I say.

He pulls me into his arms and plants a kiss on my forehead. "Only the best for my wife."

STRUM FOREVER

Chapter One

KARA

I adjust my blouse and skirt. I need to look perfect. I know Drew doesn't care—he'd say I look best in nothing—but it calms me knowing my hair, makeup, and attire are on point.

I check my makeup in the mirror. My smoky eye is still perfect, but my lipstick could use a touch-up. I dig into my bag for my *baby, you know you want to kiss me* red.

Not that Drew needs any convincing on that front.

There. That's better. I take a deep breath as I study my reflection. Why am I so nervous? I wake up to Drew every morning. He knows what I look like exhausted, hungover, and sick.

No matter what, he always tells me I look beautiful.

I throw my lipstick back in my purse. It smacks into a tampon. There are tons of tampons in here. Enough for an entire cycle.

What the hell?

My phone buzzes. Drew. He's here. I check my makeup one more time. Deep breath.

Drew is here. Nothing else matters, certainly not my

inability to stock my purse with an appropriate amount of feminine hygiene products.

Fuck, it's been so long since I've seen him. I can't do anything to contain my excitement. I practically burst out of the bathroom.

The baggage claim is crowded with people getting off the flight. Most are Bay Area tech types with hipster glasses and baggy hoodies.

A guy in a black hoodie moves out of the way.

There's Drew. I sigh with relief. Everything will be okay. He's here.

His dark eyes light up as he spots me. The exhaustion on his face is replaced with excitement.

He practically runs to me. He looks good in a tight t-shirt and skinny jeans, his backpack slung over his shoulder.

He stops next to me. In one swift movement, he drops the backpack and wraps his arms around me.

I bury my face in his chest. It's better than I thought it would be.

Drew is in my arms.

Fuck. I missed him.

"You look gorgeous," he mumbles.

I squeeze him tighter then release the hug enough I can look into his eyes. "How was the flight?"

"Which one?" He runs a hand through his hair. "Tom and Willow were making out the whole flight to LA."

"Really?"

He nods.

I laugh. "You must feel emasculated, baby, him making out with your sister in front of you."

"They *are* married." Drew shakes his head with disbelief. "She's happy. That's what matters."

"Proud of you for standing down." I rub his bicep. My

fingers can't help but trace the lines of his tattoos. It's wrong how sexy his ink-covered arms are.

It's more wrong that he ever wears a shirt. Even now, the way his chest-piece tattoo peeks out from the low v of his v-neck...

My knees go weak. My heart thuds against my chest.

"How do you look so fuckable after fourteen hours in transit?" I ask.

He raises an eyebrow, staring at me like I'm crazy. "I look like shit."

"No." I rise to my tiptoes so I can run my fingers through his short black hair. It's oily, in need of a wash. And his under-eye circles are darker than mine. Okay, I can admit it. "You look a little tired. And a little greasy. But all that means is that you need to be in the shower with me."

"Aren't we staying with your mom?"

"She went to bed before I left."

His eyes light up.

It's going to be difficult working around my mom's schedule for the two weeks we're spending in her townhouse. The place is a palace by San Francisco standards, but it's tiny by *I want my mom far enough away from my bedroom that she won't hear me fucking my fiancé* standards.

Drew can more than afford a hotel room, even a suite at a fancy hotel in SoMa, but it means the world to Mom that he's staying with us.

He leans down to kiss me. It's hungry and needy.

Somehow, I'm hungrier and needier than he is. At least it feels that way. It feels like I'll never get enough of kissing him.

I have to make up for every kiss we missed the last two weeks.

I need every inch of Drew. I need every bit of love, affection, and warmth.

I slide my tongue into his mouth and bring my hands to his waist. The fabric of his cotton t-shirt is thin enough I can feel the heat of his skin.

Fuck.

Why didn't we stay at a hotel?

⚜

THE DRIVE LASTS A MILLION HOURS. THANKFULLY, THERE'S an open space on our street.

Drew grabs his suitcase from the trunk. For a moment, his eyes go to the place next door. It's the house where he grew up. His mom still lives there.

I see her from time to time. She always acts like he doesn't exist.

That must hurt. It hurts me just thinking about it.

I squeeze his hand.

He shakes his head, his attention coming back. "Fuck, I'm jet lagged."

"Thinking about your mom?"

He presses his lips together. Okay. He doesn't want to talk about it. Hard to blame him. Drew's not really the type to talk about his feelings. It's still hard for him to admit anything has ever hurt him.

I open the door for him and lead him to my room.

Drew sets his suitcase on the bed and unzips it. "Still can't believe how fast things with my mother went to shit." He opens each drawer in my dresser, one at a time. "You have any place for my stuff?"

"Shit. I forget to clear a drawer. Let me." I grab everything from my top drawer and shove it into the second.

"Quite the organizational skills."

I nod. Usually, I like keeping things neat. But right now,

I'm itching to get Drew naked in that shower. "You want to talk about it?"

"Fuck no." His eyes pass over me. "What the fuck am I doing putting this shit away?"

I smile. "I was about to ask you that."

"God damn, Kendrick, your tits look divine in that blouse. How the fuck is it staying buttoned?"

"I'm going to be an English teacher, not a physics teacher," I tease.

"Better test it." He slides his arms around my hips. In one swift movement, he pins me to the wall. His lips go to my neck. My ear. My cheek. Then they're on mine.

His kiss is hard, needy.

He drags his hand up my torso. His fingers trace the neckline of my blouse. He undoes one button. Two. Three. That's enough for the shirt to spill open, my chest on display to him.

He slides his hand into my bra and rubs my nipple with his thumb.

Fuck, the man has magic fingers. They get better every time I see him.

He pulls back. His dark eyes meet mine. They're as hungry as his kiss. He shifts his hips so I can feel his erection. "Not sure if my hands or my cock missed you more."

"Why choose?"

He steps back, taking my hand. "This is gonna be fast. Was thinking about you the whole flight here."

Before I can respond, his lips are on mine. His tongue slides into my mouth. He groans as he palms my ass over my skirt.

We stumble to the bathroom. With Mom asleep in her bedroom, it's way too loud. I lock the door—just in case she gets up—and run the shower.

Hopefully, I can stay quiet enough the shower muffles everything.

His eyes fix on me as he undoes the last three buttons of my blouse. He nearly rips the thing off my shoulders. He nearly breaks the zipper of my skirt as he undoes it and slides it off my hips.

I reach back to unhook my bra.

His eyes go wide as the garment falls to the floor.

"Fuck, you get more beautiful every time I see you." He cups my breasts, watching his fingers toy with my nipples.

Pleasure shoots to my core. "Me or my tits?"

"Both." He leans down to kiss me—the man is nearly a foot taller than I am.

He slides his hand between my legs, rubbing me over my panties. I'm already wet, already needy. The touch sends electricity racing to my fingers and toes.

"Drew," I breathe. "Fuck me."

"This first." He pushes my panties to my knees.

His fingers brush my inner thighs. Even after all this time, I expect him to recoil when he touches my scars. But he doesn't. He traces a few with that soft touch of his.

Then his hand is on me.

I dig my hands into his chest as pleasure knots in my core. Why is he still wearing a shirt? I slide my hand under it, taking my time reacquainting myself with the hard muscles of his chest and stomach.

His dark eyes fix on mine. I hold his gaze as an orgasm builds inside me. Those expert hands of his.

Damn.

A few more strokes and all that tension knots tighter and tighter. I bite my lip so I won't scream as I go over the edge.

"Fuck, Drew," I groan. Pleasure spills through my pelvis as I come. It feels like it's been a million years. "I missed you so much."

"Missed you too." He pulls his t-shirt over his head and pushes his jeans and boxers off his hips.

He's naked.

I'm naked.

The shower is running.

Sometimes, life really is perfect.

He pulls the curtain back and helps me into the shower. Then he's there with me, the curtain in its proper place.

Warm water streams over my head and neck. My hair wets quickly. Then it's sticking to my cheeks, covering my eyes.

He laughs as he switches positions with me. He throws his head back to wet his hair.

We take turns soaping each other. We spend ages touching and kissing. It's like it's the first time. My hands still adore every inch of his skin. I trace each of his tattoos, each line of his muscles.

His fingers graze every inch of my skin. They settle on my chest. I love how much the man loves my boobs.

My eyelids press together. I groan against his chest. I press my palms against his stomach. One treads lower. It wraps around his cock.

Fuck, he's hard.

He's really fucking hard.

It never gets old. It still feels amazing that my best friend in the whole fucking world wants me as badly as I want him.

It's like a dream.

I stroke him until he's groaning then I look up into his eyes. "Fuck me."

His eyes are heavy with desire. He only barely manages to nod. His hands go to my hips.

He guides me into position—me facing the wall, him behind me. I place one palm against the wall for support.

Drew digs his fingers into my skin as his cock brushes against me.

I arch my back to grab more of him.

Slowly, he slides inside me. Each inch feels better than the last. More like I'm whole.

More like I'm home.

Fuck, I missed him so badly.

He holds onto my hips as he thrusts into me.

My eyes close. Conscious thought slips away. All the nights apart, all the afternoons I spent wishing he were there, all the dinners I wanted to brag about cooking—everything else fades away.

There's nothing in the world except our bodies in this shower.

He rocks into me with a steady motion. His thighs are shaking, his fingers digging into my skin.

He's close.

He was right. It's fast.

But I don't care. I want to feel his orgasm. I want him as wrecked with pleasure as I am.

A few more thrusts and he's there.

"Kara," he groans.

His breath hitches. His cock pulses as he comes inside me. He thrusts through the orgasm until he's spilled every drop.

When he's finished, he turns me around. His eyes find mine.

He slides his hand between my legs. "You need to come again."

If he insists.

I close my eyes and surrender to the pleasure filling my body.

Chapter Two

KARA

Drew is downstairs, scooping veggie omelets onto ceramic plates. He motions to a cup of tea on the dining table.

"You sleep well?" he asks.

"Yeah." I take a long sip of my tea. Earl Grey. My favorite. "How are you awake?"

"Jet lag."

"Let's take a walk after breakfast. Daylight is supposed to help."

He laughs as he brings the plates, and his coffee, to the table. "Kendrick, you think I don't know the jetlag tricks? Been touring for the last four years."

"But you only had your first international tour a year ago."

He shakes his head. "Can't believe the lack of respect."

"Baby, you know I think you're a rock star." I allow myself the opportunity to check him out. He's wearing a t-shirt and boxers. It's too much clothing. I need that shirt gone so I can gawk at his tattoos. And his six-pack. And those v-lines. God, those v-lines. "But you can always play a song for me, to remind me."

"Can I?"

I nod. "Woo me with your beautiful voice."

"How about if I use my mouth for something else?"

My cheeks flush. "I can live with that."

"Can you?"

I nod. It's a casual nod, but it *is* a big deal. Before Drew, I never let guys touch me, much less stick their heads between my thighs.

I was ashamed of my cutting scars. But he treats them like a badge of courage. Like they're a sign I survived something hard, not like they're a sign I'm a damaged freak.

❦

THE BED SHAKES SO HARD I'M WORRIED IT'S GOING TO FALL through the floor. It doesn't. Not the first, second, or third time I come.

After we clean up, we head to Golden Gate Park for a long walk. There's a lot to catch up on—all the little details that make up days. Mostly, I talk and he listens, but I do get a few details about the tour. There was a great show in Tokyo and an awful one someplace in China. He broke three guitar strings during a solo.

I get lost in our conversation. He must be lost too, because we're well into the afternoon when we realize the time.

My phone is packed with *When will you be home for lunch?* messages from my mom.

"Shit, we better go." I show Drew the texts.

He presses his lips to mine. "You're always making trouble, Kendrick."

I nod and lead him back home. It's a long walk, but it's nice today. It's cool, but the flowers and trees are in bloom. There are pollens everywhere.

My allergies are going crazy. I'm sneezing, I'm tired, and I'm incredibly nauseous. Usually, the nausea is more mild. At the moment, I'm about ready to throw up.

It feels like it's something worse than allergies, but it's been consistent for a few weeks. What else could it be?

At home, Mom is in the kitchen. It smells like tomatoes, meat, and pasta.

Yum.

"Hey, Kara." Mom smiles. She nods hello to Drew. "Andrew, nice to finally see you."

Drew actually blushes. He hates being called Andrew.

God damn, he looks cute with his cheeks pink. My head fills with all sorts of delicious thoughts about other activities that make him flush.

"It's just Drew, Mrs. Kendrick," he says.

"It's just Judy." She motions to the table. "I'm about to bring out the salad."

"Thanks for cooking, Mrs., ahem Judy."

She smiles. "Kara helped prepare it last night."

Oh, it's the lasagna. I've already forgotten everything about yesterday that wasn't me and Drew in the shower.

"You cooked for me, Kendrick?" He squeezes my hand under the table as he turns to Mom. "She always 'lets' me cook for her."

Mom laughs. "Kara is excellent with grilled cheese, mac and cheese, anything with cheese."

Is loving cheese a crime? Grilled cheese is fantastic. Especially with tomato soup. Maybe I like carbs more than I should. The evidence of my love affair shows in my hips, my stomach, my thighs, my—well, my everything.

Truth be told, I like my curvy figure. Sure, it would be nice to have abs, but my boobs and butt fill out a tight dress like nobody's business. If only I could do something about being five feet tall.

We take our seats and serve ourselves. The lasagna looks amazing, and I'm hungry. I've been starving lately. Usually, I'm not big on meat, but the beef smells amazing. I want to eat a million pounds of it.

And the tampons...

And the nausea.

No.

There's no way...

There's no way I'm pregnant. I had my period recently. Didn't I?

I try to work backward, to do the math, but I can't remember any specific cycle. School makes all the days run together.

It can't be possible. I'm religious with my pill.

Only traveling makes it difficult to keep track of time zones.

I want to have a family with Drew. One day. I want a little girl. I know everyone says boys are easier. I know Drew would be less overprotective of a boy. But I still want a girl. I want to dress her in those tiny Converse and cozy sweaters. I want to put her in dance classes until she finds a style she likes, the way my mom did for me.

If she hates dance, she can try soccer or karate or gymnastics. She's going to be a strong girl, physically and mentally. I can see the three of us at the park or the beach or her first day of school. I know I'll annoy the shit out of her, fussing over her hair and clothes for pictures. But she'll appreciate it when she's older, especially when she's old enough I can teach her how to tame her thick hair. Drew's hair is short, but it's nearly as thick as mine.

I can see a great life for us, the three of us...

But it's five or ten years away.

Now... he's still touring half the year. I'm still in graduate school.

Mom's voice interrupts my thoughts. "Are you going to visit your parents, Drew?"

I clear my throat. Better to focus on Drew. This is a remote possibility. "Mom, I told you about Drew's parents... what happened with him dropping out of school."

Mom looks at me curiously. She doesn't remember.

I shoot Drew an apologetic look. He acts strong about his parents being out of his life, but I know it hurts him.

He takes a steady breath. "My mom stopped speaking to me after I dropped out of Stanford to follow the band." His eyes go to the table. "I'm sure she had good intentions. But —" He shakes his head, struggling to keep his voice even. "I accepted it a long time ago. I just wish she hadn't done the same thing to Willow."

"Your sister?" Mom asks.

Drew nods.

"She was a sweet girl. How is she doing?"

"She married their drummer," I say. "She's a photographer now."

"Mom didn't like that either." Drew clears his throat. "She and Willow never had a blow up fight, but they don't talk much."

"What about your father?" Mom asks.

I clear my throat. "Mom, Drew's been traveling. He's jet lagged. I'm not sure—"

"It's fine." He looks at Mom. "He lives in Europe. He's married to a woman a year older than I am. He calls on my birthday. Sometimes on holidays."

"Oh." Mom frowns. She shakes her head, shifting to a more pleasant topic. "Christmas is next week. We can get a tree tomorrow. Hang lights. I don't know if you celebrate, Andrew... Drew."

"I do," he says.

"Excuse me." I push out of my seat to use the bathroom. I have to pee again. Already.

That's one of the signs, isn't it?

After I wash my hands, it hits me. I have a period calendar on my phone. I don't exactly use it religiously, but it should be able to help me.

Damn. The last time I entered something was this summer. But there was something during the school year. I remember asking my friend to borrow a tampon.

When was that?

I haven't got a clue.

I can't even keep track of my periods. Can I really handle taking care of a child? I've only just figured out how to take care of myself.

I try to push it aside as I return to the table. Drew and Mom are having a nice conversation about a book series I've never read. Something about mystery and action.

I settle into my seat and pick at my lasagna. It's delicious —chewy, tangy, creamy—but I'm no longer feeling well.

My gaze goes to Drew. He's smiling, cracking a joke with Mom.

He'll be a good dad. Overprotective, but good. I can see him cradling a baby, reading comics with a toddler, teaching a kid to play a tiny guitar.

But not in nine months.

Not for years.

Many, many years.

I stare at my food, forcing myself to take small bites.

Drew taps me on the shoulder.

I look up at him with hazy eyes.

"Kara, your mom was asking about our wedding," he says.

"What about it?" I ask.

"When we're gonna pick out a specific location." His eyes fix on mine. "Don't tell me you forgot the date."

"No. June twelfth. We're doing the beach. What's the rush figuring out the other details?" I take a bite of lasagna and swallow hard. There's an obvious reason to rush, but I don't want that for our wedding.

"You'll forget all about it when school picks up." Drew squeezes my hand. "You okay? You look queasy."

I feel queasy. This is overwhelming, and I'm not good with overwhelming.

I push out from the table. "I'm not feeling well. I think it's allergies." I take a step backward. "I... uh... I'm going to lie down. Why don't you guys go out, take in the city?" I lean in to kiss Drew on the forehead. "Don't worry about me. I'll be fine after a nap."

I climb the stairs to my room, collapse on my bed, and pull the covers over my head. I repeat the words to myself. *I'll be fine, I'll be fine, I'll be fine.*

But every time, they feel like lies.

※

THERE'S A KNOCK ON THE DOOR. THE HANDLE TURNS, AND Drew steps inside.

"Hey." Drew's voice echoes through the small room. "You okay?"

I nod. This pregnancy thing is a remote possibility. I think.

"You sure? I can run out to CVS and grab something."

"That's okay." I push myself up, blink my eyes a few times, and yawn. "What time is it?"

"About six. You feeling more rested?"

I nod. Sort of. My body is more relaxed, but my mind is still racing. No matter how many times I try to tell myself it's not possible, that I should just wait for my next period, I don't quite buy it.

"You're not going to believe this," he says.

"Believe what?"

He closes the door and presses his back against it. "Meg and Miles are getting married."

That's great! My lips curl into a smile. "Really? When?"

"In Vegas. As soon as possible."

I laugh. Of course, Drew is wearing a judgmental expression. He doesn't approve of them rushing.

"Why you looking at me like that, Kendrick?"

"No reason."

"They should figure out their shit. He asked us if we'd come early. He thinks Meg needs your help."

And Drew wants our vacation together. I want that too. I want a long, pregnancy-scare-free vacation.

His voice drops to something supportive and sweet. "What are you thinking?"

I clear my throat. It sounds like this wedding is happening in the next few days. This can wait. "We should go. Can we fly in tonight?"

He nods. "You sure that's it?"

No.

"Kara?"

I press my lips together. "It's probably nothing."

"Doesn't look like nothing."

"It can wait until after their wedding."

"Don't see why they can't set a date and send out invitations like normal people." He sits on the bed next to me. He leans in close enough to whisper. "Sweetheart, what the fuck is going on? You've got the weirdest look in your eyes."

Do I? I force myself to make eye contact. There's all this concern in his dark eyes.

Usually, I hate when people look at me like that. But not when Drew does it. When he does it, I know it's because he cares, because he loves me.

This *can* wait until after their wedding. It's probably nothing.

"It's romantic," I say. "Our wedding will still be nice. On the beach, with the sun shining behind us."

Of course, if I am pregnant, I'll be ready to burst in June.

And I'll have a newborn in September. If everything goes according to plan, I'll graduate this spring and start teaching this fall.

But if I'm pregnant...

Even with strict anti-discrimination laws, no one hires pregnant teachers. And nobody respects women who get a job then take maternity leave right away. Every female teacher warned us—people will give you shit about being pregnant and about taking maternity leave.

Even elementary school teachers, the ones who devote their lives to small children, get shit about having babies during the school year. As if they can pick a delivery date like magic.

Shit.

Teaching jobs are hard to come by. If I don't get hired right away, it might be two or three years before I find another gig.

Teaching may not pay as well as being a rock star, but I love it. I love middle school students. They're just starting to blossom into adults, and they're amazed by all the new ideas in books like *A Separate Peace*, *To Kill a Mockingbird*, and *Romeo and Juliet*.

Drew is staring at me with all this concern in his eyes. It must be obvious I'm worried.

I run my fingers through his short hair. "You jealous, baby?"

"No. I just don't like them interrupting my plans."

"Yeah?"

He pats the bed. "I was gonna spend a lot of time right here."

"We'll have a bed in our hotel room."

"Not the same." He stares into my eyes. "There's something you aren't saying."

I nod.

"What is it?"

"It can wait. Get the tickets to fly to Vegas. Tonight, if we can."

"You sure?"

"Yes."

Chapter Three

DREW

F ucking time zones.

I'm groggy on the flight and in the cab ride to the hotel. But I'm not groggy enough to miss that something is very fucking wrong.

Kara is tense. She tries to smile every time our eyes meet, but she's not pulling it off.

After we check in, she mumbles something about wanting to unpack, and she practically locks herself in the bedroom—the suite has a main area and a separate bedroom.

I give her half an hour to unpack then I take a shower. There's a chance I'm tired enough I'm reading this all wrong. The hot water feels amazing on my aching muscles. Not as amazing as her hands feel. Fuck, it's been too long apart. I need every drop of her.

When I'm done, I wrap a towel around my waist, and I join Kara in the bedroom.

She's sitting in the bed in the dark, covers around her waist. Her blouse hugs her more than ample chest in a way that looks hot as fuck but supremely uncomfortable.

Her big, brown eyes are filled with frustration. Her shoulders are up to her ears. There's tension in her jaw and neck.

Still, she licks her lips as she takes me in.

"You should lose the towel," she mumbles, her voice thick with desire.

My cock stirs at the thought of wiping away all her frustration with my body. God knows, I want her eyes rolling back in her head as she comes.

We have to deal with this—whatever it is—first.

I've never been good at relationships before. I've loved Kara since forever, but it took a while for me to figure it out. I was sure I was bad for her. I tried to protect her from everything, including me, but it didn't work.

She needs me.

I need her.

It's been eight months now. I still worry that I'm going to fuck it up sometimes. I haven't yet.

Mostly, it's good.

Mostly, it's better than fucking anything.

I wrap my arm around her. "Hey."

I want all of her. I want every thought in her head. I want to take the weight of every burden that weighs her down.

She nestles into my chest. Her breath is warm against my skin. "You smell good. But kinda girly."

"Used your soap."

"I thought so." She presses her lips to my chest. "If I asked you to fuck me until I stopped thinking, what would you say?"

I run my fingers through her long, dark hair. "We should talk first."

"Yeah, I figured." She looks up at me, her eyes heavy with a mix of frustration and desire. "For a rock star, you're really uptight."

"You're just figuring that out?"

She shakes her head. "You know, I hate Batman. Why doesn't he do something productive with his money instead of dressing up in spandex and hitting people? If he spent half that energy working on education in Gotham City, that would do a lot more to deter crime."

I laugh. She's trying to bait me. "Because Gotham City is corrupt. He can't trust the establishment to use the money for good."

"He could run a charity. Something. I think he prefers the city overrun with criminals so he has a reason to kick ass."

"I don't look to him as a role model."

"Uh-huh."

"When I was seventeen, maybe."

"You're not proud of yourself for beating up assholes?"

"I'm always going to protect you and Willow. You're not going to talk me out of that."

She's still baiting me. I do realize I'm easy to bait. My temper has a short fuse. But I'm never going to apologize for protecting the people I love, even if they prefer non-violence.

As far as I'm concerned, any guy who touches Kara doesn't deserve hands. Or breath.

My hand finds the neckline of her shirt. I play with it until her eyes are closed and she's purring lightly. I want to know what's wrong, but she's not going to talk until she relaxes.

I lay Kara on the bed and lie next to her. Immediately, she shifts her body toward mine, hooking her leg over my hip and cupping my cheek with her palm. The tenderness of her touch makes me warm everywhere.

Damn, her body is soft. Her tits pressed against my chest is heaven.

My cock stirs. It's impatient.

She lets out a soft gasp. "Already?"

I bring my hand to her ass to pull her closer. God damn,

our bodies feel good like this. My hands want to stroke every inch of her skin.

My hands are greedy fuckers. They want her coming again and again.

As badly as I want to pin her to the bed, hike her skirt to her waist, and plant my head between her thighs, I need to make sure she's okay first.

I press my palms into her upper back, over her shirt, and pull her body into mine. "What's wrong?"

She shakes her head.

"Kara. Whatever it is, I want to help."

Again, she shakes her head. Her hand goes to her cheek. It's hard to make out her expression in the dark, but it looks like she's crying.

She sniffles. A sob breaks through her throat.

"Fuck." She wipes her tears and buries her face in my chest.

Her eyelashes brush against my skin. I can feel her tears against my chest. She's really crying.

I need to make that better.

I bring my hand to her chin and tilt her head so we're eye to eye. "Talk to me."

She wipes her eyes and stares at her palm like it did her wrong.

I've seen it do her very, very right a number of times. Blood rushes to my cock as I replay the image of her fucking herself for my viewing pleasure.

Can't go there yet.

I squeeze her hand.

She sighs with pleasure as she rubs her crotch against mine. "You're still hard."

"You forget the part where I fuck you *after* you talk to me?"

"That's a when. It's the chronology, so it's a when."

I laugh. "Ms. K is correcting my grammar."

She nods. "I... I don't know what to say." A sob breaks up her words. She blinks away a tear. The break only lasts a moment. She brings her hand to my waist and buries her face in my chest. "I'm not seducing you very well."

"You've done better before."

She laugh-cries. I pull her closer. I need to soothe her somehow.

My hand goes to the back of her head, cradling it. "What is it?"

"I've been moody the last few weeks."

"Me too. It's hard being apart."

"But you're always moody, Drew."

Feel like I should take offense to that, but I can't exactly argue.

"And I've been craving red meat." She presses her palm against my stomach.

"You've been hanging out with Willow." My sister has been a vegetarian since she was nine or ten. She's not pushy about being meat-free, but she does so much cooking that people end up eating vegetarian when they're around her. "Same thing happens to me."

"No. It's more than that." Kara looks up at me. Her eyes fill with guilt. "I can't do this to you."

"What is it you think you're doing to me?" I shift my hips to press my crotch against hers. "Besides this."

"I'd love to help with that." She sighs. "But... I don't know if I, if it's..." She trails off. Her eyes close.

"What is it you think you're doing to me?"

She shakes her head.

Damn. I know Kara has a hard time letting people, even me, in, but this is a whole other level.

"Are you leaving me?" I ask.

"Of course not." She slides her arm under the crook of my neck. Her gaze stays on my chest or maybe my stomach.

"Are you cheating on me?" I ask. Only to prove a point. That's far out of the realm of possibility.

"No." Kara breaks our touch. She shifts to the edge of the bed and stares into my eyes. "How could you say that?"

"If you aren't leaving me and you aren't cheating on me, it can't be that bad."

"Oh."

"Now, Kara, what is it you think you're doing to me? Besides making it hard to resist fucking you." I bring her hand to my erection.

She sighs with pleasure. "Are you sure about this talking thing?"

"Unfortunately."

She finds the zipper of her blouse, undoes it, and pulls the top over her head. "Still?"

I take her in slowly. Damn, my hands want on that soft skin. Want to cup her lush tits. Want to toy with her nipples until she's purring. Want to feel her fleshy thighs pressed against me.

Kara is nothing like the women our label hires to pose in our music videos. All sixty-one inches of her are curvy perfection.

I never realized how much I like women with a little meat on their bones until I caught sight of her in a tight dress.

Way back when we were kids, she was the first girl who didn't seem icky. She was way more than *not icky*. God knows how many times I fucked myself thinking of her.

Her eyes are wide with lust. "Please, Drew." She reaches around, unhooks her bra, and slides it off her shoulders. "Please fuck me first."

I shake my head. My body has other ideas. One hand goes to her ass. It finds the hem of her skirt and stays there.

The other goes flat against her back, pressing her body closer.

Fuck, I love the way her chest feels against mine.

This time, I sigh with pleasure. I want to fuck her. I want to wipe away the pain in her eyes any way I can.

"If that's really what will make you feel better." I pull her closer. "Then take your fucking panties off."

She nods, but there's still a tear in her eye.

I run my fingers through her hair. "We're a team. Whatever it is, you don't have to carry it on your own."

I loosen her watch and slide it off her hand. She wears it to hide the scars on her wrist.

Kara used to cut. It killed me when I found out.

But I made it all about me. I should have thought about how it killed her. I got so fixed on how *I* failed her instead of thinking about how I could make things better.

Right now, she needs my understanding.

I trace the scars on her wrist. As far as I'm concerned, they're battle scars she earned being strong for everybody else.

I bring her wrist to my mouth and plant a soft kiss on her skin. She purrs. Her lips part with a sigh. I can practically hear her begging.

"Made myself a promise that night you told me you used to cut." I look into her big, brown eyes. "I already fucked it up a few times, but I did promise myself that, from now on, I'd be there any time you needed someone to be strong for you."

She stares back.

"I'm gonna do my best to stay true to that."

Her voice is barely a whisper. "I'm scared."

I slide my hand over her neck and shoulder. "You're carrying the weight of the world again."

She shakes her head.

"Yeah." I rub her shoulder. "Let me take some of it."

Her inhale is sharp. She looks up at me, her eyes heavy with the weight of something I can't figure out. Then her eyes are fixed off someplace in the darkness.

She shakes her head. Another tear rolls down her cheek. This time, I wipe it away with my thumb.

"I'm late," she whispers.

"Late for what?"

"No, Drew." Her voice breaks. "I'm *late*." She takes an unsteady breath and digs her hands into my skin.

Late.

Fuck, she can't mean—

"You're pregnant?" I ask.

She shakes her head. "I don't know. It's probably nothing. The travel or the stress of school. I switched to a new pill a few months ago. Different hormones. It's supposed to be fewer side effects, but I don't remember when my last period was. I don't have a clue."

"Do you want it to be nothing?"

"Wouldn't that be best?"

I bite my lip. I'm trying not to push as hard as I usually do. But fuck, it's tough keeping my mouth shut here. Kara pregnant—that's fucking amazing.

Us, having a family. It's not something I think about. Not right now. But fuck timing. I want that with her. I want everything with her.

"What do you want?" I ask.

"I... want a baby. One day."

"Me too." We've only discussed it briefly. We're young. We're not even married yet. It never seems like an immediate priority. But I know we both want a family. "You'll be a great mom."

"Yeah, but... what if I can't take care of a baby and myself?" She blinks back another tear. "It's not that I don't want it, Drew. I do. I want to have a family with you. I want to have a little girl, and I want to buy her every damn princess dress in the Disney store. Or every superhero costume. Whatever she wants. I want to take her to the park, and to read my favorite books to her until she figures out what she likes, to tell her about boys, or girls, if she decides she prefers girls. I want to teach her to drive, to help her get ready for Prom, to see her graduate... I want all of that. But I can't do it by myself. And I can't ask you to quit."

"I know. We'll figure it out. Don't worry."

She laugh-cries.

Okay. That's a stupid suggestion. "You want me to run out and buy a test? So you know?"

"It's the middle of the night."

Fair point.

"In the morning," she says. "Or... I don't know. I'd rather wait until after the wedding to deal with this."

"You'll feel better knowing."

"Maybe."

I take a deep breath. "It's your body. I wouldn't tell you what to do with it."

"I don't want to have an abortion," she says. "If that's what you're getting at. But I do appreciate that you... that you wouldn't try to decide for me. This is bad timing, but—"

"Fuck timing. We'll make it work."

"How?"

"I'll do whatever it takes."

She's shaking, so I pull her closer. She digs her hands into my skin like I'm her only lifeline.

Fuck, no wonder she's frustrated. This is heavy. It's good, but it's fucking heavy.

"You're not doing anything to me," I whisper. "This is good news."

"Really?"

"This is great, sweetheart. I want to have a family too."

She looks up at me. "It's probably a false alarm."

I rub her shoulders until the tension in them eases. She sighs, relaxing into my body.

"It's probably nothing," she whispers.

But I can tell she doesn't believe that.

Chapter Four

KARA

The ring of the alarm clock is cruel. Is it really time to wake up? My body has other ideas.

My mind is not at all inspired by the thought of anything that is not the bed. Especially with Drew's body in such close proximity.

The clock tells me it's ten. We're supposed to meet Meg and Miles in an hour. She needs help with her dress.

I'm not going to usurp her wedding, even if this is eating at me. It can wait a few days.

Drew grabs the offending cellphone and turns off the alarm. He rolls over so he's looking at me. His eyes meet mine. He's half-asleep.

He's cute tired.

"You can stay in bed, baby." I run my fingers through his hair. "I don't think she needs your help with a dress."

He shakes his head. "I'll go with you." He slides his arm around my waist and pulls me back into bed.

Then he pulls my body against his, my back against his chest.

He presses his lips to my neck. "My hands missed you."

Hell yes.

My back arches reflexively. I rub my ass against his crotch until I can feel him hardening.

"You carry the world around on your shoulders," he whispers. "Not gonna let you do that."

"Okay." This does feel like the world.

It's a good thing. A great thing. But it's terrifying.

"It's sweet you want to be there for your friend." He pushes my pajama bottoms to my knees. His voice gets low as he drags his fingers up my thighs. "You can take care of her if you let me take care of you."

"Drew," I breathe. "We're meeting them in an hour."

"I know. Close your eyes." He traces my scars with his thumb. "My hands have been fucking aching for you."

I press my ass against his crotch.

With his other hand, he pulls off my tank top.

I'm naked in his arms—I always sleep sans bra and panties.

His body is hard and warm. I need this release. I need this break. Everything is getting complicated, overwhelming.

I don't do overwhelming. I only do crumbling under the weight of everything overwhelming.

He rubs the spot where my neck meets my shoulders, one hand on each side of my neck.

Damn, the man really does have magic fingers. I sigh with pleasure. Bit by bit, every ounce of tension in my body releases.

"Drew," I groan. "Touch me."

His lips brush my ear. Then he's sucking on my earlobe. It sends a spark of desire straight to my core.

He drags his fingers up my other thigh, once again taking his time to trace each scar. The way he touches me makes me feel whole, accepted.

Like I'm normal.

Like I'm hot as hell.

His fingers brush my sex.

I let out a low groan. Again, I rub my ass against his hard cock.

His touch gets harder. Harder. Then he's rubbing me exactly where I need it.

Pleasure wells up inside me. The man has amazing hands. I bite my lip. I grind against him.

For a few minutes, the only sound in the room is our breaths and our groans. Everything fades away until my world is bliss. The only thing I can feel is the pleasure building in my core.

My sex clenches.

Almost.

He presses his lips against my neck. Then he's sucking on my skin. His breath is hot and heavy.

He's so fucking hard.

A few more brushes of his hand, and I'm at the edge. Then I'm there. All the tension inside me unfurls as I come.

Pleasure spreads out to my fingers and toes. He plants kisses along my shoulders and up my neck.

His lips hover over my ear. "Now, you can get ready."

I shake my head. "Hold me first."

He slides his arm around my waist and pulls me closer.

Right now, the world is perfect.

Pretty soon, it's going to be overwhelming as all hell.

But right now, it's perfect.

Chapter Five

DREW

After Kara and Meg go off to pick up dresses, Miles puts me in charge of making sure Tom and Pete show up in appropriate attire.

It shouldn't be a difficult task, but Tom likes to torture me. He spends twenty minutes trying to take charge of Meg and Miles's wedding before he admits he's already packed his plain black suit. He and Willow will be here by tomorrow.

Thankfully, Pete is easier to manage. I text him to bring a black suit. He texts back a sure.

I pick up a test at the hotel's gift shop. Figures they have pregnancy tests in the gift shop of a Las Vegas casino.

I text Kara.

Drew: How's the gown search?

Kara: Fruitful. I think she's found one. How was everything with Miles?

Drew: He's worried about me.

Kara: You were looking at me like you were going to hit anyone who got within fifteen feet.

Drew: That different than normal?

Kara: Normally, it's five feet.

No sense in playing coy here. Not like I can pull off coy.

Drew: I picked up a test.

Kara: Oh.

Drew: What the fuck does "oh" mean?

Kara: I want to spend the night with you without thinking about the future. If it's killing you, I'll take the test. I don't want to. I want a break. But I will. Tell me it's not killing you.

Drew: Not yet.

Kara: Good. I need a break.

I need to lighten her mood.

Drew: That means I can't allow you to ride the roller coaster on the Stratosphere.

Kara: Somehow, I'll live.

Drew: Or the one at the New York, New York.

Kara: What about skydiving?

Drew: Out of the question.

Kara: Gambling?

Drew: With all that secondhand smoke? No way.

Kara: But I'm feeling lucky. Want to put it all on red.

Drew: I can find a way to keep you entertained all night without leaving the hotel room.

Kara: Deal :)

❧

I MEET KARA IN THE LOBBY. SHE'S WEARING A FACE FULL OF makeup, and her hair is pulled into an elegant updo. It leaves her neck completely bare.

"Wedding makeup takes forever." She wraps her arms around me and mumbles into my chest. "This is all going to come off on your shirt."

"Might have to take my shirt off."

"Oh no." Her voice is light as she teases. "That would be awful. What if it got on your pants?"

"Not gonna object to you putting your head in my lap, Kendrick."

"Right here?"

"We'll get arrested." I press my palm into her lower back and lead her to the elevator. There's already a carriage here. We step inside. "I have a surprise for you. Close your eyes."

She looks at me like I'm crazy.

"You trust me?"

"Of course."

"Then close your eyes. I'll lead you."

She pushes her lips to one side. Her eyes pass over me slowly. She looks at me like she's going to consume me.

My cock stirs. I fucking love that look. I've had a lot of attention in my life—too much the last few years. Kara undressing me with her eyes blows everything else out of the water.

I need to get her out of that tight wrap dress.

The thing falls off her curves like it was made for them.

Her lips fall apart. She sighs lightly as she nods. "Okay." She presses her eyelids together. "We'll also get arrested for having sex in the elevator, won't we?"

"Yeah." I chuckle. Doesn't mean we have to keep our hands to ourselves. I lean in to kiss her. My hand finds the neckline of her dress. I trace the fabric until she's groaning into my mouth.

Her back arches. Her crotch grinds against mine. Blood rushes to my cock. It gets hard to think.

Can't start this in the elevator.

But I'm not about to stop.

My hands need her skin. I slide my hand into her bra, cupping her breast. Within seconds, I'm rock hard.

She's divine.

I slide my tongue into her mouth, kissing her like I'll

never get another chance to kiss her again. There's been too much heaviness. I need to feel close to her tonight.

I need to know she's mine.

My other hand finds the hem of her dress. Then it's on the soft skin of her thigh. I run my fingers over her skin. They brush over her cutting scars.

The elevator dings. Our floor. I press my palm against her panties—she's already wet—then pull it back to my side.

This needs to happen in our hotel room.

This needs to happen all fucking night.

I pull away and take a long breath. "Keep them closed."

She's panting. "Drew."

Fuck. I need inside her now. Need that dress on the floor, her lush tits in my hand, her soft ass grinding against me.

I step behind her so I can lead her.

She sighs as her ass brushes against my cock. "When did you become such a tease?"

I bring one hand to her hips and hold her body against mine.

"Drew," she groans. "I will jump you in the hallway."

And I'll let her. It's almost worth getting kicked out of the hotel. Fuck knows, I don't mind. Major perk of being a rock star—nobody bats an eye if you trash a hotel room or get caught having public sex.

But Kara is gonna be a teacher. And last I checked, schools frown on that kind of thing.

I break touch to lead her down the hallway. Her eyelids stay pressed together. She takes slow, careful steps like she expects to trip.

"I've got you." I pull her closer. A few more steps, and we're at our corner suite.

I slide the key card into the electronic lock and turn the handle.

"Can I open my eyes yet?" Kara tugs at my t-shirt.

"Not yet." I push the door open and lead her inside.

Usually, I find it hard to care about hotel rooms. Seen one, seen them all. But this suite is amazing. The curtains are drawn enough to let in the neon lights of the city. The main room has a white leather sectional, a coffee table, and a dining area. The bedroom is off to the side. As much as I enjoy fucking Kara on a couch, I need her on her back, her legs pinned to the bed.

Now.

"You can open your eyes," I say.

She gasps. Her eyes go wide as she takes in the room. "Drew, this is..." She squeezes my hand. "Thank you. It's beautiful."

She spends a minute exploring the room. The last bit of tension falls off her face. She shrugs her coat off her shoulders and tosses it over the couch.

I almost want to watch her run around with glee all night.

Almost... but not quite.

I wrap my arms around her, pulling her soft body into mine. "There's a bathtub for two with jets."

She sighs with pleasure. "After."

"After?"

"After," she murmurs. She tilts her head, offering her neck to me.

I lean down to press my lips to her skin. I kiss my way from her ear to her collarbone. She purrs, grinding her soft ass against my crotch. My cock strains against my tight jeans. I need out of these things.

I suck on her neck until she's groaning so loudly I'm sure she can't take it anymore then I lead her into the bedroom.

"This is amazing." She throws herself onto the bed, laughing as she lands on her back. "Thank you, Drew. This is exactly what I need."

I pull my t-shirt over my head and drop it on the floor. "What is it you need?"

Her eyes fix on me. She swallows hard as she pushes herself up. "You."

"Tell me how."

"Inside me."

Fuck yes. I unbutton my jeans and slide them off my hips.

Kara nods. She spreads her legs, pulling her dress up her thighs, offering herself to me.

There's no shyness about it. She knows she's mine.

I kick my jeans off my feet and climb onto the bed. I plant my body on top of hers and I kiss her hard.

She sighs. Her back arches. It presses our bodies together. Her crotch rubs against mine. The friction is fucking divine. I want inside her as soon as possible.

But first, she comes on my face.

My hands find her hips. No time to waste. It's been two weeks since I've tasted her. That's too fucking long.

I push her dress to her waist. Damn, those round hips, those lush thighs. There's no way I'll ever get enough of her body.

I pull her panties to her knees and off her feet. One hand on each thigh, I pin her knees to the bed.

Her back arches. Hell, she's shaking with desire.

"Drew," she groans.

Damn, that sound is the best music in the entire fucking world.

I drag my lips against her thigh. A tease to get her panting. Her hands go to the back of my head. Guiding me.

Her hands have no patience. My lips don't have much either. But I'm not about to rush this.

I kiss my way up the inside of her thigh and over the deep scars. I'm close enough to inhale her scent. Fuck, she smells good.

I nip at the skin of her inner thigh.

She groans. Her thighs strain against my hands, a plea I move closer.

One more time. I find the apex of her thigh, and I nip at her soft skin.

Her hands go to the sheets. She claws at them.

Now.

I run my tongue over her outer lips. She sighs with pleasure. Certain she's getting what she wants, she relaxes. Her back softens. Her thighs stop fighting my hands.

She plays with my hair.

I lick her up and down. Harder. Softer. Faster. Slower. Once I'm certain I've tasted every inch, I plunge my tongue inside her.

She groans. Her hand goes to the back of my head, holding it against her.

Fuck, I love watching the pleasure spread over her body, the way she shakes and groans and gets demanding.

Her groans get deeper. She's close. I lick her until I can't take her agony anymore then I suck on her clit.

"Fuck, Drew." She tugs at my hair, bucking her hips against me.

I suck harder. Harder. Until she cries out with a mix of pain and pleasure.

"Don't stop," she breathes.

Like hell. I slide a finger inside her. Then two. Her groans get louder. Her breath hitches.

I move my fingers in time with my mouth. Within moments, she's writhing as she comes on my face. Her moans fill the room. She screams my name again and again.

When she's done, her thighs go slack. She looks spent, but I need to see her come again.

Two more times, preferably.

I look up at her. Those big brown eyes are heavy with

desire. She's floating on a cloud of it. No stress, no heaviness, nothing in her life but pleasure.

Perfect.

I let go of all the other ways I need to take care of her. I let go of every need except her coming again.

We can get to me after that.

I give her a moment to catch her breath then I plant my face between her legs. Her thighs press against the sides of my head.

This time, I start slowly. I lick her up and down.

When she's groaning and panting, I focus on her clit and I move faster. Harder.

Within moments, she's coming again. She tugs at my hair. Her heel digs into my back as she groans my name.

This time, she doesn't collapse. She pushes herself up and moves next to me. Her eyes fill with intention.

She plants her palms against my shoulders and pushes me onto the bed. Her lips brush against my chest. My stomach.

My cock twitches. My eyelids press together as she kisses her way down my torso.

Her lips brush against my cock.

Fuck.

I shudder as she flicks her tongue against me. She teases. Fuck, how she teases.

Her hair is still tied behind her head. My hands slide to her shoulders and squeeze tightly as she takes me deeper.

Her mouth is soft, wet. And her tongue. Fuck, her tongue-

Pleasure grabs hold of me. Usually, I can last as long as she needs me to. But she's too fucking good at this.

It only takes a few moments for me to get there. I dig my fingers into her skin. My hips shift of their own accord.

Fuck.

"I'm gonna come," I breathe.

She looks up at me, her big, brown eyes filled with hunger.

She sucks harder, takes me deeper.

I let go of everything else. My hand stays on the back of her head, guiding her. My eyelids press together.

It's not just her body that's mine.

It's mine that's hers.

I'm entirely at her mercy.

With the next flick of her tongue, I come. I press my fingers into the back of her head as I fill her mouth.

Pleasure shoots through me. It's fucking everywhere.

She swallows hard and pushes herself up. Then she's lying next to me. I turn onto my side and pull her body into mine.

She presses her lips to my chest. Her fingers trace the lines of the tattoo on my shoulder—my half of our couple's tattoo. "Thank you. I needed that."

Thank me? She's got that backward.

"You don't ever have to thank me for getting you off." I pull her closer.

"Still." She looks up at me. "It's nice not thinking. Let's order room service and not think for the rest of the night."

"Let's not think in the bathtub next."

"Mmm. Yes." She nestles into my chest. "I know you want me to take the test, baby. I will. First thing tomorrow. I promise. As long as you promise you won't say another word about it tonight."

"Come here." I slide my hand around her neck and pull her into a deep, slow kiss. When it breaks, I stare into her eyes. She's relaxed, steady. That's everything. "I promise."

Chapter Six

KARA

The heel of my foot hits the sleek tile floor. I turn and pace the length of the bathroom. The huge room felt like paradise last night. The bright white bulb lit Drew in an angelic glow. Okay, and it made it easier to gawk at his sculpted body as he stripped for me.

The sleek glass counter is trendy and modern and chic. But it's no place to sit. It's no place to collect my thoughts as I press the test against my chest.

Fuck. I can't do this.

The box is on the sleek glass counter. The testing stick is in my hands, still wrapped, still not taken.

My hands are shaking so badly I can barely hold the stick. I set it on the counter. I need something cool, something to calm me, but there's nothing.

Drew is outside the door. He'll calm me. But he'll also look at me with those dark eyes of his, and I'll know I'm hurting him by making him wait.

It's not fair to him to drag this out.

This is his life as much as it's mine.

It will be *our* child.

Or it might be nothing.

God damn, is it so wrong that I want one fucking week of vacation? Is it so wrong to want one week of thinking about *now*?

Drew knocks on the door.

"One more minute." I press my palms against the ceramic sink and look into the mirror. It was a thing of beauty last night, when I watched Drew fuck me from behind, but I hate the stupid reflective surface right now.

Drew taps on the door.

"Just a minute."

"Tell me you aren't panicking."

"I'm..." Deep breath. I'm not lying to him. "I'm working on it. Give me one minute."

He says nothing, but I can feel his frustration from here. I want to let him in. I want to feel as steady as he is.

I might feel better sitting in the bathtub.

It's worth a shot.

I press my palms against the sides and climb in. For a moment, my mind goes back to last night. We spent a long time in this bathtub. I came so many times I lost track.

There's a knock. But it's not the bathroom door. It's from outside the room.

"Did you order room service?" I ask.

"No." Drew's voice is uneasy. "I'll check."

"Lucy, I'm home!" The voice is muffled by the door, but there's no mistaking Tom's chipper tone.

I have to laugh.

Of course Tom is here now.

He's always around at the best-slash-worst possible time.

Tom knocks again. "Guitar Prince, you should open up, or I'm going to have to start making out with your sister-"

"Your wife." Willow chimes in, correcting Tom.

"Yeah, you're right, kid. You're my wife. It's my marital duty to make out with you as often as possible."

Drew growls. The door opens.

I laugh.

Tom really has Drew's number. It's not exactly difficult to stoke Drew's temper, but I have to admire the balls it takes for Tom to bait him like that.

Drew's as protective of his sister as he is of me. More even.

But then Tom is right. It's his marital duty to keep her *happy*. It was part of his engagement speech.

"Give me a second," Drew says to the visitors. There are footsteps as he comes closer. The door handle turns and he steps inside the bathroom.

"What if I was peeing?" I ask.

He throws me some serious side eye. Really, it's good side eye. He's learned well.

"Okay, fair enough." I go to push myself out of the tub, but it's too slippery.

Drew is there instantly. He slides his arms under my armpits. In one swift movement, he pulls me up and out of the tub.

Damn, the man is strong. Sometimes I forget what control he has over his body—over *every* part of his body.

I look up at him. "Can we go back to the part where I'm coming until I can't take it anymore?"

"After you take the test." He runs his fingertips over my cheek. His expression gets intense, protective. "Kara, this is important. Maybe the most important thing we'll ever do."

"Do you really want to have a baby?"

He nods.

"Now?"

"Later would be easier, but now is fine, yeah. I want a future with you. I want the whole thing—the house, the white picket fence, the kids, the dog." He scrunches his nose. "Not the dog. You're allergic."

"Maybe a snake."

He laughs. "Yeah, sure. A snake."

"I don't want a white picket fence. I want a fancy beach house like Tom has."

"Not in his neighborhood. Too many vagrants and junkies."

My shoulders relax. Drew's already got this under control. Sort of. I know I can't do it on my own. But with him... that feels possible.

"Take it now," he says. "I'll keep them busy."

"After they leave."

Drew's eyes fix on mine. He stares at me like he's staring into my soul. "You've been killing yourself wondering. Not gonna watch you do that." He drops his voice. "It's killing me too."

My gaze goes to the tile floor. He's right, but I'm still not taking the test until they leave. "I'm not taking the test in front of our friends. I don't want to tell anyone until I process this, and I don't want to have to worry about their reactions or about hiding my reaction from them."

Drew frowns, but he doesn't argue.

"After breakfast," I say.

Drew slides his arm around my waist to lead me out of the bathroom.

Tom launches into a slow clap. "Embarrassing shit, Guitar Prince. You didn't even last three minutes. I timed it."

Willow nods. Her chin-length pink hair sways with her movements. "He did time it, but it's obvious you two weren't having sex. We would have heard a lot more." She nods hello to me. "Good to see you, Kara. You look beautiful. Your hair always looks good. I'm jealous."

What a sweet, lying sister-in-law I have. Well, I guess Drew and I aren't married yet. But close enough.

"Kid, she looks pretty shitty. Like she slept in that makeup. No offense, Kara. You're still hot." Tom slides his arm around his wife. He blows a wavy blond strand from his green eyes. "Your tits look bigger than normal."

Drew growls.

I shoot him an *it's fine* look, but he still pulls me closer. I can't say that I mind the proximity. His body is warm and hard. When his arms are around me, I feel safe, like everything really is going to be okay.

Willow covers her face with her palm. She laughs.

"Look at them." He turns to her. "Don't get me wrong, kid. I prefer yours. But those are fucking huge."

Willow nods. "Sweetie, you know you're allowed to have thoughts and *not* vocalize them."

"Not sure about that," Toms says.

She raises a brow.

"Let me try." He looks her up and down. His mischievous green eyes get brighter. His tongue slides over his lips. "Fuck, you're right. Thought about unzipping your jeans and I didn't—"

Willow turns bright red. "Down, boy."

Tom smiles. "You should try directing your attention a little lower."

Despite the delight in her eyes, Willow clears her throat. "We are in my brother Drew's hotel room. Not ours. And we're here to ask them to breakfast." She turns to us. "We should have called, but we're here. You guys want to get breakfast? We only got in an hour ago."

Drew is still in guard dog stance. Hard to blame him with Tom flirting in his face. It's hard for *me* to wrap my head around Tom as a sweet, faithful husband when I saw him plow through so many women.

Must be harder for Drew.

It's difficult to get over the difference in pre- and post-Willow Tom. He always seemed like he knew what he wanted, but the way he looks at her—it's like she hung the moon.

They'll be a good aunt and uncle. Tom will play with the kid. He'll spoil the shit out of the kid. Willow will be a more even-tempered caretaker. She's a little shy—we're all shy compared to Tom—but she's loving and sweet.

The tightness in my chest fades. I really love the two of them. Like they're my brother and sister.

They'll help with this.

Oh fuck. I'm crying. I turn before anyone can see. God damn hormones. Probably. "Give me five minutes to change. You guys can watch TV or talk. Whatever you want. Just keep it in your pants."

"Well, I never..." Tom feigns offense.

"No one's buying that, sweetie." Willow laughs. "You're like a puppy today."

He licks her cheek. She laughs.

"I can try that a little lower and a lot softer," he murmurs.

She turns even more red.

I grab Drew before he can start growling.

ॐ

THE AIR OUTSIDE ISN'T EXACTLY FRESH—THERE'S FAR TOO much cigarette smoke to call it fresh—but it's in the ballpark.

I inhale my last bit of not exactly fresh air as we step into the Wynn. Apparently, the restaurants here are well-known for their vegan and vegetarian options.

"Tom, you know I can order a vegetable omelet anywhere." Willow looks around the opulent casino lobby and presses her lips together. "If you guys want that five-dollar steak and eggs downtown or whatever."

"Drew doesn't eat cheap food." Tom clears his throat. "Place has great reviews and a view of the hotel garden."

"It's fine, Wil." Drew nods to the restaurant in the corner. "Looks like a nice place."

She looks at me. "He spent the entire drive talking about the vegetarian friendly restaurants." She looks back to Tom. "I'm not picky. I can get a salad or a grilled cheese anywhere."

He pouts. "You're not eating grilled cheese in Vegas. This city is known for its dining, and you're not gonna miss out on my watch."

She smiles.

They're sickeningly cute. I'm glad. I may give Drew a hard time about his temper, but I feel that same urge to protect Willow. I'll destroy anyone who hurts her.

Drew frowns as we walk through a cloud of cigarette smoke. He fans the air in front of me. Damn, this city really is all cigarettes and booze. There isn't much for a hypothetically pregnant woman to do.

Tom and Willow are a few paces in front of us. Tom looks back, studying us. His green eyes light up and connect with mine.

He shoots me a knowing look.

But there's no way he knows...

How could he possibly know?

I check my purse. The test is in there, but the handbag is zipped tightly. I wouldn't necessarily put snooping in a purse past Tom, but he hasn't had a chance. The thing has been on my shoulder the entire walk here.

"Something on your mind, Tom?" I ask.

"Nah. Nothing important." He looks to Drew then back to me. "You?"

"My stomach is growling." Okay, it's saying *Ugh, throwing*

up is a good idea, but it is saying something. "I'm starving. Hope you don't mind me copying your veggie omelet, Willow."

She throws her arm out like she's a queen presenting a crown to her subjects. "Veggie omelets for everyone."

We stop in front of the host stand. There's a small line curling around the corner—there are lines everywhere in Vegas—but Tom ignores it.

A college-aged woman in the line tugs at her friend's t-shirt. She points to Tom then to Drew and whispers in her friend's ear.

The boys have been spotted. Usually, I don't mind random shows of celebrity—sometimes it's kinda funny watching Drew turn red over the attention—but I'm not in the mood right now. I'm in more of a sit down and throw up kind of mood.

There's no way this is allergies.

Thankfully, Tom has some kind of VIP pass. Or the host recognizes him as a VIP—he *is* famous on Instagram in addition to his usual rock star thing. Helps that his boudoir photographer wife loves shooting artsy black and white nudes for his page. There's nothing showing—not that I check.

The host leads us through the restaurant to a secluded corner. The non-smoking section, thankfully. Drew pulls my chair out for me and fusses to help me sit. Tom and Willow are staring, but they say nothing about it.

The place is clean and well-lit. Our square table is adorned with a bright white cloth. Nothing about this feels like Vegas. It's more like a nice restaurant in Santa Monica. Except for the beeps and bops of slot machines fifty feet away, it could be any restaurant in our neighborhood.

I play with the menu. There are tons of fancy options, but none of them appeal. The vegetable omelet sounds like more than I can handle. Toast and plain tea is about all I can handle, but I've been eating nothing but bread the last few days.

I set my menu down. "You guys drove in?"

Tom nods. "Left around three A.M. We were up all night—"

Willow clears her throat. "It was a quick drive. No traffic."

"Pete come with you?" I ask.

Tom laughs. "No, he and Jess had to *catch up*. He's leaving sometime today. If they ever get out of bed."

"I'm sure they'll get to the couch or the shower," Willow says.

"He tell you that?" Tom asks.

"Girls talk." Willow smiles. "Not Kara though. She's probably sparing me from hearing about sex with my brother."

I nod. She's right. I feel weird talking about my relationship with Willow. I can talk about Drew, but only in a *we should do something special for his birthday* kind of way. Anything more intimate feels like a boundary violation.

Drew is fixed on me. It's like the two of them aren't even here.

He leans in. "Are you okay?"

"Yeah. Great. Just hungry," I say.

He raises a brow.

Thankfully, a waiter stops by our table with four waters. I suck on my straw. It helps ease the wave of nausea that's rising in my throat. Deep breath. I'll be fine as soon as I eat something.

Hopefully.

We take our turns ordering. Coffee for everyone else. Earl Grey for me. Omelets all around.

"This place does look good." Willow presses her lips to Tom's. "Thanks for doing so much research."

"Anytime, kid." His kiss is a hell of a lot less chaste.

Drew clears his throat. He's calm about watching his sister moan over her husband. "Did you invite us to breakfast to make out in front of us?"

"Being familial," Tom says. "The making out is a bonus for your eyes."

Willow bursts into laughter. "Where do you come up with this stuff, sweetie? You should give Drew a break, for once. You don't have to remind him about our sex life every time you see him."

Drew squeezes my hand under the table. I turn to face him. His dark eyes are intense, protective. His short hair is messy. I fix a strand that's hanging in his eyes. He never lets it get long enough to hang in his eyes.

"I like your hair longer." I run my fingers down his cheek and over his strong jaw. He's classically handsome. Good genes. Not that it matters what our kid looks like. But being attractive would put him or her at an advantage. "You should keep it like that."

He purrs as I run my fingers over his neck. "I could be convinced."

"We should get them back by making out on the table." I smile. "We could get them back even better by having sex on the table."

Drew shakes his head. He's a lot less shy with his affection than he used to be, but he's still not the PDA type.

Well, not in front of our friends.

The waiter interrupts my bliss with the coffees. They smell stronger than usual.

My stomach lurches. I push my seat back and take a long sip of water. It's not enough.

Fuck.

"Excuse me. Ladies' room."

I grab my purse and push out of my seat. The bathroom is right around the corner. It's clean, white, and empty.

I push into an empty stall just in time to throw myself on the ground and hurl into the toilet.

Fucking coffee. Okay. I can do this. Deep breath then I stand up.

I go to push myself to my feet, but it's no good. Another wave of nausea overtakes me.

I hurl again.

When I'm sure I'm done, I sink onto my feet. Sitting on a bathroom floor in Vegas. Classy. At least it's clean.

Speaking of clean, I should wipe up. As soon as I catch my breath.

The door swings open. Awesome. An audience.

"Kara, you okay?" Willow's footsteps move closer. "Are you—" Her eyes go wide. "Are you pregnant?"

Chapter Seven

KARA

Am I pregnant? That's the million-dollar question, isn't it?

Willow takes a step backward. "Sorry. None of my business. Do you want? Here-" She pulls the stall door open. She sits next to me and pulls my hair behind my head. "You have a hair tie? I don't carry them anymore. This cut is too short for a ponytail."

"Yeah. In my purse." I reach up to flush the toilet then press my back into the wall of the stall. Willow is close, and I'm sure I don't smell like flowers at the moment. "You don't have to sit with me."

"I know." She unzips my purse and digs through it. Her eyes go wide. Must be the pregnancy test. She says nothing about it. Instead, she clears her throat and hands me a hair tie.

"Thanks." I pull my hair into a loose ponytail. I'm sure Willow realizes this, but I might as well say it aloud. "I haven't taken the test yet."

Willow shifts into a cross-legged position. "Why not?"

"I only started thinking it was possible a day and a half ago." I take a deep breath. "And I'm terrified."

There's understanding in her hazel eyes. "I'm not sure how much Drew told you about..." She takes a deep breath. "About my ex raping me. I took the morning after pill, but... if that hadn't worked, if I'd been pregnant..." She presses her trembling hands together. They steady. "I wouldn't think less of you if you decided to terminate."

I shake my head. "I want to have a family with Drew. I want to teach a kid how to take on the world." My exhale breaks up the tension in my chest. I really do want a family with Drew. I can see a great future for us, for our family. But it's still as scary as it is beautiful. "Just... I thought it would be in five or ten years."

"I didn't think I'd get married at twenty-two. Or ever, really. I had pretty much given up on dating and men in general." Her expression gets dreamy. "But I'm glad I did. Tom is..."

"Tom is Tom."

She laughs. "That's about right." Her eyes go to my purse then to me. "Drew has never been happy like this. At first, I couldn't believe that it was really my brother, but it is. He loves you more than anything."

"Tom either. You should have seen him before he met you. It was like... he was always Tom, but you could tell there was something missing, that he was desperate to prove himself or to find something more. The way he looks at you... I can tell you're meant for each other."

Her cheeks flush. "Tom is amazing. But even knowing that, I was nervous about getting married. Big changes are always scary." Her gaze meets mine. "Is that why you're waiting?"

"I'm hoping it will feel less terrifying in a few days. Once I'm used to the idea."

"Give me a second." She pulls her phone from her pocket and taps the screen. "Don't hate me for this?"

I shift up to glance at the cell screen. She's texting someone.

Dammit.

"You feeling better?" she asks.

"Not better enough to move."

"Here." She gets up, wets a paper towel in the sink, and brings it back to me.

The door swings open and Drew steps inside.

"This is the women's bathroom." I shoot him a *What the hell?* look then offer the same one to Willow.

Drew shrugs. "We aren't having sex in here."

"Is that something you do regularly?" Willow makes a face like she smells something bad. "You know what? Don't tell me. I don't want to know."

"I'm the one who has to hear about your boyfriend's cock piercing," he says.

Willow flashes her left ring finger. "Hey. That's my husband's cock piercing."

Drew shakes his head. She laughs.

I laugh too. It's a full-blown belly laugh. These two are ridiculous. But they're sweet.

They're my family. Both of them. Willow is a good sister. And she'll be a good aunt.

And my mom... things are still strained between us sometimes. She'll think I'm too young to have a kid, but she will support me. She will be happy to have a grandchild.

The door swings open. Fuck. This is bad news. Only it's not a woman who is going to get security. It's Tom.

Of course it's Tom.

I burst into another belly laugh. Drew is looking at me like I'm possessed, but I don't care.

They're my family. All of them.

Drew turns to Tom. "What are you doing?"

"Wanted to be where the party is." Tom nudges Willow. "Never realized you were into orgies, kid. Should have invited Pete to have a threesome before he found someone."

Willow blushes.

God, this is hilarious. I'm laughing so hard I can barely get words out. "Yeah, Drew would totally have an orgy with you and his sister. God, would you really have a threesome with your brother?" I shake my head. "Of course you would."

Willow looks at him. "Would you?"

Tom shrugs. "Not anymore. He's engaged."

"But before?" she asks.

"Sure. If you wanted," he says. "Whatever you want."

Her eyes go wide. "Really?"

"Want me to ask Ethan? Or Kit?" Tom teases.

"No..." Willow stammers. "That's okay. I'm... I'm good with one cock at a time."

"Can always fuck you with your vibe while you're sucking me off." Tom speaks like he's mentioning the weather.

God damn, what a family.

Drew must be worried about me, because he doesn't so much as glare at Tom.

I have to hold my stomach so I don't keel over from the laughter.

"What about you, Drew? You want to have a threesome?" I tease.

"Fuck no." He stares at me like I'm crazy. "Did Miles put you up to that?"

God, Miles is ridiculous too. And Pete—he acts all quiet and sweet, but he's the filthiest pervert of them all.

All of them are my family. It's not a traditional family, but so what? It's mine, and they're going to make great aunts and uncles.

If I'm pregnant.

Tom looks from me to Willow to Drew. He makes eye contact. "You hung over or pregnant?"

"Tom!" Willow squeals.

"It's okay. She asked me the same thing," I say.

Drew clears his throat.

This does nothing to move Tom and Willow.

"I don't know yet," I say. "I haven't taken the test."

Willow leans in to whisper in his ear.

His eyes light up. He nods.

The girl has his number.

She looks at me. "We'll be at the table. If you want to skip out on breakfast, we can handle it. Just text me."

"Maybe *we* should practice the mechanics of making a baby," Tom says. "Don't want to get rusty."

"At the table?" She raises a brow.

"No, kid, don't be ridiculous. At the hostess stand."

"We already decided we're adopting, but sure, I'll play into your fantasy. Back in our hotel room. After breakfast." She kisses him then turns to me. "Good luck. Call if you need anything."

Tom follows her out of the bathroom.

Drew comes closer. He sits on the ground next to me. The expression in his dark eyes is soft.

"We have a weird family." I squeeze his hand. "But I wouldn't trade them for the world."

"Me either." His dark eyes fix on me. "Are you ready?"

"Will you read the results?"

He nods.

"Then I'm as ready as I'm going to be."

He pulls the test from my purse and hands it to me. "You can do this."

I step into the stall and take a deep breath.

Here goes nothing.

Chapter Eight

DREW

Two-minutes fifty-nine seconds. Fifty-eight. Fifty-seven.

Fuck, this is going to be a long three minutes.

Kara washes and dries her hands. She stares at the test sitting on the counter. Her big brown eyes fill with anxiety. I can practically see her neck and back tightening.

There's nothing I can do to change the results or make them come faster. But I *can* ease the agony of waiting.

I wrap my arms around her and pull her close. She's a strong person. It's easy to forget how petite she is. She barely comes up to my chest.

Her voice is a little louder than a whisper. "Are you terrified?"

Only that she's going to break. She's still shaking. I rub her shoulder with my thumb. She purrs, leaning into the gesture.

I rub a little harder. "I'm ready to know."

"You're brave."

"You too."

She shakes her head.

"Say it. You're brave."

"I'm brave *sometimes*."

"You're lucky you're pressed against me, or I'd give you a hard time about this shit."

"You should give me a hard time as soon as possible."

Fuck yeah. Soon as we deal with this.

She digs her fingers into my t-shirt, holding onto me like I'm her life vest. It feels fucking good bringing her comfort, knowing I'm taking some of the weight she carries around on her shoulders.

I'm not sure how we manage to stay alone in the bathroom, but we do. All three minutes, I stand here, holding Kara.

The timer beeps.

The test is done.

Kara takes a step backward. She looks up at me. "Are you ready?"

I nod. I am.

I take the test from the counter and turn it over.

Two lines.

Positive.

Kara is pregnant.

Fuck.

This is fantastic.

The two of us having a family—it's real. It's happening.

"Drew..." Her voice is timid. "What does it say?"

I meet her gaze. Those big, brown eyes of hers are filled with that same anxiety.

I slide my arms around her waist and pull her closer. My voice is bright, excited. "You're pregnant."

Her eyes go wide. "I am?" She takes the test from my hands and stares at it.

Moments pass as she takes it in. I'm not sure what's going

through her head. I hate not knowing what's going through her head, but I have to give her time.

"I'm pregnant," she whispers.

No sense in beating around the bush. "What are you thinking?"

"I'm pregnant." Her voice lifts. "I can't believe it." She takes a deep, slow breath and looks up at me. "This is good."

"This is fucking great."

She nods. Her lips curl into a smile. She tosses the test on the counter and jumps into my arms. "We're gonna have a baby."

I hold her closely. "Yeah, we are."

When our embrace breaks, she looks up at me. Her smile widens. Her eyes brighten. "You look happy."

"I am." I run my fingers through her hair until she looks up at me. Understanding passes between us. Kara and I are a team. We come before everything else in the world. Our family comes before everything else. "As long as I'm alive, you'll never be alone. This kid too."

"Okay."

"I'll figure this out. Trust me." I look into her big, brown eyes. "I don't want to be like my father. I want to be there every fucking second till that kid is yelling at me to give him space and locking himself in his room."

She laughs. "Are you going to tell your parents?"

"No. I don't want my mom getting in his way the way she did with me. Whatever this kid wants, he's going to get it."

"What if she hates the guitar?" Kara teases.

"With half my DNA? Not possible."

"But what if she does?"

"Then she hates the guitar. But that won't happen. I'll teach her to play as soon as she can hold a guitar."

She looks up at me. A playful smile spreads over her face. "What if she only likes rap music?"

"Then we'll soundproof her room. And ours." I pull Kara into my chest again. She's warm, and she smells good. "We should soundproof our room no matter what. I'm not gonna hold back on fucking you because I'm afraid of waking the baby."

She laughs. "Good." Her voice softens. "Do you think... for the name. Alex. Alexander if he's a boy, and Alexandria if she's a girl? After my dad."

I melt. That's perfect. "Of course."

She smiles. "Really?"

I nod.

"That will make Mom happy." She squeezes me. "I'm terrified of what she'll say."

"She'll be happy."

"You think so?"

I have to admit I'm stretching the limits of my knowledge. Kara's mom hasn't always been as supportive as she could be. But the way she looks at Kara—she'll come around.

I rub her shoulders. "Yeah, but let's not worry about it right now. Let's soak in the good news for a while."

Her voice wavers. "That sounds nice, but... maybe not the most possible."

"It's okay you're scared." I lean down to press my lips to her forehead. "I'm scared too. But I think we should continue this conversation outside the bathroom."

She laughs. "True. I'm going to wash up. I'll meet you at the table."

"I love you, Kara. We can do this."

She nods. "We can. If we do it together."

۞

TOM AND WILLOW ARE WAITING AT THE TABLE. THEY'RE teasing as they feed each other bites of toast and eggs.

They really are happy.

It's fucking weird that Tom is married to my sister. Not sure it will ever stop being weird, but I'm happy she's happy.

Tom nudges her. He practically points to us. Then the two of them are exchanging whispers.

Kara squeezes my hand. A nervous look spreads over her face.

I rub her shoulders. "They'll be happy for us."

She nods, but her big brown eyes stay nervous.

Tom rises as we approach the table. He looks from Kara to me. His eyes fix on Willow. "I told you she was pregnant."

"Tom!" She shakes her head, but she's smiling. My sister looks at me. "Is it true? Are you?"

"Yeah," I say.

Willow claps her hands together. "Oh my God. That's great! Are you happy? You look scared. But happy. It *is* scary." She jumps to her feet and hugs Kara. Then she hugs me. "I'm excited for you."

Tom nods. He hugs Kara. I try to shake his hand, but he shakes his head and pulls me into a hug.

"Happy for you two." He steps back and looks at me. "Don't worry about band shit. We'll figure it out."

Kara presses her lips together. "I... I don't want this to be the thing that breaks up Sinful Serenade."

Tom waves his hand in a *don't worry about it* gesture. "It won't. Worst case scenario, we replace Drew."

I scowl.

Kara frowns.

"Kidding." Tom looks to me. "Shit. Nothing is coming to mind, but we've got time. Enjoy your news. Go have crazy sex or some shit like that."

Willow laughs. "Sex isn't the solution to everything."

"Gonna have to agree to disagree there." Tom shoots her a flirty look. "Or I could prove you wrong."

"Later." She looks at him with adoration then she turns her attention to us. "We're happy for you. Really. And happy we'll be an aunt and uncle. Everyone else will be happy too."

"Thanks." Kara tries to smile, but it's not quite there. "Keep it between us for now. I don't want to usurp the wedding."

Tom nods. "Seriously, Kara, the band will be okay. We'll figure it out."

"How?" she asks. Her voice is dripping with anxiety.

It's a fair question. I don't own a teleporter. I can't exactly fly home between gigs, not when they're two days apart.

Something has to give. Either I'm home less or I'm on the road less.

It hits me like a ton of bricks. I can't believe I'm doing this, but I am.

I kiss Kara on the forehead. "I'm gonna make a call. I'll be back in a few."

"Is everything okay?" she asks.

"Everything is fucking great, Kendrick." I take a moment to take her in. She's scared, but there's happiness in her expression too.

Tom was right. Her chest is bigger.

Damn, her tits are gonna get huge. Can't complain about that.

I step away so dirty thoughts won't take ahold of me.

This is an obvious solution.

But I still can't believe I'm doing it.

Hell, I'm not sure my ego can handle it.

I find a semi-quiet spot and I call Ethan—he's the guitarist of Dangerous Noise, the band opening for us on the tour that starts in two weeks-and bring the phone to my ear.

I was the original guitarist for Dangerous Noise. At this point, there are only two original members of the band left.

It's normal for small bands. Most people are in half a dozen bands before one sticks.

But I'm still worried. I didn't exactly make a good impression by stealing the former lead singer's girlfriend and generally being a narcissistic prick.

Ethan is groggy, fresh out of bed. "Drew Denton? What the fuck you doing calling me?"

"How fast can you get to Vegas?"

"You getting hitched or something?"

"No. Wouldn't invite you if I was."

He laughs. "Cold. Just like Tom says."

I shake my head. Used to be that kind of thing would bait me, but it's hard to feel anything bad at the moment. "No. I need to ask a favor."

"I'm listening."

"How fast can you get here?"

"Couple of days. Tour doesn't start for another two weeks. Heard rumors you're a perfectionist, but I can't imagine you want to help me work on the Dangerous Noise set list."

"No, it's something else."

"Hard to believe *the* Drew Denton needs me."

He's teasing me. I think. Hard to say. I'm not exactly a people person. I don't know Ethan well enough to know if he's teasing or serious.

I clear my throat. Better to focus on the task at hand. "I'll need you all day."

"Damn, wish you were somebody else talking like that." He chuckles. "You're not secretly a smoking hot strawberry blond with soft lips and legs for days?"

"Brunette, but my legs do go for days," I say. "You'd have to ask Kara about the soft lips part."

Ethan laughs. "I'll be there."

Chapter Nine

KARA

I push my delicate condition aside to focus on steadying the blushing bride. She's almost as nervous as I am.

Everything blurs together until I'm watching the happy couple say I do. The reception is as gorgeous as the wedding. The chocolate cake with mocha frosting is to die for.

I eat far too much of it, considering I should be concerned about my nutrient intake. Starting tomorrow, I eat healthy, I get light exercise, and I take my vitamins. This baby is going to have the best possible start.

I'm having a baby.

It feels too grown up, but it's good. I'm happy. Scared, but happy.

I'm too tired to think about it. I need to sleep forever. Or at least until Drew works out how he's going to be around enough for us. It's weird wrapping my head around the idea that it's an *us* now.

Drew sits next to me. He runs his fingertips over my chin, careful not to mess up my tight updo. "You should call your mom."

"First thing in the morning."

"Everyone is meeting for brunch tomorrow. That's a thing, apparently."

I look up at him. "You said brunch without rolling your eyes."

He chuckles. "Call her now. You'll feel better."

"I can think of another way I'd feel better."

He raises a brow. "That so, Kendrick?"

I nod.

"I'll run the bath."

Oh, I like the bath.

I don't so much like worrying what my mom is going to say.

I know I'll feel better after I call her. But the part where I call her... that part is terrifying.

I'm only twenty-two. Moms aren't usually happy about their unmarried twenty-two-year-old daughters getting knocked up.

It takes me half an hour to psyche myself up enough to call. I dial her number. But I'm not ready yet.

I end the call before it can ring.

Mom and I are better than we were, but things are still strained sometimes. I *know* she wants the best for me, but sometimes, it feels like she wants her idea of the best for me.

My phone buzzes.

Incoming call from Mom.

Dammit, I thought I hung up fast enough.

For a second, I consider letting it ring to voicemail. But then I see Drew's slacks and boxers on the bedroom floor.

Damn him and his sexual not quite bribery.

I answer the call. "Hey, Mom."

"Kara, sweetie. How are you?" Her voice is chipper. She's doing well.

"I'm good. Tired."

"How was your friend's wedding?"

"Beautiful." I spent nearly twenty minutes filling Mom in on all the details of the wedding. Not that I'm avoiding the subject at hand.

She interjects with *awws*. It was a nice wedding.

When I run out of details, I start talking about the cake. Then the frosting.

Then I'm out of other subjects.

I have to tell her.

Fuck.

I push myself off the bed and pace the hotel room. It's a long room. It's a lot of space for pacing.

"Kara, you okay?" Mom asks.

"I have to tell you something." I need to do this fast, like a Band-Aid. Quick. Painless.

Yep, there's nothing as painless as telling your mother that you're unwed and pregnant.

It's not so bad, really. Drew and I are engaged. We're employed. Well, he's employed. I'm employable.

He's responsible. He's mature. Hell, he's the only one of the guys who does his own cleaning. Miles, Tom, and Pete all hire cleaning services.

Drew takes care of himself. He takes care of me. He can take care of our baby too.

We can do this.

I take a deep breath. "Mom, I'm pregnant."

"Oh."

I can't read her voice. Shit.

"I just found out." I tap my fingers against the phone. What do I say here? How do I convince her this is okay? "It's a good thing. We're happy."

"Then I'm happy."

Drew calls out from the bathroom. "You have an appointment with a doctor in the morning."

175

Thank God for Drew. I've never been more certain that I need him than I am right now.

"I'm seeing an OB tomorrow," I say. "We'll find out more."

"That's great, sweetheart."

"Really?"

"You're a little young, but... you know, your father and I got married and started trying for a baby as soon as we could. Sometimes, it's okay to do things early."

"Yeah?" I ask.

Her voice lifts. "You're going to be a great mom, Kara. I know it's scary. I was terrified when you were born. I thought I'd do something wrong. But the love you have for your family—it's the best thing in the world."

⚜

AFTER THE DOCTOR'S OFFICE—I'M TEN WEEKS ALONG, AND everything looks good—we get into a cab and head to brunch.

"Think they're tired of sleeping together already?" Drew asks.

"Not in a million years." I rest my head on his shoulder and intertwine my fingers with his. "Do you want to tell them or should I?"

"I will." He squeezes my hand. "Unless you object."

"No. You should tell them." I press my eyelids together and soak in the vibrations of the road. "In thirty weeks, we're going to have a baby."

"Yeah."

"There are about two weeks until your tour starts."

"I've got it under control, Kara. Don't worry."

"You want to tell me how?"

"I'd rather tell you once I'm sure this will work." He lowers his voice. "In case I fuck it up."

"Okay." My breath feels sharp. I don't like the uncertainty, but I *can* respect that Drew wants to be sure before he makes a promise.

It's his way.

After a few quiet minutes, we arrive at the restaurant. It's surprisingly quaint, like a hipster version of Denny's. Everyone else is here. They're at a long table in the middle of the room. Meg and Miles are sitting on the end. They're wearing the relaxed smiles of two people who spent the entire night knocking boots.

Tom jumps out of his chair when he sees us. Willow follows, a few paces behind.

He hugs me hello and whispers in my ear, "nobody knows you're knocked up."

Willow play-swats him then takes her turn hugging me. "You do have that glow about you."

"It's the glow of good nausea medication." The doctor prescribed something that is safe for the baby. It still feels like a dream. I'm having a baby. We're having a baby. In seven months, we'll have a baby. "But thanks."

"No, it's more than that." Tom gives me a quick once-over. He turns to Willow. "They *are* bigger."

She laughs, somehow endeared by her husband's bluntness and inability to mind his own business. Okay, it's hard to deny that Tom is charming in a very Tom kind of way.

She kisses him on the nose then turns to me. "Do you know how far along?"

"We're going to announce it in a few minutes." Drew motions to the table. "Sit down or you'll blow our cover."

They do as they're asked.

Drew turns to me. He rubs my shoulders as he stares into my eyes. "You okay?"

"Still breathing."

"Want to get this over with?"

"Please."

Drew nods. He presses his palm into my back to lead me to the table.

I smile as I take my seat. "Congrats again, you guys. You look very married."

Meg smiles. She stares at her rings with delight then turns to Miles and plants a peck on his lips.

He slides his hand behind her neck and kisses her deeply. She pulls back an inch, murmuring something about *not in front of our friends*. Within seconds, she's kissing him back.

Then the two of them are making out like no one is watching.

"Think he'll ever get tired of that?" Tom asks.

"Fuck no." Pete nods hello to me and Drew.

Jess too. "You look pretty, Kara. I couldn't figure out how to tame my hair after all that hairspray. I'm impressed you did."

Pete exchanges a look with Jess. God knows what they're communicating. I'm not sure how anyone communicates anything with the dark-haired bassist. I've known him for nearly two years, and he's still an enigma.

Drew leans in to whisper. "Now?"

I nod. "Now."

He stands up and addresses the table. "We have an announcement."

"You're getting married too?" Jess claps her hands together.

Drew shakes his head. "No. We're... Kara's pregnant. Almost two months along. We're excited, but it means some things are gonna change."

"Give everybody a minute to be happy for you." Tom

stands up. He offers Drew his hand to shake. "I know I already said it, but this is fucking awesome."

"You told Tom?" Pete cocks a brow in a gesture that says, *you know he can't keep his mouth shut, right?*

Tom laughs. "He didn't exactly have a choice. Long story. Fill you in later."

Pete shoots him an inquisitive look.

Tom shrugs.

Pete looks at me. "That's great, Kara. You're going be a great mom, and Drew's gonna be a really protective dad. But it's good. Kids need love *and* boundaries."

Miles calls out from his side of the table. "That's great, Kara."

"Yeah. It is." Meg smiles and mouths, *are you okay?*

I nod. "Hope we're not usurping your wedding."

"Don't worry. I know how to steal spotlight back." Miles winks.

Meg laughs. She leans in to kiss him. This time, he's even more obvious about making the kiss hot as hell. He slides his hands to her ass, pulls her into his lap, and presses his lips to her neck.

She groans loudly enough to draw the attention of everyone here.

Only there's no one but us and a few confused staff members. None of them are looking at the group with that, *oh my goodness, celebrities are weird* stare. It's more, *kids these days*.

Drew looks me over carefully. I must look okay, because he steps backward and nods to Tom. "Shall we?"

Tom taps his fingers against the table. He pushes himself up. "Yeah." He blows a kiss to his wife. "Order without us. Could be a while."

"Sure, sweetie." She smiles until Tom and Drew walk

away, then she's pressing her lips together, her brow knotted with worry.

Yeah, that looks about right.

Willow shakes it off when she catches me staring. "I'm sure it will be fine. Tom's really excited. He kept talking about how when we adopt in a few years, we can adopt an older kid or older siblings—usually, older siblings can't get any placement—so our kids will be similar ages."

"You and Tom have already talked about adopting?" Jess asks.

"Yeah." Willow smiles. "He's always wanted to adopt. Because of his parents and being in foster homes." She clears her throat. "Uh, your wedding was really nice, Meg. And your tattoo looks awesome." Willow places her hand over the tattoo on her chest—a glass heart, broken and bleeding. Drew has the same one on his shoulder. "I should have warned you about these. Guys love staring."

"I'll protect you, Princess." Miles squeezes Meg.

"Likely story." Meg traces the lines of her new ink—the words *Be Brave, Love* in script on her chest. It matches the tattoo on Miles's chest.

It's all very sweet.

But not sweet enough to distract me from Tom and Drew's conversation. They're just outside the restaurant.

It looks tense.

Really tense.

"I'm sure Drew isn't gonna quit." Miles laughs. "He needs the money now."

Pete chuckles. "They'll work it out. Tom cares about family more than he lets on. The band's a family. It's not gonna fuck us up if Drew takes time off. We'll figure something out."

Miles clears his throat. "You suggesting we replace Guitar Prince? He'd never go for that."

"His ego can handle it," Pete says.

"You angling to pick up the mantle?" Miles teases.

"Fuck no. Give me a bass guitar or give me-" He turns to Jess. "Well, there is something else I like my hands on."

"Don't tease." She presses her forehead against his.

"Who's teasing, baby? I've got the day free." Pete smiles ear to ear. He presses his lips to her neck.

She groans. Her eyelids press together as she tugs at her skirt.

Miles clears his throat again. "Damn, don't need to hear you come this often, Steele. At least keep it down this time."

Pete shakes his head. "No way in hell."

Miles raises a brow.

Pete winks.

At least they're in good spirits. I can't get the worried feeling out of the pit of my stomach. I take a deep breath, but it doesn't help.

"Excuse me. I'm going to get some air." I push myself from the table and find the back entrance.

It doesn't open up to anything fancy—just the parking lot —but it's quiet and it's empty. I press my back against the walls and scan the windows to check the view. Once I'm sure no one can see me from inside, I sink to my feet and bury my head between my knees.

Too much is happening.

A month ago, I had the next few years figured out. I was going to take a teaching position in Malibu at the school where I did my student-teaching, marry Drew, and spend my weekends and summers with him on tour. He'd fly home as often as possible. The constant stop and go would be hard, but we could do it for a while. Until everyone in the band wanted to slow down.

Sinful Serenade is big, but they're not big enough to pull

off a multi-year hiatus. I can't be the person who holds them back from reaching their full potential.

A tear stings my eye. Damn pregnancy hormones.

I let it fall. I spent years trying to stay in control of my feelings. All it got me was a bunch of ugly scars to line my thighs.

I was running from my feelings until Drew forced me to confront them. I was running from everything I wanted.

There are footsteps. I wipe my tears with my sleeves and push myself to my feet. No sense in embarrassing myself in front of a stranger.

Only it's not a stranger. It's Meg.

She crouches down to wrap her arms around me. "Are you happy? Besides the crying in a parking lot thing?"

"Terrified. But also happy."

She squeezes me. "Then I'm happy too." She helps me up. "Your boobs are going to get even bigger. How will you ever find clothes that fit?"

I laugh. "I wasn't worrying about that."

"You should have told me you were pregnant instead of letting me go on about wedding dresses and cake. I feel like an asshole."

I shake my head. My eyes are still stinging with tears. "Fucking hormones." I use my other sleeve this time. "Your wedding is important. And cake is fucking amazing."

She laughs. "That's true."

"And you picked an amazing cake."

She nods. "It really was good. I ate so much of it. I never want sugar again."

"That sounds about right."

She smiles and leans closer. "You know you can always tell me the truth. No kid gloves, okay?"

"Okay."

"Holy fuck, you're gonna be a mom!" She hugs me again. "It's really cool."

It is. I can see that part—I can see myself cradling a baby, dressing her in those adorable tiny Converse, playing peeka-boo, and when she's older, teaching her to read.

"Miles likes to play cool, but we were going through this too." She lowers her voice. "I wasn't sure I could survive us being apart so much. School is hard. I don't have time to visit. Sometimes, it feels like a part of me is gone with him. And that's when we're apart a week. When it's longer–" She shifts her weight between her legs, leaning against the wall. "I was worried. The next five, ten years, I'm going to be stuck at whatever hospital will have me. It's nothing compared to having a child, but it's hard."

"You weren't sure about the wedding?"

"Yeah. You couldn't tell?"

"Figured it was normal cold feet."

"Maybe it was." She looks up at the blue sky. "Change is hard. Even when it's something good."

I copy her position, leaning against the wall and looking up at the sky.

"Did you cut your caffeine down to less than 200 milligrams a day?"

"Yeah, but no future Doctor Smart. Is it still Smart?"

She nods.

"No future doctor right now. Just my friend, Meg."

"Miles talked to Tom about slowing down. At least, I figured he talked to Tom. It does seem like Tom's in charge of everything, but I've never really looked into it."

I laugh. "He is."

She turns back to me. "I know that slowing down won't be enough. You'll need him around to raise a baby with you, but you can figure it out. You can come on the road some of the time. He won't quit the band. Hell, I won't let him."

"You're going to convince Drew of something?"

"Yeah, you're right." She nudges me. "He's almost as stubborn as you are."

"Almost?"

She laughs. "Five percent more."

"At least ten."

"You know what, for you, fifteen percent."

I laugh. "I'll take it."

She shifts away from the wall. "I don't know if Miles and I will ever decide to have kids. We're both on the fence. But... whatever we decide, even if my life looks nothing like yours in ten or fifteen years, you're going to be my best friend." She squeezes me. "You're stuck with me."

I squeeze her back. I'm lucky to have this much love in my life. Even if it's overwhelming sometimes. I break the hug and look at her. "Go have sex with your husband."

She squeals. "Can you believe he's really my husband now?"

"You've never looked happier."

"This marriage thing is great."

"It's been a whole twelve hours."

"Twelve amazing hours." She leads me back into the restaurant.

She nods to the table. Pete, Jess, Willow, and Miles are sitting, not at all hiding how they're staring at us.

Meg shakes her head. She motions to Drew and Tom talking outside. "Go be with your baby daddy. You two are living happily ever after. I won't allow anything else."

"We're not married. We're living in sin."

"So it's a sinful ever after. That sounds more fun anyway."

I laugh. It does sound more fun.

I lean in to whisper. "Promise you won't start touching my stomach and talking about miracles."

"Cross my heart and hope to die." She nudges me toward

the other door. "Talk to him. You two have to do this together."

She's right. I nod goodbye to everyone as I pass.

I need to know Drew has this under control. I need to know it's going to be okay.

Please let it be okay.

Chapter Ten

DREW

Kara steps outside. She's still shaking. It's almost imperceptible, but then I notice everything her body does.

Tom turns instantly. His brows knit together. The guy doesn't exactly hide his feelings.

"Did you..." Her eyes go from Tom to me. "Could one of you convince me this is going to be okay?"

Fuck. I must be neglecting something if she's looking to Tom for reassurance, but I can't promise yet.

Tom stares at me like I'm about to turn into The Incredible Hulk. "Drew..."

I move close enough to Kara that I can look into her eyes. "I promise it's going to be okay. Meet me tonight, after dinner."

Her eyes fill with confusion. "Where are you going?"

"To make this work." I brush her hair from her face. There's still a lot of apprehension in her eyes. "I need to make sure it will work."

Tom shakes his head. "If you need to go, do it. But don't

be all enigmatic and shit. I can fill her in." Tom shakes his head. He turns to Kara. "How do you put up with him?"

"Good body," she says.

Tom nods in agreement. "And the shit about him being good with his hands?"

She smiles. "That too." Kara stares into my eyes. "I trust you, baby. But I'll feel a hell of a lot better knowing more."

I want to tell her more, but I'm not sure I can say it aloud again.

I pry my lips apart, but the words don't fall. I need to get over this fast. I only have twenty minutes to spare.

I pull Kara into a tight hug. "You okay hanging with Tom and Willow for the rest of the day?"

She nods into my chest. "What is it you're doing?"

"Finding a way to be in two places at once." I lean down to kiss her. It's short and sweet. God, how it's sweet. Whatever happens, I'm not losing Kara.

I'm not giving up on our family.

If I have to choose between her and the band, it's her by a landslide. But I'm doing every fucking thing I can to make sure it doesn't come to that.

Gonna have to admit it in about nineteen minutes.

She takes a step backward. "Go make it happen, baby."

Tom shoots her a *really?* look.

She returns it.

"Don't look at me. He's your baby daddy," Tom says.

"He's *your* brother now." She teases Tom.

"Brother-in-law." Tom shakes his head. "Can you believe my poor wife has to put up with this shit?"

Kara smiles, her mood lightening. "No, I can't believe she married you. I have no idea why she did that."

"Course you do." Tom nods goodbye to me and leads Kara toward the restaurant. "I'm a fantastic lay. And I'm hot as fuck."

She laughs.

"Plus, I'm rich."

"I think she actually likes you for you."

"And you don't?" Tom asks.

Kara laughs. "You've grown on me."

"No, only on her," Tom says.

Kara bursts into a fit of laughter.

Tom opens the door for her. Once she's inside, he turns back to me. "Don't fuck this up, Guitar Prince. She's the best thing that ever happened to you."

The nickname is meant to bait me. Or it was. At this point, it's more of a pleasant familiarity.

Truth is, I deserve the nickname. I put guitar, and what I wanted for the band, ahead of everything else for far too long.

Not anymore.

THE LIGHTS IN THE CLUB ARE ON. THEY TURN THE STAGE into someplace normal. It's not a pedestal, but a place to stand and practice.

I know how to practice. The guitar laid out for me isn't nearly as good as mine, but it's more than enough for this.

I take the stairs one at a time. The stage feels bigger like this. The room too.

Can't remember the last time I was this nervous getting on a stage. Don't think I've ever been nervous getting on a stage in an empty room.

But, fuck, if I don't get this right...

My only choice is getting this right.

I sling the guitar over my shoulders, pull a pick from my jeans, and tune the damn thing. The familiarity of practice takes over as I work my way up the strings. Then it's scales.

My friends might think I'm a diva. Maybe they're right.

But it's not about my ego. Not usually. I love the strings of a guitar, the way they feel against my fingers, the way they respond to me. Playing is the only thing that makes sense.

Until Kara.

I close my eyes and play the first intro that comes to me. It's the song I know best. *No Way in Hell*. Must have played this song a few thousand times by now. It's our biggest hit to date. Fans riot if we go too long without playing it.

Thank fuck it's one of our most fun songs. My fingers fly over the fretboard. Music flows through the room. It bounces off the walls and back into my ears.

By the time I finish, I'm in a trance. I play another half a dozen songs. Each flows into the next. My hands are always a few steps in front of my head. They lead the way as I finish the last song on our set list.

The stage lights are bright enough that it's hot. I'm dripping with sweat. I lift my shirt to wipe my forehead.

There's Ethan, standing in front of the stage, his guitar slung over his shoulder.

He cocks a brow. "Don't need the sexual favor, Denton. I'm happy to be here."

His lips curl into a smile. I don't know Ethan too well, but I know the type. His cocky attitude is a front. Got no clue what he's hiding behind it, but then people aren't my expertise.

Guitar is.

The man knows his way around the instrument, and he's willing to help.

I motion for him to join me on stage. "Of course. I am *the* Drew Denton."

Ethan laughs as he climbs the steps to the stage. "Heard a lot about you from everyone but you."

"Anything good?"

"Couple of rumors about you having a threesome with Tom, but I think Tom started those."

"Undoubtedly."

"He's real fond of you. Though he'd never admit it."

"Don't tell him, but I'm fond of him too."

Ethan smiles. "My lips are sealed." He plugs his guitar into the amp and pulls a pick from his jeans. His voice drops, that *this is a secret and it's serious* tone. "Mostly, I heard that you're an asshole who gets into fights."

"Mostly, that's true."

"Still?"

"Still an asshole, but I don't get into fights."

Ethan laughs. "Fair enough. I think Kit's fond of you. But then, he keeps his cards pretty close to the vest."

I stretch my fingers. Tap my toes. I need to rely on my people skills. Only I don't have people skills. I offer Ethan my best smile. "You know any Sinful Serenade songs?"

"A few."

I raise my brow.

"You guys write good shit. You especially. Not that your ego needs stroking. After all, you are *the* Drew Denton."

I smile. He's already on board.

Asking for help isn't the worst thing in the world.

That's a good thing. I'm gonna have to get better at it quickly.

I keep my voice steady. "How do you feel about filling in for me?"

His blue eyes go wide. "Full time?"

"Here and there. A handful of shows this year. More in the future. If you want."

Those eyes light up. "Fill in for Sinful Serenade? Fuck yes."

"You'll play two and a half hours straight some days."

"My hands have plenty of stamina." He rolls his shoulders back and tests his guitar with a few chords. "Teach me before I change my mind."

That, I can do.

Chapter Eleven

KARA

Tom is the same bundle of energy he was this morning. I've got no clue how Willow deals with it every day. Sure, it's nice when you're in a good mood. But when your stomach is in knots from a mix of morning sickness and fear your fiancé is about to give up everything else in his life for you...

I stay ten paces behind as he leads the way through one of those casino passageways. The Luxor to the Mandalay Bay. I think. I lost track of which casino was which a long time ago.

It's been a busy day of decidedly un-depraved activities— The Atomic Testing Museum, The Neon Museum, and an amazingly relaxed tea shop with a large non-smoking section. I appreciate how much the Steeles are trying to keep me from feeling like a third wheel.

But I've had enough. I need my bed and I need Drew in it, his hands on my skin, his voice in my ears as he convinces me this is going to be okay.

Smoke wafts into my nostrils as we step onto the casino floor. The lights and sounds wake up the tension headache that has been dormant for ages. My shoulders and back tense. My neck is in agony.

"Tom, it's been fun, but I'm about ready to crash." I undo the tie holding up my hair in the hopes of easing the strain on my neck. It's about one percent better.

"Nope. Your baby daddy wants to make a gesture." Tom checks something on his phone. "And I've got to nail the timing."

"Sweetie, why is it *you* have to nail the timing?" Willow asks.

"Cause I'm the rhythm section," he says. "Well, me and Pete, but he's busy... sure we can all guess what he's doing." He pulls her into a quick hug-kiss combo then he turns to me. "You got another half-hour in you?"

I can do another half-hour if it ends with Drew explaining how he's going to make this work.

"Good." Tom's smile lights up his soft green eyes. He turns back to Willow and whispers in her ear.

"Oh." She turns to me with a smile and offers me a thumbs-up.

Okay, everyone knows what's happening except me.

Awesome.

Tom motions for me to follow as he steps into the closed door of the hotel theater.

Drew's in a theater.

My stomach settles. Drew won me over by stepping on stage and singing for me many months ago.

The stage is what he knows, where he belongs.

This might work out.

I follow Tom and Willow inside. The venue looks like it seats about a thousand, but it's hard to say with all the lights off.

There are two figures on the stage, but they're barely silhouettes.

"Any day now," Tom taunts.

The stage lights turn on. That's Drew, standing in front of a microphone in jeans and a tight t-shirt. He looks as yummy as always.

His expression is nervous.

He must be scared for me to see that all the way back here in the cheap seats.

A guitar kicks in. But that doesn't make sense. Drew isn't holding a guitar, and the sound is live, not pre-recorded.

My brain has no time to contemplate it. Drew wraps his hands around the mic, brings it to his mouth, and he sings.

It's all over.
I'm ga-ga out of my head,
One of those idiots
I always made fun of.

Drew is singing for me.

The same song he used to win me over that night.

I push past Tom and Willow to get closer to the stage. My body moves of its own accord, no thinking necessary.

Drew is singing for me.

Singing about being in love for me.

My heart melts as his voice flows into my ears. Drew may not be the best singer in the world, but I can feel every word in my soul. I can feel every bit of emotion in his voice.

The song fades into the outro. Right away, another starts. Only this isn't a Sinful Serenade song. It's one of his songs.

He never shares those. With anyone. He won't even sing the lyrics in front of me.

The other stage light goes on. There's a man with dark hair and bright eyes playing the guitar part. I barely recognize Ethan, the Dangerous Noise guitarist.

He's playing Drew's part. In Drew's song.

I'm not sure what it means. It's hard to concentrate on

anything but how much I want to dive into Drew's voice and stay there forever.

This time, he stops after the song fades into the outro. He sets the mic back in its stand and turns to me.

"We learned about a dozen of these, but I'm guessing you got the idea." He jumps off the stage so he's standing in the aisle, ten feet away from me.

"I can listen to you sing another dozen songs."

He nods.

"After you explain?"

He takes a step closer. "After I explain, I'm going to take you backstage and make you come."

"After that."

"Afraid I've got the entire night dedicated to making you come."

My lips curl into a smile. Already, all the tension in my shoulders is relaxing. "I can live with that."

He moves close enough to touch me. His fingertips skim my wrist, the scarred one. He looks into my eyes. "This tour, Ethan is going to fill in for me any time I need to be home with you. I'm going to be there every doctor's appointment, every time you get scared. Every time you need me, we're going to be together."

"And after that?"

"Got four session musicians lined up."

"Someone else is playing for you?"

He nods.

"Really?"

"Yeah."

"But you're not leaving the band?"

"Not unless I get kicked out." He looks toward Tom. "Not going willingly." He brings his gaze back to me. Brings his palm to my cheek. "You come first, Kara. Our family, that comes first. But you were right, Sinful Serenade is our family too. As much as I hate to admit it, we need them."

I stare up at him. "Explain the details."

"First year or so, I want to be there, at home with you. After that, I'll still go on the road, but we'll never be apart for more than a week. I'll fly home or you'll come with me. It won't be easy. It will be a lot of trial and error, but we'll make it work."

Drew's letting someone fill in for him while he stays home with me, with our family.

But then he's going back.

I'm not derailing the band. Not derailing him.

He rubs my cheek with his thumb, wiping away a tear. "That a happy tear?"

I blink, and my lashes are heavy with happy tears. It's an obvious solution, but I wouldn't have ever guessed Drew would be willing to do it.

He's more protective of his role as the guitarist, the best musician in the band, than he is of anything.

But he's still the band's guitarist, because the band is so much more than the music. It's a family.

All eight of us are a family.

Drew wipes another tear from my eye. "I love you. I want a life with you and with all our family."

"I love you too."

He squeezes me. "You're gonna be a great mom, Kara."

"You think so?"

"I fucking know so."

"Really?"

"Really."

I rise to my tiptoes to press my lips to his. He tastes like home. He always does, but in this moment, it's more potent. It's exactly what I need.

Wherever we are, that's home.

He's my home, and I'm his, and together, we're going to be this baby's home.

"You're going to be a good dad," I whisper.

"I'll be there whenever you need me, honey. Anytime. I'll make it work."

I nod. "We're really doing this. We're really having a baby."

He smiles. "Yeah, we are."

I kiss him again for good measure.

ROCK FOREVER

Chapter One

WILLOW

"What are you looking at, kid?" Tom presses his back into the mirrored elevator wall. He looks me up and down, his green eyes lighting up.

Why am I reading an email on my cellphone when my husband is eye-fucking me?

God, he's really my husband.

It's been two months, but it still feels like a dream. Like it's too good to be true.

My gaze goes to my wedding band and the huge, three-stone engagement ring sitting atop it. It's not a dream.

He's mine.

Tom pushes off the wall. "You're gonna make me insecure at this rate."

"Is that right?"

He nods. "You better remind me that you prefer me over that cellphone."

I better. We're riding the elevator back to our hotel room. This email can wait.

We've been helping Kara and Drew all day. They've got a

lot on their plate, what with her being pregnant, but he made his big gesture. They're both happy.

It's our turn to tend to each other.

Only my gaze refuses to leave my cellphone.

I can't keep this from Tom.

I can't delete it.

I have to do something, but I'm not sure what the right call is.

"Don't tell me it's more interesting than this." He slides his hands around my hips and pins me against the elevator wall.

Then his hips are against mine. His lips are on mine.

My eyelids press together as his tongue plunges into my mouth. My husband really is a hell of a kisser. It's hard to believe he avoided locking lips most of his life.

I'm so overwhelmed with need and affection I nearly drop my phone. My other hand goes to the back of his head, playing with his wavy dark blond hair.

I want to kiss Tom forever.

We're married. I get to kiss Tom forever.

He shifts his hips so I can feel his erection then he pulls back and stares into my eyes. "What's the verdict?"

"I think I need a little more evidence to be sure."

He cocks a brow and shakes his head like I'm as ridiculous as he is.

I am. His zest for life is contagious.

This time, he's faster, more aggressive. Hands on my hips, he pins me to the wall.

His crotch grinds against mine.

His hands slide under my t-shirt and go flat against my lower back.

He sucks on my bottom lip.

What the hell was I looking at on my phone? I can barely hold onto the damn thing at the moment.

Ding. The elevator slows to a stop. Our floor.

Tom breaks our kiss, but he stays pressed against me.

"What's a phone?" I mumble.

He smiles. "It's been miserable keeping my hands off you all day."

"You have a funny definition of 'keeping my hands off you'."

"Was being polite in front of Kara."

"That was your idea of polite?" I laugh. Making out with tongue *without* any over or under the clothes touching is probably Tom's idea of being polite in front of Kara.

My eyes meet his. Sure enough, there's nothing but playful sincerity in those mischievous green eyes of his.

He ignores the open elevator and the people standing outside it and slides his hands to my ass. "You're my wife."

I nod.

"This is my marital duty."

God, I love the sound of that. It's been a long day. I'm glad we could help Kara and Drew through the stress of an unexpected pregnancy—I'm still overwhelmed that I'm going to be an aunt in seven months. I can't imagine how scared she is that she's going to be a mom—but I've had enough of everything besides me and Tom.

I slide my phone into my purse. This *is* important, but it can wait until after. Sure, I joined Tom for the last week of his international tour, but that still leaves a solid three weeks to make up for.

Three weeks of kisses and hugs and orgasms we owe each other.

He takes my hand and pulls me into the hallway. We pass a group of twenty-something women in cocktail dresses and teetering heels.

A few months ago, I would have been jealous of their long legs and ample chests. Before we got together, I would have worried Tom would go home with one of them. By all accounts, he was the world's biggest manwhore.

But, right now, I'm utterly secure with my relationship. Tom has been with plenty of women, but he's never cared about any of them.

He's mine, and I'm his, and he's never shy about reminding everyone around us of those two facts.

The girls stare at Tom. Specifically, at the erection straining against his jeans. It takes longer than usual for anyone to recognize him.

My husband is usually quite the obliging celebrity, but today he hasn't got a hint of patience.

He pulls me closer. "What the fuck are you waiting for, kid?"

"Uh... aren't you Tom Steele?" one of the women asks.

He offers a polite smile. "Yeah. Nice to meet you. Write the label if you want an autograph. Don't have time today." He nods goodbye. "If you'll excuse me, I need to fuck my wife until everyone on this floor can hear her coming."

The girl turns the same color as a tomato. I'm not doing much better on the blushing front.

My cheeks are burning.

Dammit, I'm hot everywhere.

One of the girls lets out an orgasmic gasp.

Tom is smiling from ear to ear. What can I say? My husband knows every button he has to press to get a reaction.

Damn, I love the way he presses my buttons.

He squeezes my hand and motions toward the hallway. "Don't tell me you don't want to be under me, screaming my name."

"I don't."

Tom cocks a brow.

I offer the girl a smile and turn back to Tom. "I want to be on top of you, screaming your name."

His smile widens. "Could never deprive my wife of what she wants."

"Promise you'll always say it like that."

"Like what?"

"Like we're newlyweds."

"We *are* newlyweds."

"Promise."

He nods. "I promise, kid." He leans closer.

"Promise you'll always call me that."

"Even when we're eighty."

I ignore our audience and press my body against his. His clothes—the usual hoodie, t-shirt, and jeans—get in my way, but I can still feel every hard inch of him.

Damn, I want him out of those jeans.

It's been a while since we had to sneak around, but I still get a thrill from being with him this openly, from kissing him like no one is watching.

But people are watching, and I don't want those people following us to our hotel room.

Tom doesn't give a flying fuck about our audience. If anything, he's angling to give them a show. He kisses me hungrily. His hands go to my ass. He lifts me into the air. My attempt to wrap my legs around his hips is messy, but I figure it out.

He pushes me against the opposite wall.

I'm not aware of much besides his tongue in my mouth and his hands against me. Even over my jeans, the touch makes me burn with heat.

It's been a long day. No, it's been a long few days and a long week before that. Yes, I have to deal with this email thing soon, but it can wait until tomorrow.

Everything else can wait until tomorrow.

The giggles and groans stop. The elevator doors close and the carriage whirs.

I peek my eyes open as I break the kiss. Sure enough, the giggling girls are gone.

"You gave them something to think about tonight." I motion for him to set me down.

He does. But he keeps his hands against my ass, keeps me pressed against his erection. "Gotta make sure my wife comes every day." He motions for me to follow him to the hotel room.

This time, I do. The damn thing is all the way at the end of the hall. The only downside of a corner suite is that it's in the corner.

The opposite corner of the elevator.

By the time we get to the door, I'm on fire. These clothes are far too much. His must be worse. God, I don't have a clue how he's walking with the way he's fighting those jeans.

Tom unlocks the door and pushes it open. "My eyes are up here, kid."

"Uh-huh."

He pushes my coat off my shoulders. His lips go to my neck. His kiss is soft, tender, the Tom only I know.

"I remember something about your wife coming every day."

He unbuttons my jeans and slides them to my knees. "Have I missed a day?"

"What about when we're apart?"

"Prefer to do it myself. With my cock, or my mouth, or my hands." He presses his palm against me, over my panties. "But I'm not picky. It can be your hand. Or a vibrator. As long as you come, I'm happy."

"Even if you aren't there?"

"Yeah. Course I prefer when you let me watch or listen." He rubs me harder. "Fuck, you're wet."

Pleasure floods the spot. I can only respond with a groan.

My hands go to his shoulders. The hoodie. I suspected it was evil, but now I'm sure. It needs to be gone.

My hands struggle to find the zipper. It only gets more difficult as he rubs me with his palm.

"Tom," I groan.

"Say it again."

"Tom." I find the zipper and pull it down. Then I push the thing off his shoulders. "Please. I need you."

"Say *that* again." His voice gets heavy, breathy.

All this time, and he still needs to feel needed.

I can barely pry my eyelids apart to look up at him. Those gorgeous green eyes of his are fixed on mine. There's vulnerability in them.

How the hell did I get so lucky to find Tom? He's...

He rubs me harder. His voice gets rough. "Say it."

It's hard to think much beyond *he's Tom*. But there's no better way to describe it.

He's everything.

I stare back into his eyes. "I need you."

"Fuck, Willow." He pulls me into a deep kiss, still teasing me with his finger.

I *do* need him. And now. I break the kiss so I can pull his t-shirt over his head. After one long, sweet moment of gawking at his body, I undo his jeans and push them off his hips.

Then the boxers. Only enough that I can see his tattoo. *Willow*. My name in a curvy script over his hipbone.

My name on his body forever.

I trace the letters with my fingertips.

Tom kicks off his shoes. He pushes his jeans and boxers to his feet. Then they're gone, along with his socks.

He does away with my t-shirt. My bra. He takes his time exploring my chest. He traces the lines of my tattoo—he does it nearly every time he sees it—then he drags his fingers up my torso.

He cups my breasts with his hands. I used to feel like small breasts meant I was missing out, but I love the way his hands envelop me.

The way his eyes go wide as he plays with my nipples.

God, he's good at this. Pleasure shoots to my core with every flick of his fingers.

He stares into my eyes with a wealth of affection. Right now, I'm the most important person in the world. The only thing that matters in the world is the two of us together.

My hands go to his hips, but that's not enough. I need him feeling good too.

I brush his cock with my palm.

He shudders. His lips part with a sigh. "Willow."

I watch his reactions as I tease his tip with my thumb. First the flesh then the metal balls of his apadravya. He groans every time I touch it.

Never thought I'd be with a man with a cock piercing. Certainly never thought I'd marry a man with a cock piercing.

But I fucking love this thing.

His pupils dilate as I wrap my hand around him and stroke him.

He squeezes my nipples. Harder. Hard enough I have to bite my lip to take it.

Tom brings his hands to my wrist and sets it against my side. Then he's unbuttoning my jeans. In one swift movement, he slides them, and my panties, to my feet.

I kick my shoes off. Then the rest.

No more clothes in the way. We're naked in front of each other. We've been here a hundred times—more even. Every time, it feels exhilarating, intimate, loving.

Every time, it feels hot as hell.

I let Tom lead—he's damn good at it. He shifts onto the

bed on his back then he pats the spots in front of each shoulder.

He's telling me to sit on his face.

I did ask to come on top of him.

My sex clenches at the memory of his tongue. It's only been a few days, but my body is greedy.

I'm greedier. I need more than coming on top of him. I need him coming under me too.

I crawl up the bed next to him. His eyes are still wide with desire. He's still in that *fuck, I need you* daze.

My lips find his. His kiss is hard, hungry, needy. He groans into my mouth. His hands slide to the back of my head, pulling me closer.

Damn, he tastes good.

I press my palms against his chest as I break the kiss. It takes a bit of careful maneuvering to swing my thighs over his shoulders.

I sit on him, facing his feet, and I plant my hands outside his hips.

His hands go to my hips. His mouth goes to the inside of my thigh. "Fuck."

I plant a kiss on his stomach and watch his muscles tremble with anticipation. I kiss lower. Lower.

I trace the lines of his tattoo with my tongue.

His fingers dig into my hips as I brush my lips against his cock. He tastes good here too. Like soap and like Tom.

He kisses his way up my thigh. He gets closer and closer then his lips are on me. He licks me with patient strokes. Every flick of his tongue sends another wave of pleasure through me.

I surrender to his movements, sinking deeper into the bed, my sex pressed against his face.

He groans with pleasure as he licks me. It feels so fucking good.

I have to have him feeling this good too.

I take him into my mouth.

He groans against me. He licks harder, faster. His hands are firm against my hips. They hold me in place against him.

I play with his piercing with my tongue, reveling in the way his thighs shake and his fingers dig into my skin. Then I take him deeper. Suck harder.

He licks me, and I suck on him. The sensation of giving and receiving at once is overwhelming. Not just physically, but emotionally too.

We never keep score. All of me is his, and all of him is mine.

Pleasure flows between us the same way love does.

My thighs squeeze against his ears as my sex clenches. I'm close, but I want him coming with me.

Tom can last a hell of a long time, but I know how to get him off quickly. That piercing is like a turbo button.

I flick my tongue against the metal balls until he's shifting his hips to drive his cock deeper into my mouth.

His thighs shake.

He plunges his tongue inside me.

I forget any intentions of anything at all. My body takes over as I wrap my hand around him and suck harder. Harder.

His tongue flicks against my clit. Again. Again.

There.

My sex clenches. Everything unwinds. I can feel the orgasm all the way in my fingers and toes. The only thing I can do to contain it is groan against him and suck harder.

He's close too.

I can feel it.

I press my hand against his thigh to steady myself. I need him coming. I need to feel his orgasm.

Tom doesn't stop. He licks me again. Again. He goes harder. Faster. Until I dig my nails into his thigh.

I flick my tongue against him a few more times then I take him as deep as I can, sucking as hard as I can.

Another orgasm rises up inside me. I press my thighs against his ears.

There. I dig my nails into his thigh as I come. Pleasure rolls out to my toes. My sex clenches with aftershocks.

I suck harder.

He starts to shake. His fingers dig into the flesh of my ass, lifting my body away from his.

Then he's groaning my name into my thigh.

"Fuck, Willow." He sucks on my tender skin.

His breath hitches.

His feet curl.

Then he's there, his cock pulsing as he comes in my mouth. That, too, tastes good. Salty and sweet and Tom.

I wait until he's finished, and I swallow hard.

Tom sighs with pleasure as he pulls me up and into his chest.

I nestle into his body.

He runs his fingers through my short hair and looks down at me. "You're fucking perfect."

"It's my marital duty too." I press my lips against his chest. "To make sure *you* come every day."

Chapter Two

WILLOW

My phone is still in my purse, still beckoning me. I can't say it beckoned me all night—my husband's body had every ounce of my attention —but it's been calling me all morning.

It called me as I brushed my teeth and dressed, and as we walked to the cafe a few hotels down.

And now that Tom is meeting Ophelia in the lobby, my cell is tempting as all hell.

I pull it out and scan the emails. The first, to start.

I hope this email isn't an imposition, but I recognize your model and I was wondering if you'd pass along my contact information. There is no easy way to say this, but he looks a lot like my son. It's a messy story, but I lost him many years ago. My boyfriend was not the kind of man who should be around a child. The state was right to take Tommy away. But I wonder about him. I miss him dearly. I'd love to hear from him, to know he's doing well.

- Liberty Wright

And there's her contact information—she included every- thing about her save her social security number.

She lives in Las Vegas now.

Tom's birth mother lives in Las Vegas and she wants to contact him.

We've exchanged a few more emails. She had no idea Tom was in a band, that he was even famous. A friend of hers who was looking for a boudoir photographer showed her my website.

What a mortifying way to stumble on your long-lost son. There are many, many half-naked pictures of Tom on my site and on my Instagram. What can I say? The camera loves him almost as much as I do. The sexy pictures are enough to keep his fans wanting him and wanting our relationship to succeed at once.

She's sincere. She wants to speak with Tom.

He's still carrying around all this baggage about being in foster care, about being adopted. Everything worked out-Ophelia is the best parent anyone could ask for—but he went through a lot of pain along the way.

It might be good for him to meet her. To realize that his birth mom did love him.

He'll never agree to it. If I ask, he'll say no, and that will be it.

If our roles were reversed, Tom would push me to do it.

But will he forgive me for setting this up? I can't do anything that risks losing Tom. Even if it will be good for him. Even if it will help close a wound that still hurts him.

My thoughts are interrupted by Tom and Ophelia's arrival. He's not as bouncy and energetic pre-coffee, but they're still quite opposite. She's much more like Pete—calm, even, assured, and completely obsessed with sex.

Her hair was teal the last time I saw her. Today, it's a vibrant shade of orchid.

I slide my phone into my purse and rise to hug her. "Your hair looks great. Did you sleep well?"

Tom shakes his head. "Go tell her."

Ophelia smiles. She motions for Tom to sit. When he does, she takes her seat. "I didn't do much sleeping."

"Did Ellie come with you?" I ask.

Tom looks at his mom and cocks a brow. "You didn't tell her?"

"Tell me what?" I slide my phone back into my purse.

By all accounts, we're staying in Vegas through Christmas. Until the start of the tour even.

That buys me a week and a half.

But I don't like this hanging over my head.

"Sweetheart, your wife doesn't want to hear about my sordid affairs." Ophelia smiles.

"And I do?" Tom asks.

"You understand what it's like to enjoy something casual." Ophelia turns to me. "I'm afraid Ellie and I wanted different things."

"Oh?" I ask.

"Ellie was three or four women ago." Tom shakes his head. "And I thought I slept around."

I laugh. "There's no shame in sleeping around."

"Thank you." Ophelia nods to me then she turns to Tom. "Is your brother coming or is he *held up* in his hotel room?"

"Do you ever get tired of talking about your children's sex lives?" Tom clears his throat, but it does nothing to hide the blush forming on his cheeks.

"She likes embarrassing you," I say.

Ophelia mocks incredulity the same way Tom does. It's amazing how much they have in common when their dispositions are so different.

She's a great mom. And Tom adores her. Everyone adores her.

Maybe it's better to delete these emails and pretend they never happened.

I feel for Liberty, I do, but I can't do anything that will hurt Tom more than it helps him.

"You okay, sweetheart?" Ophelia asks. "Don't tell me you're pregnant too. Not that it isn't wonderful, having children, but you're still young. You and Tom work nonstop. You can't do that if you have a child. God knows how your brother is going to manage balancing work and child rearing. It's hard enough when you have a normal job."

"No, I'm not pregnant." I try to shake off whatever unpleasant expression is plastered on my face, but I can't be doing a good job because Tom and Ophelia are still looking at me with concern. "I have an IUD."

"Nothing is one hundred percent except eating pussy," Ophelia says.

Tom presses his palm into his forehead. "You do this on purpose."

"Willow, sweetheart, how does Tom talk when I'm not around?"

"He's not as filthy as Pete," I say.

"God damn, both of you. Can't we talk about the weather or a movie or something for once?" Tom turns even more red. "Even Pete and Jess talk about *The Hunger Games* sometimes."

"Are you eavesdropping while they're... talking about other things?" I ask.

"Eavesdropping? No. I wish I had to try to hear him." Tom shakes his head. "Fucker still lives for phone sex."

"And I'm the one with a dirty mind?" Ophelia shakes her head with mock incredulity, exactly the way Tom does. "You shouldn't call your brother a fucker."

"What should I call him? Peter, like you do? He hates that," Tom says.

"You'll understand if you have kids." Ophelia hails the waiter and orders coffees for the table. Once we've all given him our orders, she turns back to us. "There's no rush. And there's nothing wrong with deciding you'd like to stay child-free. Don't give into pressure from anyone. Including me."

The tension in my chest relaxes. Ophelia is the most supportive person I've ever met, maybe even more supportive than Tom. She's the opposite of my mother, who pushed for her way so hard we're no longer communicating.

She was even worse with Drew. They haven't spoken a word since he dropped out of college. She pretends like he doesn't exist.

If Liberty is anything like my mom, Tom is better off never knowing about this email.

But if she really has cleaned up her life, if she's even half as supportive and sweet as Ophelia, then meeting her would be a good thing.

In theory.

"We're gonna adopt," Tom says. "But not for a while."

Ophelia's smile is ear to ear. Her whole expression is soft. "You are?"

I nod in agreement.

I swear to God, she melts.

"Tom, you don't... are you sure?" she asks.

"Have I ever done anything I wasn't sure about?" he asks.

"And you, sweetheart?" She looks to me.

"Yeah, I am." I squeeze my hands together. All this talk of family and children only highlights this decision. What the hell am I going to do? I need to know where I stand. "How long do you want to stay in Vegas?"

I've had enough of the city. I miss my bed, miss California, miss the smell of the ocean air.

Tom shrugs. "Meg and Miles are leaving late on Christmas. They want to do a big Christmas thing with everybody. Her parents are here. And he wants Ophelia there too. Probably 'cause they're both suave perverts."

Ophelia smiles, charmed by the comparison. "Miles still has a lot to learn about seducing women."

"Think he's got it figured out, being married and all," Tom says.

"You ever meet any adult man so fixated on his mother settling down?" Ophelia asks.

I shake my head. "No." There's nearly a whole week to the 26th. I'm not really a fan of Christmas—too many awful memories of awful family encounters. I don't mind spending it in Las Vegas. And that does buy me time to figure this out.

But I want to be home.

I want everyone else's problems off my back for a while, so the entire world is only me and Tom.

With his celebrity, it can be hard to shut out the world. The only place we can do it for sure is our house. Or on some private beach on some sunny island, him lying on the sand and frolicking in the waves in the world's skimpiest bathing suit.

Or frolicking in the waves in nothing.

That would be perfectly fine.

Ophelia's phone beeps with a text alert. She checks it and smiles. "Your brother and his fiancée will not be joining us."

Tom shakes his head. "He's making us look like a boring married couple just cause we're respectable enough to get out of bed once a day."

"You sound jealous," I say.

Tom pouts. "No, just... he was the boring one with the girlfriend."

"I doubt he was ever the boring one," I say.

"Yeah." Tom taps his fingers against the table. "We're gonna have to get some more sex toys. Show him up."

Ophelia chuckles. It's funny. She has the same deep chuckle Pete does.

The brothers are such opposites in most ways, but both of them take after their adopted mother.

"I'm not complaining," I say. "But I don't think you'll ever come out as more depraved than Pete."

"Yeah, I guess." Tom shakes his head. "You think he's ever going to marry her?"

"They've only been engaged a month," I say.

"And?" Tom raises a brow.

"Pretty sure she's the one making him wait," I say.

Tom cocks a brow. "You're holding onto gossip?"

"A few things," I admit.

Tom looks to Ophelia. "Can you believe my wife? She's supposed to tell me everything."

"This is why I never got married." Ophelia pats Tom on the shoulder. "Women need to be mysterious. Let her have a few secrets."

Tom raises a brow. He pushes himself up. "I'm going to use the restroom. Try not to gossip too much while I'm gone." He leans down and plants a kiss on my lips.

It's only a peck, but that's enough to overwhelm my body. There's only one way to describe the feeling. I'm loved.

Can I risk a single ounce of Tom's affection? Even to heal a wound that still cuts him?

Ophelia waits until he's out of earshot then turns to me. "Sweetheart, I don't know how you keep up with him."

I smile. "Sometimes, he runs circles around me, but Tom is... Tom is Tom."

"That he is."

The waiter arrives to drop off our coffees and assure us that breakfast will be here shortly.

"He takes great care of me," I say. "Every place we go, he makes sure there are vegetarian options. He gets me a coffee every morning. And sometimes, he wakes up with... well, never mind about that part."

Ophelia chuckles. "I'm glad the two of you are happy together."

We are. Really happy.

But still, I feel like I have to make this connection happen.

I check to make sure the coast is clear, and I lean a little closer. "What made you decide to adopt?"

She frowns. "My parents kicked me out after they caught me screwing one of my friends from church. It was a different time then, though that still happens."

"I'm sorry." I can't believe I've never heard this. "That must have hurt."

"At first. But you can't live your life waiting for people to accept you. You know that, after everything with your mother."

I nod. She's right. Some people are never going to change their minds. It's possible Tom will never change his mind about his mother, that he'll always see her as a druggie who abandoned him.

"Once I was mature enough, and financially stable enough, I knew I wanted to help kids who were in dire straits. I had a few other foster kids before Tom. They eventually reunited with their parents. It was great for them, but it broke my heart. I adopted Tom the second I could."

"Did he really call you ugly when you met?"

She laughs. "Yes, he did."

"What a little shit."

"That's Tom."

I play with the fabric of my jeans. "His mom, she was a drug addict?"

Ophelia nods.

"Why didn't she try to get custody back after she cleaned up?"

"It was part of a plea agreement. She had to choose

between jail and giving up custody. She had little chance of getting custody behind bars. It made more sense to give it up. I think she knew that it was best for Tom that she not be his caretaker." Ophelia's expression gets quizzical. "Is there something you need to know about her?"

"Maybe."

"Sweetheart, I love you as much as I love my sons. You *are* my daughter now. But whatever it is, you should talk to your husband about this."

"I know."

"What do you want with his birth mother?"

"Maybe nothing. Maybe... maybe it would be good for him to meet her."

She presses her lips together. "And where do you fit into this?"

"He'll never do it on his own."

She nods. Her eyes fix on me, an expression that demands I explain. "What happened, sweetheart?"

"Liberty contacted me."

Ophelia's brows turn down. Her forehead screws with frustration. "And Tom doesn't know about this?"

"It was from my photography website. She didn't know he was my husband. She only hoped to pass along her contact information to a model, so he could contact her if that was what he wanted to do."

Ophelia leans back into her chair. "Quite the awkward way to find your son."

I nod.

Her voice is low, like she's sharing a secret. "Willow, she didn't give him up because she was seventeen and she knew he'd be better off. He was eleven when the state took him, and he was beaten within an inch of his life. It wasn't her. It was her boyfriend who did it, but I don't think that matters much to Tom. All he knows is that his mother didn't protect him."

"I know."

"He's not curious about what happened. He knows that his birth mother didn't think enough of him to get clean or to leave her abusive boyfriend."

"It's not that easy to leave someone abusive."

"She had a son."

"It fucks with your head. You think he loves you, that he doesn't mean it. You think that there's no one else who can help you, who even cares. Or you don't realize how bad it's gotten." My palms slap the table. I'm nearly shouting, but I have to get this out. "Sometimes, you've already lost all your friends and your family and he's the only person you have."

Ophelia frowns. "Sweetheart, I'm sorry. I didn't—"

"It's okay. I know you didn't mean offense. Nobody ever does." Nobody ever thinks about what it's like when you're in the middle of it. They act like it's easy to leave, like women stay with abusive men because they're stupid or weak.

I take a deep breath. I don't like reliving that part of my life, but running from it doesn't do me any good.

I blink back a tear. Stupid fucking memories.

"Think about what you do. Tom might not forgive you for this. And I'd hate to see anything come between the two of you."

Right on cue, Tom steps into the restaurant. He zeroes in on me like I'm the bat signal and he's Batman.

He practically runs over. "What's wrong, Willow?"

Shit, it must look bad. He only drops the nickname when things are really dire.

"Something insensitive I said. I'm sorry, Willow. I wasn't thinking, but there's no excuse." Ophelia pushes herself up. "I'll take my turn in the restroom."

Tom slides next to me on the bench seat. "What did she say?"

I shake my head. "Something about abusive relationships."

He frowns. "Why the fuck were you talking about that?"

I don't have an explanation that won't give this away. I don't want to lie. "It just came up."

He pulls me into a tight hug. "It's okay. No one is ever going to hurt you again."

With Tom's arms around me, I give myself a few moments to cry. Those memories don't sting as badly as I used to, but they still fucking hurt.

"Never," he whispers.

He's helped me overcome my past. I want to do the same, but not if it means losing him.

I tug at his t-shirt, pulling him closer.

Whatever happens, I can't lose Tom.

Ever.

Chapter Three

TOM

Willow only eats half her omelet and one slice of toast. She drinks her coffee with timid sips. My wife is nearly as addicted to caffeine as I am. That shit isn't like her.

There's no sense in prying with Mom. She's never spilled a secret in her life. But there's something real strange about the apologetic look on her face.

Ophelia isn't the kind of woman who apologizes for shit.

What did she say that upset Willow?

Neither of them shows any signs of confessing. Better to wait until Willow and I are alone. If it's serious—and it's fucking serious if she's crying at breakfast—she won't want to talk about it with an audience.

Our conversation is all small talk. Mostly Willow asking Ophelia about the woman she's dating. Ophelia plays nice about it, but it's pretty obvious she's describing a Vegas fling.

After we finish eating, we head to one of the indoor shopping areas. It's meant to look like some other place. There's a fake sky painted on the ceiling, bright blue with puffy white clouds. The shops are designed to look like a little town in

Europe. Venice, I guess. The fake canal that intersects the shops gives that away.

Vegas is a weird fucking city. I enjoyed the hell out of it back when I spent my nights drinking, dancing, and taking a stranger or two home. But now it seems as hollow as the fake plastic trees lining the streets.

At least Willow is taken with the faux Venice shops. She looks up at the painted-on sky, her lips curling into a smile.

"It's like living in Los Angeles. The sky is blue every day." She slides her hand around my waist and looks up at me. "You don't like it?"

"It's fine." I shrug. Don't think I can like any place where she's hiding something from me.

Mom stays quiet, and she stays a few steps in front of us. She's up to something, but then it's not like she's gonna tell me. Better to accept that I'm in the dark.

She nods to one of the shops. It's a chain I've seen at other malls. The place sells upscale casual and business casual women's clothing. Mom used to drag us to the mall and make us wait during her shopping expeditions.

Pete and I were such miserable little fucks. I don't know why she took us anywhere.

He was quiet, but I complained every other step. She never bent to it. Not once.

She's not gonna tell me shit, no matter how much I beg.

I pull Willow closer. "You want to go in?"

"Not really my style." She moves closer, looking up at me, those hazel eyes of her filled with uncertainty. "Unless you think I need a shift dress."

"I think you need no dress." I slide my hands to her ass. "No panties. No bra. Could keep going."

"To what?"

"No coat. No socks. No tights."

"Just shoes?"

I smile. "Yeah. Just shoes."

"You want me naked except for my Keds?"

I nod.

"Not heels or something?"

"You wear your Keds. I'll wear my Converse. It will be kinky canvas shoe shit."

"That's a thing?"

"We'll make it a thing."

She smiles back, but it can't hide the frustration in her eyes.

"Fuck. Whatever Mom said, I'm sorry." I run my fingers through her hair until a sigh escapes her lips. Damn, I love the way she sighs with pleasure. I need more of it. Need it louder. Need to feel how much she's mine.

Her voice is low, a whisper. "I'm not thinking about that anymore."

"What are you thinking about?"

She looks down, pressing her lips together.

There's a hand on my shoulder. It's not hers—those are around my waist—so what the fuck is it doing there?

I turn to face whoever it is that's touching me. It's an occupational hazard. Didn't always mind so much, but who the fuck is dense enough to touch a guy when he's embracing his wife?

It's a teenage girl. She's young, but she's old enough to know better.

"I... I... I'm sorry." She steps closer. "I just wanted to say I'm a big fan of Sinful Serenade, and I..." She looks back to her friends—another half-dozen teenage girls—standing in the corner. "Could you take a picture with us?"

Willow steps backward. She motions, *go for it*. She never gets jealous. She growls when fans, female fans at least, touch me without asking, but she doesn't get jealous.

I look at the girl. "Yeah, sure. If you do me a favor."

Her eyes light up. It's not that kind of favor, honey. This girl must be fifteen or sixteen. She knows what a wedding band is.

She knows what a couple looks like.

If she's a fan, she knows I'm married.

I turn back to Willow. She's wearing that same frustrated expression. Her eyes are on her cellphone. Again. A lot of people pull their cell out every time they get a spare second— I certainly look at mine more than I should—but not Willow.

It was the same thing last night.

And this morning.

She's not texting anybody. She's not doing anything but staring at the screen, frustration filling her eyes.

Someone tugs at my hoodie. Sure enough, it's the girl. Usually, I like talking to fans. I wouldn't have any of the stuff I have if it weren't for people who like our music. Or people who like Tom Steele, famous drummer.

I exploit my celebrity. So fucking what? You gotta do something if you want to stay in people's minds. And I'm happy to be the fun, hot bad boy who's good for a night but certainly not good for bringing home to Mom.

Everyone has an image, whether they're aware of it or not. Everybody projects something to the world. At least I'm in charge of mine.

But why the fuck does everybody think they can touch me without asking?

Don't have the patience for this shit right now. Don't have the patience to ask her for a favor—to stop touching people without asking first.

But I know my role. I gotta do this shit if I want the band to keep going, and we can't afford to drop anything else with Miles and Drew wanting us to slow down our tour schedule.

My shoulders relax. Slowing down sounds nice. I won't admit that to them, but it sounds like fucking heaven. More time with Willow, just the two of us—what the fuck else could I want?

I grit my teeth and oblige. After I'm done posing with the teenagers, I nod goodbye and send them on their way.

Willow is leaning against the railing, her hands folded over her chest, her eyes on the fake sky.

She brings her gaze to meet mine. Her lips curl into a half-smile. "You look pissed."

I shrug.

"Usually you hide it better." She slides her hands under my hoodie and presses her palm flat against my stomach, over my t-shirt. "I hate it too."

"What?"

"When girls touch you." She pushes off the railing and rests her head against my chest. "Why don't you ever ask them to stop?"

I shrug.

"Doesn't fit the Tom Steele brand?"

"Why don't you and Mom shop without me? I'm not in the mood for the celebrity shit right now."

She looks up at me, her hazel eyes filled with affection. "Is something wrong?"

I nod.

"What?"

"My wife's upset but she won't talk to me."

"Oh. I'm just thinking about something."

It's that fucking asshole who hurt her. Can't believe I agree with Drew about something, but that fucking asshole doesn't deserve oxygen.

I hate that he's still breathing.

I hate that she has to wonder if he'll show up on her doorstep one day.

Part of me wants to arrange to have him killed or arrested, something to make sure he's gone forever. But Willow would never forgive me if she found out. She's a good person. She doesn't want to hurt anyone, not even the man who nearly destroyed her.

I slide my arm around her waist and pull us to a secluded corner. Once I have my back to anyone who will walk by, I lean closer.

Her expression is vulnerable, needy. "It's not about Bradley."

"What's it about?"

"A decision I have to make. It's really not anything you need to worry about." She rests her forehead against my chin. "Let's have some fun first."

"Which kind of fun?" I slide my hands under her coat and pull her close. I need the reminder that she's okay.

She lets out a slow exhale, takes in a long inhale. But I can't feel her heartbeat. Not yet.

I pull her closer. I press my lips to her forehead.

"Any kind of fun." Her fingertips find my forearms. "I just want to be with you right now."

"You're scaring me, kid."

She sighs, but it's with relief. "It's really not a big deal."

"What did Mom say?"

"It's not about that."

"But what?"

"Just something about how women who are in abusive relationships should know to leave." She turns away from me. Her voice wavers. "She didn't mean offense. I'm not bothered. Really."

Yeah, but I am. Not by what Mom said—though she does know better—but that it ever happened.

It still hurts her.

It's not fair that I can't wipe that pain away. Dwelling on it, or on how badly I want the guy who hit her to stop breathing, doesn't help either of us.

Fuck, she's got enough of that from Drew. Not that I blame him. I would have killed that asshole. I don't know how Drew stopped himself.

I pull her closer. Close enough she squeaks. Her hands go under my shirt. The touch is soft, a *yes*, a *please* even.

We should have the better kind of fun.

I need my hands on her body, starting with those sexy shoulders and ending with... well, fuck, not ending with anything until I've had every inch of her soft skin, until she's come so many times she asks me to stop.

I need her body against mine so both of us know that nothing is ever hurting her again.

I press my cheek against hers and whisper in her ear. "Let's go back to our hotel."

"Are you sure? I don't want to be rude." She rises to her tiptoes and presses her lips to my ear.

Fuck. I pull her closer.

She moans as she sucks on my earlobe. It feels fucking amazing. I can't do anything but dig my fingers into the fabric of her jeans.

I groan. "You keep doing that, and I'm gonna fuck you in the nearest empty room."

"We'll get arrested."

"You say that like you think it matters to me."

She takes a step backward. Her lips curl into a smile. "We can't all be rock stars. Some of us have reputations to maintain."

I nod. She's a photographer—a fucking amazing photographer—and she has a business to run.

"Then how about we talk?" I ask.

Her lips press together. Her gaze goes to my crotch. "Maybe we should go back to the hotel room."

Hard to blame her for staring at my erection. The tight

jeans make it painful, but it's well worth it for the excitement lighting her face.

She still looks at me like I'm a present she's desperate to unwrap. It's different than the way other women look at me. Yeah, she's appreciating my body, but she sees more than that.

She sees me. She sees every part of me and she's still here.

I'm warm everywhere. I've never cared about anything the way I care about Willow. Not even the band.

I nod to the fake canal behind us. "Let's talk first. On the gondola."

"Won't people gawk at the celebrity doing a cheesy tourist attraction?"

"Dunno. Where's this cheesy tourist attraction? I only see a fucking amazing replica of the actual canals in Venice."

She laughs. "Okay. Let's talk on the gondola." She bites her lip nervously but her eyes stay bright.

I send my Mom a text updating her on our plans—she texts back a suggestion we skip the ride and go back to our hotel room-and lead Willow to the ticket booth. Turns out, charm and celebrity don't do much to help us skip the line. But money does. I pay for the VIP passes then we're up.

A man in a striped shirt and straw hat introduces himself with an obviously made up Italian name. Okay, sure. We'll buy into that.

Willow is smiling. I can't complain about anything with her smiling like that.

He helps her onto the gondola. Then me. He looks at me with recognition, but the guy plays his role and stays zipped about all matters of celebrity.

"Honeymooners?" he asks.

Willow squeezes my hand. She traces the outline of my wedding band with her thumb. "Close enough."

I melt. I still can't believe it means as much to her as it does to me, that she's my wife and I'm her husband.

That we're together forever.

I can feel her affection everywhere.

I press my forehead to hers.

Her breath is steady, but she's not close enough. I slide my arms around her waist and pull her closer.

Need to know what it is that's weighing on her.

Can't take any more shit weighing on her. Between Meg and Miles throwing an impromptu wedding and Kara being knocked up, we've had enough of other people's problems.

Don't get me wrong. I love my friends. Just wish they'd deal with their shit for once.

Or at least not fight my help.

The gondola guy starts singing in Italian. Willow looks up, her hazel eyes going wide. Her smile goes wider.

I lean close enough to whisper. "You like this cheesy shit?"

She nods.

"Want to tell me what it is that's on your mind?"

"No."

I cock a brow.

"Your mom does the same thing. And your brother." She brushes my hair from my eyes. "It's cute how the three of you share so many mannerisms."

"Cute?"

She nods.

"Gonna make me prove I'm not cute?"

Again, she nods.

"I'll do it here."

"The boat will tip over!"

"So?"

She laughs. "Okay, do it here. I dare you."

Shit. I hate backing down from a dare, but I have to admit she called my bluff. I'm plenty in the mood for her body under mine, her strong legs wrapped around my hips, her nails digging into my back as she screams my name.

What the fuck am I trying to do here?

Thoughts of baseball do nothing to help the situation. Don't know shit about baseball.

I shake my head. Clear my throat. Takes a minute, but I get my senses back.

She laughs. "You're backing down from a dare."

"No. Just want to wait till we're alone."

"Uh-huh." She smiles ear to ear. "You don't have anything to prove to me. You're still the most outrageous person I know."

"Thank God."

She nods. Her expression softens, more serious. "Do you want to be here for Christmas?"

"Don't care where I am as long as I'm with you."

"Really?"

I nod. The last few years, I've spent half my time with my surroundings blurring together. Another hotel, another venue, another Thai restaurant, another woman at another club—it's all felt the same until Willow showed up in my hotel room.

I knew she was different that first night. It still took me a while to realize she was exactly what I needed.

"We won't have much family here," she says.

"We have the band and Ophelia. Who else do we need?"

"Do you ever think about your biological parents?"

My stomach clenches. Which of them would I think about—the father who walked out when my mother got pregnant or the mother who couldn't be bothered to stay sober long enough to fucking do anything? "No."

"Never?"

"You ever think about how your dad moved to Europe and married some French chick three years older than you?"

"Yeah, I do."

She does? Her eyes are wide, this mix of frustration and something else. I don't get it. Usually, body language is easy to read. Usually, I know exactly what she wants.

But now, I don't.

She's getting at something, but what?

Hard to focus when she brings up my birth parents.

Why the fuck would she bring them up?

"What are you getting at, kid?" I ask.

"I still think about my dad and my mom all the time." She frowns. "Sometimes, I think about getting back in touch."

"Why would you do that?"

"Because they're my family, Tom. I grew up with them. The only person I've known my whole life is Drew. I don't have any old friends from high school. I only have one friend from college." Her gaze goes to the bottom of the gondola. "I decide that it isn't worth the hurt, but I do think about it."

"Nobody who hurt you deserves your thought."

"Sometimes people who love you hurt you." She looks up at me. "You've hurt me."

Fuck, I have. The thought guts me. I can't stand that I've hurt her.

She presses her fingertips into my cheek. "It's okay. I know you didn't mean to. I'm sure I've hurt you before."

"No."

"Really?"

"Never." I lean into her touch. I can feel that everywhere too. She's soft. She's warm. She's fucking alive now. Not like before. Not like when she was running from everything.

And I am too. A whole different part of me is awake.

Willow bites her lip. "I'll probably hurt you one day. Without meaning to. That's what happens when you give someone your heart. Sometimes they stumble a little."

I trace the lines of the tattoo on her chest—a shattered

glass heart. She's a strong person to survive everything she's been through, but I'll always worry about her breaking like that tattoo.

I'll always need to make sure she's pasted back together.

"Do you ever think about talking to your birth mom?" she asks.

What the fuck? "To do what?"

"It weighs on you. The way she let you go so easily. Maybe she had her reasons. Maybe she still loves you."

I shake my head. The gondola is turning. Feels like the whole fucking world is turning.

Why would I want to talk to my birth mom? *Why'd you let your boyfriend beat me when he came down off his meth high?* isn't exactly productive conversation.

There's nothing to say. I meant nothing to her. Nobody thought anything of me until Ophelia.

There aren't many people who care about me, about the real guy and not the celebrity, but there are enough.

Willow is enough.

But what the hell is she getting at? "Why are you bringing this up?"

Her brow knits. "Thinking about family and Christmas. Things are changing. Drew and Kara are having a baby. And I... I've never liked Christmas. Lots of bad memories. My parents always fought like cats and dogs."

"Yeah?"

She nods. "This is our first Christmas together."

"We're gonna celebrate with our friends."

"Is that enough?"

"You're all I need, Willow." Even if I've got no fucking idea what she's after.

She nods, but I'm not sure I buy it.

Still, I pull her closer. It makes my whole body warm. It's

not just heat, not just how much I want her athletic body under mine, her hazel eyes filled with pleasure.

Don't just want to fuck her.

I want to make love to her.

Want to savor every single second of it.

I don't even care that *make love* is the cheesiest phrase in the history of the universe.

"We're really grown-ups, huh?" she asks.

"Speak for yourself, kid. I'm a rock star."

"You do your new manager's job."

"Only till he learns."

"What a load!" She laughs. "You're going to do it forever."

"You run your own photography studio."

"True."

"You're grown up."

She turns to me. "You are too."

"We should celebrate with some grown up fun." Need whatever it is she's getting at gone. Need everything between us gone. Need every inch of her pressed against me.

She smiles sheepishly. Her gaze passes over me, stopping at my chest, then making its way back to my eyes. "Are you sure Ophelia won't mind?"

"She already texted, telling me to go fuck my wife."

"She did not."

I show Willow the evidence.

She laughs. "Well, ignoring her advice would be rude."

"Don't have to convince me."

Chapter Four

TOM

I t's a ten-minute walk back to our hotel room. I'm in no
mood for celebrity shit. I keep my hood and my
sunglasses on. Fuck looking like a tool. Nothing is
getting in the way of me connecting with Willow.

Nothing is getting in the way of me reminding her how
good sex feels.

Or reminding myself.

Never felt shit beyond pleasure during sex before. But
with her... with her, I feel everything.

With her, I'm whole.

It's fucking cheesy shit, but I don't care. I need our bodies
locked together.

I need her eyes glued to mine as she screams my name.

God dammit, I need her screaming my name.

She clings to my waist. She's brighter now. She's smiling.
But there's something there. And I need that
something gone.

Finally, we get to our hotel room. I unlock the door and
push it open. No wasting time. I slide my hands around her
hips and pin her to the door.

She looks up at me with hungry eyes. Her hand slides around my neck. Her touch is soft, affectionate.

No more words. No more questions about what it is that's on her mind. If there's one thing I'm good at, it's using my body to get the message across.

She rises to her tiptoes to press her lips into mine. God damn, her lips are soft, and she kisses me like she'll never get enough of it.

I won't ever get enough of it either.

I slide my tongue into her mouth. I want to take my time with her, to get her panting and desperate before I give her what she's craving, but I need this now.

She arches her back, moaning into my mouth and digging her fingertips into my skin. Her hands go to the back of my head. She holds me close, kissing me harder and deeper.

When the kiss breaks, she stares at me. Her hazel eyes are filled with need. "Fuck me, Tom. Now."

"Fuck yes." I don't waste any time. I do away with my hoodie. Then my t-shirt.

She presses her palms against my chest. Her eyes fill with need as she rakes her hands over my torso. Her hands feel fucking amazing on my skin.

We're touching, connecting.

Nothing else feels this good.

I do away with her coat. Then the t-shirt. The bra. I pin her to the wall, my bare chest pressing against hers, and I kiss her hard.

Willow groans as she kisses back. She's as hungry and needy as I am. The way she presses her fingertips into my neck, with all this gentle affection-

Fuck, I need her right now.

I unzip her jeans and push them off her hips. She kicks them, and her shoes, off.

I want inside her, but I can't rush this.

Need to make sure she's ready.

Her back is arched. Her crotch is pressed against mine. She's sighing like she's desperate.

I rub her over her panties. For a moment, she groans into my mouth. Then her lips break from mine and she's moaning into my ear.

"Now." She sucks on my earlobe. "I need you inside me."

She sucks harder. Her hands dig into my hair, pulling my head into position. My eyelids press together as pleasure overwhelms me. She knows how to fucking work me. Other women never bothered to figure it out.

But Willow realized it before I'd ever even touched her.

Fuck. I slam my hands into the wall, rocking my body into hers. The friction of my jeans is equal parts pleasant and painful.

She unzips my jeans and presses her palm against my cock, over my boxers. Somehow, I get harder.

I push her panties to her knees and run my fingers over her. She's wet. She's fucking dripping. Usually, I'd make sure she comes first, but I can't fucking wait.

I do away with my jeans, kick our clothes out of the way, and wrap my hands around her ass.

Need to know she's mine. Need to feel it everywhere.

She gasps as I lift her and press her against the wall. Her hands slide around my upper back.

"Tom," she breaths.

Yes.

I watch need fill her expression. Her eyes are heavy with it. Her lips are pursed like she can't do anything but groan.

I hold her hips, guiding her body towards mine. My cock strains against her. The brush of her folds sends me panting.

Fuck. I need to be inside her.

Her eyes press together. Her fingertips dig into my skin. "Tom, please. I need you."

God damn, I love the sound of that.

Slowly, I shift inside her. One inch at a time, she envelops me.

I shift deeper. Deeper.

She groans as I press my body against hers.

She feels so fucking good. I keep her pinned against the wall as I thrust into her. Slowly at first. Then faster.

Harder.

Her mouth goes to my ear. She sucks on my earlobe, her hands digging into my back, her hips shifting in time with my movements.

There. That's it.

Feeling how badly she wants my pleasure, how badly she needs us pressed together—that's fucking everything.

My last conscious thought falls away. All I know is Willow. Her lips on my skin. Her skin against my fingertips. Her folds enveloping me.

She sucks harder. Harder. Hard enough I lose control.

My grip tightens around her hips. I move faster.

She pulls back to gasp. Her eyes meet mine. She brings her hands to my hair and she stares into my eyes.

The intimacy of it leaves me breathless.

Then she's kissing me, and I know my lips will be pressed against hers until we're both finished. I move faster, harder.

Until she's groaning into my mouth.

She's almost there.

Her thighs squeeze my hips. Her hands tug at my hair.

She groans enough I feel the vibrations everywhere.

I can feel her coming, feel the way she pulses around me, the way it pulls me closer, deeper.

I keep the same rhythm until she's finished, and then I move faster. Harder.

I need all of her.

Need to come inside her.

She holds on tightly, still kissing me, still groaning into my mouth.

The world is the two of us.

No secrets, no hiding shit, nothing but us connecting.

Pleasure takes hold of me. Can't do anything but soak it in. She's fucking soft. Still fucking wet. Still fucking moaning into my mouth.

Still fucking mine.

With my next thrust, I come. The intensity of it makes me pull back. I have to groan. Have to gasp. Have to take in all the affection and need in her hazel eyes.

She squeezes me as I fill her.

Fuck, I feel my orgasm everywhere. I'm still shaking when I'm finished. She's still shaking when I set her down on the ground.

She wraps her arms around my waist and rests her head against my chest.

I hold her back. We'll have to clean up in a minute, but right now, the universe is the two of us.

Whatever it is she's hiding doesn't matter.

She purrs as I stroke her hair.

Willow, fuck, Willow.

"I love you," she mumbles into my chest.

"I love you too."

But that doesn't tell me shit about what it is that's wrong.

Chapter Five

WILLOW

My cell buzzes with a text alert. It's unlikely it's anything important. I'm tempted to ignore it in favor of shutting out the world.

Enough of the world.

I need to stay in this hotel room with Tom forever. I need to forget about every other thing that exists.

He leans against the wall and meets my gaze. I'm cleaned up and halfway into my clothes, but he's still naked.

Very naked.

He raises a brow. "What's on your phone that's so interesting?"

I check the device. It's a text from Jess.

Jess: Sorry we missed brunch. We were held up. You guys want to join for dinner? We found a great place in Chinatown with a lot of veggie options. Ophelia is non-committal about it. Pete says she wants to go out and get laid.

Willow: Did he say get laid?

Jess: God knows I'm not repeating what he said. I can barely think it. You want to come?

Tom's brow is knitted with frustration. He sees through me. He knows I'm up to something.

I'm not going to lie to him. That's not the kind of marriage I want.

But I can't tell him until I've made up my mind.

"It's Jess," I say. "Inviting us to dinner."

"Are they chafed?" Tom rolls his eyes.

"You're jealous."

"No." He looks to the ground. "Just kinda rude that they only show up when it's entirely necessary."

I have to smile. I can't believe Tom is jealous of anyone's sex life. It's not as if ours is lacking in any way. We're together all the time and it always ends explosively.

"Is that all?" I ask.

He shrugs. "You're off someplace. Tell me where."

Oh. Maybe that's why he's jealous. He thinks they tell each other everything, that they never keep secrets.

"Do you want to meet them for dinner?" I side-step the conversation entirely.

"Sure."

I text her a confirmation. "Why does everyone fuss over feeding me?"

"Cause you're sweet. Everybody wants to take care of you."

"It makes me feel difficult." After I nail down a time for dinner, I set my phone in my lap. Tom is still looking at me, still demanding I explain. I can't keep this from him for much longer. "I'm fine eating whatever."

He says nothing. His green eyes stay fixed on me.

There's no way Tom will agree to this. My only option is to surprise him.

Will he want that?

Will he forgive me?

My gaze drifts to the lion tattooed on his chest. The

design snakes down his shoulder and arm, all the way to his wrist. He's never said as much, but I put the pieces together. He got it for Ophelia, when she was sick.

Because she was the only person who ever thought he meant something.

He still carries that around on his shoulders. Even now, he's trying to get this out of me because he needs to help other people to feel important.

He needs to know he's loved.

I need to do this.

I pry my eyes from him to look at my phone. I already have Liberty's information saved. I keep my expression casual as I text her.

She texts back immediately with a time and a place.

Tomorrow morning, a breakfast spot a little outside of town. All I have to do is say yes, and Tom will see his birth mom for the first time in a decade.

Deep breath. I look up at Tom. "Breakfast tomorrow at nine? Found a nice place just outside town."

"Was planning on spending the morning fucking you until we were too tired to move. But sure, we can do breakfast at some place just outside town."

"Great."

"Why are we doing this?"

"It's a surprise."

"A good one?"

Hopefully. Maybe. My confidence falters, but I keep a smile on my face. "Time will tell."

Tom raises a brow. "Okay. If you promise you'll fill me in on whatever *this* is tomorrow."

I can do that. "I promise."

I text her a *yes*.

It's happening.

God, I hope this is the right decision.

Tom nods to the bathroom. "Gonna shower."

"Sure. You want to do anything between now and dinner?"

"Want you to join me in the shower. The rest we can figure out."

My stomach clenches. It feels like I'm lying to him. And if I'm lying to him, I don't deserve the ecstasy of being pressed against the tile wall with my hands wrapped around his cock.

"You've never kept a secret before," he whispers.

"It's just a surprise."

He studies my expression and takes a step backward. I'm not sure if he believes me.

I'm not sure if this is the right call. But helping him heal the wound that's still causing him pain is worth the risk.

"You coming?" His voice is bouncy, but there's a neediness in his eyes.

He needs that closeness too. Hell, maybe he needs to prove to himself that he's still a stud settled down.

Whatever his intentions, I want to be pressed against him in the shower.

I'm not wearing much. I pull my t-shirt off my head and push myself off the bed.

"Of course I'm coming. But it's up to you how many times," I say.

⚜

FOR THE REST OF THE AFTERNOON AND EVENING, I PUSH aside everything but the moment. I soak in every second of fucking Tom in the shower, of a lazy afternoon taking in the flowers and the water shows of the Bellagio, of dinner with Pete and Jess.

I especially soak in the night pressed against Tom in our giant king bed.

At eight a.m., my damn alarm ruins everything. I jolt out of bed.

Tom wraps his arms around my waist and pulls me back under the covers. "What's the rush?"

I start with the easiest thing to explain. "I need to pee."

He mumbles something I can't make out then lets me go. I do my usual morning routine in the bathroom and return to the main room.

Tom is sitting up in bed. His wavy hair is falling over his face. He looks good just rolled out of bed. He looks tempting.

He's my husband and he's insatiable. I can have him whenever I want him. It's not a temptation, really.

It's an invitation.

But I can't have him now. Not with this hanging over our heads. It will be over in a few hours. He might be pissed at first. He might leave without considering talking to Liberty, but he will know that she did love him.

That she still regrets how everything happened.

I don't expect him to forgive her. I don't expect them to form any kind of relationship. I don't expect anything but him hearing, from her, how much he mattered to her.

He needs to know how much he matters.

He needs to know he's wanted.

"Good morning." I offer him my best smile then I turn to my half-unpacked suitcase. What do you wear to meet the woman who gave birth to your husband then lost him to the state? Jeans and a sweater can't be too far off.

Tom looks at me funny. Even through a yawn, his eyes stay fixed on me. He runs his hand through his hair. "You're still hiding something."

"It's a surprise."

I dress and check my cell—Liberty is going to be early—then get to work on my makeup. I don't usually wear much more than eyeliner and a little lip gloss, but I need something to occupy my hands and my mind.

Tom follows my lead. By the time I'm done with my makeup, he's dressed and sitting on the bed.

"This is a good surprise?" he asks.

I haven't got a clue. "I hope so."

He looks at me like he doesn't believe me. But still, he leads the way to the hotel parking lot and to our car.

Still, he drives according to the directions I read off my phone.

Still, he parks in front of the quiet restaurant.

He turns to me. "You're nervous."

"Yeah."

"You gonna tell me what we're doing here?"

"Then it wouldn't be a surprise." And he'd leave without giving it a chance.

"Okay." He raises a brow, but still, he gets out of the car, opens the door for me, and hits the electronic lock.

I check my phone one last time for posterity.

She's here.

We're here.

So here goes nothing.

Chapter Six

TOM

I slide my keys into my jeans pocket and open the door for Willow. Know it's old-fashioned, but I like making sure she knows I'm taking care of her.

Especially when she's shaking with nervous energy.

Gotta say, this doesn't seem like a good surprise.

I like a good surprise—an *I'm naked under my coat* kind of surprise—but this whole morning is giving me a sinking feeling in my stomach.

Willow clears her throat. Her eyes go to her phone again then the thing is in her purse. She wipes her palms on her jeans. She taps her toes together. Look at that. Our sneakers match. Both are dark blue, almost navy.

You'd think that kind of thing would happen all the time, but we both own so many pairs of canvas sneakers we almost never match.

Fuck. I'm fixating on sneakers instead of whatever it is that's making her lips purse like she's about to throw up.

She looks up at me, her smile doing nothing to hide the fear in her eyes. "Let's go in." Her eyes go to the *Please Wait to be Seated* sign and she shrugs. "It's pretty dead."

Okay...

Guess it makes perfect sense that we're at some empty Denny's knock-off twenty minutes off The Strip.

I don't like to hold my tongue, but I'll give her the benefit of the doubt.

Willow presses her lips together as she takes a step into the restaurant. She looks around the room. It's a pretty average diner, with booths along the walls and tables in the middle. Everything is an unpleasant shade of brown.

Her gaze fixes on a table in the back. There's a woman in a suit. It's hard to say from here, but I'd have to guess she's in her thirties or forties.

There's clear recognition on my wife's face. What the hell? The woman might be another photographer. Something like that.

Not that there's any reason for us to meet with a photographer. Unless her surprise is *I want someone else to shoot our homemade porn. It's hard to get the angles right on my own.*

Not sure how I feel about that idea.

She looks back to me with a weak smile. "I love you, Tom. Whatever you think here... I love you."

What the fuck?

We take another few steps forward, and the woman comes into focus. She's about 40. She looks like a professional woman in that designer suit, her gray reading glasses framing her blue-green eyes, her hair a mix of gray and mousy brown.

She's cleaned up nice and she's quite a bit older, but there's no fucking doubt in my mind.

Liberty.

My mother.

What the fuck is she doing here, and why does every single fucking piece of evidence point to Willow being complicit in it?

Willow's expression is hesitant. She's staring at me like I'm a ticking bomb and the counter is down to single-digits.

Liberty doesn't say shit. She's staring too. But I don't give a fuck about the expression on my face.

How the fuck...

"Tom, I... she emailed me a few months ago about your photograph on my website. She didn't know I was your wife."

"We weren't married a few months ago."

"She didn't even know you were famous."

"You fucking knew about this at our wedding?"

Her brow furrows. Her eyes turn down. "I wasn't sure what I was going to do."

My stomach drops like a stone. I can't think. Can't move.

I stare back at Willow. Her expression is remorseful. Loving, even.

But...

She's kept this from me for months.

"That part in our vows about us not having secrets. Was that bullshit?" I've got a lot of practice keeping my voice even. It's taking every bit of control to do it here.

"No, Tom... I didn't want to put this on you. I thought I'd tell her to go away, but she's... she misses you. She loves you. She's sorry, Tom. I wanted you to hear it. Hear that it was all a mistake."

Of course it was a fucking mistake.

According to Liberty Wright, my entire fucking existence was a mistake. I was the worthless shit that got in the way of her meth paradise with her drug dealer boyfriend.

I was the thing in the way.

So what if she's wearing a suit and her hair is clean and her teeth are fixed?

Now she can look respectable while she calls me a piece of shit.

Now that I'm the one with the tattoos and the wild hair, everybody else can judge me as the piece of shit too.

Willow is talking. She's saying something with a soft voice and apologetic eyes, but I can't hear a fucking word.

Everything I've told her... how the fuck could she do this to me?

I...

I have to think, but I fucking can't. I step backward. Then I do it again. Again.

There's the bathroom around the corner. I push inside. It's a small room with two stalls and old ceramic sink and mirror.

It's empty.

I take a deep breath, but that doesn't do shit to calm my heartbeat or bring my stomach back to its rightful place.

How... why...

What the fuck?

My hands are on the paper towel dispenser. I hurl the thing at the wall. It bounces off. I throw it again. Throw it until the top falls off and paper covers the floor.

The mess doesn't help put my thoughts in order.

It doesn't make this clear.

Willow is my wife. Willow is my everything. How could she fucking do this to me?

I'm shaking my head but nobody can fucking see me here. Nobody but me. I need to smash the mirror so my green eyes look less crazy. Or so they stop mocking me at least.

I need to break something.

Gotta get out of here before I break the only thing that matters.

Only two places the world makes sense. Now that it doesn't make sense with her, I'm down to one.

I need to be there.

Now.

Chapter Seven

WILLOW

Something is wrong.

Scratch that. Everything is wrong. I'm sitting across from Liberty, saying nothing. What is there to say? *Sorry, my husband still thinks you're the devil. Guess this was ill advised.*

He's still in the bathroom. It's been too long.

This is wrong.

Liberty stares at her phone. She has nothing to say either. What could she say? *Sorry I ruined your husband's childhood with my drug addiction. Couldn't find the motivation to get clean, so it didn't happen until the state of California forced me into rehab. And I chose dodging jail time over custody of Tommy.*

She still calls him Tommy. Like he's ten. Because he was barely north of ten when he was beaten so badly a teacher called Child Protective Services.

God, this was a mistake.

I should have asked him.

Yes, Liberty deserves a second chance, but that was Tom's decision to make. Not mine.

Fuck. I pull out my phone and send him a text.

Willow: You okay?

Thirty seconds pass and he doesn't respond. So I call. It rings all the way to voicemail.

I call again.

Again.

Ten times, and every time, I get voicemail.

Finally, Liberty speaks. Her voice is dull, defeated. "He's not ready to forgive me. I understand that."

No wonder she lost her son so easily. The woman gives in like it's nothing.

"Why don't you go talk to him?" She suggests. "If he wants to leave without ever seeing me again, I understand."

"I'm sorry," I say, but I'm not really apologizing to her. It's to Tom.

Where the hell is he?

"Sure. I'll... let you know." I push off the table and make my way to the bathrooms by the entrance. I knock on the men's room door. There's no answer.

Here goes nothing.

I step inside the bathroom. The paper towel dispenser is broken on the floor. Like it was thrown. Like someone wanted to break something.

Shit.

He's not here.

I do another scan of the restaurant but he's nowhere to be found. He's not outside it.

The car isn't here either.

I stare at my phone. Still nothing from Tom. It hasn't been long enough for him to get to any of our friends. Even to his brother or his mom to tell them what an awful mistake he made marrying me so the three of them can decide to excommunicate me from the Steele family as a unit.

Fuck.

I call a rideshare, cross my fingers, and wish for Tom to be in our hotel room.

☙❧

NO FUCKING LUCK.

He's not here. There's no sign he was here. The room is exactly as it was when we left an hour ago.

I plant on the bed. Tears well up in my eyes. There's no sense in blinking them back.

How did I get this so wrong? It's obvious now. I wasn't thinking beyond myself, beyond what I saw of Liberty—a woman broken by an abusive relationship, who turned to drugs to cope and forgot everything else.

That wasn't what Tom saw. It certainly wasn't what he experienced.

God, I hope this isn't as fucked as it feels.

I call Tom again.

Nothing.

I call five more times.

Still nothing.

I can't sit here feeling sorry for myself. I need to find him and make sure he's okay. Bad things happen when people run off like that.

If he got himself into trouble because of me...

If he did something he can't take back...

There are two other people who know Tom well enough to know where he might be. Only one of them is staying in our hotel. His room is down the hall... somewhere. I check my phone for the info.

Room 2113.

No problem. I grab a tissue and do as much as I can to wipe off my smudged makeup then I make my way to Pete and Jess's room.

Deep breath. I shouldn't be nervous to talk to Pete. He's practically my brother. So what if he's intimidating with the dark hair and the dark eyes and the perfect eyeliner—he really wears it well—and the way he always knows exactly what to do?

He would have told me this was a terrible idea if I asked.

I should have asked.

I should have listened when Ophelia tried to talk some sense into me.

I knock. There's no answer, so I grab my cell and call. It rings to voicemail.

I knock again. I call again. I do both fucking things at the same time.

The door pulls open. Pete is standing in front of it with only a towel wrapped around his hips.

The towel isn't doing anything to hide the fact he's hard.

I interrupted my brother-in-law and his fiancée having sex. That makes this better.

"Fuck, Willow. What happened?" He motions for me to come in and takes a step backward.

"I... uh... I don't want to interrupt." I press my phone to my chest.

"It's fine. Just give me a minute." He nods to the couch in the corner.

Their room is the same suite we have. Pete goes into the bedroom. I can hear him saying something but I can't make out the words.

It's probably best I can't make out the words. I'm embarrassed enough without adding his filthy mouth to the equation.

Probably best I spend this moment figuring out how I'm going to explain rather than speculating on his sex life.

He returns to the room wearing jeans—only jeans—and he takes a seat on the other side of the sectional couch.

His dark eyes fix on me. Instead of speaking, he gets up, pours a glass of water, grabs a box of tissues, and brings both to me.

His voice is steady, even. "I'm guessing you're looking for Tom and not trying to invite yourself to a threesome."

I can't bring myself to laugh at his joke. Nothing feels funny right now. I nod and take a long drink of water. It helps soothe my throat.

My breath slows. Only by one percent, but I'll take a percent right now. By the time I'm finished with my water, I'm up to three percent, give or take.

"Where's Jess?" I ask.

He smiles. "Jess is a little tied up right now."

Oh God.

Pete chuckles, that same chuckle Ophelia has. "Probably shouldn't tease, given how much you look like you're gonna cry." His expression softens. "What happened?"

"I fucked up."

"Can't be that bad. You'd have to try to lose Tom."

I shake my head.

"You'd have to try hard."

"So you... she's in there and she's..." I clear my throat. If I'm going to dodge admitting this, I should do so with clear words. "You've got her tied up in there?"

Pete chuckles. "That's what concerns you right now?"

I shake my head.

"Would it make you feel better if we talk about everything I'm gonna do to Jess when you leave? Don't mind as long as I can do it loud enough she hears."

I shake my head.

"Didn't think so."

"So those restraints that were in Tom's room... you used them too?"

"Have my own." He raises a brow. "If you want to talk

259

about bondage, I'm game, but I'm gonna use more descriptive language."

"No... I... I fucked up, Pete. I fucked up so badly."

"Tell me what happened."

"I... I brought Tom to meet his mother."

Pete's brow furrows. Frustration spreads over his face. Usually, it's hard to read him, but not right now.

He might as well scream, *yeah, you did fuck up*.

He gets up to grab his cellphone. "Haven't heard from him. You two get into a fight or—"

"He just left. He looked like he'd seen a ghost."

"Well, you—"

"I know. I shouldn't have. I just thought maybe if he met her and he realized she was sorry about everything... that maybe he'd realize he's loved."

"Tom knows he's loved. He has you."

"But he still—"

"You don't have to apologize to me. I'm not the one who flipped and ran off. And we both know Tom would have done the same thing you did." Pete's dark eyes light up with revelation. "Only one place Tom would go to figure shit out."

"Where?"

"I'll text you the directions." He taps a few things on his phone then looks back to me. "Tell him what you said to me. He might be mad, but he'll forgive you."

I shake my head. I don't know that.

"Go make up with your husband." He motions to the door. "I can come if you want, but it's gonna be awkward when I stand there watching you two have makeup sex."

"That wouldn't be awkward for *you*."

He smiles. "Course not. But it would be awkward for you. And I'd hate to wait any longer to get my mouth on—"

"That's enough."

He motions to the door. "Call me if you need backup."

"Okay. But, um, you can finish before you come—ahem—before you leave."

He nods. "Good luck, Willow."

"Thanks."

God knows I need it.

Chapter Eight

TOM

✤

I'm not aware of much beyond the sticks in my hands, the way they tap the drums or smash the cymbals. Beyond my foot pounding the pedal of the bass drum until the entire fucking amphitheater is shaking.

The music—if I can be so generous as to call my thrashing music— bounces off the walls and echoes back into my ears. This is shit playing. I'll feel better if I focus, if I play our entire set list all the way through, but I can't focus on shit.

Don't want focus. I want loud. I want noise. I want my drum kit screaming.

Eventually, I'm gonna get tired. That's what logic suggests. But I've been going for a while, and I still have a head full of steam.

I better smack these fucking things harder. Hard enough I could break the kit.

Even in my pissed off state, this sounds too much like noise. I can't stand the shitty noise.

I start to focus. First, the loudest song we have. As loud as I can play it.

There. Better. I don't sound like a drunk fifteen-year-old

who's never held a pair of sticks before. More like a tipsy twenty-year-old who's only been playing for a few months.

I bring it all the way up to sober twenty-something who knows his way around a drum kit.

Then all the way to Tom Steele, bad ass God of a drummer.

The music bounces off the walls and back into my ears. But there's another sound too. The door opening. And footsteps. They're fast.

I can't bring myself to look up. Can't bring myself to stop playing. Even as the footsteps move closer, as a sob breaks up the music.

It must be a fucking loud sob if I can hear it over the music.

"Tom."

That's Willow.

I drop my sticks instantly. Then I'm on my feet.

She's standing in front of the stage. Even with the stage lights on, I can make out the redness in her eyes.

She's been crying.

She's been crying a hell of a lot.

"Oh my God, Tom." She looks up at me. "You're okay."

I don't like that she's crying. Don't like that she's hurting. I'm still pissed about all this, but I need her not hurting. Now.

I move away from the drum kit. She's already climbing the steps to the stage. She practically throws herself into my arms.

"I was scared. I thought... I don't know." She presses her hands into my t-shirt. Then her cheek. "That something bad happened."

She's been crying so hard her tears wet my t-shirt. I wrap my arms around her and pull her closer. She smells good. Like Willow. Like home.

But what she did...

Fuck, I don't know what to do here.

"I'm sorry." She looks up at me, her eyes still dotted with tears. "I'm sorry I sprang that on you. Liberty seemed sincere and I thought... I thought you'd feel better once you heard from her about how much she regrets what happened. That maybe you'd feel more wanted, more loved."

I stare back at her. The words aren't making sense yet. I'm still foggy from the haze of playing.

Her voice is soft, a whisper. "I'm sorry." She buries her face in my chest for a long moment then she's looking into my eyes. Her voice gets louder, stronger. "But you can't do this to me, Tom. You can't run off. Bad things happen when people run."

There's fear in her hazel eyes. A lifetime of fear.

Dammit. I hurt her. It fucking aches that I hurt her. It doesn't erase everything else I'm feeling, but it's a hell of a lot stronger.

I hate when she hurts.

I nod.

She nods back. "You don't have to talk to me now. You don't have to talk to me for a month if that's what you want. If you ask me to leave now, I will." She swallows hard. "But you have to tell me you're okay. You have to tell me where you're going. Okay?"

"I'm sorry, kid." I run my fingers through her short hair. Already, I'm melting. It's hard to stay mad at Willow.

I don't think I've ever been mad at her before.

It feels right having her in my arms. Only other thing that feels this right is sitting behind my drum kit.

I pull her closer. Closer. Until her breath is steady.

"Your heart is beating slower," she says. "It was racing before."

I nod to the drum kit.

"You're sweaty too." She slides her palm over my bicep. "Not that I'm complaining."

"Yeah."

"Usually, you take your shirt off when you're drumming. Or is that for the benefit of the crowd?"

"Half for me, half for them." I look down at her. I would feel better to hold her without my shirt in the way of skin to skin contact. Without any of her clothes in the way.

But we have to discuss this. It's a big fucking deal.

I'm out of my haze. I'm calm enough. I make eye contact. "Start from the top again."

She takes a deep breath. "You sure?"

"Yeah."

"About three months ago, Liberty contacted me. Through my photography site. A friend of hers was looking at boudoir pics and she thought you looked a lot like the boy she had when they were younger. Liberty has your picture everywhere. She shows it to everybody. She thought it might be her son, and she wanted me to pass her contact information along."

"Why didn't you tell me?"

"At first, I thought I'd tell her to go away."

"Don't do that, kid. Don't make decisions for me."

Her expression softens. Her eyes brighten. "You called me kid."

I raise a brow.

"When you're really upset, you don't."

I let out a low laugh. "Guess that's true."

"I thought I could spare you from that pain. But then she said a little more about you, about what had happened." Her eyes fill with empathy—she's too fucking kind—then they're back on mine. "I guess I thought of what happened to me. That maybe she had been trying to leave her abusive boyfriend but she'd never figured out how. That she had just made a lot of mistakes that kept snowballing."

It's hard to think of Liberty as anything but the woman who didn't give a shit about me. Hard to use the word *mom* or *mother* to describe her.

I don't know whether I should melt over Willow seeing the best in people or shake my head over her getting taken for a ride. I don't like anyone fucking with her. I'll destroy anybody who fucks with her.

But I can't deny that her version of events could be true.

"I was waiting for things to slow down," she says. "But they never really do."

I nod.

"I knew she lived in Vegas. So I thought while we were here... I knew you'd say no. That doesn't excuse it, but you still walk around with a chip on your shoulder, like you're still sure everyone is going to think you're worthless." She reaches up to run her fingers through my hair. "I thought maybe if you met Liberty and saw that it was all mistakes, that she always wanted you and thought you were valuable... I thought maybe you'd stop feeling that way."

My last bit of resistance melts. It's impossible to stay mad at her. I'm not sure Willow has a selfish bone in her body.

But that doesn't make this okay.

Still... "Have to admit, I'd have done the same thing."

She smiles. "And I'd have been pissed about it."

"I don't need anybody but you loving me."

"You have your mom and Pete."

"That's three times what I need."

"Drew loves you." She laughs. "He'd never admit it though."

"Then how do you know?"

"I just do. And Miles. And Meg and Kara. I'm not sure about Jess. She hasn't known you very long, but she seems fond of you." Her voice drops. "You've helped me move on from my past. I thought maybe I could do the same."

"I don't doubt your intentions, kid. But I don't want shit sprung on me."

"I know. I'm sorry." She slides her arms around my waist. "I'm glad you're here. I thought I lost you."

"Never." I take her hand and bring it to the tattoo on my hip. "This is forever." I point to her wedding ring. "This too."

"You promise?"

"Course."

She looks up at me. "Do you remember that night I was trying to leave your bed, and you pulled me close and asked me to promise not to leave you?"

"That was the first night you blew me."

She blushes. "I'm trying to be romantic."

"You asked me to come in your mouth."

She laughs. "That's true."

"You said *please*." Fuck, that was hot.

"That's also true."

"Fuck, you're giving me ideas."

Her voice drops to something sensual. "I like all your ideas."

"Here?"

She nods. "Unless you want more time to yourself to think."

"No."

"You don't want space?"

"Not from you."

She raises to her toes and presses her lips to mine. Relief floods my lips as I kiss her back.

She's mine.

Whatever happens, she's always mine.

When the kiss breaks, she stares deeply into my eyes. "I was terrified I lost you. I'm not sure I can survive without you. You're my oxygen. I can't believe I did anything to risk that." She runs her fingers through my hair. "If you don't want to meet Liberty again, that's okay. As long as I don't lose you."

"Never."

She tugs at my t-shirt. "Promise again."

"Never, kid. You'll have to try a hell of a lot harder to get rid of me." I run my fingers through her hair. It's hard to think anything besides how much I want her body against mine, but I have to get this out. "Not sure if I'm ever gonna want to see Liberty again."

She nods. "We have a few days if you change your mind. And if not, that's okay. I sympathize with her, but you always come first."

"Now that isn't true."

She smiles. "You know what I mean."

"Yeah, but I'd like to demonstrate what it's like when *you* come first."

She nods. "Please."

"Say it again."

"Please, Tom. I need you."

Fuck.

I kiss her and the rest of the world melts away.

❧

Back in the hotel room, I order breakfast for us. We shower together.

I used to hate it when women felt the need to jump in the shower with me. We were done with our *relationship*, and we didn't need to play house. Not like those women looked at me as anything but a shiny trophy, a rock star boyfriend to show off to their friends.

But damn, I love when Willow gets in the shower with

me. Love running my fingers through her short hair. Love the way she squeals and fusses over me using the products for color-treated hair.

I especially love pressing my lips to her neck and running my hands over her wet skin.

No sense in wasting this opportunity. I hold her body against mine and stroke her to orgasm.

God damn, I love that part most of all.

By the time we're done, breakfast is waiting outside our door and it's cold.

We're wearing those ridiculous white plush robes, sitting on the couch and sharing everything. It's a standard spread—scrambled eggs with vegetables, fruit, toast.

She stirs sugar and almond milk—of course they have almond milk here—into her coffee and takes a long sip. "It's freezing."

"I wonder how that happened?"

She smiles. "Quite the mystery."

Her robe slips off her shoulder. It falls open enough to show off her chest tattoo and the tops of her breasts.

Damn, already getting ideas about having her again.

She spreads jam on her toast, rips it in half, and hands one piece to me. "Did you think about it at all?"

"When would I have thought about it—when I was fucking you on that stage or when I was getting you off in the shower?"

She blushes. "When we were walking back to our room."

I shake my head. "Was thinking about fucking you in the shower."

"You were not."

Okay, I wasn't. Truth is, I wasn't thinking much. Hard to think much after sex.

Her eyes meet mine. "Where's the convertible?"

"At the venue." I tear my half-piece of toast into quarters. "Shouldn't have bailed like that."

Her eyes fix on mine. "It was okay, but—" She shakes her head. Her wet hair lands over her cheeks. "Don't do it again. Please."

Damn, she's polite. She should tell me to go fuck myself for that. Shit she pulled was bad, but nothing excuses leaving her stranded at some random diner.

Her gaze goes to her wedding ring. "You don't have to decide now."

"Don't have anything pleasant to say to that woman."

She nods. "We don't have to talk about. We don't have to talk at all."

"Yeah?"

She laughs. "I meant something like *watch a movie*, but we can do that too." Her eyes meet mine. "You're more insatiable than usual."

"Don't like feeling distance between us."

"Do you feel distance right now?"

I nod. "*This* is between us."

"Yeah." She chews and swallows a bite of her toast. Her eyes meet mine then they're back on her food. She hides behind her coffee cup. "That ball is in your court, sweetie. It's whatever you want to do."

"You really think something positive can come out of me talking to my biological mother?"

"If you're open-minded about it."

Quite a fucking if.

She finishes her coffee and refills it from the pot. Her fingertips curl around the handle, but she doesn't pick it up. She stares at it.

I take a sip of my coffee. This means a lot to her.

It's really hard to get my thoughts to do anything but

scream *no fucking way*. I never thought I'd see my mother again. Never wanted to.

Mostly, I remember her high. But there are a few bits and pieces before she started doing drugs. Before she started dating another loser who hit her or me. She's a magnet for that type of guy.

I never compared her to Willow. Not for a second. Willow was a kid with a warped idea of what love is. She didn't *have* a kid she had to protect.

But it's not like my mother asked her boyfriend to hit her.

It's not like it was her fault.

Of course Willow empathizes.

She's a good person. A hell of a lot better person than I am.

She looks up at me. "Maybe I'm wrong about Liberty, but she really seems like she's turned her life around. And she really seems sorry and like she wants to know you now. If you think you'll get something out of hearing how much she regrets what happened... then yeah, you should meet her. But if it's only going to stir up old pain, then I'll tell her it's not happening." She traces the handle of her coffee cup. "I only want to help close that wound that still hurts you."

What the hell is she talking about?

"You still don't quite believe you're worthy of love." She scoots closer. "Which is ridiculous, because you're the greatest person I've ever met."

"Must not have met many people."

"I've met enough." She rests her head on my shoulder. Her voice is low, needy. "I still can't believe my luck that you're my husband."

I run my fingers through her hair until she's purring. "Okay."

"You sure?"

"Yeah. But not a surprise this time."

She nods.

"No more surprises unless they involve you naked."

"What about me in lingerie?" she teases.

"I can live with that." Getting all sorts of fucking ideas about that.

"I'll arrange it later. For the day after tomorrow." She looks up at me. "You're all mine tomorrow."

"What if someone else needs me?"

"Too bad. I need you." She presses her lips to my cheek. "I'll lock you in this room if I have to."

Can't complain about my wife locking us in our hotel room.

Fuck, I should throw away the key right now.

"Sounds like it's a plan." She smiles. "I suppose you'll need your strength. You should eat."

I do.

We talk about nothing as we finish breakfast. I'm about ready to practice being locked in this room when there's a knock on the door.

Room service always announces themselves.

So who is that?

"I'll get it." Willow pushes herself up. She cinches her robe then answers.

Of course, it's my brother and his fiancée. They have that just-fucked look about them.

The always have that just-fucked look about them.

Pete smiles at Willow. "Told you it would be fine."

She nods. "Thanks for your help."

Jess brushes her blond hair behind her shoulder. "Hey Tom, Willow. You look cozy. Sorry about before." She blushes.

"Don't worry about it, baby." Pete slides his arm around her waist and pulls her closer. "Only gave Willow ideas." He winks.

Now, Willow is blushing.

Pete chuckles. He's too good at this shit.

"We're meeting Mom for dinner tonight. You guys have to come," Pete says. "After you *come*."

"Why are you so interested in other people's sex lives?" I ask.

"Yeah, I'm the one overly invested in other people's lives." Pete shakes his head. He looks to Willow. "You believe this shit?"

"He might have a point here, sweetie," Jess says.

"That's cold. You gonna make that up to me?" he asks.

"You guys want something besides exhibitionist thrills?" I ask.

"Love you too." Pete blows me a kiss.

Willow looks at me. "I think they want to confirm this dinner thing."

"Yeah. Dinner. Sure," I say.

"Be nice." Willow mouths, *please*. "I went to Pete when I couldn't find you. He knew where you'd be."

Shit, guess I do owe him one. Hate to admit that relationships have stolen a lot of the time my brother and I used to spend together. Last few months were the first time we'd lived apart since Ophelia adopted him.

"Thanks for that," I say.

He replies with his usual nod. "One more thing." He reaches for something—a shiny pink gift bag, the same shade as Willow's hair.

Jess claps her hands together. "It does match really well." She smiles. "This is for you guys." She turns back to him. "An early Christmas present?"

He chuckles. "Yeah."

"Enjoy." She hands it to Willow then turns back to Pete. "Can my early Christmas present be you wearing your glasses twenty-four seven?"

He shakes his head. "They'll get in the way."

She murmurers something and presses her lips to his.

Okay, that's enough of that.

"Come on, kid. They'll do this all day." I motion for Willow to come inside then I nod goodbye to Pete and Jess. "It's how they get their jollies."

She laughs, but she still nods goodbye and closes the door.

Willow sets the hot pink gift back on the table.

"Is it from Pete or both of them?" I ask.

She looks at it. "No card. Hard to say."

Damn. Not sure I want to know what it is if it's from him. But there's no time like the present. "Open it."

She smiles. "Yay, I love gifts!"

I laugh. God damn, I love the joy in her expression.

She pulls the hot pink tissue from the bag, reaches inside, and pulls out a box.

A box of bondage restraints.

Oh fuck.

She pulls a sticky note off the front and reads it. "Trust me, you don't want your old restraints back." Willow laughs. "Not that I doubted he was using them."

I raise a brow.

She shakes her head. "Nothing important." She studies the box. It's a full kit—blindfold, handcuffs, under the bed restraints. "I know I was skittish about it at first, but if you want to tie me up, I'm game."

She looks up at me and her eyes light up.

Fuck, my cheeks are burning.

Her mouth drops open. "You're blushing."

"Yeah."

"You never blush."

God damn, I am blushing. My cheeks are burning.

"Why?" She moves closer. "You're not shy about *anything*."

She's right. I'm not shy about anything. Usually.

But right now, my gaze won't budge from the floor. "I don't want to tie you up. I'm not against the idea. Not at all. But I..." I clear my throat. "I want you to tie me up."

She gasps.

Her eyes are as big as the fucking moon.

I run my hand through my hair. God damn, this must be how other people feel all the time, all nervous and vulnerable. It would be awful with anybody else. But with her, it's tolerable. It's almost nice. "If you're into it."

God damn it, I must be red. I finally manage to look my wife in the eyes. Her face is lit up with enthusiasm. She bites her lip.

Her pupils dilate. "I want to."

"You sure?"

Her voice lifts. "Positive. You want to do it now?"

Fuck, I'm already getting hard. I nod. "Now is good."

Her gaze goes to my crotch. "Now is very good."

Chapter Nine

WILLOW

The woman staring back at me in the mirror is some other version of myself. Her eyes are lined with black. Her lips are red. Her black lingerie does amazing things to her broad shoulders and slim hips.

The woman is a sex goddess.

I'm a sex goddess.

Or at least, I want to be one. Tom always makes me feel like the sexiest woman in the universe, but usually, he's the one leading. Usually, he insists on it.

This time, I'm leading. I'm more than leading. I'm tying him to the bed and... well, I'm not sure what I'm doing after that.

I stare back into the mirror. I'm going to tie my husband to the bed and have my way with him.

I can do that.

My heart is beating hard enough I can feel it in my fingertips. I'm not sure I know how to do this. It can't be *that* complicated. Cassandra passed down a lot of trashy books. I skimmed the bondage scenes—I didn't exactly have a positive experience with a man forcing me to submit—but I got the gist of them.

It's not really about force. The submissive partner gets off on losing control, but he's the one in charge of the scenario. The dominant partner has to read him, to make sure he's getting off.

I'm not sure I'll be any good at it, but I want to try.

I want Tom to have every bit of pleasure in the world.

There's something appealing about the thought of him bending to my command. Usually, he's in charge of the entire universe. If I'm in charge of him... commanding the King of the Universe is a lot of power.

I check my reflection one more time for good measure. There's no ifs, ands, or buts about it. I look hot.

I can do this.

I really, really want to do this.

Deep breath.

I make my way to the bedroom. The lights are off but the curtains are open. The sun—it's already mid-afternoon—streams in through the windows. I can see the mountains off in the distance. They're red, burnt orange even, against the bright blue sky.

The serenity of the view assures me.

The room is empty except for the bed, and that's got nothing on it but sheets, restraints, and Tom.

He's sitting at the edge of the bed, in his boxers, his feet planted on the floor. His eyes are on me. His eyes are wide with this amazing mix of enthusiasm and lust.

He presses his palms into the bed. He's already getting hard.

Damn, how I want that.

I want to watch his eyes roll back in his head as he comes.

I'm in control. I get to decide when he comes. And he doesn't come until I'm done enjoying the ride.

Heat pools in my core. I'm not sure if I can pull this off, but I'm starting to like the thought of it.

A lot.

"You sure about this?" I ask.

"Fuck yeah." He looks me up and down. "You look hot."

"I know." I slide into his lap, my knees planted outside his hips. I look *him* up and down. His lips are parted. His green eyes are hungry. I need that hunger. All of it. I make my voice confident. I'm in charge. "Kiss me."

His kiss is so intense I forget to breathe.

I can feel him getting harder. I grind my crotch against his as I slide my tongue around his. Dammit, that feels good.

I kiss him until I can't take it anymore. Then I take his hands and bring them to my chest. "Take off my bra." My voice is half-whisper, half-command.

Still, he obliges me. He groans as he slides my bra off my shoulders.

I bring my mouth to his ear, breathing hot and cold until he shudders. "Touch me."

I can't tie him up until he's touched me properly.

Tom's eyes stay on mine as he plays with my chest. There's no teasing today. He goes right to what he knows I like. His thumbs brush against my nipples lightly. Then harder. Harder.

Perfect.

I groan. "Don't stop."

Every touch sends another wave of pleasure to my core. It's hard to believe I'm the one in charge when he's playing me like an instrument.

I let my eyes close and soak in sensations of his hands on my chest, his body against mine, his hard cock under me.

Tension builds in my core. It's difficult to think about anything but how badly I need to come.

I take his hand and slide it down my torso, into my

panties. Then his finger is brushing against my clit, and it feels so good I can't think at all.

I can't lose control yet. I'm the one in charge.

I have to give him an order.

"Make me come," I breathe.

He rubs me with his index and middle finger. No teasing here either. He goes right to the spot that always gets me off.

I'm already close. I squeeze my legs. My inner thighs press against his hips. There's not much room for his hand to maneuver, but it's not doing anything to slow him down.

Tension knots in my core. So fucking close.

I bring my hand to Tom's hair and I tug. "Fuck, Tom."

Then I'm there. The tension hits a fever pitch, and it releases. My sex pulses as pleasure spreads to my limbs.

I revel in the aftershocks of my orgasm for a moment. That's enough for me. It's his turn.

I push him onto the bed. My hands go to his hips. It's a lot messier than when he does this, but I manage to get his boxers off his feet in one gesture.

He's already shaking. Already needy. Already fucking hard.

The under the bed restraints are more hardcore than the wrist cuffs, but the way he's spread over the bed is inviting.

I take one cuff and secure it around his ankle. He lets out a low groan as I secure his other ankle. The cuff is loose enough it won't cut off his circulation but tight enough he can't get out of it.

He looks up at me with a needy expression. "Fuck, Willow."

I press my lips to his ankle, just above the cuff. My eyes stay on his as I kiss my way up his leg. All the way to his inner thigh.

Then I've got to focus on my task at hand.

He groans as I flick my tongue against him.

Again.

Again.

I take him into my mouth, only the tip, and I play with his piercing with my tongue.

He tastes good. He always does.

His body takes over. His hands go to my hair. He tugs at it, holding me in place. But today, he doesn't get to do that.

I pull back and kiss my way up his torso. His hard body feels good against my lips. But it's more than his six-pack, or his chiseled chest, or his soft skin.

It's Tom.

My husband.

My everything.

I plant my knees outside his chest and reach for the left cuff. There. I grab it and start to secure his left wrist.

His right hand goes to my hips. He pulls my body over his, pulling my crotch over his mouth.

His tongue flicks against my clit. Hard to turn that down, but *I'm* in control.

I press my hands into his shoulders and push myself back. My eyes find his. "Not until I give you permission."

"Fuck." His pupils dilate. He just barely nods.

I work to secure his other wrist and spend a moment taking it in. He's tied to the bed, completely bound, completely under my control.

He's giving me all his trust.

The thrill of that has my body buzzing. I wasn't sure I deserved his trust after this morning, but he forgave me.

He still loves me.

He still trusts me as much as he did yesterday.

I press my lips to his neck. I know he wants his mouth on me, but he doesn't get that yet.

I suck on his earlobe until he's groaning my name. His eyelids press together. His fingers curl into his palms.

He tugs at the restraints but only enough to test them. When the cuffs pull at his wrists, he sighs with pleasure.

He really fucking likes being tied up.

And I really fucking love how much he likes it.

He turns his head, offering his ear to me. I lick, suck, and nibble until he's groaning in agony then I move to his other ear.

He groans as I push his head into the bed.

"Fuck, Willow." His hips shift as I tease his other ear.

His expression is hazy, lost in pleasure. It does things to me. It makes it really fucking hard to keep teasing him. But I need more of his ecstasy. I need to keep him feeling good for as long as possible.

I make my way down his chest. Then it's my tongue against his cock. He tastes so fucking good. I want to take him deeper, want to feel him coming in my mouth.

But not yet. I suck him off until he's groaning and shaking like he's almost there.

His groan is more agony than pleasure as I pull my mouth away, but his eyes are still hazy. He's still lost in how good this feels.

I flick my tongue against him one more time then I make my way up his body.

I plant my knees outside his chest and plant myself over him. My hand goes to his head. I guide him into position.

He moans against my inner thigh. Then his tongue is on me. He licks me up and down. His tongue plunges inside me again and again.

He moves faster than usual. He's hungrier, needier.

I shift my body, bringing my clit to his mouth.

He licks me until I'm at the edge. The tension in my core calls all my attention. For a moment, I forget about control entirely and I surrender to the sensation. The tension knots so deeply it hurts. It hurts in an amazing way.

With his next lick, I go over the edge. Pleasure spreads out through my core. All the way to the very tips of my fingers and toes.

No more teasing.

He needs to be inside me now.

I shift into position, checking Tom's expression to make sure he's still lost in pleasure.

He is.

Dammit, I love the way his eyes are hazy, the way his lips look are parted with a sigh. He's never this relaxed, this lost in sensation.

I plant my hands on his chest and lower my body onto his.

Tom groans as his cock strains against me. I tease myself with his tip again and again.

Again.

"Fuck, Willow." His nails curl into his palms. "Fuck me."

Fuck yes.

But first, I tease more. I tease until I can barely keep my eyes open. I tease until I can't take it anymore.

I spread my legs wider as I slide onto him. I take it slow, so I can feel every inch of him, feel the way my sex stretches around him.

There's no resistance today. I'm dripping wet. I'm desperate for him to come.

Using my hands for leverage, I slide myself over him again and again.

My eyes stay glued to him. I watch pleasure fill his expression. Watch his shoulders and chest shake as he gets to the edge.

For a moment, our gazes meet. So much passes between us—love, need, trust. He's always mine and I'm always his, but right now, he fucking feels like mine.

The pleasure on his face is intoxicating. I forget about

how much I want to come with him. I only know that I want him to come.

I move faster, deeper, harder.

His hips shift up and down to match my movements.

"Fuck, Tom," I breathe. My cheeks flush as I issue the command. "Come inside me."

He groans with bliss.

A few more thrusts, and he's there. I watch his eyes roll back, his lips part with a dizzying mix of groans and sighs.

His cock pulses as he fills me.

I don't stop until I'm sure I have every drop of him.

My hands fall to my sides. After I catch my breath, I shift off him and undo his restraints, one at a time.

He wraps his arms around me and pulls me close. With his chest against my back, he presses his lips to my neck.

"Fuck, that was amazing." He sucks on my skin. "You're amazing."

I nod and nestle into his chest. My eyelids press together. That was amazing, but it was exhausting too.

I take Tom's hand and slide it between my legs.

This time, he doesn't need any instructions to get me off.

Chapter Ten

TOM

My wife is true to her word. Except for dinner with Pete and Jess, and Mom, we spend the next twenty-four hours alone together.

Of course, dinner involves Pete and Jess announcing that they're getting married on Christmas Day. It's only half a week away, but they already have almost everything planned. They want me and Jess's sister standing with them at the altar, but beyond that, they don't need help.

Fucker makes a point of asking me to *not* help.

Everybody still thinks I'm bossy and over-involved.

Hard to care at the moment.

Hard to care about much beyond seeing my mother tomorrow.

Usually, I know exactly what I want. Usually, I know exactly what I can manage.

But with this...

I've got no fucking clue.

Chapter Eleven

TOM

❧

Dammit, I'm sweating bullets here. I don't ever sweat like this. Not after a three mile run. Not after an hour of lifting. Not even when I try and fail to beat Willow at a race across the pool.

Not that I notice much sweat in the water. When I carry her to the nearest empty room afterward, I sweat like hell.

But not like this.

I wipe my palms on my jeans. We're already here. It's the middle of the afternoon. Not a breakfast or a lunch meeting, but a tea. That was Willow's idea.

Nobody would accuse her of being anything other than a genius.

God dammit, I don't back out of shit. I don't. But I can't do this.

I stare at the door of the tea shop. I tell my hand to make contact, to push or pull it open or whatever it is the sign on the door says.

But I can't.

Willow is next to me. She's looking at me with those

expressive hazel eyes. I can't bring myself to look back to see if she's disappointed.

Already had enough of one woman's disappointment.

I shouldn't be nervous. However good Liberty cleaned up, she's not gonna have as much money as I do. Or as much fame. Or as cool a job. I made something of my life without her help. It shouldn't matter what she thinks of me.

But it fucking does.

It doesn't fucking matter that I'm a millionaire rock star. Doesn't fucking matter that I play the drums as good as anybody ever has.

Sure as fuck doesn't matter that I have several million Instagram followers.

Fame doesn't matter to me on a normal day. Only makes me feel like my career is more a bullshit popularity contest.

Like I'm nothing but a celebrity.

Forty-year-old women aren't impressed by rock drummers.

Fuck. I shouldn't care if I impress her.

But I do. I already feel like that kid who was never good enough. Already feel like a miserable shit.

I can already hear her screaming that I'm getting in her way.

Can already feel her asshole boyfriend's fist.

Dammit, I can't breathe.

I take another step backward. My heel hits the curb. I stumble, but I stay upright.

Willow is watching me. I can feel it. But I still can't look at her.

"We can go." Her voice is calm, but it's uncertain. "If that's what you want."

Her hand curls around my arm. She rubs my bicep with her thumb. Even through my hoodie and t-shirt, I can feel the heat of her skin.

The day locked in the hotel room was a fucking great idea. This isn't.

She rubs my arm over my hoodie. With her other hand, she reaches up to brush the hair from my eyes.

She's looking at me. I know she is, but I still can't look at her. I have to stare at this damn tea shop.

"Hey." She moves closer. "Talk to me, sweetie. What are you thinking?"

I shake my head.

It's not like me to be tongue-tied. Usually, my thoughts make it from my lips without spending nearly enough time in my brain. I get myself in trouble that way.

But this...

I don't fucking have a clue.

She runs her fingertips over my cheek and chin. "Tom. Talk to me."

"I can't." Even that is hard to get out.

"You can't do this or you can't talk?"

"Talk."

"How about if I ask yes or no questions and you can nod or shake your head?"

Sounds reasonable. I nod.

She laughs. "You're doing it already." She presses her palm against my cheek, presses her cheek against my chest. "Do you want to call this off?"

I shake my head.

"Okay. Good. Do you want to stay here?"

Fuck, guess I do. I nod.

"Liberty is inside, in the back room."

My heart nearly stops.

Willow drags her fingers to my neck. There's all this affection in her touch. I soak in as much of that as I can.

"Do you want to go back to our hotel room and get naked?" she asks.

I nod.

Her voice lifts. "Right now?"

No. This is too heavy. I shake my head.

"Do you want to go inside the shop?"

No. But I don't want to leave without doing this. Don't want to spend the rest of this trip wondering if I made the wrong call. Don't want to spend the rest of my life wondering what could have been.

I'm not a *what could have been* kind of guy.

I nod.

"You'll probably want to talk to her, but I won't stop you from sitting and staring." Willow's hand squeezes mine. "You look cute staring."

"You shouldn't make fun of your husband in his time of need."

She traces my wedding band with her thumb. "I guess I shouldn't." She looks up at me. "Are you ready?"

This time, I manage to look into her hazel eyes. She's worried, yeah, but she's not disappointed.

If anything, she looks proud.

Not many people have ever been proud of me. I know Ophelia is, but she's not the type to remind me constantly. She's more tough love.

"Yeah, I'm ready." I squeeze her back.

"You don't have to."

"I know. I want to." Sort of.

Willow nods. She keeps her hand glued to mine as she pulls the door open and leads me into the cafe. We go all the way to the back room.

It looks smaller than it did before. I *know* the tables are spread out, that there's plenty of room, but it still feels like the walls are closing in.

Liberty is sitting at a round table, her attention glued to her cellphone. She barely resembles the woman I knew when

I was ten. Her eyes aren't fuzzy the way they were twenty-four seven.

They're clear.

They're nearly the same as mine. Hers are more blue. Mine are more green. Her hair is darker, grayer, but the nose, the chin—I can see myself in her face.

There's no doubt this woman is my mother. My biological mother, at least.

Willow squeezes my hand. She pulls the chair for me and motions for me to sit.

I do. My fingers tap the table. I can't help the gesture. I don't want to.

"Thank you for coming, Tom." Liberty's voice is soft, the one she used before the drugs and the bullshit. "It's great to see you."

I stare back at her. Words aren't fucking happening. I can barely nod.

"Willow tells me you go by Tom now. Is that right?" she asks.

"Yeah." Only ten year olds go by *Tommy*.

"Willow has been great." Liberty looks at my wife. "You're very lucky to have her."

At least we can agree on that. "Yeah."

"I don't know where to start." Liberty's eyes go to the table then they're on mine. "Do you have any questions for me?"

Nothing polite. Hell, nothing that will fly in a nice joint like this. I have nothing to say to Liberty. I'm still not sure why I'm here. I guess it's because I trust Willow.

She thinks it's a good idea.

But I'm still not seeing the value.

My fingers tap the table. "I'm not here because I want something. I'm here because my wife convinced me it was a good idea, and I trust her more than I trust anybody else."

Liberty nods.

"You fucking manipulate her again, and I'll ruin you." My hand curls into a fist. I unclench and stretch. Then my fingers are tapping the top of my thigh.

Liberty half-smiles. "You were always protective."

If she says so.

Willow squeezes my other hand. She looks from Liberty to me. "You can say what you're thinking, sweetie. Even if it's ugly."

"I'm thinking that it's real nice you cleaned up and got your life together, but that hasn't got shit to do with me. You never gave a fuck about me, so why do you want to see me now?" Dammit, I don't like being vulnerable around somebody I can't trust. My heart is in my throat. I can barely breathe.

This fucking sucks.

Liberty doesn't recoil. I need to say something that hurts more, so she's the one who runs away.

"I deserve that," she says.

What?

Her voice is heavy with regret. "I don't expect forgiveness. Honestly, I just wanted to see you and know you were okay. I didn't even know if you were still alive."

"Except for this meeting, I'm fucking peachy. That all?"

Willow squeezes my hand. Her hazel eyes are filled with concern. They're so full, they look like they're gonna drop off her face.

Don't give a fuck what my mother thinks of me. But this is hurting Willow. That's not okay.

This woman has already done enough to fuck up my life. Now she's hurting Willow.

I'm not going to do anything that will make Willow hurt worse.

"I want you to understand what happened," Liberty says. "That it wasn't your fault or anything you did wrong."

My fingers curl into a fist.

"Is that okay?" she asks.

A deep breath does nothing to calm my temper. I'm not this guy. I don't get pissed at the drop of a hat. Don't lose it.

Fuck, I hate feeling like this guy.

"Yeah," I mutter.

"You were wanted, Tom. Even after your father left me. I knew my options, but I wanted a child. I wanted you." Her eyes go to the table. "Do you remember when you were little? My mom would watch you sometimes."

I remember an older woman with grey hair and kind eyes. "She have a smoker's cough?"

"Yes, that's her. Chastity." Liberty shakes her head. "You would think she'd end the tradition of naming women after virtues with a name like Chastity, but she didn't."

Can't say I'm too invested in this story, but I do remember Chastity. Bits and pieces of her. A wrinkled smile, that deep smoker's cough, the low roar of the TV. She always watched soaps as background noise.

"You were small. You might not remember. But she took care of you when I was at work. I was a secretary. It was long hours sometimes, but I didn't have much choice. We didn't have much money." Liberty looks up at me. "She loved you. We both loved you. I was always happy to get home to you."

Don't remember this. "Then why do I remember you high constantly?"

"She died when you were five. From there..." Her voice drops. "From there, everything turned. I was in and out of work. I dated a lot of guys who didn't treat me too well. But I didn't have any money. I didn't have a choice but to use the only card I had."

What the fuck is she talking about?

Willow breaks the silence. "Tom, she's saying she was out of money and she had to move in with a guy. She had to use her sexuality to keep a roof over your head."

Guess the apple doesn't fall far from the tree. Maybe I should thank her for teaching me that particular lesson. I owe half my success to how hard I sold myself as *Tom Steele, sex god, the ultimate one-night stand.*

Liberty nods. "The drugs were David's thing. They made it easier. And they made it easier to take how poorly he treated me. If I'd realized he was so violent with you..." Her eyes go to the table. "I don't deserve forgiveness. Back then, the drugs mattered to me more than anything else. Have you ever known an addict?"

"Yeah." Not admitting any more than that.

"Drugs warp your priorities. When I was high, I didn't even realize I had a son. The state was right to take you away. I had no plans of stopping. Things were only getting worse with David. If he hadn't been arrested, if we hadn't been arrested—"

"What for?" I ask.

"Possession with intent to distribute. Child endangerment. I testified against him, but part of my plea agreement meant I had to give up custody." She wipes a tear from her eye. "It wasn't because I didn't love you, Tom. I knew you were better off away from me. In another home."

Yeah, in a bunch of homes where other people looked at me like a piece of shit or a punching bag.

Willow squeezes my hand. The warmth of her skin calms me but not enough.

This is too much to process.

It's easier hating Liberty. It's easier pretending like she doesn't exist. I'm not sure I'm ready to forgive her, to see her as anything but the woman who abandoned me.

"Your wife tells me your adopted mother is a sweet

woman," Liberty says. "Are you happy you're part of her family?"

"Yeah. But don't think that excuses anything."

"I don't," she says. "I know nothing will excuse what happened. I wish I had a better explanation than drugs, but that's the truth. It took me years to get sober then years to clean up. I have a job now, a home, a life. But I still fall asleep regretting what happened every night."

I force myself to meet her gaze. Force myself to think of Liberty as my mother. To try to remember her before the drugs.

There's a hint of something. I can see a smile, hear a laugh. Can see us on the faded carpet in some tiny apartment in the desert, watching reruns on a shitty TV with worse reception.

I can see us at the park.

Can see a trip to the beach, running around in the sand.

But that's dwarfed by the memory of fucking David and his fucking fists and that hazy look in Liberty's eyes.

God dammit, I hate drugs. Picked the wrong career to avoid them, but I've fucking made it work.

"You were a good kid," she says. "You deserved a good home."

What? "I was?"

"Yeah." Liberty's smile is sad. "You got into some fights and occasionally got a bad grade, but it was nothing out of the ordinary. I always considered myself lucky to have such a great son."

"What?"

She nods. "You were wanted, Tom. You were loved."

I look to Willow. This sounds too much like something she would say. Sure enough, there's a hint of guilt in my wife's eyes. No doubt about it, she fed Liberty lines.

But Liberty's voice is sincere.

My mother's voice is sincere.

"You sometimes got into trouble for being bossy." Liberty laughs. "From what Willow says, it doesn't sound like much has changed."

"You were talking about me?" I ask.

"Only bits and pieces." Willow's eyes turn down. "I should have asked first."

"Guess it's all on *TMZ* and shit." I tap my fingers against the table. It's a fucking weird feeling, hearing my mother tell me I was wanted and loved.

She practically threw me away.

But then I've seen drugs make a person do far, far worse.

Willow clears her throat. "Liberty had no idea who you were."

"Really?" I ask.

"Sweetie, you sound a little conceited. You're not *that* famous." She smiles and presses her lips to mine. Then she's close enough to whisper. "Are you okay?"

"Close enough." I press my palm against her back and hold her body against mine. Usually, I don't give a fuck who's around—now that we're not hiding this from Drew, I take every bit of affection I can with Willow—but it's fucking weird holding her in front of my mother.

"I love you," she whispers.

"I love you too."

Once we're back in our proper positions, Liberty offers a weak smile. "I have to admit that I'm still not sure who you are beyond what Willow has told me. I only listen to country music and I don't follow any celebrity gossip."

"He's only c-list," Willow teases. "If that." She squeezes my hand.

I squeeze back.

"You do well?" she asks.

Not like me to stay quiet when I have the chance to brag. But I don't want to mention specifics. "Really well."

Liberty smiles. "You seem like you've become a nice young man. A lot of tattoos, but they look good."

Willow laughs. "She likes your tattoos."

Damn, she's enjoying this. But that's better than it weighing on her.

Liberty smiles. "I'd like to hear about your life. If you don't mind."

"What about it?" I ask.

"Everything," she says.

"Starting now or from the beginning?"

"Everything."

I start at the beginning. From my very first foster home to landing with Ophelia, getting in fights, sleeping around. I talk about Pete, about the band, about Ophelia's cancer scare. Don't hold much back, even the parts about how much I've hated Liberty, about how I never felt like anyone gave a fuck about me until Ophelia.

When I'm done, Willow is still squeezing my hand and Liberty is still listening with rapt attention.

Then it's her turn. She tells me about her life, about getting clean, about finding an administrative job out in Riverside then eventually taking a position in Las Vegas at one of the casino chains.

She even asks Willow about her life, about her photography. We must spend an hour or two talking when Liberty says her goodbye.

"Thank you, Tom. It's been great talking to you, but I should go. I'm incredibly late for a meeting." Liberty smiles. "I've got something for you." She pulls a small, wrapped present out of her bag. "It's a photo album of when you were little. I understand if you don't want to keep it, but take a look for your grandmother's sake. She would have hated me for losing you."

Liberty stands. Willow and I stand too. How do you say goodbye to the woman who sorta feels like your mother?

I'm not the type to analyze this shit. It's better to do what feels right.

I offer her my hand.

She shakes.

Willow follows my lead. "Maybe we can see you again before we leave. If you're in town."

Liberty nods. "I'm always in town. I *can* get you a discount if you'd like. Not that you need one. I'd love to talk more. I can tell you more about what happened if you'd like to hear that." She looks to me. "Thank you for coming, Tom. And you too, Willow. You're a lovely couple. I can't remember ever seeing two people who looked at each other with as much love as you two do."

I guess my mother isn't the fool I thought she was. Not if she can see that.

Willow smiles and squeezes me tighter. We watch Liberty walk out of the cafe.

My stomach settles as she walks out the door. Not sure how I feel at the moment. Too much is swirling around my head.

Willow looks up at me. "You want to look at the pictures?"

"Later."

"Your heart is beating really fast."

I nod.

Her voice gets low, sensual. "I can help you calm down."

"That's not gonna make my heart beat any slower, kid."

She laughs. "Are you saying you don't want to?"

"Fuck no." I run my fingers through her hair. "Here?"

"We can drive out to the mountains, find an empty road, and lower the convertible roof."

Fuck yeah. "Marrying you was the smartest thing I ever did."

"You're just now figuring that out?"

"I realized it the moment I said *I do*."

She smiles. "Me too."

Chapter Twelve

TOM

Willow drives. It only takes a few minutes for us to find a road that leads out into the desert.

We roll the top down. The rushing air is cold, but the bite feels good. It wakes me up. It drowns out every other sound, forcing me to sort through my thoughts.

It's going to take a while for all this to feel normal.

It's going to take a while to reconcile the two versions of my mother—the drug addict who abandoned me and the one who came before and after that, who really did love me.

I keep my eyes on the bright blue sky as memories wash over me. There was a lot of time before the drugs when things were better. I was young. It's hard remembering much, but it *is* there.

I break open the photo book and flip through the pages. I recognize Chastity and I recognize the five-year-old kid in Liberty's arms. That's me. And we're fucking happy.

She's happy.

She loves me.

It's gonna take a long time for that to feel normal. Gonna take a long time for me to forgive her enough we can have a relationship, but looking at the big yellow sun and the beige expanse of desert, I believe I'll get there.

Willow squeezes my hand. It brings me back into the moment. I watch the wind blow her short hair all over her face. She looked good with longer hair. She looked like my friend's little sister.

But the short, pink hair—it's all pink now—does something for her. Between that and the chest tattoo, she *should* look like an edgy punk rock chick. But she doesn't. She still looks sweet, like a kid dressing up as a rock star for Halloween.

I'm not sure anything could change how sweet she looks, even full sleeves of ink and eyebrow piercings.

She rubs my index finger with her thumb. Another finger brushes against my wedding band. I fucking love the way she's always tracing it, like she's reminding herself we're married.

Us being married makes everything else look small. Even this thing with Liberty.

It's hard thinking about my mother. It hurts.

But no hurt could ever compare to how good it feels knowing Willow is mine.

She looks at me for a moment. Her lips curl into a smile then her eyes are back on the road.

It's too loud for conversation.

She tries anyway. "What are you thinking?"

I nod to the road that leads off the freeway. It's half a mile away.

She nods back. "You get such good ideas, sweetie." She pulls onto the road. The car slows enough the racing air is a murmur instead of a scream. "I hope this leads somewhere private."

I cock a brow. "So we can talk?"

"Of course. What else could I mean?" The delight in her

eyes gives that away. She drops her voice to something more serious. "What are you thinking now?"

"I believe her. That she's sorry. That she loved me. That it was the drugs that fucked things up."

"Really?"

"Yeah."

She's fucking beaming.

"Don't have to brag about it."

Willow shakes her head. "I'm not. I wouldn't." She takes a curve around a hill, then she pulls onto a side street.

There are no structures on the horizon. We're out of view of the main road.

It's private enough for us to communicate properly.

My eyes go to the sky. It's bright now, but it's winter. The sun sets early. "We're going to have to do this fast if we want to get out of here before it gets dark."

Her voice is confident. "Then you'll have to get me off fast."

I unbuckle my seatbelt and turn to her. "When did you start talking dirty?"

"You don't like it?"

"Fuck no. I love it." I undo her seatbelt and pull her into my lap. Her knees plant outside my hips. "Just worry you were getting tips from Pete."

Her lips curl into a smile. "I might have."

"Should kick his ass for saying dirty things in front of my wife."

"You'll have to kick his ass frequently."

"Now I'm going to have to think about my brother when we're having sex."

She laughs. "You offered to have a threesome with him." Willow runs her hand through my hair. "It can't bother you *that* much."

She's enjoying this.

I can't exactly object to her on my lap, her hands on my skin. I let my eyes close for a moment, and I soak in everything—the sun, the cold air, the warmth of her body.

Her lips on mine.

My mouth parts to make way for her tongue. She's leading. It's not often she leads. Right now, I want her leading. I want to feel her desire.

I want to feel like I'm hers.

I blink my eyes open as the kiss breaks. She's looking down at me through heavy lids. Her hazel eyes are filled with affection and desire. Her pink lips press together then part with a sigh of pleasure.

I need my hands on her skin. I need to feel more of her. I press my palm into her lower back and pull her body closer. Then I reach up and run my fingers over her cheek.

She leans into the gesture. Her eyes close. Her lips part with a sigh, a louder one this time.

"Thank you for pushing me." I cup her palm with my cheek. "But don't fucking do it again."

"I won't."

"I understand why you did this, kid, but I don't need anybody else loving me." I stare into her hazel eyes. Now, they're wide. They're fixed on mine. "I have you."

"But-"

"No but. The way you look at me every morning, that's more than enough to convince me I'm loved. That I matter."

I unbutton her jeans and push them off her hips. She lifts her ass, her pelvis pressing against my stomach, her chest pressing against my forehead.

Damn, not gonna be able to think for much longer. Blood is fleeing my brain at an alarming rate.

I grab her panties and push them aside. There. My fingers find the lines of her tattoo. *Tom* in curly letters. She never even jokes about how she could add to it to make it *Tomorrow* or *Tomato* or some other shit like that.

I trace the lines again and again. "That's better than any reconciliation with any person who ever hurt me."

She groans. "You're making conversation difficult."

"You're making things *hard*." I bring her body onto mine so she can feel my hard-on.

Her groan gets louder. Still, she looks me in the eyes. "I'm trying to be a supportive wife."

"As opposed to?"

"Jumping your bones when you're trying to talk about something important."

"Never gonna complain about you jumping my bones."

"I know." She slides her arms around my shoulders and grinds her crotch against mine. "But this is important. I love you so much, Tom. I love you so much it takes my breath away."

"Me too."

"I don't know what I'd do without you." She presses her fingers into the back of my neck. Her voice is low, needy. "I'm not sure I'd survive."

"You don't have to. I'm always going to be yours."

She presses her lips to mine. "I'm always going to be yours."

"You still want to adopt kids one day?"

She smiles. "I haven't changed my mind since Ophelia asked about it a few days ago." Her fingers slide into my hair. "I want to enjoy our life together, just us, for a while first. But one day, in five or ten years, when I'm ready to take care of someone else, then yes. I want to have a family with you, but I still have a lot to learn about taking care of myself."

"You're gonna be a great mom."

"You're gonna be a great dad." She plays with my hair.

"But I think it's bad luck to say this kind of stuff before sex. It's an incantation for birth control failure."

I laugh. "What makes you think we're having sex, kid?"

"Hmm, I wonder." She grinds against my erection. "How can you concentrate with that thing?"

"Practice."

"Those six weeks of celibacy?"

"Every fucking inch of my body wanted yours." I press my forehead to hers. "Whatever happens in our lives, even if adoption doesn't work out, if kids don't work out, I'll have enough love. Your love is more than enough."

"Is it cheesy if I ask you to make love to me?"

"Very."

"I'm going to do it anyway. Make love to me." She presses her lips to mine. "You're my everything, Tom."

"You're my everything."

She's right. Words aren't enough to express this. Sex isn't enough to express it either. I could spend every minute of every day telling her I love her, and that wouldn't be enough.

Fuck, that's cheesy as all hell.

But it's true.

Willow kicks off her shoes. I push her jeans and panties to her feet. Then they're gone, and she's nearly naked on my lap.

My body takes over.

I unzip my jeans and push them off my hips. Then the boxers. Usually, I'd warm her up first, but she's already wet and I need inside her. Now.

I bring my hands to her hips and position her body over mine. She slides her hands into my hair. Her knees spread wider.

My tip strains against her.

I stare into her eyes as I bring her body over mine. Slowly, I slide inside her. I can feel every fucking inch of her stretching to take me.

It always feels like more than sex with Willow, but right now-

Fuck, right now, I'm home.

I do away with her sweater, her blouse, her bra. She does the same with my hoodie and my t-shirt.

Then her chest is pressed against mine. The skin on skin contact fills me with something I can't explain. This closeness, this wholeness.

Fucking cheesy shit, but still, I don't care.

We stay pressed like that, bodies working together, tongues dancing together. It doesn't take long for pleasure to well up inside me. Usually, I can hold off, but right now, fuck.

Right now, I need her to come with me.

Need to feel her pulsing around me.

I slide my hand around her hip and rub her with my fingers. She breaks our kiss to groan.

Her eyes meet mine. "Tom." She slides her hands into my hair then pulls me into a deep kiss.

Then she's groaning again.

"Fuck, Tom." She presses her forehead to mine. "Come for me."

Fuck yes. I rub her harder. "You too."

She nods then she's moving faster, taking me deeper, rocking her hips to use my hand like it's her plaything.

I bring my other hand to the back of her head and pull her into a deep kiss.

A year ago, I wouldn't have believed I could have been this guy with a house and wife and all this fucking love in my life.

Would never have believed I could feel like this.

I always thought women wanted me to show them the world, but it's the other way around. Willow showed me the whole fucking world.

Fuck, Willow.

I kiss her deeper. I can't hold off any longer. I rub her harder. I groan into her mouth as an orgasm takes over.

Then she's breaking the kiss to groan. She's coming with me, holding my hand against her just where she needs it.

I can feel her pulsing as I come inside her.

Her groans vibrate across my chest and neck.

When she's spent, she collapses on top of me. Her eyes meet mine, this look of affection that says, *I love you.*

I don't even need words with her.

I use them anyway.

"I love you, kid."

She runs her hands through my hair. "I love you too."

PLAY FOREVER

Chapter One

JESS

The Tesla is quiet as a mouse. It's a well-needed oasis of calm after the last few days.

Dinner with Tom and Willow was enough to put me in a *need silence now* state of mind. I enjoy my almost brother-in-law and his wife, but the man takes up a lot of energy.

My fiancé is nothing like his brother in terms of conversation. He's a man of few words. Except when the topic shifts to sex.

Then he can fucking talk.

Pete turns to me. His lips curl into a smile that lights up his dark eyes. He knows I'm thinking dirty thoughts about what his mouth can do.

I clear my throat. I'll tell him exactly where I want his mouth... once we're someplace private. Well, private and stationary.

"I still can't believe you stopped for a charge in Barstow. We could have tested Peeta's stamina." I run my fingertips over the dash. "Why did I let you drive my car again?"

"You're sick of driving downtown in traffic."

"Sounds like a ratchet."

He chuckles. "Suggesting I used illicit means to convince you?"

I nod.

"You want to take over, do it. I'm sure Peeta likes having your hands around him."

I shake my head. I'd rather have my hands on him.

Right now. Then for the rest of the night.

Ahem. "Peeta loves threesomes. He missed you."

His chuckle is deeper this time. "*He* missed me?"

"I missed you too. But who do you think consoled me on my drives home from school, when I was lamenting that you wouldn't be there?" I pat the dash.

Pete chuckles. "I'll destroy him if he's moving in on my woman."

"He'd never."

"Doesn't sound like it."

I take him in again. The black hair, the dark eyes, the soft lips, those strong shoulders, and the tattoo peeking out of his v-neck—the one he got for me.

God damn, it's good to see him. He's been on tour the last four weeks. He flew in for one weekend—it was closer to a day—but we spent the rest of the time apart.

He's only been back a few days. We've spent most of that time tending to our friends' sudden plans. First, Meg and Miles decided they wanted to get married in Las Vegas. Then Kara and Drew announced a pregnancy. Now, Tom and Willow are up to something.

I love our friends—they're sweet and supportive in a way my family never has been—but I need some quality time alone with Pete.

I need a few days in our hotel room without interruptions.

And without clothes.

So I'm not sure why we're driving away from our Las Vegas hotel room. "Where are we going?"

"Any reason you ask?"

No sense in playing coy, not with Pete. "I would like to have sex with you."

He smiles. "I like when you're direct."

"I'll stoop to unzipping your jeans."

"Stoop?"

"It's tacky."

"Not complaining."

"Well, what if I went down on you?"

"Baby, is that supposed to be a threat?"

"Maybe." Now that I'm thinking semi-straight, it's not a very convincing threat. It's more an invitation.

It's a very, very appealing invitation. But I'm not nearly reckless enough to attempt it while the vehicle is moving.

"You really think I'll stop you?" he asks.

Of course he won't.

He smiles. "You're gonna make me crash poor Peeta."

He's right. It's a terrible bluff. But maybe I can convince him to park the car in some empty lot right away.

I need our bodies joining. I need my lips pressed against his and his cock buried deep inside me.

I need him. Period.

I recline my seat and look out the sunroof. It's well past sunset. The stars are starting to shine bright against the dark sky. The moon is big and silver.

My first semester of law school is done. Grades are in—somehow, I managed straight *A*s. There isn't much to worry about until Spring semester starts in January.

There's another week and a half until the band starts touring again, but Christmas and New Year's Day are in the middle of that.

I need more time for us.

A sign announces that we're leaving Las Vegas. "Where *are* we going?"

"It's a surprise."

"A good surprise?"

"You'll like it." He smiles. "I can pull off on a side street if you can't wait to get your hands around me."

God, he's not even trying and he makes it sound hot as hell.

I can wait. I don't want to wait, but I can. If I change the subject immediately. "Tom was acting cagey."

"Tom's always like that."

"Yeah, but more than normal."

"I think Willow is up to something."

"How can you tell?" She's such a sweet woman. I can't imagine her up to anything.

"Guilt's all over her face." He glances at me. "Neither of them knows how to hide their feelings."

"You say that like it's a bad thing."

He shakes his head. "They're cute."

"You miss living with him?"

"Sometimes." He plants his hand on my knee then drags his fingertips up my thigh. "Prefer my new roommate."

"Who you calling a roommate?" I grip the edge of the seat as his hand slides under my skirt. It's incredibly difficult to get anything but a moan off my lips. "Should I move into my office?"

I'm wearing tights, but I can still feel all the heat of his skin.

"That's gonna make it hard for me to live up to my promise to make you come every day." He presses his palm between my legs. "But I'll try."

"You wouldn't object?"

"Doesn't matter. You aren't going to do it." He rubs me over my tights.

"Pete," I groan. "You're going seventy miles an hour."

"You want me to stop?"

No, but— "I want to get wherever we're going alive."

He nods. Slowly, he drags his hand down my thigh and brings it back to the steering wheel.

"I won't be upset if you turn around and go straight to our hotel room." I press my knees together to calm the heat racing through my body. It not at all helpful. I'm burning with desire.

It's still hard to believe it's possible to want another person this much. To trust another person this much.

His voice is steady, deep. "You should make me feel special if you want in my pants."

"Should I?"

"Yeah."

"How about if I say, *fuck me*?"

"Saying it like that won't do shit for you."

I laugh. His directness is still refreshing. Pete isn't like anyone else I've known. He's more authentic, more honest, more caring... fuck, he's better in every conceivable way.

He's certainly more of a tease. I like teasing back, but I haven't got a clue where we're going or for how long. What if it's hours until we're alone in our hotel room?

I'm already close to pushing my tights to my knees and bringing his hand to my thigh.

The man is skilled, but I'm not sure he's skilled enough to drive and get me off at the same time.

His dark eyes are on the road. There's a smile on his lips. His loose grip on the steering wheel is effortless.

He's having fun.

I make my voice low and seductive. "Fuck me."

He chuckles. "That a command or a demonstration?"

I'm not sure. The backseat is a perfectly good location. Or the passenger seat. But not while we're speeding down the highway. "You're not going to tell me where we're going, are you?"

He shakes his head.

"How long will it take to get there?"

His eyes go to the clock. Then to the sign on the side of the road. "Another twenty minutes."

Between that, whatever it is we're doing, and the return trip, that's a long time until we'll be naked in our hotel room.

He looks so fucking hot in his tight v-neck. And the eyeliner.

God damn, I created a monster. He wears it every day now. I can barely look at him without taking off my panties.

Pete chuckles. "Jess, how many times do I have to remind you? If you're gonna have dirty thoughts about me, you should do me the decency of describing them to me."

"You're driving."

"And?"

"And I still want to get there alive."

He smiles. "I like you confident."

"You like me flushed and wanting."

"You don't?"

"I plead the fifth."

૭⊱૭

SOMEHOW, I'M EVEN MORE FLUSHED AND WANTING WHEN we pull off the freeway. We're in Henderson, a city known mostly for its proximity to Las Vegas.

What the hell are we doing here?

Pete keeps his hands on the steering wheel. He offers no clues except a mysterious smile.

We've lived together for months, but the man is still quite the enigma. I like the way he's always surprising me, but I crave a better read on his head and his heart.

After a few minutes of driving around the city streets, we pull into the parking lot of a warehouse type building. According to the sign, it's the factory for a popular chocolate brand.

What the hell?

I like chocolate as much as the next girl, but I haven't got a clue why we're at a factory well after business hours. The building doesn't even look open.

And why would I want to see inside a chocolate factory?

Pete turns the car off and unbuckles his seat belt. His eyes meet mine. He cocks a brow.

"What is that supposed to mean?" I ask.

He shrugs as if he has no idea what we're doing here.

"You're up to something."

"Not yet. But it won't take long if you make due on those threats to suck me off in the car."

How does he say it with such an even voice, like he's talking about the weather?

It still shocks me, what a filthy mind my fiancé has.

It still shocks me, the way I consider taking him up on all his offers. My eyes pass over him—from his messy black hair to his narrow waist, all the way to his all-black Converse, then back up again.

I want to take him up on his offer.

Badly.

But, for some reason, there are other people here.

I undo my seatbelt, grab my coat, and open the door. "Later."

He chuckles as he gets out of the car, locks up, and makes his way to me.

It's cold tonight. I pull my coat tighter. But that doesn't warm me up nearly as much as his arm around my waist.

His body feels so good next to mine.

I don't think I'll ever get tired of him holding me.

He leans down to press his forehead to mine. Then it's his lips.

We've kissed plenty since we've reunited—we've spent most of our free time kissing, touching, or fucking—but my lips still miss his.

Dammit, he tastes good.

When he breaks the kiss, I'm panting.

I look into his dark eyes and run my fingers over his cheeks and chin. "Can we do this all night?"

"Always."

Why did we get out of the car? We could be naked already.

A car in the parking lot turns on with a roar. Oh yeah, there's the little matter of us having an audience and me not wanting to get arrested for public indecency. That would end my career as a lawyer before it began.

I force myself to take a step backward so I won't be tempted to mount Pete. "Okay, let's do this." Whatever it is we're doing here.

"Let's." He takes my hand and leads the way around the building and through the entrance of a gated courtyard.

There are lights everywhere in every color of the rainbow. Most are white and red. They're adorning all the plants in the courtyard.

All the cacti.

It's a cacti garden. A cacti garden decorated with Christmas lights. There must be a thousand adorned plants here.

It's the best thing I've ever seen.

I squeeze Pete's hand. "I love you."

His hand isn't enough. I nearly throw myself into his arms. I press my lips to his, a peck at first then something longer, deeper.

He groans as he kisses me back.

I'm acutely aware there are other people here, but I need the affection that's pouring between us.

It's just a kiss. If people object to a couple in love kissing, that's their issue.

A Christmas cactus garden is perfect. No one else would have found this for me. No one else even notices my love of the prickly plants.

I slide my arms around his, soaking up the affection in his dark eyes. "I love you so fucking much."

"You love me or the cacti more?" He smiles, teasing.

"There are a lot of cacti and only one of you."

"That put me at an advantage or a disadvantage?"

I shrug in my best attempt at playing coy.

He runs his fingertips over my cheek. "Baby, you're going to hurt my feelings."

"No, I'm not."

His lips curl into a smile. "No, you're not."

"You know I love you more than anything else."

"Even law school?"

I nod. My voice is honest, open. It feels good not holding anything back. "Of course, I love you because I know you support me and you'd never try to come between me and school."

"Diplomatic answer."

"Am I wrong?"

He shakes his head. "Just appreciating what a shark you are already."

"I've been practicing."

"How about you practice in your pencil skirt and blouse next time?" His lips press together, his eyes filling with desire.

The look in his eyes makes me feel hot as hell.

"You like me in a suit?" I've only worn my suit around him once or twice. It's hard to believe it made much of an impression.

He nods, his eyelids heavy. "You all prim and proper? Fuck yeah."

"You want to debase the prim and proper law student?"

"You want something different?"

I shake my head.

"Fuck, the ideas I had about tearing off that blouse and pushing that skirt to your waist." His voice is low, nearly a growl.

He presses his lips to mine. Then his tongue is in my mouth and his hand is between my legs.

He presses his palm against me. Just like in the car, my tights and underwear are in the way.

My body aches for his hands. My body needs more of him, needs to make up for all this lost time.

I break our kiss. "Pete, this is a nice place."

I groan though my flimsy objection. The truth is, I like when he touches me in public. I like the way it makes me feel dirty and naughty.

He pulls back enough to look me in the eyes. "You want me to stop?"

No, I want him to go. I want him to press me against the wooden fence and fuck me until I'm screaming.

But this *is* a nice place, and there *are* people here.

I break the kiss and look into his dark eyes. "You think about anything besides sex?"

He takes my hand and leads me down the courtyard path. "Besides you?"

"And besides the bass guitar?"

He chuckles. "Don't do this to me, Jess. Don't use that tone of voice talking about the bass."

I laugh. "I did not use a tone."

"Understand if you're jealous, but I'd rather have my hands on you."

"Really?" I have no doubts about how much he enjoys touching me, but the man fucking worships that instrument.

He nods.

"I apologize to the bass guitar for any offense. I must have been jealous. It's had your hands for most of the month. I've been missing out."

He smiles. "And I'm the one who can't think of anything but sex?"

"Absolutely."

He slides his arm around my waist, pulling me closer.

The garden is amazing. I let the lights wash over me. A tall tree is decked in white. The tiny cacti that surround it are dressed in purple. A succulent is lit up in green.

The cold air can't do anything to chase the warmth from my body. It's not just the heat of desire—though God knows I can feel that. It's the warm embrace of affection and love.

It's still hard to believe it's possible to love someone like this, to trust someone like this.

He has my heart, and I trust him to take care of it.

We do three circles around the garden, walking hand in hand the entire time.

I'm shivering when we stop. I don't feel cold, but I can't deny the goosebumps on my arms and neck. I can't deny the way my shoulders are shaking like they're desperate for warmth.

Pete pulls me into a tight embrace. That helps. I'm still shaking, but now half of it is from desire.

He brings his mouth to my ear. "There's a single-stall bathroom in the lobby."

I have to laugh. He points out every bathroom where we can have sex.

"Don't tell me you aren't thinking about it." He slides his hand under my coat then under my skirt. His fingers skim the seams of my tights, sending a dizzying rush of pleasure up my spine. "I can tell you're wet even with all this fucking fabric in the way."

"I'm thinking about how you were fucking that slut in the red dress when we met."

His voice drops to something low and demanding. "When we met?"

"When I broke up your slutty bathroom sex."

"Baby, you sound judgmental."

No. Maybe. Okay, a lot. "I don't like thinking about you with other women."

He smiles. "You're jealous."

"Maybe." Definitely.

"Maybe?"

"Okay, I'm jealous. Are you satisfied?"

"Yeah. You're cute jealous." He chuckles. "Does it help that I didn't enjoy it?"

That does help. I nod.

"I don't think about anybody but you." His lips skim my neck. "Don't you want to destroy all my previous memories of bathroom sex with how fucking amazing this is?"

I laugh. "You should be the lawyer cause that's a hell of a spin."

He chuckles. "That right?"

"Yeah."

"Don't have a college degree. Can't go to law school."

"You're smarter than half the people at law school."

He kisses his way up my neck. Then his lips are on my earlobe. "That's just priorities."

"Priorities?"

"Getting you off comes first."

"Let me guess, then the bass?"

He nods. He's teasing but he's dead serious at the same time.

Again, I have to laugh. The tension that's been lingering

in my shoulders for this entire trip melts. He makes me feel easy and free.

He makes me feel alive.

For once, I'm seriously considering this bathroom sex thing.

I rise to my tiptoes so I can press my forehead to his. "You're like a comic book character sometimes."

"Which one?"

I raise a brow.

"Oh? Mr. Peter Parker?"

"Of course."

"Then, baby, let me shoot my web all over you."

I laugh. "Ew."

He teases. "You want it here." He runs his hands over my hair and cheeks and neck. "Here. Here. Here. You want to be all tangled up in my web."

I shake my head. "This is your worst seduction to date."

His voice is a playful challenge. "Is it?"

I nod.

He steps backward and takes my hand. "Then don't follow me to the lobby."

The man knows how to call a bluff.

I try to hold off enough to tease him. The sight of him is still thrilling. It's been too long.

I hate him being away. I know he lives for his music, and I'd never dream of getting between him and the band, but I fucking hate him being thousands of miles away.

I take my time soaking him in. His long bangs fall to one side of his eyes. And the eyeliner... God damn, the man belongs in eyeliner. It frames those gorgeous coffee-colored eyes, highlighting every hint of emotion in them.

Those eyes light up as he smiles. "Don't make me get started without you."

"You don't mean you'd touch yourself in the bathroom?" I bite my tongue. Of course he means that.

He nods, his smile getting wider.

Damn, he'll do it too. He'll probably take pictures in the mirror and send them to me to torture me.

As much as I'll enjoy that torture, I can't allow it. I need his body again.

He takes another step backward and raises a brow. "Last chance."

I'm only human.

Chapter Two

JESS

Six months ago, I was a normal girl with a normal life.

More accurately, I was a miserable, lonely girl who had just decided to abandon everything she was used to—her home, her family, her ex-boyfriend, her friends—to start over in Los Angeles.

But I certainly wasn't the type of girl who entertained the idea of having sex in a public bathroom.

Yes, this is a particularly nice bathroom. It's small. It's clean. It's secluded.

But it's still hard to believe I'm utterly without reservations about screwing my fiancé in a public bathroom.

The heat racing through my body collects in my core. There isn't a single part of me that wishes things went differently.

Pete turned my life upside down. He turned me upside down. But then he put everything back where it belonged.

He leans against the wall. His eyes pass over me slowly, drinking me in.

His deep voice gets rough, commanding. "You want me to fuck you, baby?"

I nod.

"Say it."

"Fuck me."

"How?"

"Put me up on the counter and fuck me until I'm going crazy that I can't scream your name."

His eyes flare with desire. I can barely believe the stuff that comes out of my mouth now.

The man is an excellent teacher.

"God damn, Jess." His hands go to my hips. He lifts me and places me on the counter.

Then he's on one knee. He unzips one of my wedge boots and pulls it off my foot. Then the other.

His dark eyes stay glued to mine as he drags his hand from my ankle to my knee, all the way to my inner thigh. The thick tights do little to dampen the heat he builds.

I need his hands on my skin.

I need him inside me.

Now.

He pushes himself up and looks me up and down. It's slower this time. He's relishing it.

His tongue slides over his lips. "Take off your tights."

It's a struggle, but I do. The things land on the floor. So much for those. He really is destructive to my undergarments, but I can't say I have any complaints.

"Take off your panties."

Fuck yes.

I slide them to my knees. They fall off my feet, landing on top of my tights.

His hands curl around my knees. The man has too much patience.

I love him in control. I love him leading.

But I can't take the teasing tonight.

I grab his t-shirt and pull him closer. Then my arms are

around his chest.

I press my lips to his and I kiss him. I kiss him like I'll never get another chance to kiss him again.

There's only a week and a half until he's back on the road.

A week and a half isn't much time together.

His hands go to my hips. They pull me closer. Closer. Close enough I can feel the erection straining against his jeans.

I groan into his mouth then my hands are in his hair. Fuck, I love his hair. It's thick and it's dark and it's just long enough to grab onto.

He pulls back to press his lips to my neck. His hands find the neckline of my dress and pull it down. I hate to lose a bra on vacation— I've only got one more with me—but I need his hands on my skin too much to care.

I use one hand to balance. I use the other to push my dress off my shoulders. The sleeves collect at my elbows. There's no way I'm going to manage to remove my bra, but that thing needs to get out of the way.

Now.

I grab onto his shoulder for balance. My eyes meet his. "A little help?"

He smiles. "And you insulted my seduction."

He unhooks my bra and pushes it off my shoulders. Then his hands are on my chest, his fingers playing with my nipples.

I tug at his t-shirt.

He watches my reactions with lust in his eyes. His thumbs brush my nipples. The touch gets harder, rougher.

I press my thighs against his hips. I can't take much more waiting. I need our bodies joining.

But this feels too good.

I let my eyelids press together. I let my hand wander over his t-shirt then under it. I press my palm against his stomach and trace the lines of his muscles all the way up his chest.

Then I blink my eyes open so I can trace the lines of his tattoo.

Real

I love him, real.

He loves me, real.

We're engaged and life is fantastic, real.

"Pete," I breathe. "Don't make me beg. Not here."

His eyes fix on mine. His breath gets heavy, needy.

"Fuck me."

"After you come on my face."

Desire races through me.

I nod a frantic yes. He presses his lips to mine for a hard, fast kiss then his lips are on my neck, my collarbone, my chest.

His mouth closes around my nipple. He flicks his tongue against it until I'm groaning then he moves to the other.

My hand slips from the counter, but I don't fall. He's already got hold of me, of my hips. He lowers himself to his knees and plants himself between my legs.

He plants a kiss on my inner thigh. Another. Another.

I press one palm into the edge of the counter to steady myself. The other goes to the back of his head.

I can feel his breath, hot, then cold, then hot again.

Then his mouth is on me. He licks me with soft, slow movements. He takes his time sucking on my lips as he makes his way to my clit.

"Fuck." I bite my tongue so I won't scream. He's good at this.

It feels as intimate as the first time, him between my legs. I spread my knees wider, opening myself to him.

His movements stay soft and slow.

Tension knots in my core. It gets tighter, tighter, so tight it hurts.

I tug at his hair. I bite my tongue to muffle my groans.

He reaches up. His fingers skim my chest, my neck, my chin. Then they're on my lips. His thumb hooks over my bottom lip as his fingers slide into my mouth.

I suck on his fingers to keep myself from screaming.

My climb is beautiful agony. Tension knots tighter and better and harder.

Then I'm there. My eyelids press together as pleasure spills through my body. The world is a dizzying shade of white, so bright and beautiful it's blinding.

There's nothing bad in the world.

Only pleasure.

My thighs press against his head as I revel in the after-shocks. Finally, I blink my eyes open. He's looking up at me with a contented expression. He's proud of himself. He should be.

But he doesn't get to stand around content. He needs to be inside me.

He wipes his mouth with the back of his hand and pushes himself to his feet. His hands curl under my knees.

His eyes fill with desire.

My hand slides to the back of his head. I pull him into a deep kiss. The taste of me on his lips only makes me more desperate to have him.

When our kiss breaks, he brings his gaze to meet mine. "Wider, baby. I want to split you in half."

I spread my legs.

He holds onto my hips as he brings his body toward mine. He's close enough I can hear every inhale and exhale. I can feel all the heat of him.

His cock strains against me.

Yes.

Now.

My eyes stay glued to his. Slowly, he slides into me. I can feel my sex straining to take every inch of him.

I can see it in his expression—he has every inch of me.

Damn, that feels good. Like I'm home. The intimacy of this, him inside me, our eyes locked, takes my breath away. Right now, I'm sure there's nothing between us.

That nothing will ever come between us. Not for long.

God, I hope I'm right.

He holds me tightly as he moves with deep, slow thrusts.

I stare back at him for as long as I can manage. The bliss building in my core is too intense. I have to close my eyes.

I have to moan his name.

He lets out a low groan.

I say it again, a little louder this time.

His lips part with another groan. His eyes meet mine. His expression is a warning and a plea at once.

I dig my hands into his hair and I pull him closer, so his cheek is against mine.

My mouth goes to his ear. I whisper, "Fuck me, Pete."

He sucks on my neck as he moves harder, deeper. I wrap my legs around his hips to keep my balance.

Damn, he feels good.

I suck on his earlobe until his groans get louder. "Harder."

"Fuck, Jess." His hands slide around my waist. He pulls me off the counter.

My feet hit the ground. Then he's turning me around so I'm pinned to the counter. I place my hands on the slick surface. My eyes find his through the reflection. He's behind me, his hands on my hips. We're both needy and panting.

We're both watching.

I arch my back, offering myself to him again.

He holds me in place as he thrusts into me.

He moves harder, faster. I reach back so I can feel his skin against my hand. My palm presses against his hip, the one with the intricate tattoo.

He only shares that with me.

I have every part of him, and he has every part of me.

I watch his expression through the mirror. His eyes fill with pleasure then they flutter closed.

His fingers dig into my hips as his breath hitches.

He's close, but he nearly always waits for me. I haven't got the faintest clue how, but he does.

His hand slides around my thigh. Then it's between my legs.

He strokes me as he fucks me.

"Pete." It's much louder than it should be, but I can't bring myself to care. Right now, I can't feel anything but bliss.

And what fucking bliss.

My sex clenches. Almost. I rock my hips to meet his movements, to press my clit against his fingers.

I soak in the sensation of him inside me, his hand on me, his breath on my skin.

Then I'm there. I bite my lip to keep from screaming as I come again. The orgasm is intense. I can feel myself pulsing around him, pulling him closer and deeper.

He presses his lips to my neck, groaning against my skin as he thrusts hard and fast.

His teeth scrape against my skin—barely enough to hurt —as his cock pulses. He's there too, groaning and thrusting through his orgasm.

When he's finished, he kisses my neck and repositions our bodies so we're face to face.

He kisses me hard and deep. "Fuck, I missed you."

"I missed you too."

Neither of us brings up that we've had days together. It still feels like we're filling some empty spot.

But right now, we're together.

Right now, the world is perfect.

Chapter Three

PETE

Jess is lying on her side, hugging a pillow to her chest. She's half-asleep, half-awake. She yawns and pulls the pillow closer. Lucky pillow is pressed against her chest.

I settle on the bed behind her. I can already feel the warmth of her body. We spent the entire night pressed together, but I still want her closer.

This whole fame thing is a mind fuck. I'm not sure it will ever get any easier.

Only a few things in my life make sense. She's the most important.

I run my hands through her long blond hair. She lets out a soft moan. Her shoulders shake. Her feet rub together.

Damn, her shoulders are tense. She shouldn't have any hint of tension left. She should be as spent as I am.

I slide my arm around her waist and pull her closer. Sex may not be the best way to fix this, but I'm more than willing to give it a shot.

I press my lips to her neck. "What's wrong, baby?"

She lets out another soft moan. Her back arches, her ass

pressing against my crotch. I love the way she moans when I call her baby. Wherever we are, whatever we're doing, it puts her under my thumb.

My hand slides over the curve of her hip. I pull her closer, holding her lush ass against my crotch. My cock stirs from the contact.

I guess I'm not spent.

Jess lets out another groan. "You're going to kill me."

"You complaining?"

She shakes her head. "I was so busy the last month that I managed to convince myself that I was okay with you being away."

"I missed you too." I don't think I've ever missed anyone the way I missed her. The next four months of touring are going to be hell.

"I guess I can thank Kara for getting knocked up." She laughs. "You guys will have to slow down."

"Might even take a year or two off."

"Really?" Her voice perks. She shakes her head. "I mean, you should do whatever works best for your life and your career."

"And gets me in our bed, at home every night?"

"If you insist."

I chuckle. She's not good at playing coy. I appreciate that she doesn't want to get in my way, but part of me wants her to beg me to stay.

Part of me wants to agree to that promise. Touring half the year is exhausting. Everything blurs together until I've got no sense of time or place.

I run my fingertips over her cheek. "You upset I'm leaving in two weeks?"

"It's only a week and a half, but no. Are you?"

"I don't being away from you."

"You'll have to visit more. Me too. I can spare a few weekends."

"Yeah?" Our last tour was international. That made it hard to visit. Jess is in school all week. It's nearly impossible to squeeze in any time when the flight is twelve hours and five time zones.

"Yeah. But that's not what's bothering me." She takes a deep breath. Her exhale is heavy enough she shakes. "My dad and sister are flying here in a few days. I don't think he should be in Vegas."

She has a point. The man is fresh out of rehab. He should be in some dry county, not in a city where people walk around with vodka slushies in guitar-shaped plastic cups.

"I'll figure that out," I say.

"How?"

Not sure yet, but— "I will. Trust me."

"I can't believe it, but I do." She plays with the edge of the sheets. "That cactus garden was amazing." Her voice lifts. It's soft, bright. "I can't remember the last time I enjoyed anything about Christmas."

"I'm glad."

Satisfaction spreads through me. I always hated Christmas with my dad. Every year was the same. He was drunk and miserable and looking for someone to take it out on. Ophelia turned all that around. It wasn't about presents. She never spoiled us. It was the way she made the day about love, family, connecting.

I want to do that for Jess. I want to replace all the pain in her life with pleasure. With joy. When she's happy, the world makes sense.

"I've hated Christmas for a long time," she says.

"Your dad?"

"Yeah. The entire holiday season was an excuse to get

trashed." Her voice drops to a whisper. "I always got caught up helping him hide it."

I rub her shoulder until she lets out a sigh of pleasure. "You don't have to take care of anybody this year."

"What about myself?"

"That's my job."

"Is it?"

I push the strap of her tank top off her shoulder. She lets out a low groan, her back arching as her ass presses against me. "Pete..."

Damn, this is going to get derailed fast. Blood rushes to my cock, but I keep my hand on her neck. We need to have this conversation.

"I thought you were worn out."

She sighs with a mix of pleasure and irritation. "You're an insufferable tease."

"You want me to stop?"

"No." She turns to face me. Her blue eyes fix on mine. "Never."

I brush her hair behind her ear. "I'll take care of everything with your family."

"Like telling them to stay in New York?"

"If that's what you want." It's not. As much as her dad and sister hurt her, Jess still loves them, still misses them.

She shakes her head. "Why are we staying in Vegas for all this? The wedding is over. We could go back to our place in Venice Beach and soak in the sun." She sticks her tongue out. "I hate Vegas."

"Of course you do."

"Everything smells like smoke and people drink on the streets." She raises a brow as she makes eye contact. "What about it is good?"

"Shows."

"Which shows?"

"*The Thunder from Down Under*? Don't you want to see hot Australian guys strip to nothing?"

She laughs. It lights up her bright blue eyes so they shine the way her hair does. It's nearly white-blond now. I was never into the platinum blond thing before, but with Jess's light features, the nearly white hair is angelic.

She is my angel. Last I checked, angels are naked. I should get her naked right away.

She shakes her head. "You're thinking about sex."

I grab her ass and bring her closer, so her crotch presses against my erection. "What gave it away?"

She groans then bites her lip, considering it. Finally, she shakes her head, clearing her throat. "I'll be too chafed for tomorrow."

I chuckle. When we met, she was shy about sex. Now, she's direct, blunt even. "If you're not into Australian guys, we can get tickets for Chippendale's."

"If you'll go with me."

"That a bluff?" She must know I'll do it.

She holds strong, shaking her head. "No..."

It *is* a bluff. She should know better.

I roll over to grab my cell off the bedside table. "You free tomorrow night?"

"Pete!"

Can't see too well without my glasses or contacts. I have to squint to make out my cell screen. Still, it only takes a minute to get tickets on my phone. "VIP tickets. Best in the house. We can meet the performers after the show."

Her cheeks turn red. She hides behind her palms. "You have no shame."

"True."

"I'd rather you do the striptease."

"Won't last very long. Only wearing these." I bring her hand to the edge of my boxers.

She slides her hand below my waist, cupping my cock over the fabric. Fuck, that feels good. I need her now.

Her voice is heavy, breathy. "I had a point, but it's slipping from my mind."

Me too. But what the fuck was it?

She slides her hand to my thigh. It only draws more blood to my cock. My skin burns from her touch.

I need her hands on my skin. Need my hands on her skin. *That* makes more sense than anything else. Even playing bass guitar.

She slides her other hand around my neck. Her forehead presses against mine. Her voice is low, sweet. "I wish we could fly to an island in the sun until the tour started. Just the two of us, swimming and sunbathing."

"Nude?"

"Of course." She pulls away enough to look me in the eyes. "We never got to explore Hawaii together."

"Say the word and I'll buy tickets for tomorrow."

She shakes her head. "We're stuck with my family."

"There's a whole week between Christmas and the start of the tour."

She bites her lip, considering it. "You always take care of me."

"Of course."

"What do you get out of that?"

My brow furrows. What kind of question is that?

Does she really doubt my feelings for her?

I try to shrug it off, but my shoulders stay tense. I can deal with a lot of shit, but her doubting my affection is not on the list.

Her blue eyes bore into me. There's no accusation in them. Her expression is earnest.

Okay. Words aren't my strong suit, but I'll answer the best

I can. "Makes me feel good. Don't you like taking care of me?"

She nods. "You rarely let me." She drags her fingertips over my chest until they get to my tattoo. "You're stronger than I am."

"It's strength that you can admit things hurt you, that they're hard for you." I slide my hand around her neck, cupping the back of her head. "I was broken before I met you. You stitched my heart back together."

"Really?"

"Yeah."

It's hard to wrap my head around my high school sweetheart and my best friend fucking each other behind my back. Hard to feel like I'm not lacking in some way.

But Jess erases all that. She erases all the fame bullshit. She erases that sense I get on the road—that there's nowhere I belong.

When I'm with her, everything makes sense. I don't doubt myself. I don't give a fuck about our surroundings.

I belong with her, wherever she is.

"I can't remember the last time things felt this normal." I press my lips to hers. She tastes good. And the way she moans into my mouth and squirms against me—that's fucking normal.

When I'm with her, I don't have to put on airs, don't have to have my guard up.

I can finally breathe.

She pulls back with a deep, low sigh. "Having sex in the bathroom at a cactus holiday garden is normal?"

I nod.

She laughs.

I see her point. Maybe we're freaks, but in a great fucking way.

Before Jess, I had resigned myself to only feeling whole

when I played. It wasn't the worst thing in the world. I spent half of my waking hours playing music. Spent enough of the rest working out or reading that I stayed busy.

Her eyes meet mine. "You know, for once, you look like you're thinking about something besides sex." She drags her fingertips over my chest. "This is a rare moment."

I laugh. "It is."

"Want to share?"

I run my fingers through her hair. "The last time I felt like this, like I belonged somewhere, was when I stepped on stage for the first time."

Her eyes brighten. "Yeah?"

I nod.

"You're too sweet."

"Should I say something dirty?"

She laughs. "I'll never say no to that."

I bring my mouth to her ear. "You want to come on my hand or my cock?"

She lets out a needy sigh. "Your cock."

Not gonna leave the woman wanting.

⚜

THE WEIGHT ON THE BED SHIFTS. THE COVERS PULL TO ONE side. Then there's light streaming through the window.

Fuck, I can barely see anything without my glasses. I never get used to waking up nearly blind.

Jess is sitting on the other side of the bed. She stretches her arms over her head in an adorable yawn.

I move close enough to slide my hand under her tank-top.

She shudders with pleasure. Her voice is a low murmur. "My alarm is going."

There *is* the faint sound of some Amy Winehouse song. It's far away, not much of an alarm. Could swear she uses something else as her alarm tone, but it's too early for me to put those pieces together.

I try to check the clock on the bedside table, but the neon green numbers are a blur. Squinting does nothing to help matters.

"It's eight thirty," she says.

"That's early." I tug at her tank top. "Come back to bed. Want to get an early start on my goals today."

"I'm a goal?" Her voice is incredulous.

"I make you come every day."

"And that's an obligation?"

Not sure if she's teasing or serious. Either way, I need to set the record straight. I push myself up so I can press my lips to her shoulder. "Fuck no. It's a privilege."

She lets out a low moan. She's considering it. She only needs one more nudge to be convinced.

"It's my favorite part of the day." I suck on her skin as I trace the neckline of her tank top.

Her groan is low and deep. She arches her back, pressing her chest into my hands.

She wants me.

No, she needs me.

But the damn phone rings again.

She sighs as she breaks my touch. "I should get that. It might be Ophelia."

"We're not meeting her until ten."

"It might be Dad or Madison. Who else would call this close to Christmas?"

She's got a point. Still, I want her naked on top of me. Still, I want her coming on my hand.

It felt like a part of me was missing this last month. I need to remember what it feels like to be whole.

Jess answers the call with a nervous, "Hello."

I throw her an inquisitive look and grab my glasses so I

can study the expression on her face. She's frowning, but when she catches me staring, she waves me away.

I don't like her frowning, but I know better than to pry when she wants space. I make use of the time doing my usual morning routine. When I go back to the main room, she's done with the call.

Her blue eyes are hazy with frustration.

Something is wrong.

Something bad.

She nods hello then her eyes go to the floor. "Excuse me. I should brush my teeth." She pushes past me to step into the bathroom.

What the hell?

She doesn't hide things from me. Not anymore. I'm sure as hell not going to let her deal with this, whatever it is, on her own.

It takes a few minutes for her to step out of the bathroom. She has that same miserable look on her face. I'm going to wipe it off, whatever it takes. The way her shorts hug her hips encourages *one* method, but I do have other tools in my arsenal.

I rub her shoulders. "What happened, baby?"

Her chest heaves as she takes a deep breath. Her gaze goes to the floor. "I can't believe it."

"What?"

"I lost my scholarship."

Her brows are knit with frustration. She looks like she's going to break. But why? There's an easy solution for this.

"I'll pay your tuition," I say.

She takes a step backward. "No."

What the fuck does she mean, *no*? We're partners. It's our money.

Jess crosses her arms over her chest. "Don't look at me like that."

"Like what?"

"Like I kicked a puppy. You're not paying my tuition."

"You're right. I'm not paying your tuition. *We're* paying your tuition."

She presses her lips together. Her blue eyes get intense. "I appreciate how generous you are—"

"This isn't fucking generosity. That money is *ours*. Everything we have is ours."

She looks down at her engagement ring. "I want to feel self-reliant." Her frustrated expression softens. "It's important to me to feel self-reliant. I know you understand that."

Yeah, I do. But it's important to me to get as much of Jess as I can. If she takes on a part-time job, I'll get less of her. If she's got loans weighing on her mind, I'll get less of her.

Whatever she decides, I'll get less of her.

It's *our* money.

This is ridiculous.

"If we were married, would you let me pay your tuition?" I ask.

She looks at me carefully, judging my intentions. She rolls her shoulders back. She shifts her weight between her legs. "I suppose I would."

"Then marry me in Vegas. This week. Fuck, we can do it today."

She looks at me like I'm crazy.

"Come on, baby. Marry me here. Marry me now."

Chapter Four

PETE

J ess's brow furrows. She stares through me. "No."

No? Uh-uh. I'm not accepting that answer.

"I'm not marrying you so you can get your way."

"We're engaged."

"No, Pete." She folds her arms. "I still have my scholarship from the school. I only need to come up with a quarter of my tuition. And I'm coming up with it myself."

"Fuck the tuition. Marry me here."

She blinks. Her face screws with frustration. "What?"

All of a sudden, it's obvious. I don't want to wait any longer for us to start our lives together. Sure, she's mine now. I'm hers now.

But us being husband and wife...

Fuck, that would be amazing.

"Take the fucking money for the tuition. I'll still want to marry you now," I say. "You're what makes sense, Jess. I want to know this is forever."

Her brow softens. "I love you, Pete. But you need to stop pushing me about this."

"It's our money."

"That you earned."

"And when we get married and your law firm makes ten million a year, will that be all your money?"

"No. Of course not..." She looks at the ground. "I... I want to feel self-reliant. It's important to me."

I swallow hard. There's still a lot of frustration on her face. Pushing her won't help either of us.

My fingers curl. Not quite fists but halfway there. I respect that she wants to be self-reliant, I do, but she needs to understand that it's not about getting my way.

I need to help her.

She needs to understand that I want to marry her because I love her.

I plant on the bed and press my palms against my thighs. My hands are itching to play or to get her off—the two things they do well. "I hate seeing anything in the way of your success."

"I'll get a loan. Or a job."

"No."

She folds her arms. Her eyes flare with frustration. "What the fuck do you mean, *no?*"

Shit. She's pissed. Hard to blame her, but it's not like that.

I meet her gaze. "I can't stand seeing you any less than I do now."

Her expression softens. "That's a sweet reason for being controlling."

"I'm not controlling."

"Would you prefer pushy?"

"Fine." Can't exactly deny that. "But you're being stubborn."

She raises a brow. Her expression shifts so it's half-frustrated, half-playful. "*I'm* being stubborn?"

I nod.

"It happened two minutes ago. Give me some time to figure it out before you swoop in to save the day."

I pat my lap.

She presses her lips together. "Is that a good idea?"

"Want to hold you right now."

Her eyes light up. There's still a heaviness to her expression. She's still frustrated.

But she does come closer.

She does sit on my lap.

I wrap my arms around her as I look up at her. "If we get married today, we can go on our honeymoon tomorrow. We can have our week on the beach."

Her tongue slides over her lips. "You're very convincing when you want something."

I slide my hand behind her neck. "Baby, I'm not trying to manipulate you. There's a problem. I have a solution. Money isn't good for much beyond comfort and fixing problems."

I lean in to kiss her.

She groans, her lips parting for my tongue, her hands going to my shoulders. When she pulls back, she stares into my eyes.

Her fingertips skim my cheek. "I appreciate that you want to help, but I want to figure this out on my own."

"I still want to marry you, even if you refuse to use our money to pay your tuition."

"We're engaged. What's the rush?"

She must feel it too. She must feel that ache for more. However much of her I have, I always want more. "I want the world to know you're mine."

Her expression softens. "You've gotten very possessive."

"You like it."

"I admit nothing."

"It's embarrassing begging my fiancée to marry me."

She smiles. Her voice lifts. "You can beg much better than this."

True. My hands go to her hips. One sides around her thigh, between her legs. "This how I should start?"

"Aren't we meeting your mom?"

"In an hour."

She looks down at me. "I don't want to rush our wedding. We're always squeezing things into breaks in our schedules. Not this."

I *will* convince her. Today. Tomorrow at the latest.

I want to respect her decisions, her independence, but I'm going to take care of her.

I press my palm against her. "You need to come on my hand."

She looks at me a little funny, unsure of my motives.

Uh-uh. Can't take any more uncertainty. Can't take any more space between us.

I slide my fingers into her shorts and rub her over her panties. My lips go to her neck. I kiss my way to her ear then I suck on her earlobe.

She groans. All that frustration on her face melts. The tension in her shoulders melts.

"Take off your clothes, baby. All of them."

"Pete, I..."

"I want to make you come. There's no ulterior motive. You want to come on my hand?"

She bites her lip. "Yes."

"Then take off your fucking clothes. Now."

She holds my gaze for a moment. She's not convinced yet.

I drag my fingertips over her thigh. I press my palm into her lower back and pull her into a deep kiss.

She kisses back. Softly at first. Then harder. Then her tongue is in my mouth. Her hands are digging into my shoulders.

She groans as she pulls her tank top over her head and pushes her shorts over her wide hips.

God damn, I love those hips. I love the way they feel against mine. I love the way they feel in my hands.

I help her push her shorts to her feet. Then they're gone.

She wraps her arms around my shoulders as she straddles me.

She's in my lap wearing nothing but her glasses.

This is exactly where we both need to be. Why can't she see how much I can help?

If we get married today, we can do nothing but this for the next week and a half.

I have to think of a way to convince her.

After this.

Usually, I tease her until she's begging me to stop. Not today. Today, I need to feel her against my hand. I need her eyes locked on mine as she screams my name again and again.

I kiss her hard. I love the softness of her skin, the way she groans into my mouth as my fingers get closer.

She digs her hands into my hair, holding my head against hers. She needs this release.

She needs *me*.

I brush my fingers against her as softly as I can. She shudders. I do it again and again.

Each time, she shakes a little harder, kisses a little deeper.

When my thumb brushes against her clit, she breaks free of the kiss to groan.

Her eyes bore into mine. Her expression is needy. "Please."

Fuck yes. I stare into her blue eyes as I rub her.

She lets out another groan. One of her hands tugs at my hair. The other sinks into my shoulder. It feels fucking amazing, her hand on my bare skin. The look of pleasure on her face feels better. Fuck, that feels better than anything.

I rub her a little harder, a little faster. She holds my gaze as her eyes fill with pleasure. The bliss is all over her face—in the way her eyebrows relax, the way her eyes get heavy, the way her teeth sink into her lip.

"Pete." She tugs at my hair.

"Louder."

She's too busy groaning to get out a word. She lets out incomprehensible grunts. Then her fingers dig into my skin and she screams my name.

God damn, I love the way my name sounds on her lips.

I rub her harder. "Louder, baby."

"Pete," she groans. "Please don't stop."

Never. I bring my free hand to her chest. I play with her nipples as I stroke her.

Her eyes press together. There's beautiful agony all over her face. I steady my speed so I can soak in every second of it.

She screams my name again and again as she comes. The way it falls off her lips makes it hard to stay in control. Makes it hard to do anything but pin her to the bed and drive my cock deep inside her.

Her eyes blink open then they're on mine. She doesn't say anything, just presses her lips to mine.

Right now, she's mine.

I need more of that. I need her mine forever.

Chapter Five

PETE

M om is sitting at a roomy booth, her attention on
her cellphone. When she puts it away, she
shoots us a knowing look.

I shrug. Not like I can put anything past her.

Jess blushes. She tries to play cool, but she runs her words
together. "Good morning, Ophelia. Did you have a nice
night?"

Mom smiles at Jess then she shoots me an equally
knowing look. *Such a sweet girl. What is she doing with someone as
depraved as you?*

Jess hasn't quite figured out how much my mom likes to
sleep around. I can't say that I think about it often, but she
likes to remind me and Tom every chance she gets.

She thinks it's funny to make us blush.

"What?" Jess looks at me. "What are you two signaling
telepathically?"

"Nothing, sweetheart. You don't need to hear the details
of my night." Ophelia picks up her menu. "It was the usual.
Went to a bar, met a woman, took her home."

"Oh." Jess blushes. "I thought you were seeing someone."

Ophelia shakes her head. "No, I'm afraid I've never wanted to settle down." She folds her menu and sets it aside. "Peter and Tom are all the commitment I need."

"I'm twenty-three," I say. "He's twenty-five now. I'm not sure you can play the single-mother card anymore."

"Yet, you still need your mother's advice constantly." Ophelia shakes her head in mock outrage. She looks to Jess. "Is he this stubborn with you?"

"Much worse." Jess looks to me then to Mom. "But he's very handsome, so I put up with it."

Mom laughs. "A woman after my own heart."

I clear my throat.

Mom lets out a deeper laugh. "Are you really jealous, sweetheart? I don't think anyone could steal Jess from you."

Fuck, am I jealous? Mom *could* steal just about any remotely bi-curious woman. But it's not like I ever doubt Jess's commitment or devotion.

I don't think about my ex too often anymore, but I do think about what happened, especially when I'm on the road. She and Kyle made it sound like their sordid affair was the inevitable result of the distance.

It was an excuse, but sometimes, I can't help but wonder if there's some truth to it.

Will Jess get tired of the distance? Of the fame bullshit?

Whatever happens, I'm not losing her.

I squeeze her hand. The way she squeezes back sends those doubts running for the hills.

"Why is it the two of you look distressed?" Ophelia asks. "When it's so obvious you just had sex."

Jess turns bright red.

I blush too.

Ophelia chuckles, amused. The three of us are silent until the server comes to take our orders. It's the usual breakfast stuff— eggs, toast, bacon, coffee.

Jess looks from Ophelia to me. "I guess I can see where you got your dirty mind."

"Me, dirty? Where did you get that idea?"

She shakes her head. "No one is believing that."

"It's true," Ophelia says. "You can protest better than that, Peter."

I chuckle. I used to hate it when she called me Peter. It was what my dad called me. But after ten years, it feels like home.

I take in Jess's expression. She's still a little awkward about Mom's sex comments, but she's smiling.

The server drops off our coffee. Jess fixes hers with plenty of cream and sugar and takes a long sip. She sighs with pleasure.

This is my chance. Not sure it will work, but I'm willing to try it.

I take a sip of my black coffee. Not great, but not bad. "Jess and I were talking about getting married while we're here."

"*We* were talking about that?" Jess raises a brow.

"Okay, I was talking about it," I say.

Mom cuts in. "What's the rush? Let your poor girlfriend—"

"Fiancée," I correct.

"Let your poor fiancée enjoy her life for a while. You're only twenty-three. Why do you need to get married this week?"

It's hard to explain. I need everything with Jess. I need it now.

I need to convince her, but this isn't the fucking way to do it.

I run my hand through my hair. "I'm sorry, baby. Don't mean any harm. Just want you to be my wife now."

Her gaze goes to her engagement ring then it's back to my

353

eyes. "I'll think about it. But only if you agree to table the conversation for the rest of the day."

I can live with that deal. I nod.

"You swear? You bring it up once, and I'm going to flip." She pulls her long hair behind her back.

"Cross my heart and hope to die," I say.

She looks at me sideways. "I still can't decide if you're being sweet or pushy." She slides out of the booth. "Excuse me. Ladies' room."

I watch her walk away. The way her hips sway as she struts is fucking captivating.

Ophelia waits until Jess is out of earshot. "What is wrong with you?"

"What?" It's not a crime gawking at your fiancée. It would be wrong not staring at Jess's perfect ass.

"You know more about women than this." Ophelia takes a long sip of her coffee. She shakes her head with disapproval. "The woman is clearly mad for you. What's the rush?"

"You'd understand if you'd ever wanted something serious," I say.

"You've known her what, four months?"

"About that."

"Give it a year."

"Tom didn't."

Ophelia shakes her head. "You're not a follower, Peter. You never have been. Don't try to pin this on your brother."

Can't argue with that.

"You keep pushing her and you'll push her away."

"She lost her scholarship. She doesn't want me to pay."

"So you marry her?" She lets out a chuckle. "I guess that is one way to solve the problem."

"I do want to marry her."

I'm not like Tom, Miles, or Drew. I never saw the appeal of casual hook-ups. Don't get me wrong—I still tried to fuck my way out of my misery, but I always knew, deep down, that it would feel empty. I've always wanted forever. But Cindy cheating—that fucked everything up.

I always knew, deep down, that Cindy and I weren't forever. When I tried to imagine a life together, some part was missing. With Jess, everything is clear. I can see us in that house on the beach in ten years. I can see her getting home from a long day in court, tired and achy, and me throwing her on the kitchen table, pulling her panties to her feet, and planting my head between her legs.

I can see us traveling every place in the world together, collapsing in our hotel room at night, peeling each other's clothes off before bed.

A lot of what I see is sex, sure, but there's more too. I see her walking at graduation. I see her squealing over her first job, her first win in court, her first law firm of her own.

I see a future for us.

I want her as my wife.

Ophelia clears her throat. "You really want to get married now?"

I nod.

"Then you need to convince her you want marriage, that you're not doing this to trick her into getting your way."

I know that much. The tricky part is the how.

Jess struts back into the restaurant. Sometimes, I get lost staring at her. Not sure which part of her I like the best—the angelic hair, the clear blue eyes, the librarian glasses, the narrow curve of her waist, the round flare of her hips, or the lush ass.

It's got to be the tattoo on her back. The one she got for me. *Real or Not Real.*

We both know this is real.

Just need to make sure the world knows it's forever.

She slides into the booth next to me and presses her forehead to mine. "Talk about me at all?"

"Mostly, Mom was telling me I was being an idiot," I whisper.

"She's a smart woman."

I nod. "Yeah, she is."

Jess looks up at me. "I do want to marry you. But I'm not sure I want to marry you in Vegas this week."

I press my pointer finger to my lip in the *shhShh* gesture. "Promised someone I'd table that conversation."

Her lips curl into a smile. "True." She leans back to a *Mom is watching us* appropriate distance. Her gaze meets Ophelia's. "Thanks for talking some sense into him."

"Sweetheart, nobody can get through that gorgeous head of his. But I did try."

Jess smiles. "That's all I can ask."

⚜

WE SPEND THE AFTERNOON AT A NEARBY AQUARIUM. WE spend the evening walking the fake Parisian streets and eating scallops and steak—and plenty of vegetables for Jess-at a secluded French restaurant.

After dinner, we take a tour of the fake Eiffel Tower. It's cold enough and quiet enough—not many people are in Las Vegas half a week before Christmas—that we have the tiny metal vista point to ourselves.

She squeezes my hands, taking in the view with delight in her eyes. The Strip is a dizzying mix of neon. The mountains to the west are low against the horizon. It's too bright to make out any stars, but the big silver moon hangs low in the desert sky.

This city is a real wealth of sensation. I wouldn't mind a week and a half on a quiet island with Jess. For a rock star,

I'm not big on the whole sleep all day, party all night thing. I'd rather spend my time reading or practicing or making Jess come.

Especially making Jess come.

I let the sights and sounds of the day wash over me as I hold her close. Must have seen a million things, a million people, a million signs.

One stands out.

It's perfect.

It's enough to convince her.

Chapter Six

JESS

✣

We wake at an ungodly hour—it's so early the sky is still lit by neon rather than by the sun—eat breakfast in our hotel room, and take a cab to the Stratosphere Hotel.

Pete tries to play coy. Well, my fiancé pulls off mysterious well. He very much succeeds at playing coy. Still, I get the feeling there's something up his sleeve.

The horrifying hour of the day gives it away. No normal person would awake before eight A.M., especially in Sin City.

Thankfully, the early hour means the casino is quiet. Well, quiet by casino standards.

We're here for the main attraction—the viewpoint at the top of the hotel's hundred-something-story tower. I have to admit, it will be nice watching the sun rise over the desert. It would be nicer watching the sun rise from our hotel room, especially if we were naked in bed—

Dammit, when did I become such a sex-crazed maniac? Before Pete, I thought about sex a few times a day. Like a normal person. My ex, Nathan, wasn't exactly Casanova, but it was pleasant enough. Occasionally, I craved it. But now, I can't get enough of it.

No, that's not right.

I can't get enough of Pete.

There's no line for the observation tower at this time of day. But there is someone else in the clean, white elevator. He's wearing a bright blue hotel vest emblazoned with the hotel's name. He looks at Pete with recognition in his eyes, but he speaks only about the history of the tower and the city.

I absorb nothing. It's much too early for history. I rest my head against Pete's chest and soak in the feeling of his arms around mine. We don't have enough time together. I need every second of it. I need every ounce of him.

My ears pop three times during our ascent. I take a deep breath and swallow hard. There. That's better.

The elevator stops at the floor for the observation deck.

Pete squeezes my hand. His palm is usually cool and steady. Right now, it's not.

He's sweating.

He presses his lips together and shifts his weight between his feet.

He's nervous.

Why?

He looks at me with an utterly inscrutable expression. "You ready?"

"Ready for coffee." I smile. "But the view should be nice too."

"There's a rollercoaster. You want to look down 100 floors?" he asks.

"One hundred and eight floors," the elevator guy corrects. "There's also a slingshot ride at the very top of the tower. You get a 360-view of the strip. We have a great all-inclusive package. You can purchase it at the gift shop."

Pete smiles at me. "What do you say, baby? You want extra thrills today?"

It's too early in the morning for thrills. "I'll think about it."

There's a lightness to his expression, but there's no mistaking the nervous energy in his eyes. He shoves his hand into his pocket, takes it out, tries his back pocket, takes it out.

Has he ever been this nervous?

I don't think so.

What the hell is he up to? And why is he up to it this early in the morning?

The elevator boy is looking at us expectantly. Okay, we've been standing here for long enough. I squeeze Pete's hand and lead him onto the observation deck. Half of it is inside. The other half is outside the glass doors.

The view of the city is gorgeous. The sky is a soft shade of blue. The sunrise casts orange over half the sky. The other half is bright with the neon lights of the casinos.

This early, there are only about half-dozen people here— a few tipsy frat boys laughing over tchotchkes in the gift shop and a family of tourists in matching *Las Vegas, Nevada* t-shirts.

At first, Pete's whole *we're normal* thing didn't make any sense. Normal people don't swoon over cactus holiday gardens. They certainly don't have sex in public bathrooms at cactus holiday gardens.

But right now, this feels normal. A very Las Vegas kind of normal. We're up high enough that nothing else can get to us. No one— not family or friends or fans—knows where we are.

The world is ours.

There's some brave soul on the observation deck. It looks cold out there. But the guy is wearing something warm. A coat. No, a cape.

A white, studded cape.

He turns, and everything shifts into focus. He's an Elvis impersonator. Huh? That's strange, but in a *totally normal for Las Vegas* kind of way.

Pete slides his arm around my waist. "You want to say hello to The King?"

Uh... Why not? "Sure."

Pete chuckles, but there's something different about it. He's still nervous.

I study his expression. He's actually blushing. My goodness, is it hard to do anything but stare at his flushed cheeks. I nearly walk into the glass door.

Deep breath. I can ogle my fiancé later. Say when we aren't a few thousand feet above ground.

He pulls the door open for me. "After you." His voice is confident, but that nervousness is still there.

I force myself to focus on my footsteps. It's cold out here. Really cold. That's one way to wake up. Goosebumps spread over my neck. My eyes nearly burst open.

The Elvis impersonator looks to us. "Hello, Little Lady. Are you Miss Jessica James?"

What the hell? I look to Pete for a clue, but his expression gives nothing away.

"Yes, I am." I cinch my coat tighter.

Elvis looks to Pete. "And are you Mr. Peter Steele?"

"I am." Pete smiles.

"Just call me The King." The man is doing his best impersonation of Elvis Presley's exaggerated drawl. "Now, I hear the two of ya'll are getting married right here, right now."

What? "We are?"

Pete nods. "It's not legally binding."

Okay...

Elvis steps in. "It's our 'I Was Just Kidding' package. You get the entire ceremony without any of the legality."

I Was Just Kidding Package? God, Vegas is a weird place. But that does sound familiar. I could swear I read a few signs on casino wedding chapels—marriage was on my mind all day yesterday—that offered some version of a just for fun ceremony.

Because everyone associates weddings with fun and not with stress and family drama.

"You can back out." Pete slides his arms around my waist. "But I want to show you how special this can be, even if it's the two of us, and Elvis, in our jeans at the crack of dawn. What matters isn't the decorations or the venue. It's the two of us promising each other forever."

My heart threatens to melt. His words are sweet and his voice is earnest.

I know he loves me, that he wants to marry me. But I'm still not entirely convinced of his motives here.

He's used to getting his way.

Still, I'll play along. It sounds sweet. I nod. "Okay. I'm willing to try."

The King guides us into position. Of course, he's the offi- ciant. "Alright, darling, it's real cold out here. So I'll make this quick. We're gathered here at the top of the Stratosphere to celebrate a really beautiful love. Now, I hear ya wrote your own vows."

Pete nods.

"But I... I didn't know." I shake my head. This is ridicu- lous. We're having an impromptu fake wedding. Of course I don't have vows.

"You can wing it, baby." He squeezes my hand.

Okay, I can do that.

My lips curl into a smile. I love how ridiculous this is. I love that he's trying to show me what he feels for me rather than trying to convince me he's right.

It feels like the sky is lighter already. It's a softer shade of blue. It's more streaked with orange.

The wind howls. It *is* cold. Just like at the cactus garden, I can barely feel the chill of the air. I'm too overwhelmed by the warmth of his love for me.

I take back anything I said about us being normal.

My fiancé is not a normal man. But I love him even more for what a weirdo he is.

Pete stares into my eyes. Already, he's blushing. "I'm not an eloquent guy. Even when I write a song, the words are simple. I don't know how to make words into something beautiful. The best I can do is speak from my heart."

His gaze goes to the sky as his cheeks get pinker.

Damn, he's never this shy. Ever. It's incredibly endearing.

He lets out a nervous laugh then his eyes are back to mine. "I was broken when I met you. I didn't know what I wanted. I didn't know how to turn the world into a place that made sense. It used to be that I could pick up my bass and everything would click into place. But that had stopped. For the first time, I didn't know where I belonged. I didn't know what I wanted. The first time I made you smile, I knew what I wanted. I wanted more of your smile. I wanted more of your laugh. I wanted more of your satisfaction, every fucking kind of satisfaction. I didn't ever want to fall in love again. But you stole my heart. Now I can't think of anything I want more than knowing you're mine forever."

My heart does melt. I'm warm everywhere.

His eyes bore into mine. "I guess that's a really selfish vow, but it's true. I want to spend my life making you happy. I'm going to spend my life making you happy, whatever it takes."

He's blushing still, but his eyes aren't nervous anymore. They're filled with a delicious mix of excitement and enthusiasm.

My heart is beating so fast I can't keep up.

His words wash over me. He *is* eloquent. Maybe it's not a

typical, MFA in poetry kind of eloquence, but the rawness of his words is beautiful.

I squeeze his hand. "I don't know how to follow that."

He smiles. "Usually, I let you go first."

Nerves flee my body as I laugh. Of course he's making a sex joke at a time like this.

Of course I'm laughing off the tension in my shoulders.

He always puts me at ease.

Okay, I'm winging this. I can do that. I take a deep breath as I collect my thoughts. "I remember thinking that I'd never met anyone like you. Now, I'm sure there isn't anyone in the world like you. There's no one else who can make me laugh the way you do."

I build up my courage to force myself to look into his dark eyes.

"There's no one else who can make me come the way you do."

My cheeks burn, but I press on. I want to get everything I'm feeling out. He needs to know how much I love him.

"There's no one else who makes me feel easy and free. I'm not sure what my life is going to hold, but I know I always want a place for you in it. I want to fall asleep with you every night and wake up with you every morning. I want to do whatever it takes to hear your laugh in my ears. You make me stronger, and better, and I want to repay the favor every day for the rest of my life."

"Baby." He slides his arms around my waist. He moves closer. Then his lips are on mine.

My hands dig into his hair as I kiss him back.

Elvis objects, mumbling something about how we aren't at that part yet, but neither of us listens.

Every inch of me is on fire. He was right. The venue doesn't matter. The decorations don't matter. What matters is the two of us promising each other the world.

He's already given me the world.

I really do hope I can repay the favor.

When our kiss breaks, I'm panting. The sky *is* brighter now. The clouds glow with orange light.

"Usually, we wait to exchange rings and say I do," Elvis says. "But I can tell the two of you are ready to kiss some more."

Yes, we are. I nearly jump into Pete's arms, and I kiss him like the ship is going down.

His words are still washing over me.

Every part of me melts as he kisses me. When we're finished, I'm a puddle. I'm mush.

He looks into my eyes. His fingers skim my cheek. "What do you think?"

I nod. "Let's do it here. For real." My gaze goes to the Christmas lights strung up inside the deck. I hadn't noticed them before. "On Christmas."

"There's a private balcony a few floors down."

My smile gets wider. "Perfect."

"Let me take care of everything."

"Except the dress."

He nods. "Except the dress."

My heart is soaring. We're really getting married. It's really going to happen. And it's only a few days away.

I look up at him. "You mean all that?"

"Every word."

I tug at his t-shirt. It's much too early—and this is much too romantic—for my inhibitions to get in the way of words spilling from my lips. "I need you to fuck me. Somewhere I can scream your name as loudly as I want."

He slides his arm around my waist. "I have an idea. If you're game."

"Yeah?"

"I want to tie you up again."

The flush in my cheeks spreads all the way to my chest. "Oh."

"Want to force you to take all the pleasure I want to give you."

Well, when he says it like that.

I nod. "Hell yes."

Chapter Seven

JESS

❦

The cab is crawling. The odometer reads *twenty-five miles per hour*, but that must be wrong. It must be the angle.

I need to be in our hotel room, in our bed, right away. My knees knock together. My feet tap the floor. My wedge boots are heavy enough that each tap is more of a thud. I make a note to myself to buy a nicer, lighter pair of boots, but it flies right out of my brain.

My brain is screaming *I need to be tied to his bed now*. Though it's not really his bed. It's not even our bed. It's the hotel bed.

Somehow, that makes it hotter, dirtier.

I'm always at his mercy, always under his command, but making it actual and physical—it's more than hot as hell. It's freeing, captivating, and intense.

Pete chuckles. "You ready for something?"

A pang of desire shoots straight to my core. I open my mouth to speak but words refuse to form.

Thoughts swirl around my head. There's a lot to consider. A wedding, even a straightforward wedding at a venue that does ten weddings a day, means decisions and stress. My family is arriving in two days. Then it's Christmas Eve. Then Christmas.

I said Christmas, that we'd get married on Christmas.

That's only four days away.

In four days, I'll be a married woman.

It's a good thing—hell, it's a great thing—but it's quite the change.

My life has changed a lot in the last year. Most of it has been for the better, but it gets exhausting keeping up. I need a break from everything swirling around my head.

Pete rubs my shoulder. "What are you thinking, baby?"

"That I'd like a break from thinking."

He smiles. "Lines up with my plans for the rest of the day."

Uh... I'm already forgetting how to think anything but *yes, please, now*. My body is on fire with want. It's difficult to get words out. "All day?"

He leans in to whisper. "I'm going to make you come until you beg me to stop."

I nod. Yes, that's quite a plan. He really does have shit under control.

He presses his lips to my neck. It's soft then it's harder. "I want you relaxed today." He sucks on my earlobe. "And we both know I always get what I want."

He does.

My thoughts turn to dust as he presses his palm against me. He rubs me over my jeans, groaning lightly as he nibbles on my ear.

We're in the back of a cab. The driver can glance in the rearview mirror to watch.

The exhibition of it sends a thrill to my core. My lips part with a sigh of pleasure. This already feels good enough to chase away my thoughts.

I soak in the movements of his hands and lips for the rest of the ride. Then we're at the hotel. He takes his time shifting away from me. His dark eyes are filled with desire. There's something else too, something commanding.

He undoes my seatbelt and opens the door for me.

I'm in a daze of lust as he slides his arm around my waist and leads me through the hotel lobby.

This time of day, the elevator bank is quiet. He leads me onto an available—and mercifully, empty—elevator and taps in our floor. The elevator rises.

Pete turns around and gives me a long once-over.

I unbutton my coat reflexively.

He slides one hand around my waist, then it's under my sweater, against my lower back. His hips press against mine— he *is* hard—then they're pinning me against the elevator wall.

The intensity of his stare melts something in me. His eyes are brimming with desire. It's fucking amazing.

He leans in to kiss me. God, what a kiss. My lips part to make way for his tongue. Then our tongues are dancing. Kissing him is always intoxicating, but this is something else.

We're really getting married.

This is really forever.

His hand brushes the waist of my jeans. Then my jeans are unbuttoned, unzipped. He slides his hand into my panties.

I groan into his mouth as he strokes me. All that stuff about musicians being good with their hands—it's all true. I'm almost there already.

The elevator dings. Our floor. He pulls his hand away then buttons my jeans and my coat.

He plants a long, slow kiss on my lips.

When he pulls back, he smiles a truly evil *damn, do I enjoy teasing you* smile. I only catch my reflection for a minute. It's enough to see that I look as flushed and desperate as I feel.

I might be in over my head here.

I squeeze his hand on the way to the hotel room. "What if it's too much, if I want you to stop?"

"Say stop." He unlocks the door and whisks me inside. "This is about bringing you pleasure, baby. It's not about depriving you of anything."

His voice is low and steady. Mine feels scattered and weak by comparison.

I try to cultivate all the confidence I have. "I like when you give me orders."

"I know." He looks me up and down. "Take off your coat."

I leave it hanging on a chair.

His voice shifts, deeper and more demanding. "Strip to your bra and panties. Slowly."

Hell yes. I watch delight spread over his face as I hang my sweater and blouse over my coat. It's hard taking off my boots, socks, and jeans in a graceful manner, but I manage.

I rub my thighs together. Then my palms. There's a desperate ache in my core. Nothing will satisfy it except for him.

"Fuck, you get more gorgeous every day." He pulls my glasses off, gently, and sets them on top of my jeans.

He takes his time running his fingers over my body. Every brush of his fingers winds up the tension in my core. I'm still on the edge, still in need of release.

He sighs with pleasure as he cups my ass. Then he's lifting me into his arms. He carries me to the bed.

He sets me on the bed and presses his lips to mine. "You're nervous."

"A little." Okay, a lot.

He runs his fingertips over my cheek. "You're in control of this. If there's anything you don't like, tell me to stop. Doesn't matter how much I'm enjoying it." His expression gets intense. "Promise?"

"I promise."

He smiles that same evil smile. It lights up his face. His dark eyes are practically shining.

He sheds his coat on the armchair in the corner. My gaze goes straight to the erection straining against his jeans. It's not mine yet. It's not mine until he sees fit.

Pete pulls something from the bottom drawer of the dresser. It's the same restraint that was under Tom's old bed at the Hollywood place. He's been hoarding it.

He hooks it around the headboard. His eyes meet mine. "Take off your bra."

I nearly fling it aside.

He motions, *come here*.

I do. Then his fingers are on my wrist. His touch is soft as he cuffs me. He moves to the other side of the bed and cuffs my other wrist.

I'm tied to the headboard.

I really am at his mercy. The revelation sends another pang of lust to my core. I do my best to sit up straight, my back against the headboard.

My eyes stay on Pete. He takes his time stripping. First the shoes and socks. Then the t-shirt. The jeans.

He slides his boxers off his hips.

Mmm. He looks so fucking yummy naked.

I press my fingertips into my thumbs. I'm wound up. I need release.

His expression intensifies as he wraps his hands around my ankles. Slowly, he pulls my body toward his. I push off the headboard. Then I'm flat on my back, my ankles on the edge of the bed.

Pete places himself between my legs. His eyes stay on mine as he drags his fingertips from my ankle to my knee then all the way up my thigh. Slowly, he drags his fingers back to my ankle.

He does it again and again. Each time, he gets closer.

His fingertips skim the peak of my inner thigh. My sex clenches from the proximity. I need his hand on me. The wait is torture. It's beautiful, sweet, delicious torture, but it's torture nonetheless.

He presses his palm against my inner thigh. "You want to come on my hand, baby?"

"Yes."

His fingertips skim my sex, feather-light. I shudder. My heels knock into the mattress.

He does it again and again.

He does it until I'm writhing on the bed.

"Please," I breathe. My eyes catch his. There's that same intensity in his stare.

He likes being in control. But there's more to it than that. There's a tenderness, a focus. He's fixed on *my* pleasure.

His breath hitches as his touch hardens.

It only takes a few moments of his fingers on my clit to push me off the edge. The unbearably taught tension releases as I come. I shudder and shake and scream his name. Pleasure spreads to my toes. I feel the release everywhere.

I'm not sure I've ever needed an orgasm as badly as I needed that.

He drags his fingertips over my thigh for a moment. Then he's rubbing me again.

It's intense. My eyes close. My breath gets heavy, impossible to control.

There's no way for me to contain this. I try squeezing my toes into the sheets, but that doesn't help. All I can feel is the intensity of the orgasm building inside me.

I bite my lip.

Almost.

Then I'm there. I scream his name as I come again. It's faster and harder than the last orgasm.

The look in his eyes is clear. He's going to make me come again. I'm not complaining—not even close—but I want this to end with him coming inside me, not with me begging him to stop stroking me because I can't take it anymore.

I press my knees together. My voice is needy. "Fuck me."

He runs his fingertips over my inner thigh. His voice is commanding. "Not until you come on my face."

I groan.

He leans down to press his lips to my ankle. "Twice to start."

To start?

The man is trying to kill me.

He drags his lips up my calf and over my inner thigh. I squeeze my toes. I'm already overwhelmed with pleasure.

But there still isn't a single molecule in my body that wants to protest.

His breath is nearly as heavy as mine. He moans against my inner thigh. It's amazing music.

But then there's this other music. Something familiar. One of those bands he likes.

His phone. It's ringing.

He ignores it, moves a little higher, nips at my skin.

The phone rings to voicemail. It stops for a second then it's going again.

And there's something else. Someone is knocking on the door. It's not the polite knock of the staff. It's frantic, desperate even.

Pete pushes himself up. Frustration fills his expression. "You okay tied up while I check that?"

I nod. There's something appealing about being tied up waiting for him.

He grabs the towel from the bathroom, cinches it around his waist, and goes to main room.

With the bedroom door open a sliver, I can hear the faint

whisper of conversation at the door. It's a woman's voice and she's crying. She's frantic. She's really familiar.

That's Willow.

Before I can contemplate what it is that's wrong, there are footsteps coming closer. Pete steps into the room.

His tongue slides over his lips as he looks me over. "Should be five minutes. Want me to untie you?"

That sounds like an eternity, but the breather will do bounds for my stamina.

I shake my head. "I think I need the break."

He smiles as he throws off his towel and slides on his jeans. Only his jeans, no boxers.

He's naked under his jeans.

His fingertips trail over my ankle. "Don't think I've changed my mind about you coming on my face."

This time, he closes the door. It's for the best. I don't want to eavesdrop on their conversation. I'm sure it's about Tom. You'd think that, with what Nathan did to me, I'd get antsy about how close Pete is with his brother's wife, but there isn't a single part of me that doubts his fidelity.

He's mine and I'm his. In a few days, the world and the state of Nevada will know it.

I let my mind go wild imagining his body on top of mine, his deep voice in my ears, his cock buried inside me.

He does things to me. He wakes up this demanding, blissful part of myself.

Their voices quiet. Then the front door opens and his footsteps come closer.

This time, he pushes the door wide open.

He leans against the frame. "Spread your legs, baby. I want to look at you."

I do. Again, he looks at me like I'm a masterpiece.

His dark eyes are filled with delight. He looks as hungry as I feel.

Pete moves closer. Then he's on the bed. His hands curl around my inner thighs.

He pins my legs to the bed and brings his lips to my skin. He kisses his way to the apex of my thighs.

Then his mouth is on me.

He licks me up and down again and again. Each time, his motions get faster, harder.

I groan as pleasure builds in my core.

I try to reach for him reflexively. But I can't. My wrists are bound. The reminder sends another shockwave of desire through me.

I'm at his mercy.

His fingers dig into my flesh as he licks me. His strokes get shorter. faster. He starts to focus on the spot that always gets me there.

His tongue flicks against me again and again.

I shudder.

I shake.

Almost.

My knees fight his hands. I'm so fucking close.

But his mouth moves away. I sigh with frustration.

The fucking tease.

He takes his time sucking on my lips, plunging his tongue inside me, playing with different speeds and pressures.

My sex clenches. I'm still at the edge. I can't take this anymore. I need to come. "Please."

He's there immediately. He starts soft then gets harder. Harder.

My breath hitches as I race toward an orgasm. A few more flicks of his tongue and I'm coming. I press my legs against his head.

"Fuck, Pete." I groan. "Fuck me. Please."

He murmurs something against my thigh. His teeth scrape against my skin. Then his mouth is on me again.

I've barely recovered from my last orgasm. But his soft, wet mouth feels fucking good.

My eyes close. Almost.

Almost.

Fuck. I scream incomprehensible things as I come.

The man doesn't waste any time. He pushes himself up and shimmies out of his jeans. His eyes fix on mine as he slides his hands under my ass.

With one strong motion, he thrusts deep inside me.

My body floods with relief.

With his next thrust, I forget everything in the world but the two of us.

I stare into his gorgeous brown eyes. This really is where we belong.

His voice is low and needy. "Come on my cock, baby. I want to feel your cunt pulsing around me."

My conscious mind is gone. My body really is under his command. I nod. I arch my hips to meet his movements. Again. Again.

The tension in my core knots. With his next thrust, I'm there. I can feel my sex pulsing around him, pulling him closer and deeper.

"Fuck, Pete," I groan. I blink my eyes open to look into his. "Come inside me."

He groans with pleasure as he lowers his body onto mine. He plants his hands outside my shoulders. His lips go to my neck as he thrusts into me.

His movements get harder, faster. I can feel his orgasm in the way his body shakes against mine. The muscles of his torso clench and relax. His thighs too.

I lift my hips to push him deeper.

Then he's there. He groans my name as he comes inside me. His breath goes wild as he finishes.

He presses his lips to mine with a deep kiss. Every feeling

inside me pours into him. Every feeling inside him pours into me.

I can feel our love in my soul.

Gently, he undoes my restraints and checks my wrists.

Then his arms are around me. His body is against mine. I nestle my head into his chest and I exhale every heavy thing in my body.

He runs his fingers through my hair.

"Would you really spend that much time making me come if I let you?" I ask.

"Yeah. You want me to?"

I shake my head. "I'm not sure I can move."

He chuckles. "We don't have to go anywhere for a while."

That sounds like a hell of a plan.

Chapter Eight

PETE

J ess falls asleep in my arms. There's a real pride of accomplishment from making my fiancée come five times. Knowing I wore her out enough she can't even keep her eyes open is icing on the fucking cake.

I use the time to make arrangements for the wedding. The hotel-casino has a few standard packages, but I want things special for her. I demand enough extra to frustrate the poor wedding planner, but it's not as if I'm rude about it.

My imagination goes wild thinking about me and Jess tying the knot at the top of the stratosphere. She'll look like an angel in some curve-hugging ivory dress, her blissful expression lighting up her face.

The ceremony is going to be simple and elegant— deep red roses, teal ribbons, the city skyline as our backdrop.

The reception is cocktails and cake. In our case, it's mocktails and cake. I don't want her worrying about her dad's sobriety. I don't give a fuck about what it is that's in the champagne glasses when we toast.

What matters is that we're toasting to the rest of our lives together.

The bedroom door doesn't open until well past lunch time. Jess is still naked. She's not even wearing her glasses.

She stretches her arms over her head as she yawns. Her eyes scan the room then they're fixed on me.

She smiles. "You used up all my energy."

Damn, I'm not sure it's possible to smile wider than I am right now. This, the two of us in our hotel room together, getting married in a few days—it's fucking perfect.

I motion for her to come here.

She squints, trying to make out the gesture.

"Come here."

She shakes her head. "I don't have anything left." Her smile widens. "You have to promise to be good."

"Good?"

"Chaste."

"Don't think I can do chaste. Not if you're naked."

"I suppose I'll have to put on clothes." She grabs her glasses and slides them on. "Looking at anything interesting?"

I take in all the curves of her body. "Very fucking interesting."

She blushes. "I mean... on your computer."

"Scheduling our wedding."

"Already?"

I nod. "It's done. Sunset on Christmas."

She sighs with pleasure. "It's done, all that planning, like that?" She snaps her fingers.

I snap mine. "Like that."

"You're amazing."

Again, I motion for her to come here.

She bites her lip, considering it. There's delight in her eyes, but there's exhaustion too. She takes a step backward. "You're trying to kill me."

"Absolutely."

"You didn't just exhaust me. You also worked up my

appetite."

"Get dressed. We'll stop by Tom and Willow's room before lunch."

"Is everything okay with her?"

"It will be."

"But you want to check, just in case?"

I nod.

She smiles. "You're a good brother."

"Do what I can."

"You do more than what you can. I... I've been a pretty shitty sister to Madison the last few months."

"She slept with your ex."

"Yeah, but she apologized. I forgave her."

"Don't apologize for your feelings, baby. Just because you forgave her, it doesn't mean you have to trust her."

She chews on her lower lip. "You make it sound easy."

"It's not easy." I know it's not easy for Jess to put herself first. She wants to take care of her sister and her dad. Even after everything they've done to hurt her, she still worries about their well-being. "This is our wedding. It's your chance to be selfish."

She nods. "I'll think about it." Her eyes go to the pink gift bag sitting on the table. "What is that?"

"A present for Tom and Willow."

She raises a brow. "Do I want to know?"

I chuckle. "Up to you."

"It's the same color as her hair."

It is. That was luck. I found the thing in some closet at our apartment. I nearly forgot I'd brought this with me. It's supposed to be for Christmas, but after what Willow told me, I'm pretty sure they need it today.

"Okay, I'll bite." Jess's eyes meet mine. "What is it?"

"Bondage kit."

Her cheeks flush. "Because we... Oh god. She knew I was

tied up in the bedroom?"

"She got the gist."

The flush spreads to her chest. Her nipples harden. She presses her thighs together. Jess can play as coy as she wants. We both know she gets off on the exhibitionism.

"You've turned me into a pervert," she whispers.

"Pervert was always inside you."

"Yes, I often have a pervert inside me." She laughs.

I chuckle. I love her bad jokes. "I only brought out your inner freak." My eyes pass over her body. I'll never get enough of those round hips of hers. I'll never get enough of any inch of her, but fuck, do I love the way her lush ass feels against my hands.

"Uh-oh." She laughs as she takes a step backward. "I know that look."

I feign innocence.

"I'd better get dressed if I don't want to suffer death by orgasm."

❧

EVEN WITH WILLOW IN TEARS, I NEVER DOUBTED THAT SHE and Tom would be okay. But I have to admit I've been worried. I stay worried until we check on them.

They're okay, great even. Once they get past their embarrassment, the present will keep them busy. We make plans for dinner. I call Mom to confirm.

Jess is still in a daze. I take her to a secluded bistro for lunch. Then we head to the suburban part of town to take in a movie in a quiet, dark theater. I honor her wish not to die from orgasms and keep my hands off her.

It's difficult, but I do manage.

❧

ALL THESE LAS VEGAS RESTAURANTS RUN TOGETHER. THIS place is nicer than average. The lights are dim. The walls are a mix of cream and black. There's a chandelier hanging over our long dining table.

It's a ridiculously long table for five. But this is the only private room in the place.

On a normal night, I don't mind the occasional dinner interruption.

Tonight isn't a normal night.

Tonight has to be perfect.

The rest of the week has to be perfect.

Jess rests her head on my shoulder as she marvels at the exceptionally long table. Her eyes light up.

At the moment, I'm on exactly the same page.

My brother's voice grabs my attention.

"Damn, get a room, you two." Tom steps into the room. Step isn't quite the right word. He saunters into the room like he owns the place.

Most of the time, he does own the room. Not tonight. Tonight is about Jess.

"They're cute." Willow steps in after him. She looks at me and mouths, *Thank you*.

I nod back. Tom's always been a guy with good spirits, but he was never happy, not really, until he met her.

Jess perks up. She takes in Tom and Willow's smiling expressions and sighs with relief. She's been worried too.

I wait until they're seated across from us. "How did you like your gift?"

Willow blushes.

I can't fucking believe it, but Tom is blushing.

He stumbles over his words. "You realize that it's rude to ask people if they liked their gift." He shakes his head. "Damn. You ever think about anything besides sex?"

Jess laughs. "It's ninety-nine percent sex."

"Baby, you wound me." I squeeze her hand.

"No, I don't." She smiles. "You like everyone thinking you're this depraved sex god."

Willow runs her fingers through his hair. "I can't believe you're jealous."

He groans as she drags her fingers over his earlobes. I look to Jess to make sure she isn't disturbed by their PDA—it's not like they're able to turn it off—but she's smiling.

She presses her forehead to mine. "I love your family. They're not like mine. They're open and honest and wonderful."

I lean in to whisper. "They're your family too."

"Damn, don't you two get chafed?" Tom shakes his head.

Willow laughs. "You're incredibly jealous."

"No." Tom pouts. "I can do the same thing." He slides his arms around his wife and pulls her into a deep kiss.

She melts into the gesture.

"I'll fuck you right here if that's what you want," he mumbles.

Willow turns red. She shakes her head.

Jess laughs. "Tom, you're so funny. Don't you realize everyone thinks you and Willow are the cutest thing ever?"

When he pulls back, he's smiling. "Course they do. We are the cutest thing ever. But we're not a boring married couple. We're as exciting as you two perverts."

I look to Willow. "Did you like it?"

She stammers. Her cheeks flush. "Uh. Yeah. But I don't know if that's really dinner table conversation."

"Course, you two probably prefer to use your dinner table for fucking," Tom says. "Any place in your house you haven't fucked?"

"No. You?" I ask.

Tom shrugs, conceding my point.

Okay, time to go for the kill. I shoot Jess a *watch this* look then I turn back to Willow. "What was it like, being in control of the man who never lets go of control?"

Willow's jaw drops in surprise. "How did you know? I mean... that's really not..."

Jess squeezes my arm. Her laugh fills the room. "You're incorrigible."

I feign innocence as I shrug.

Her blue eyes fill with delight. "Not buying that for a second." She looks to Willow. "If you ignore his questions, he'll stop."

Willow laughs. Her eyes meet mine. "You're more like Tom than you let on. It was... interesting. And that's all you're getting, so you can go back to whispering about your very active sex life."

"They get their jollies from talking about it in front of us," Tom says. He looks to Jess for confirmation.

She clears her throat. "I plead the fifth."

He looks to me.

I raise a brow. Tom sticks his tongue out.

"You two never turn it off." Mom steps into the room. "I could hear you by the hostess stand."

I shrug.

Tom adopts an *it wasn't me* expression.

"What bullshit." Mom shakes her head as she takes a seat.

"Nice to see you, Ophelia. Your dress is beautiful. Hot date tonight?" Jess squeezes me, a little harder this time. Her tone is light, but there are nerves in her eyes.

We're about to tell them we're getting married on Christmas. We're asking them to spend Christmas celebrating our relationship instead of holiday cheer. I know they won't mind, but Jess isn't used to that kind of support.

"I wouldn't exactly call it a date," Mom says.

We go through the usual vacation small talk for a few

minutes. The server stops by to drop off drinks and take our dinner orders. Then he's out the door.

I lean in to whisper in Jess's ear. "You want to do it or should I?"

She presses her finger to my chest in the *you* gesture.

Tom, Willow, and Mom are joking about something.

I wait for a lull in the conversation then I clear my throat. No sense in beating around the bush. "Jess and I are getting married. On Christmas. At sunset."

Willow squeals. "Really? That's romantic. Where?"

Tom shoots me that *this shit true?* look.

I nod. "At the Stratosphere. They have a private balcony for ceremonies. It's just gonna be family and the band."

"But on Christmas?" Willow sighs dreamily. She looks to Tom. "Isn't that nice?"

He nods.

Mom raises a brow. She looks to Jess. "Sweetheart, weren't you telling him to shove the marriage plans yesterday?"

Jess nods. "He's very convincing."

"He paying for your tuition?" Ophelia asks.

"Technically, it's all our money, legally, once we're married." Jess cocks her head to one side. She chews on her lip, thinking. "There are a few 'women in law' scholarships I want to apply for. They're all merit-based. If I don't get any of them, I'll find a loan. If, somehow, I can't find a loan, then I'll use *our* money to pay the rest of my tuition."

She will? Fuck, that's fantastic. Knew I'd convince her eventually, but I didn't think it would be this easy.

"Don't gloat, sweetheart. Even you don't look good smug," she says.

Ophelia chuckles. "I'm happy for you two. If you're as sure about this as he is."

Jess beams. "I'm one hundred percent."

I melt.

Chapter Nine

JESS

Pete's eyes close the moment he hits the bed. He looks cute half-asleep. I want to climb in next to him and forget the rest of the world.

But I have to call my sister. I have to tell her I'm getting married. I have to ask her to spend Christmas at my wedding.

I run my fingers over my phone. Pete insisted on holding my hand while I called, but he looks exhausted.

He stirs enough to blink one eye open. Then the other. His expression is fuzzy, the haze of semi-consciousness.

"Sleep." I lean down to press my lips to his forehead. "I can handle this on my own."

He mumbles something, then his eyes are closed. I'm not sure how he has any energy left after how thoroughly he fucked me all afternoon.

I need to let him rest.

I take a deep breath and step into the main room. It feels huge right now. My thoughts have nowhere to go.

What will Madison say?

She's romantic but she might be jealous. She might not be happy for me. She might not want to come.

She might not want to be my maid of honor. I can ask Meg, Willow, or Kara to fill in, but it's not the same. Madison is my sister. Pete will have Tom standing with him at the altar.

God, my hands are sweating. I'm going to drop my phone.

It's past midnight in New York. I need to do this now.

If I'm lucky, I'll get voicemail.

I take a deep breath and dial.

Madison picks up after one ring. "Hey, Jessie. Is everything okay? I'm so excited for Vegas. Do you want to go to any clubs while we're there?"

"Yeah, everything is great." My heart is beating so loudly I can hear it in my ears. She sounds happy. She'll be happy about this. Dad too. I can do this. "I have to tell you something. It's good."

"Yeah?"

"Pete and I are getting married here. On Christmas."

"OH MY GOD!" Madison's shriek pours from my cellphone speaker.

It's loud enough I have to press the phone to my chest and take a deep breath.

Even with my phone at my chest, I can hear her shrieking.

"Oh my God, Jessie. That's amazing. And romantic. God, he's so hot. I'd hate you if I didn't love you."

Why did I expect her to react with judgment?

I close my eyes and take a deep breath. I *know* Madison is happy for me, but there's still something in the way. It was half a year ago that she slept with my boyfriend, but it's still between us. Yes, I forgive her. I love her.

But it's still hard to trust her.

It's not like she'd sleep with Pete.

Would she?

I shake my head to shake off the thought. He'd never consider it. I *know* she wouldn't do that to me again, that she only did it because my ex convinced her our relationship was over, but the thought refuses to leave my brain.

I bring the phone back to my ear. "Thanks. We're excited."

"Are you nervous? I'd be so nervous."

"I am."

She squeals again. "Oh, Jessie. It's like a fairytale. A wedding on Christmas. With the hottest guy in the universe. I mean, I know you like other things about him, but you have to admit that he is fucking fine!"

The tension in my shoulders eases as I laugh. She really is happy for me. A little jealous, maybe, but I can't exactly blame her.

I'm relaxed enough to stoke her jealousy. "He fucks much better than fine. I'd say he fucks expertly."

She sighs that *if only* fangirl sigh of hers.

I make my voice as confident as I can. "I want you to be my maid of honor."

"OH MY GOD, REALLY?"

"Yes. But you'll need to tone it down a little. I'm sure you've woken Dad up."

"He's up."

"This late?"

"It's not that late. But yeah. He's had a lot of insomnia since he got out." Her voice drops low enough to remind both of us that he got out of rehab and not some fun, cushy vacation. "Mostly, he watches TV in his room."

I remind myself that this call isn't about my dad's sobriety. It's about my wedding. This is the one time in my life where I'm expected to be selfish.

"How about if I fly in early?" Madison says.

I would love help with the dress. Madison is good with clothes. "If it's not an imposition."

"Of course not! I want to be there to help. You only have

three days. Hold on." She taps something on her computer. "There's a flight tomorrow morning. It gets in at ten A.M. your time zone. I'll take a cab to your hotel and we can spend the whole day taking care of everything. Okay?"

"Okay."

"Great! Jessie, I'm so happy. Are you happy? You sound tired."

"We got up early."

"Oh, sure. Wait... are you pregnant? You'd tell me if you were pregnant, wouldn't you?"

"No, I'm not pregnant."

"Oh. Good. You should probably wait until you're done with school. If you guys have kids. You are, aren't you?"

"Oh, I..."

We've never talked about it.

Ever.

The subject has never come up. Not once. Not even on the way home from brunch, post Drew and Kara's pregnancy announcement.

We've never talked about whether or not we're having kids, and we're getting married in three days.

"I'm sure you'll figure it out," Madison says. "Do you want me to get Dad or do you want me to tell him?"

"You can get him."

My voice is empty, hollow. It's hard to breathe.

What if we want different things? Pete was right when he said he always gets what he wants. He doesn't compromise often. And there's not really room for compromise here.

It's black and white. You have kids or you don't. And nobody should have a kid they don't want. I know how awful it feels when one of your parents looks at you like you're the thing that ruined their life.

I've never thought about raising children. It never appealed to me.

My eyelids press together. I can see me and Pete at the altar. I can see us dancing arm in arm, his dark eyes filled with love and wonder.

I can see our life together. And it doesn't involve children.

Dammit, what if we're not on the same page?

Madison's voice flows through the speakers. "Guess I spoke too soon. Dad is asleep. Should I wake him?"

"No, it's late."

"I'll tell him... well, I guess I'll be leaving at the crack of dawn, so I'll leave a note or something. You okay, Jessie? Did I say something wrong?"

"No... I... I'm just tired."

"Oh, yeah. I guess I should get to bed. My flight is in less than six hours. I love you! Goodnight."

"You too."

She ends the call.

My mind works overtime. What the hell is wrong with me? I'm usually more responsible than this.

I moved in with him, I agreed to marry him. Fuck, I agreed to marry him in four days, and we've barely talked about our future.

It's not just kids... we don't talk about how long he'll keep touring. We don't talk about whether I'll spend my summers on the road with him or doing internships. They're expected, but I can't bear to give up three months with him.

We don't talk about any of it.

Okay. I won't let anxiety envelop me. All I have to do is talk to him.

That's the only solution. Period.

I step into the bedroom.

He's lying on his side, his e-reader pressed against his chest, his eyes closed. He's in his pajamas. Well, he's out of his clothes. He sleeps in boxers most of the time. But he's wearing his glasses.

He's already ready for bed.

Hell, he's practically asleep.

His chest heaves with his inhale and falls with his exhale. He turns toward me with a mumble. "You coming to bed, baby?"

"After I brush my teeth."

He nods.

"You look like you're about to fall asleep."

"Not too asleep for you to come on my hand."

The man is insatiable. I'll give him that much.

I brush my teeth, change into my pajamas, and slide into bed next to him.

I want his body close, but not for the sexual release. I want every inch of his skin pressed against mine.

I want to know this is okay.

I pull off his glasses and set them aside. He's all the way to three-quarters asleep now. I have no doubts that he's conscious enough to get me off. He can probably do that in his sleep.

But he's far too asleep for this conversation.

I nestle into his chest. His body is warm. He looks even more serene in his sleep.

I trace the lines of his tattoo as I take him in. We've figured out everything so far.

But what if we can't figure out this?

<hr />

THE PHONE IS RINGING. NOT MY CELL. NOT PETE'S CELL.

It's the hotel phone.

Dammit, it's loud.

I blink my eyes open. The blackout curtains do wonders to keep the room dark. My eyes go to the alarm clock on the bedside table. If I squint, I can make out the time. Ten something.

That must be Madison.

Pete stirs. He rolls over. His hand goes to my waist. He murmurs something I can't make out. Knowing him, I'm sure it's something like *Don't leave the bed, baby. Not until I make you come.*

Right now, he's mine. But after we talk about this...

He might not be mine anymore.

I grab my glasses from the counter and slide them on. The phone is still ringing. I need to get it before it wakes him up.

I grab the thing and bring it to my ear. "Hello."

"Hello, there's a Madison James here to see you." The front-desk person speaks with a calm, even voice. "Would you like me to send her to your room?"

"No. I'll meet her at the lobby. Thank you."

"Sure, Ma'am. Have a good morning."

I set the phone back in the receiver.

Pete pushes himself halfway up. He blinks his eyes open and looks at me. "Where you going, baby?"

"Madison is here."

"Already?" He yawns through the word.

"Already." I lean down to kiss him goodbye. This is what our life is like when he's home. I get up early to get ready for school. He tries to pull me back to bed, but he doesn't try hard enough to make me late. I need our life to stay like that. I need it to stay *our* life. "We're looking at dresses. Might take all day."

He nods as he falls back to bed. His voice is still a sleepy mumble. "You okay?"

Maybe. I don't know. But he's nowhere near awake enough for this conversation, and Madison is waiting.

I shouldn't buy a dress if it's possible we'll call off the wedding.

But I can still look.

This will be okay. If he wanted kids, he'd have said something. Wouldn't he?

His hand curls around my wrist. He tugs gently *come back to bed*. His fingertips brush my skin.

It's quite the inviting gesture.

"I have to go. Maddie is waiting," I say.

He nods as his arms curl around a pillow.

Chapter Ten

JESS

✦

After a round of squealing *I missed yous*, Madison and I grab coffee and breakfast at the hotel Starbucks. The two of us are tired enough that I enlist backup. I hate to interrupt Meg during her honeymoon, but I do need help, and she just did the impromptu Vegas wedding thing.

Jess: I hate to drag you away from screwing your husband, but do you think you could help me with picking out a dress?

Meg: Oh yah! Miles told me last night. Congrats! When is the wedding?

Jess: Christmas.

Meg: That's sweet. Why the hell didn't Miles give me that detail? The man can be a total fuck-face sometimes, but I love him. He is my husband.

Jess: You're perfect together.

Meg: A lot of people say we're tall.

Jess: You are tall.

Meg: Thanks. Where are you right now?

Jess: Hotel Starbucks.

Meg: Stay there! I'll be fifteen minutes. I know just the shop.

I use the fifteen minutes to catch up with Madison and to order a coffee for Meg.

She's bouncier than usual when she steps into the cafe. "Hey, Jess. You look nervous and happy. It's very bride-to-be." She turns to Madison. "Uh, Madison, right?"

"That's me." Madison's eyes glaze over as she takes in Meg. "Meg, was it?"

"Yes." Meg glances at the unclaimed coffee. "Is that mine?"

I nod.

"You're the best." She takes a small sip of the coffee, testing the temperature. Then she's at the counter, adding sugar and cream. "Wow, a Christmas wedding. There's today, tomorrow, then bam, you're getting married."

"Sound familiar?" I tease.

She nods. "All too familiar. Are you terrified? I was."

"A little," I admit. A lot, with this hanging over our heads. I try to push it aside. Assuming we work this out, I'll need a dress. Today is my only chance to find one. "I know I want to be with him, but it's fast."

"Very fast." Meg motions to Madison. She mouths, *is she okay?*

My sister is still standing there, star-struck. She's staring at Meg's cleavage. Well, at the *Be Brave, Love* tattoo on Meg's chest.

I make an excuse for my sister. "She just flew in from New York. She's tired."

"You want another one of these?" Meg shakes her coffee cup.

Madison blinks, only barely roused. "Uh, no. That's okay. Should we grab a cab?"

"Let's," I say.

This early in the morning, the line for cabs is short. We

chat about Meg's impromptu wedding as we wait. She really pulled shit together on short notice. It's admirable.

Madison asks her a million questions on the ride to the boutique. Slowly, my sister shakes off her slack-jawed, star-struck stare. She shifts into *let's do this* mode. Madison loves clothes and fashion. She already has a million ideas about my dress.

She's still talking when we arrive. "You're very, um, pear-shaped, Jessie. A strapless dress can help draw the eye up."

Meg practically pushes her out of the cab. "No way is she drawing the eye up. Have you ever seen the two of them together?"

"Only a little," Madison admits.

"He's always staring at her ass. In a pervy, *I'm picturing you naked, thinking about spreading your legs* way too." Meg crinkles her nose. "I guess I can't really talk with the way my husband is always sucking on my neck."

I laugh. "He is! Doesn't that bother you?"

"I like it. As long as he doesn't do it in front of my family." She pulls the door open and waits for us to step inside the shop. "He's respectful in front of my parents. It's not like him at all."

The place is bright and cheery. The white and ivory dresses that line the walls glow in the sunlight.

I drop my empty coffee in the trashcan. My hair is a mess. I must have a tie somewhere in my purse.

"You should wear something that accentuates your hips." Meg's eyes go to said hips. "You have assets. Show them off."

Madison looks around the room. "Whatever will make you feel confident and beautiful."

I consider the question as I pull my hair into a French braid. When I'm busy with school, I barely think about my appearance.

But when I'm with Pete... it doesn't matter where we are

or what we're doing. He always looks at me like I'm the most beautiful woman in the world.

I copy Meg's words. "I have assets. I want to show them off."

Madison turns to Meg. "Does he really stare at her ass that much?"

"More," Meg says.

My cheeks flush. "I'm right here."

"You love it. You two are both pervs. You're perfect for each other." Meg winks. "You want to look with us, or do you want us to take charge?"

I motion to the other side of the store. "Divide and conquer."

Madison nods. She giggles as she follows Meg to the rack of dresses on the left. I get to work with the rack on the right.

Before Mom left and everything went to hell, I was a normal little girl. I thought about weddings and princesses and fairytale castles. But I didn't think much about the dress. More about Prince Charming whisking me away from my life.

I guess, even then, I realized things weren't exactly peachy keen.

I fall into a trance as I flip through dresses. Each is beautiful but completely different. I haven't got a clue how to start narrowing it down.

Or if I'm even going to need a gown.

What if he's a hundred percent sure he wants kids?

I'm not going to keep him from the life he wants.

Madison's squeal echoes around the room. "Come here, Jessie! We found it. It's perfect!"

I take a deep breath. I'm not sure I'm ready.

"It really is nice," Meg agrees.

Madison holds the dress up. It's a strapless mermaid

gown. The ivory bodice is sleek and beaded. The tulle skirt flares into a dramatic fishtail.

It's beautiful.

"Let's try it now! If it's perfect, we'll be done for the day. Yeah?" Madison asks.

She has a point. "Okay." I press my palms together. Already, my heart is racing. This dress might be my wedding dress. If we...

No, I can't think about that right now.

I need to focus.

Madison leads the way to the dressing room. It's decorated in shades of pink. The mirrors are in ornate, silver frames. It's straight out of a princess castle. It's almost too cute.

Madison pushes her short blond hair behind her ears. "You want me to help you get into the dress?"

"Please." I haven't got a clue how to lace the corset back.

My sister pulls the curtains to one of the dressing stalls. The thing is the size of my old apartment and it's just as pink as the rest of the store.

Madison laughs. "The place has a theme." She takes in the hot pink walls and shakes her head. "And I thought that we had it bad."

She works at a fancy boutique in midtown Manhattan. It's nearly an hour and a half on the Long Island Rail Road then the subway, but she loves it.

"How is work?" I ask.

"I'm assistant manager now." She hangs the dress on a hook. She's holding something else too—a longline bra. "I'm saving up to get my own place. I'm not sure if I can afford Manhattan, but I can't take that commute anymore." Her lips curl into a frown.

"I worry about Dad too."

Her hair falls in her eyes as she shakes her head. "He's

doing better. And... well, you were right. He's fifty. He needs to stand on his own two feet. We need to have our own lives. There are all sorts of fashion internships in Manhattan. I'm never going to move on if I'm always racing to Penn Station to make the last Babylon train."

"I'm happy for you."

She smiles. "Thanks, but today is about your dress. And your wedding to the hottest guy in the universe." She clears her throat. "Sorry. I should probably stop reminding you that I've had dirty thoughts about your groom."

"Yes. You should. But I don't blame you." The man is dripping with sex appeal.

Madison blushes. She shakes it off. "Okay, girly. Strip to your panties. You *are* wearing panties, aren't you?"

"Would you really want to know if I wasn't?"

"You're right. I wouldn't. But for the sake of this crinoline-" she nods to the underskirt hanging on the rack— "I'd suffer through the knowledge enough to grab you some bridal lingerie."

"I am wearing panties."

She sighs with relief. I guess my reputation as a sex-crazed pervert has preceded me.

Usually, I feel nothing but pride about how often Pete and I make each other come. But with this *do you want kids* question hanging over my head, sex feels like a terrifyingly loaded subject.

Again, I remind myself to focus. It doesn't work. Half my attention stays on the possibility of us calling off the wedding.

By this time tomorrow, it could be over. No more Jess and Pete.

I'll be alone again. But it's much worse than solitude. I'll be empty and joyless without him.

Fuck. I have to focus.

I take a deep breath and undress.

Madison helps me into the longline bra and the crinoline underskirt.

She gives me a quick once-over. "You really do have a nice figure. How come I have such a flat ass?"

"Because you have those." I point to her ample chest. "It wouldn't be fair if you got T *and* A."

She laughs, her voice as lively as it was before Nathan fucked up our relationship. "You're right. It wouldn't be fair." She loosens the corset lacing. "I guess I'll have to wear something low cut when I get married, to show off *my* assets."

"Absolutely." I laugh, but it's only at fifty percent.

"Ah. Got it." Gently, she pulls the neckline of the dress open. "Usually, it's easier to step into a dress. But with this one hugging your hips, I think we should pull it over your head. Put your arms up at your ears."

I do.

She gathers the dress around her hands. Then she's lifting it over my head and pulling it over my arms and down my torso.

All I see is the ivory lining.

Shit. The dress hits my glasses all wrong. They fall to my stomach. Then they're on the ground.

"Don't move!" I squeak.

"Glasses?"

"Yeah."

"Stay there." She drops to the floor and reaches under my skirt. "Got it."

I can hear Madison moving, setting my glasses on the stool behind us.

She tugs the dress over my hips and knees. Even with the back unlaced, the dress is snug on my hips.

I can't quite make out the details of my reflection. Without my glasses, all I see is the light bouncing off my dress.

"Give me a second." Madison moves behind me and gets to work lacing the dress. "Take a deep breath."

I do. She pulls the lacing snug, so the dress is hugging my waist and my chest.

"There. Done." Her voice brightens. "It looks perfect, Jessie. Let's go to the big mirrors."

"Okay. But I need my glasses."

She reaches for something. "Got 'em."

Madison takes my hand and leads me to the main room.

There are two mirrors in the center of the room. Madison leads me between them. I can only get the gist without my lenses. The ivory dress hugs my chest, waist, and hips, then flares out at my knees.

Meg jumps from her seat. "Oh my God! You look amazing, Jess."

"She can't see yet." Madison brandishes my glasses. She turns to me. "Are you ready to melt?"

"Yes."

Gently, she slides my glasses onto my face. It's always a little disarming when the world goes from fuzzy to sharp. I blink a few times to help my eyes settle.

With my hair pulled behind my back, my eye goes straight to the sweetheart neckline. The curve is flattering on my less than ample chest.

The dress hugs my figure like it's made for it.

It's beautiful.

I'm beautiful in it.

A tear stings my eye. Then another. My fingers go to my cheeks, but it's not fast enough to keep the tears from falling off my cheeks.

I'm not sure if these are happy tears or *fuck, what if this doesn't work?* tears. I let them fall until I'm crying so hard I can barely speak. "It's perfect."

Madison throws her arms around me. "It's perfect."

Then Meg takes her turn hugging me. "It *is* perfect, Jess. You look amazing. And hot."

I laugh. "Thank you."

"He's going to tear that thing off you the second you're alone," Meg says.

"Is that a wedding night tip?" I ask.

She laughs. "No, we waited until we were in our hotel room. The corset back is complicated, but Miles is a singer. Not as much dexterity." She wiggles her hand. Her cheeks flush. "Not that I have any complaints."

Emotions well up in my chest. I'm excited, but I'm also terrified.

Meg and Madison help me find accessories, but I'm not really paying attention. The question is burning into my brain.

I need to talk to him.

I need to talk to him now.

⛥

I SEND PETE A *CALL ME* TEXT BUT MY PHONE STAYS SILENT.

I'm in a daze all afternoon. I barely hear anything Madison or Meg says.

Thankfully, Madison is as good with hair and makeup as she is with clothes. She leads the stylists.

We're halfway through hair and makeup when my phone buzzes. Pete.

Pete: Everything okay?

Jess: I think so, but I need to talk to you.

Pete: Did you get a dress?

Jess: Yeah. Everything is ready, I'm all measured. I just have to call the shop to confirm.

Pete: You waiting for something?

Jess: To talk.

Pete: You're scaring me, baby.

Jess: Do you really get scared?

Pete: When it's about you? Yeah, I get fucking terrified.

Jess: Where are you?

Pete: Getting a suit.

Jess: Didn't you bring a suit?

Pete: Wanted something special.

He's amazing. We have to work this out. All other options are inconceivable.

Jess: Send me the address.

Pete: Promise you'll be okay.

Jess: I will. After we work this out.

He sends the address.

I press the phone to my chest. My updo is still only half-done, but I can tell the style will work.

My makeup looks good. A little dark, but good. I should wait until the stylist is finished, but I can't wait anymore.

I nod a thank you to the hair stylist. "This will be fine. I can imagine it, and it's great. Just brown eyelashes and liner on the day. Okay?"

She nods.

I grab my purse and my coat. "Um, I'm gonna go. You guys okay without me?"

Meg smiles. "Go fuck your groom."

"We're only going to talk," I say.

Madison laughs. "Come on, Jessie. No one is buying that story."

Chapter Eleven

PETE

I'm going fucking crazy.

If she wants to call this off...

My heart won't survive if she calls this off. Not sure my body or my mind will do much better.

I'll still have my bass, still have my books, still have my friends, still have Mom (no doubt, she'll tell me I did this to myself by pushing Jess too hard), still have the band, but...

Fuck. Can't entertain this thought. If it comes to that, I'll find a music shop, grab a bass and an amp, find a practice room, and play until my hands are bleeding.

I've been dumped once. That was enough to make me realize there's no talking someone into or out of loving you.

Usually, I'm incredibly fucking persuasive. But that won't do shit for me if she wants to call this off.

The sales guy eyes me nervously. That *what the hell is with that dude?* look. He doesn't recognize me. Usually, it's a relief to be a normal guy and not a famous musician. Not right now.

At the moment, I'm more than willing to cash in my celebrity.

God damn, I don't like shit I can't control.

My heart will be dust if she leaves me. There won't be enough of it to stitch it back together.

Fuck. Anything beats standing here waiting. I try picking out a tie that will match our colors—teal and dark blue, like the ocean—but there's never been a less interesting subject in the history of the fucking world.

The bell rings as the door to the shop opens.

Light surrounds Jess. It bounces off her blond hair, casting her in an angelic glow.

That can't hide the frustration in her expression.

Is that *I have a secret* frustration or *I'm about to leave you and I don't want to hurt you* frustration?

"Hey." Her voice is barely a whisper.

The guy at the counter looks from her to me. "Your bride?"

Fuck, I hope so. I nod.

He smiles at Jess. "Why don't you help him with the tie? He's been staring for ten minutes."

Has it really been only ten minutes? Feels like it's been ten years.

She smiles back to the guy then she comes close enough to whisper. "Uh, you've got some shades of blue-green there. Is that our color theme?"

She's talking about the wedding like it's still on.

That's good.

"Color of the ocean," I say.

Her eyes light up as she smiles. But there's still all this frustration on her face.

She grabs the dark teal tie then she looks to me. "This should work."

I nod. She's wearing makeup. Half her hair is pulled behind her head. The other half is hanging over her chest in soft waves. "You look gorgeous."

"Thanks." She gives me a long once-over. "You look jump your bones handsome in that suit."

"You'll have to keep it in your pants during the ceremony."

She smiles. "That will be harder for you than it is for me."

Haven't got a doubt about that. In fact, whatever this is, we *will* get through it. We have to. After-I nod to the dressing room.

She raises a brow. "You have a one-track mind, Steele."

"You want to talk. That will give us privacy." It doesn't hurt that the stall door goes all the way to the floor.

She presses her lips together. Her cheeks flush.

I check that the sales guy isn't looking, and I lead her into the dressing stall.

She locks the door. "It's hot in here, huh?" She hangs her coat on the hook on the door.

I nod.

Her eyes go to mine as she pulls her sweater over her head. I haven't got the faintest clue what she wants to talk about, but it suddenly seems less important. Her tank top hugs her chest and waist. The neckline is low enough that the lace of her bra peeks out.

"Put me out of my misery before I tear off the rest of your clothes." Need to get this out before any more blood goes to my cock. I'm already getting hard. "You want to call off the wedding?"

"No. Of course not."

Every muscle in my body, save the one, relaxes.

Her brows screw together. "Did you think I wanted to?"

"Haven't got a clue what you're thinking, besides that you want me naked."

She laughs. "You should take off the suit."

"Should I?"

She motions to her rosy lips and cheeks. "Don't want to ruin it."

"You sure you can keep your hands off me?"

"I'll do my best, but I can't make any promises." She smiles, but there's something missing.

Still, I strip to my boxers.

She chews on her bottom lip as her gaze goes to the ground. "There's no easy way to say this, so I'll blurt it out."

"Okay."

She looks up at me. "Do you want kids?"

Huh?

That's not what I expected. Not sure what I expected, but it wasn't that.

Four months living together, and neither of us broached the subject. All the talk about Kara being pregnant and Drew needing to take time off from the band, and neither of us broached the subject.

I run my fingers over her cheek. "No, I don't. Do you?"

She sighs with relief. "You don't?"

I nod. "I don't."

It's not something I think about.

There have only been a few things I've wanted in my life. I wanted my dad to respect me. When I realized that was a lost cause, I wanted to make music. Wanted Ophelia to be healthy. Wanted someone to call at the end of the night.

Now, I want Jess. Fuck, how I want Jess. I want every inch of her, every thought in her head. I want to make every one of her hopes and dreams come true.

I hope I'm reading her right. She's smiling. Her shoulders are relaxing.

"Do you?" I ask again.

"No. I don't. I thought... well, we never talked about it. I thought maybe you... I don't know. That you figured you'd get your way. Or that you assumed I wanted kids."

"The way your ex thought you'd give up everything for him?"

She bites her lip. "It's not that I think you're like him-"

"I know, baby. You don't have to tip-toe around my feelings. Guess we should have had this conversation before we planned a wedding."

She laughs. "Yeah. I guess I never think about it."

"Me either."

"We both like to work."

"Yeah." I'm not under any illusions about how many hours she'll work after school. I hope she's not under any illusions about how much time I'll devote to music. Only two things make sense to me— taking care of her and playing the bass. Not willing to give up either. "I want a lot of you, Jess. But I want you to soar too. I like that you're ambitious. I'm never going to get in the way of that."

"What if I work 100 hours a week?"

"Might ask you to cut back to 80." I slide my arms around her round hips and pull her body against mine. "I'll promise to make good use of the other 20."

She lets out another sigh of pleasure. "Do you think Sinful Serenade will be like the Rolling Stones? Are you going to keep touring until you're 70?"

"Trying to suggest I won't be dead sexy at 70?"

She shakes her head. Her blue eyes brighten. "I was terrified I'd lose you." She blinks and there's a tear in her eye. "Fuck. Sorry. This wedding stuff is exhausting."

"Don't have to apologize for your feelings."

She nods. "You're right. I'm not sorry. But I am out of emotional energy." She buries her head in my chest.

I wrap my hands around her and I hold her until her muscles relax. "You need a break?"

She nods. "You don't think it's bad that I don't want to have kids? That it's selfish?"

"No. But I wouldn't care if it was. I want all your love."

She laughs. "What if one of us changes our minds?"

"You think you will?"

"No. But stranger things have happened."

"You're the sun in my fucking sky, baby. I know you don't think I'm the most compromising guy, but I'm going to do what it takes to make you happy."

"You're too sweet. Sometimes, I don't think I deserve you."

"You do."

"Yeah?"

"I never feel as whole as I do when I'm with you." I run my fingers through the hair hanging over her shoulders. "You deserve every inch of me."

Her cheeks flush. "Do you mean-"

For once, I don't mean it sexually. "No." I take her hand and press it to my chest, over my heart. "You're my home, Jess. You're everything."

She nods. "You're my home too." She presses her forehead to my chin, drags her fingers over my chest. "I was terrified. I love you so much. I don't know what I'd do without you."

"You'll never be without me." I bring my fingers to her chin and pull her into a kiss.

Need pours into me as she kisses back.

I let my voice drop to something seductive. "Of course, you can have every inch of me." I drag my fingers over her shoulders. I need our bodies connecting again.

Her voice drops to something low and needy. "Don't tease me."

"Who's teasing?" Fuck knows, I'd like to take her against the wall. Now.

That makes sense. No matter how hard I try, nothing makes more sense than Jess groaning my name as she comes.

"Let's finish this conversation first." She looks up at me.

"I only started imagining my future the last six months. I was thinking on the ride here. I know what I want. I want to come home to you. If that's only six months out of the year, that's okay. But it would be nice to know how long you think you'll be doing the rock star thing."

"Doing the rock star thing?" I cock a brow.

"You know what I mean. How long do you think the band will be touring?"

"Another ten, fifteen years. Maybe less. Maybe more. We're gonna have some breaks, some long ones. Drew should be home with the baby. And Tom and Willow want to adopt in a few years."

She smiles. "Okay."

"Try not to gloat about it."

"No, I'm not! I want you to soar too." She reaches up to run her hand through my hair.

No one has ever cared this much about my success, no one but Mom. It means the fucking world to me, how much she wants my happiness.

Jess's eyes fix on mine. "Of course, there's not as much room to fly higher when you're already a millionaire rock star. But I know that playing music means everything to you. You can't give that up."

"I won't."

"Promise?"

Damn, she's fighting for me.

I fucking melt. "In some way, shape, or form, I'll always play."

She presses her lips to my neck. "Good."

The proximity of her body makes it difficult to focus on conversation. I want that tiny tank top gone. I want her breasts in my hands, her lips parting with a sigh of pleasure.

"You could become a DJ," she teases.

"If you want to hurt me, there's a better way."

She looks up at me. Her expression is bright, determined. "It would keep you in town."

"You baiting me?"

She feigns innocence. "No. I really think you'd excel at the clubs."

"Baby, you're being cruel."

She smiles. "I guess I better make it up to you." She drags her fingers over my stomach.

Her touch sets me on fire. Her fingers drift lower. She traces the waist of my boxers.

She rises to her tiptoes and presses her lips to mine. Always feels amazing kissing Jess—like I could consume her —but there's more to this kiss. I can feel her relief. I can feel how much she needs me.

My shoulders relax as I slide my hands under her tank top. Part of me was worried I'd lose her.

Part of me was fucking terrified I'd lose her.

I unhook her bra. I push it, and her tank top, off her shoulders. She groans into my mouth as I palm her breasts.

She rubs me over my boxers. Damn, that feels good. Good enough that I'm not gonna last long.

She breaks from our kiss. Her eyes fix on mine. They're determined. "I want to suck you off."

I let out a grunt of approval.

She drags her soft lips over my neck. Her palm presses against my hip. She guides me until my back is against the wall.

Jess lowers herself onto her knees. She looks up at me with a hungry expression, wetting her lips with her tongue as she pulls my boxers to my knees.

My hand goes to the back of her head. I tug at her hair until it spills over her shoulders. My cock pulses.

The woman is perfection. And she's mine. She's gonna be my fucking wife.

Jess lets out a soft groan as she brushes her lips over my cock. Sensation overwhelms me. My hands beg me to spur her on. She's looking at me like she wants to devour me.

No way I'm rushing this.

I dig my hands through her hair as she teases me. She does it again and again. Until I'm shaking.

She stares into my eyes as she takes me into her mouth.

Fuck.

She's still wearing her fucking glasses.

She encompasses me with her soft, wet mouth. Her eyelids press together for a moment. Then they're open and she's focused on me.

God damn.

I tug at her hair as pleasure spreads through my body.

"Fuck, Jess." My gaze goes to the mirror. I watch her work. But that isn't enough.

I need her feeling good too.

I slide my hands down her chest, playing with her nipples. She groans against my cock, sucking harder, taking me deeper.

My last conscious thought slips away. My hand slides to the back of her head, guiding her deeper. Deeper.

She sucks harder. Flicks her tongue against my tip again and again.

Her eyes fix on mine, this look that fucking commands me.

I keep my eyes glued to hers as I race towards an orgasm. My legs shake enough I can barely stay standing. I press my back into the wall. I tug at that gorgeous hair. I squeeze her nipple.

"I'm gonna come in your mouth, baby."

She groans, sucking harder, taking me deeper.

Then I'm there. I groan, my cock pulsing as I fill her mouth. I feel the orgasm all the way in my fucking toes.

Fuck.

My brain is mush. My hands fall to my sides.

She pushes herself up and gets back in her bra and tank top.

Then her lips are on mine. She sighs with pleasure and need between kisses. Her tongue slides into my mouth. Her hands dig into my hair.

She looks up at me. "We should go before we get arrested."

I nod.

I'm putty. Whatever she wants.

Chapter Twelve

JESS

Thank God for room service. We spend the entire night and most of the next day in bed. If it weren't for the little matter of me needing to be present to pick up my dress—the tailor has to make sure all the alterations fit right—I'd stay pressed against him until the last possible minute.

The dress is perfect, like a dream. I lose half an hour staring in the mirror, imaging what it will feel like walking down the aisle, imagining the look in Pete's eyes when he sees me.

This is really happening.

It's really happening tomorrow.

The rest of my errands blur together. Madison does most of it. She helps me pick out a short ivory dress and matching shoes for the rehearsal dinner.

She's taking care of the dress, the agenda, and tonight's rehearsal dinner-slash-bachelorette party.

Wait, bachelorette party?

Madison stays mum about party details all afternoon.

Even on the way to dinner, in a much too fast yellow cab with our lives flashing before our eyes, she stays silent about the debauchery she has planned.

The event isn't quite a rehearsal dinner. It's not quite a Christmas Eve gathering. It's a combination of the two.

The cab drops us off at the Excalibur, the hotel that looks like a cartoon version of a Medieval castle. Madison leads the way through the casino. We're at one of the restaurants, in a private room.

The sand-beige walls are covered in red tinsel and tiny white string lights. There's a massive Christmas tree in the corner, adorned with white and gold ornaments.

And everyone is here, at one long table.

It's overwhelming how packed the room feels. With friends. With family. With love.

Dad gets up first. Thanksgiving was only a month ago, but he already looks much stronger. There's more color in his face. He's put on some weight. His clothes fit better.

He looks healthy. Tired, but healthy.

There's some awkwardness as he moves toward me. It's going to be a long time before this scar fades. Right now, I'm not worried about his recovery or how lying for him, for years, hurt me.

Right now, I'm happy my dad is here for Christmas. And for my wedding.

I throw my arms around him and squeeze tightly. "How was your flight?"

"Long." He steps backward. "You look beautiful, Jessie. I can't believe you're this grown up."

I blink back a tear. I can hardly believe it either. "I'm glad you're here." I wipe my eyes. Thank God for waterproof makeup. I'm going to be bawling on and off for the next twenty-four hours. "We're having a dry reception."

He nods.

"Will you... will you walk me down the aisle?"

His expression fills with a mix of relief and joy. "Of course, Jessie. I never thought you'd ask." He smiles. "I have something for you." He reaches for something on the table, a small wrapped box. "This was your mother's. It's something old and something borrowed." He hands me the box.

I look to Pete. He's at the front of the table. He's leaning against his chair, his eyes fixed on me.

"I thought we said no presents," I say.

"Afraid no one listened." He nods to a stack of presents under the tree.

"Those are for us?" I ask.

He nods.

I look around the room. Everyone is smiling. They're happy for us. And they're waiting for me to open this.

Okay, I can do that. I peel off the wrapping and open the lid. It's a necklace, a beautiful silver chain with a diamond pendant. I can remember Mom wearing it a few times. It was for special occasions.

"Thank you." I wipe a tear from my eyes. I always figured Mom took this with her. I hug Dad again for good measure.

He steps out of the way.

Then Madison takes her turn hugging me. "I should have given you this earlier. You don't need to open it now. But it's something new and something blue." She leans in to whisper in my ear. "It's a blue thong that says *I do* in crystals. You can wear it tomorrow if you want."

She steps back with a wink.

Okay, not opening that in front of my father. Or in front of my groom. Pete shoots me a *let me in on the secret* look.

I shake my head. He's going to enjoy discovering that surprise.

I set the present on the table. "Thanks, Maddie." I better not linger on thoughts of him tearing off my dress and ripping off my bridal panties. I have an entire night to get through.

Tom and Willow take their turn. He's back to his usual bouncy, mayhem-causing self.

He hugs me then nudges Pete. The brothers hug. It's the usual guy, *we don't want to get too close* hug.

Willow hugs me. "I'm glad to see you two happy." She steps back and turns to Tom. "Can I?"

"Go for it, kid."

She pulls an envelope from her purse and hands it to me. "It's a helicopter tour. It's *Jurassic Park*-themed. We went on it, and it's amazing."

Tom shoots Pete a knowing look. "If you can manage to drag yourself out of bed and into your clothes."

Pete chuckles. "Can't make any promises."

"It's perfect. Thank you," I say.

Willow smiles. She looks to Tom. "I told you they'd like it."

"Twenty bucks says they don't make it," Tom says.

"Deal." She shakes his hand then they're back in their seats.

Meg and Miles step up next. They take their turns giving me and Pete hugs.

Then Meg hands me a small, wrapped box. "Wait until the honeymoon to open this." She leans in to whisper. "It's a couple's vibrator."

"What was that, Princess?" Miles cocks a brow.

She nudges him. "He's full of shit. He picked it out. Actually, he picked out one for us, and it's very..." She clears her throat, blushing as she smiles. "You'll like it."

"Only like?" Miles teases.

"You'll like it a lot," Meg corrects. She squeezes me again. "Hate to see Tom win any bet, but there's no shame in staying in bed all week." She, too, winks on her way back to her seat.

Next up are Kara and Drew. When they dropped the *we're pregnant* news, they looked more worried than happy. Right now, they're beaming.

She pulls something from her purse. Tickets—five of them. "Hope you're up for a fun night." She brandishes the tickets—they're for the hotel's male strip revue, *The Thunder from Down Under*.

I look back to my groom. "You had something to do with this?"

He's grinning from ear to ear. "We missed Chippendale's. Figured you'd prefer doing something with the girls."

I have girls. I really do have girls. Willow, Meg, Kara, and Madison are here for me. They're happy for us.

They're my friends. My family.

Shit, I'm crying again.

I've never felt this loved or accepted.

I hug Kara again. "Thank you."

She laughs. "Don't thank me until you see the tiara."

"And the sash!" Meg chimes in.

God help me.

ॐ

DINNER IS FULL OF LOVE, CONGRATULATIONS, AND GOOD food. We don't leave until the last possible moment.

The girls turn me into a properly mortified bride-to-be quickly.

The sash isn't bad. It's a white piece of satin with the word, *Bride*, in silver letters.

But the tiara.

Oh lord, the tiara. It's quite the novelty item. Usually, a

421

tiara has gems at each point. This one has plastic penises at each point.

Every time I catch my reflection, I burst into a fit of laughter. And a few tears.

By the time we're at the venue, I've laughed so much my stomach is aching.

It's a small theater, and our table is right in front. I have primo seats to watch a bunch of Australian hunks strip.

What a life.

The girls take turns taking selfies with me as the venue fills. Slowly, the lights go from bright to dim.

A cocktail waitress stops by to take our orders and drop off waters.

Meg and Willow pass on alcohol.

Madison orders some special drink with a ridiculous name for herself. She orders another for me. "It's your bachelorette party. You must."

"Okay." She has a point. "But just one."

Kara orders a club soda. She looks at me. "How are Drew and I the last to get married?"

Meg laughs. "Drew would marry you in a heartbeat."

Kara nods. "I know. But we have our date in June. I'll be nearly eight months pregnant, but fuck it—that's life."

"You can have a honeymoon, babymoon combination," Willow says.

"A babymoon?" Madison asks.

"You go away before the baby. I'm not sure it ever caught on the way honeymoons did." She turns to Meg. "When do you and Miles leave?"

"About an hour after the wedding." Meg shoots me an apologetic look. "We might miss the last dance."

"We might miss the last dance." I laugh. "I'm not sure how much reception I'll be able to take before I drag my groom to our hotel room."

Kara laughs. "You look like such a nice girl, Jess, but you're just as much of a pervert as he is."

"And you aren't?" I ask.

She nods. "True."

"We're all sex freaks," Meg says. "But it's not our fault. Those Sinful men would turn any reasonable woman into a pervert. Sorry, Madison."

Madison laughs. "It's okay. I'm not jealous."

"Not at all?" Meg asks.

"Maybe a little," Madison admits. "They're all fucking hot."

"I'll drink to that." Kara lifts her water glass.

We take turns toasting our waters until the waitress drops off cocktails.

Damn, that's sugary. And full of booze. It's some mix of tequila, lime, passion fruit, and grenadine.

The lights dim. For a moment, the room is full of shrieks and screams—it's quite reminiscent of the moment in a Sinful Serenade show when Miles or Tom strips—then it's silent.

The stage lights turn on. The curtain pulls open. Half a dozen tall, built men step onto stage wearing loose pants, sneakers, and fedoras. They thrust to an 80s rock song.

It's ridiculous and hilarious.

A few more sips, and it's really, really hilarious. At the end of the song, the men pull off their snap pants to reveal tight black briefs.

They're good looking, sure, but none of them have anything on Pete.

I really would prefer a striptease from him.

But a bachelorette party with my friends laughing beside me- that's good too.

I relax and let the excitement of the night wash over me. The alcohol does help with my *fuck, I'm getting married tomorrow* nerves.

423

By the end of the show, I'm giddy and a little bit drunk.

Everything is a blur of *good lucks* and *I'm happy for yous*. Then Meg and Madison are walking me to my room, making sure I drink plenty of water, and helping me into bed.

I'm getting married tomorrow.

It's really happening.

I fall asleep next to my half-naked groom.

Chapter Thirteen

PETE

The coordinator pops her head into the room. "Five minutes, gentlemen." Her voice is even, calm.

She's good at her fucking job. Wish our stage manager was that calm when he announced five minutes. Damn, if I had to deal with the way Jim screams that we're going to miss curtain, that the crowd will get restless if we don't hurry up and get ready to wait for the crew to finish setting up our gear-

Fuck. I'm about ready to throw up as it is.

Five minutes.

Five minutes till I marry Jess.

My hands are shaking. All of me is shaking. I turn so I won't get any shit from Tom. He's been with me most of the day. It's been a long day.

I've felt every minute of nerves. The God damn things are a snowball, getting bigger and bigger the closer we get to show time.

Tom laughs. It's friendly rather than mocking. He nods to a bottle of whiskey on the back table. "Take a shot. It will relax you."

"No."

There's some quaint name for this room. The groom's quarters. Something to make the space seem grand and impressive when it's really a small, white room, decorated only with a few chairs and a table. Hell, there's not even food in here—not that I want to attempt to eat anything.

I barely managed to eat lunch.

"I've never seen you this nervous." Tom nods to the booze again. "You sure?"

"Yeah." I shrug my shoulders and take a deep breath. That should help with the nerves, but instead, I feel airy. "I want to be lucid for every second of this."

Tom smiles. "Have you always been this cheesy?"

"You tell me."

He nods. "You have. That how you got a nice girl to marry you?"

"Not sure. How did you do it?"

"Fuck if I know. You have any insights? I know you think about shit besides sex when you're sitting around looking pensive."

"Occasionally."

My brother's green eyes are lit up with mischief. But he's nervous too. It's all over his face.

The man is a ball of manic energy. It's good for drums. But it also means he's a ball of nerves before every performance.

Especially the big ones.

Usually, I'm the steady one. Usually, I talk him down.

"Fuck, playing the Grammys was nothing compared to this." Again, I shrug my shoulders. Again, it does nothing to help me feel like I'm touching the ground.

"You were nervous?" Tom asks.

I nod.

"Couldn't tell."

Tom adjusts my tie. He's an inch or two shorter than I am, but right now, there's something tall and imposing about him.

"You're gonna be good at married life." His voice is encouraging.

This is a pep talk.

Or something.

I nod. "Two months and you're an expert?"

"Yep." He positions the knot. "It's all about making her happy and making sure you make decisions together. You already got that figured out."

"Right."

"Fuck, Pete. I think you're actually green. You gonna be okay?"

"You're an asshole."

"I know. But are you?"

He's right. I don't get nervous. I don't know how to deal with it.

"Take a deep breath. Here." He grabs a bottle of water and hands it to me. "I know you don't want to drink it. Do it anyway."

My hands are shaking enough I'm worried I'm going to spill. But fuck it. I down the water bottle in a few gulps.

I take another breath. Another. Another.

That's better.

The coordinator pops her head in. "One minute. You ready?"

Tom looks at me, shaking his head as if to say, *you've got it bad.* He nods to her. "Yeah. We'll be ready."

"How were you as fucking calm as you were before your wedding?"

"Kept thinking about Willow." He smiles. "That made everything else fade away."

Fuck, my brother is a genius.

I close my eyes, take a deep breath, and let my mind fill with thoughts of Jess. My mind goes straight to Jess naked, screaming my name. That helps with my nerves. But fuck, it would be awkward walking down the aisle with a hard-on. I steer my mind to more appropriate places.

The way she curled up next to me last night.

The smile on her face all through dinner.

Her blue eyes lit up with joy as she took in the cactus garden.

I work backward through a thousand other happy memories. Her jumping into my arms as she agreed to marry me. Her falling off then getting back on her surf board at our lesson. And again, at our other lesson. Took her a while to get the hang of it, but she was laughing, having fun.

That's gonna be our life together.

We might fall off, might land messy, might make fucking fools of ourselves—but we're gonna have fun. We're gonna be happy.

"You're up, Tom." The coordinator pulls the door open. She looks to me. "You ready, Pete? Only one more minute."

Tom looks at me like he thinks I might back out.

I nod. "Yeah. Ready."

Tom pats me on the shoulder. "Good luck, man." He steps out of the room.

I can just hear him and Madison exchanging a hello. Their words blur together.

It's just them.

Then me and Mom.

Then Jess and her dad.

Then it's us at the altar. We're really fucking getting married.

Time is that same strange mix of fast and slow. It's similar to being on stage, only more intense, more terrifying, and utterly without a task to occupy my mind.

There's another knock on the door. It's the coordinator. She's saying words, but I'm not hearing them. I can see her mouth moving, but I haven't got a clue what she's saying.

Mom is standing there in a short teal dress. She smiles and offers her arm. "You ready, Peter?"

For some fucking reason, that calms me.

I nod and take her arm.

Mom is close enough she can whisper, "I'm proud of you. She's a lovely young woman. You're good together." She smiles. "Don't fuck it up."

I laugh. Ophelia never changes. "Very encouraging."

She nods.

We turn the corner, and we're at the aisle. There are about a dozen people on each side of the rose-lined aisle. Their chairs are decorated with teal ribbons. There's teal everywhere.

The soft pink light of sunset flows in through the windows.

I manage to take in the smiling faces of my friends and family. Then I'm there. I'm at the altar—it's fucking gorgeous with its mix of teal ribbon and red roses—on the groom's side, next to Tom, opposite Madison.

They're both smiling.

Mom plants a kiss on my cheek. "Good luck, Peter."

She takes her seat.

Everyone stands as the wedding march starts.

Time fucking stops.

My heart is beating loud enough I can hear it pounding between my ears. Not sure how my feet are staying on the ground because I'm light enough to float.

Everything else fades away when Jess rounds the corner. She's with her dad, but I can't see anything but her.

Light bounces off her nearly white hair. Off her ivory dress.

My eyes fix on hers. She's always an angel, but today, she's even more beautiful. Her hair is in some elegant updo. Her makeup brings out her light features. Her blue eyes are shining. Her long earrings catch the light.

And that necklace, the one that belonged to her mom, draws my eye straight to her chest. That dress. Fuck, that dress. It hugs every inch of her from her chest to her knees then it juts with an elegant flare.

Don't know much about clothes, but I do know that dress was made for her.

Fuck is her figure on display. For a second, my thoughts get dirty—gonna have a hell of a time stripping her out of that dress—then they bounce back.

She's a fucking angel.

My angel.

My bride.

I can feel my cheeks at my ears. I've never smiled this wide before. Certainly haven't done it for this long. She has that same wide, goofy smile.

As fucking perfect as that dress is, my eyes fix on hers. All the love in the air passes between us. With my next breath, I exhale my nerves and inhale her excitement.

She's there. At the altar. Her father kisses her on the cheek. Then he's sitting down and she's standing opposite me.

I take her hands.

She's still staring at me. I'm still staring at her. The officiant is saying something to introduce us, but it's not registering.

There's nothing in the world but Jess.

The officiant is saying my name. He's looking at me. "Peter has prepared his own vows."

Dammit, I'm blushing. Mom must have put the man up to calling me by my full name.

Jess squeezes my hands a little tighter. She's enjoying my blushing. Can't say I have cause for complaint.

Hope I memorized this as well as I thought I did.

I focus every ounce of my attention on Jess. "My entire life, there have only been a few things I've wanted. Mostly, I've wanted to make music. Everything else felt peripheral. But then I met you. And you blow everything out of the water. I want you in a way I've never wanted anything. I can't promise you that life will be easy. I know it's going to be hard sometimes. But I can promise that, whatever happens, I'll be there, by your side. I'll hold your hand through every challenge. I'll celebrate every victory with you. I promise I'll make you laugh every day. I promise to show you the world, and to let you show me the world back. Mostly, I promise to live every day to the fullest, with you by my side. Whatever life has in store for us, I know I want you as my partner."

She mouths *I love you*.

I mouth it back.

The officiant turns to her. "Jessica."

This time, she blushes. Nobody calls her Jessica.

She looks to the ground for a moment, then her eyes are on me. "I'm not good at memorizing things, and this dress doesn't have pockets, so this is a little shorter."

The crowd laughs.

She squeezes my hands. "You make me feel like I can take on the world. I want to make you feel like that too. I promise to do whatever I can to make you feel like you're soaring. I promise to hold your hand through thick and thin. Pete, you bring out the best in me. I promise to do everything I can to bring out the best in you too."

She sighs with relief.

The officiant turns to me. "Peter Steele, do you take Jessica James to be your lawfully wedded wife?"

Tom hands the rings to the officiant. Then the officiant is

handing me the ring.

I slide it on Jess's finger. "I do."

He turns to her. "Do you, Jessica James, take Peter Steele to be your lawfully wedded husband?"

She smiles as she slides the ring onto my finger. "I do."

"You may now kiss."

I kiss her.

I kiss her like her lips are oxygen. Because they are. She's my oxygen. She's my everything.

And now, she's my wife.

᪣

AFTER AN HOUR OF PICTURES, WE JOIN THE COCKTAIL AND cake reception. Without booze, the drinks are mostly sugar water, but nobody is complaining.

The coordinator turns on the music and announces our first dance. "This will be Pete and Jess's first dance as husband and wife."

Billy Joel flows through the speakers.

Jess turns bright red. Her eyes meet mine. "You didn't."

"I did."

She laughs as she slides her arms around my waist. It's hard slow dancing to *Piano Man*, but we make it work. It's especially hard telling my hands not to roam over every inch of her—that fucking dress is divine—but I keep things chaste.

The song switches to another Billy Joel hit, *We Didn't Start the Fire*. Then someone is tapping me on the shoulder.

Jess's dad. "Can I cut in, Son?"

"Of course."

Her eyes catch mine. She mouths, *You did this?*

I nod.

She smiles at me. Then she's dancing with her father. I

hang back enough for all the guys to congratulate me. I appreciate the sentiment, but my attention is still on Jess.

My angel.

My wife.

Fuck, it's unreal.

This time, the song switches to *Happy Together* by The Turtles. The officiant rolls out our cake.

Jess claps her hands together. "Already?"

"Why wait?" I slide my arm around her waist. This time, I allow my hand a moment to soak in the curve of her hip. God damn, that dress. I love it so much I'll have to restrain myself from tearing it off.

Everyone gathers around the cake. There's another round of congratulations and everything was beautiful and all that shit about how we're a perfect couple.

It all blurs into white noise. Jess still has all my attention. Her expression is still blissful.

She looks at the cake curiously.

I lean in to whisper, "It's carrot. Because you love vegetables."

She laughs. "I'm not sure cake ever counts as a vegetable."

"Sure it does."

She cuts one side of the slice. I cut the other. Together, we scoop the slide onto a ceramic plate. There are already two forks laid out for us.

We each cut off a bite of cake then we hook our arms and we feed each other the dessert.

It's good cake. Sweet, rich. It tastes like carrot, spice, and cream cheese.

She smiles. "Okay, I like vegetable cake."

"I know, baby."

"You know everything?"

"No." I lean in to whisper, "But I know a hell of a lot about what you like."

Chapter Fourteen

JESS

❧❦❧

The world goes quiet as the elevator doors press together. The silence is bliss. Weddings are exhausting.

"You tired, baby?" Pete slides his arms around my waist. In one swift movement, he pins me to the elevator wall. His lips go to my ear. "You can't sleep until I'm done with you."

Despite my total lack of energy- "I have no plans to sleep tonight."

He chuckles. "You don't think I'll wear you out?"

I have no doubt he'll wear me out, but it's more fun to tease him back.

In my towering heels, I'm almost as tall as he is. I press my cheek against his, reveling in the feel of skin on skin as I bring my lips to his ear.

Damn, what was I about to say? His skin feels good against mine. It's distracting. Right now, all these clothes are in the way of more skin on skin contact. He's in his suit. I'm in my wedding dress.

It still doesn't feel real. I hold my left hand so my ring can catch the light. There's my engagement ring, and under it, my wedding band.

"We're married," I whisper.

"We are." He presses his lips to my neck.

"You're my husband."

He kisses his way to my shoulder. "You're my wife."

"Fuck, this is the best dirty talk I've ever heard. Say something filthy."

"Want to lay my wife on the bed and pry her legs apart, so I can taste her cunt."

"Yes." Damn, I'm on fire. "Do it again."

He sinks his teeth into my skin. Soft at first then harder. "Been waiting to bite you until you were my wife."

"Mmm." I reach for something to steady me as he presses his hips against mine. The dress is a thick fabric. I can't feel any of the angles of his body. Only the weight of it. Only the sharpness of his teeth, the softness of his lips and tongue. "You didn't want to give me a hickey."

"Yeah." He sucks on my neck. "You look like an angel."

"Aren't angels asexual?"

"They have immortal bodies. Doesn't mean they can't fuck like rabbits." He drags his lips up my neck and over my chin. Then he's kissing me hard. "You look fucking divine." He slides his hands over my hips and ass. "Most beautiful bride in the history of the world."

The elevator dings as we arrive at our floor. Thank God. I need us out of these clothes.

I need my husband naked.

I need my husband inside me.

God damn, those words are marvelous.

Pete slides his hand around my waist and leads me down the hallway. We pass a group of college girls decked in cocktail dresses and heels.

They squeal, "Congratulations!" as they pass without a single word about celebrity.

"For once, I get all the attention," I say.

"You can keep it. Just keep that dress. We can go out as newlyweds every week." He gives me a long, slow once-over. "Fuck going out. We'll stay in as newlyweds."

The man is wise.

He stops in front of a corner room. I do a quick scan of the hallway. There are no doors for forty feet in either direction. This must be a hell of a suite.

Pete pulls a key from his pocket and unlocks the door. He slides his hands under my ass. "You want to do this right?"

It takes me a second to catch on. What can I say? I'm tired and all my thoughts are of him taking off that suit. He wants to carry me over the threshold.

A smile curves over my lips. "Let's."

I slide my arms around his upper back. He scoops me, holding me against his chest. It's not the first time he's carried me. Not the second, or the third, or the twelfth, but it's the best time.

I squeal with glee as we cross the threshold. He kicks the door closed then sets me down.

The room is huge.

It's the size of our house—it's always been ours, but now the state of California will recognize it as ours too. The foyer opens to a wide main area with a kitchen, a dining room, a den, and a balcony with a Jacuzzi.

"You like it?" He places his body behind mine and presses his lips to my neck.

"I love it."

"I love you." He drags his fingers over my shoulders and upper back.

His fingers find the corset lacing of my dress. He pulls the bow undone then gets to work unlacing the dress.

CRYSTAL KASWELL

"I love you too." I tilt my neck, offering it to him.

Words are great. Don't get me wrong. Most days, I live for words. When I'm not studying, hanging out with Pete, or getting some kind of exercise, I'm reading.

But right now, I don't want words. I want his lips on my body. I want his hands on my body. I want his body on my body.

I want him. Period.

He drags his lips over my neck until his mouth is hovering over my ear. "I *do* want to feel my wife come on my face."

"Mmm."

"Want to taste your first orgasm as a married woman." He loosens the lacing enough to push my dress to my hips.

I shimmy out of it. I'm desperate to be out of these clothes now, but my husband is patient.

He's seamless about unhooking my longline bra and peeling it off my torso. He's just as slow with the crinoline.

Pete slides his hands under my ass, scoops me into his arms, and holds me against his chest.

He carries me to the couch and lays me flat on my back. I'm in nothing but my heels and my thong, and he's still wearing all those clothes.

His eyes pass over me slowly. Then he's undoing his tie and tossing it aside. Then the jacket. The shoes.

He drops to his knees. His fingers trail over my ankle. He unbuckles my shoe and pulls it off my foot. Then he moves to my left foot and does the same.

Pete takes his time dragging his fingers up my legs. Those hands... damn. I'm on fire. Every brush of his skin against mine makes me needier, hungrier.

He traces the outline of my thong until he gets to the crystals that spell *I do*. "Jess." He looks up at me. "Fuck, that's perfect. Too bad I have to destroy it." He leans down to press his lips to my hip.

438

Then he's got the side of my thong between his teeth. I laugh and squeal as he pulls the panties all the way to my feet.

He tosses the underwear aside.

"Take off more clothes," I breathe.

"Which ones?" He raises a brow.

"All of them."

He smiles. "Anything for my wife."

Fuck, I love the way it sounds on those luscious lips of his.

The man remains a tease. He takes his time undoing the buttons of his shirt and sliding it off his shoulders. Then his hands are on the buckle of his belt. He undoes it, tosses the leather thing aside, and steps out of his slacks.

My husband is wearing only black boxers and black dress socks. He motions to the socks and raises a brow.

I laugh. "Very sexy."

He sits on the couch, next to my feet, and pulls off his socks. "Been thinking about getting you out of that dress all night." His hand curls around my ankle. He drags it up to my knee then pushes my knee off the edge of the couch. "Been thinking about tasting you all fucking night."

He presses his lips to the inside of my knee. Then he's dragging his lips up my thigh. He moves faster than usual, groaning against my skin, digging his fingers into my flesh.

Then he's there, his mouth on me. Damn, that feels good. I let one leg hang off the couch. I drape the other over his shoulder.

I haven't got a hint of patience today. I need to come. I need to come on my husband's face.

God damn, it's so romantic.

I rock my hips to match his movements. He groans with appreciation as his hands go to my ass. He holds me, guides me, licks every fucking inch of me.

Pleasure pushes me toward an orgasm. The man is fucking amazing with his mouth. And he's my husband.

That makes it better.

It makes it so much better.

He licks me up and down again and again. He does it until I'm close enough I'm dizzy.

"Please, Pete." I dig one hand into his hair. "Make me come."

His mouth closes around my clit. He sucks softly. Then harder. Harder. Harder.

Fuck.

The intensity of it has me breathless.

He sucks harder.

I tug at his hair. I scream his name again and again, my sex pulsing as I come.

He presses his lips to my thigh, giving me a quick break, then his mouth is on me again.

His tongue flicks against my clit. The sensation is softer, more gentle. I stay at the edge. I stay on the brink of another orgasm. I stay heavy with pleasure.

Then he licks me again, and I'm there.

"Fuck, Pete." I tug at his hair, holding his lips against me as I rock my hips. The orgasm is fast and intense. My sex pulses so hard the world goes white. Every part of me feels good. Feels free. "Fuck me. Please. I need you inside me."

I toss my glasses on the coffee table.

He pushes himself up and pushes his boxers to his knees. Damn, my husband is naked on the couch. That's quite an inviting sight.

I wrap my hand around his cock. He shudders with pleasure. His lips part with a groan. I need him inside me. But first I need him at my mercy.

I bring my lips to his cock. He groans as I take him into my mouth. He tastes good. I love the feel of him in my mouth. I love the way his eyes go hazy with need.

He plays with my nipples as I work. Each flick of his fingers sends another pang of pleasure to my core.

It spurs me on. I suck on him until his hips are lifting.

Fuck, I can't take it anymore. I need him inside me.

I push myself up. My hands go to his shoulders as I straddle him.

He presses one palm between my shoulder blades, pulling my body into his.

His mouth closes around my nipple. He teases me with his tongue. Fast flicks, slow flicks, soft sucking, hard sucking. By the time he moves on to the other nipple, I'm panting.

"I want your cock inside me," I groan.

He guides my hips, bringing my body onto his. His cock brushes against my sex.

He looks up at me with those dark eyes. The intensity of his expression takes my breath away.

I need him in a way I've never needed anyone.

His eyes stay locked on mine as he slides inside me. Every second of it is ecstasy.

I'm having sex with my husband.

I need to kiss my husband. I lean in to press my lips to his. He kisses back.

We stay pressed together, breaking the kiss only to groan or pant. He guides me over him, so I take him with deep, slow movements.

I focus on his breath, his groans, the way his shoulders shake, the way his fingers dig into my hips, the way his wedding ring feels against my skin—smooth and hard.

He slides one hand up my side. It rests at the top of my neck, cupping the back of my head.

His dark eyes get intense. His voice is low, deep. "Come with me, baby."

"Rub me."

He brings his other hand to my clit and rubs me.

Damn. A few stokes and I'm at the edge. The tension inside me is tight enough I can barely breathe. Still, I inhale deeply.

I hold his gaze. His eyes are heavy with lust. His lips are parting with a sigh.

He's almost there.

I fall over the edge first. The next flick of his fingers sends me tumbling into an orgasm.

"Fuck, Pete." I rock my hips against his, reveling in the pleasure spreading to my limbs. I can feel my sex pulsing around him, pulling him deeper.

Then he's there too.

"Jess," he groans.

He tugs at my hair, pulling most of my updo undone. His eyes stay glued to mine. The intimacy of it is dizzying. I can see everything in his soul. He can see everything in mine.

When I'm spent, I collapse on top of him.

I hold him close until my breath steadies. I can hear his heartbeat, his inhales and exhales.

He brings his lips to my ear. "My vows were going to end with, *I promise to make you come every day*, but I didn't want to embarrass you in front of your dad."

"You should have kept it in there." I take his hand and trace his wedding band. We're really married. I'm really part of the family.

"Yeah?"

I nod. "Your mom-"

"She's your mom too now."

I smile. "Ophelia would have loved it. And God knows, Miles would have loved it. Drew too. I think he'd appreciate the, uh-"

"The determination?" he offers.

"Yeah."

"What about Tom?"

"I think he's jealous."

Pete raises a brow. "Tom's never been jealous of anyone."

"He is. But I'm sure he feels the same, ahem, drive to satisfy Willow." I lean into his chest. "When I first met your friends, I thought they were only being nice because I was your girlfriend. But it's not like that. They were welcoming me into the family. All of you, all eight of us, we're a family. The love and support I feel from everyone is overwhelming."

He presses his lips to mine. "Whatever happens with Sinful Serenade, the eight of us will always be a family."

I nod. "I know you'll move on to other things one day. But right now, I'm glad the band is going strong. I'm glad you get to spend so much time with your family. Even if it means you're away half the year."

His dark eyes fill with affection. "Plus, you want more phone sex."

I laugh. "It's not Sinful Serenade unless *someone* is having loud sex."

Notes On Sinful Serenade

Thank you so much for joining me and the Sinful Family on this amazing, five-book journey. It's been a hell of a ride. When I started writing *Sing Your Heart Out*, I had no idea that I'd end up writing five books about Sinful Serenade.

This series is very personal to me--it's filled with loving jabs at Orange County (my hometown), Los Angeles, and KROQ, it's very much inspired by my love of music and lyrics and the way they convince us we're human, and it's full of the kinds of characters and stories I've always wanted to write. I'm thrilled the series has connected with so many readers. I hope to supply you with captivating tales of tattooed rock stars and the strong women who capture their hearts for many years to come :)

Please do stay in touch by signing up for the Crystal Kaswell mailing list. You'll get exclusive alternate POV scenes from all four Sinful Serenade novels! You'll also get exclusive teasers and news on new releases and sales.

Want to talk books? Awesome! I love hearing from my readers. Join my Facebook Fan Group here or contact me through Facebook or Twitter.

Sinful Ever After is the last book planned in the *Sinful Serenade* series. Don't dismay! The Sinful Serenade guys will also be appearing in the spin off series, *Dangerous Noise*. The first book, featuring guitarist Ethan and his heroine Violet, *Dangerous Kiss*, is available now.

Sinful Serenade *Sing Your Heart Out* - Miles *Strum Your Heart Out* - Drew *Rock Your Heart Out* - Tom *Play Your Heart Out* - Pete *Sinful Ever After*

Dangerous Kiss Teaser

ETHAN

***

Get Dangerous Kiss Now

The woman across the bar is staring at me with lust in her eyes. Is that *oh God, he's hot* or *damn, this is my chance to fuck a famous guy?*

No way to tell from here.

I shoot her a *maybe you can fuck me* look.

She sighs with pleasure. Her tongue slides over her lips.

She's objectively hot. Tight dress. Big tits. Dark hair in carefully messy waves. Violet always wore her hair like that, only hers was that gorgeous shade of strawberry blond.

What the fuck? Violet's not getting space in my brain. Not tonight.

Nothing is knocking me out tonight. Not even that nagging feeling in my stomach, reminding me that I always feel emptier after.

That I miss how intimate sex felt with Violet.

Coming to our old hangout spot was a mistake. But I'm here now. I'm not gonna wallow. Either I take this woman around back and spend half an hour making sure we both

447

enjoy ourselves or I go home and practice the songs I need to master before our show in San Francisco.

I run my hand through my dark hair—that always works —and shoot the woman another smile.

She looks me up and down, licking her lips as her gaze settles on my crotch. She's practically screaming *I'd like to suck you off, anyplace that works for you.*

At this point, I know the drill backwards and forwards.

She moves closer. Her expression gets nervous. Too nervous for *I've never picked up a guy before,* especially given her age. Nothing wrong with an older woman—she looks about thirty—but they don't usually get nervous picking up guys.

Fifty bucks says she's about to ask if I'm really Ethan Strong.

A hundred bucks says she follows up with something about how she'd never screw a stranger, but she feels like she already knows me.

Hell, a thousand bucks says she mentions something about my skill with my hands.

It's true—I am fucking fantastic with my hands.

She shimmies her hips as she moves closer. Her eyes find mine. "I hate to ask, but are you really Ethan Strong?"

Damn. So much for a night of anonymous sex. I'm about to become the story she tells all her friends.

I smile my megawatt smile, the one I use to win over the crowd. "That's me. What's your name, sweetheart?"

"Natasha." She laughs. "You're so funny in interviews. Do you get that all the time?"

Yes. I smile back at her. "Not as often as I'd like."

"I normally don't do this kind of thing but I feel like I can trust you." She squeezes my bicep over my leather jacket. "Oh listen to me, I forgot to start with the best part. You're so good in Dangerous Noise. Your hands must be talented."

"You can be the judge of that, sweetheart." I try to hold

my smile, but it's getting difficult. This is such bullshit. She must realize it too.

There. I manage to smile wider. If I'm going for this, I have to hold up my end of the *rock star fucks groupie* bargain.

She gets her fantasy. I get a few minutes out of my head. We both come. Yeah, I'm using her, but she's using me too.

It's win/win.

Usually.

Right now, I'm having a hard time convincing my body to get in gear. This whole place screams of Violet. And the contrast between the way Violet stared at me—she saw every fucking inch of me—and the way this woman is looking at me, like I have *famous guy* tattooed on my forehead, is underlining how much this is bullshit.

I have to move closer. I have to slide my hands to her ass and whisper in her ear *I shouldn't do this, sweetheart*—to be honest, I've already forgotten her name—*but there's something special about you.*

That's my usual move.

I shrug my shoulders to shake off my funk. It's been almost two years since Violet left. Doesn't matter that no one compares to her. I'm not looking for a new girlfriend. I'm not looking to fall in love.

I'm not interested in love. That's more bullshit.

"This bar is getting crowded, huh?" she asks. "How about we go back to your place?"

Uh-uh. Nobody comes back to my place. But that doesn't mean I'm gonna leave her wanting. I turn on the charm. "My sister's in town. How about we go back to your place. Or-" I slide my arm around her waist "—we could go around back."

"Okay." She grabs at my shoulders.

"I like your dress, sweetheart." I play with the spaghetti strap going over her shoulder. This is happening. And it's gonna feel good. Period. Violet doesn't enter into the equation. "Have to apologize in advance for how I'm going to destroy it."

She lets out a needy sigh.

I lead her through the side door. No sense in wasting time. I need to stop thinking.

I pin her to the wall.

She rises to her tiptoes to kiss me. I turn so she gets my cheek. From the sound of her whine, it's not what she wants, but that's too bad.

Her lips go to my neck.

I close my eyes.

Need to get into this. But my head keeps filling with thoughts of Violet—of her soft, red lips sucking on my neck as she climbs on top of me.

My cock springs to attention.

Uh-uh. I may be a manwhore, but I'm not tacky enough to think about my ex when I'm fucking a stranger.

I pull back to take a long look at this woman. Whatever her name is.

Her tongue slides over her lips. She wants me. Badly. Usually, that's enough.

But right now...

Damn, what the hell is wrong with me? I close my eyes and force my thoughts out of my brain.

She tugs at my t-shirt and runs her fingers over my chest.

There. Pleasure starts pushing everything else away.

I can do this.

Her hand goes to my jeans. She undoes my belt. Pulls down my zipper.

Then she's jumping back, hiding behind me. The side door is swinging open. Someone is stepping into the alley.

Better call this now. Shit's not happening with her. I should go home and practice those new songs. I should wait until I'm someplace that doesn't remind me of my ex to pick up a one-night stand.

I rebutton my pants and fasten my belt.

There's a woman in front of the half-open side door. She's on her knees, pressing her hand over her mouth.

Poor girl doesn't know her limits. It's been a long time since I drank enough to throw up but I don't remember it fondly.

She's a champ. She coughs but she doesn't gag. It takes a minute, but she manages to push herself up and brush off her dirty knees.

No-

I rub my eyes. There's no way in hell that's her.

I must be seeing things.

Violet blinks back at me. "Ethan?"

Fuck, that's her voice. I'd know it anywhere. Her hair is different—it's cut short, a severe bob with neat bangs—but those green eyes give her away.

"Vi?" I ask.

Her eyes go wide. They're more red than green at the moment. She's been crying. Or trying not to cry. Violet never was the type to cry in front of other people.

She grabs for the door but it's already shut.

"Fuck." She takes a step backwards.

Her makeup is the same—heavy enough to scream *leave me alone,* light enough to show off the adorable freckles on her cheeks and nose.

The woman paws at my arm. "Ethan." She says my name like we're old lovers, not strangers. "Do you know her?"

I swallow hard. Yeah. I know her. I know every inch of her.

Violet's eyes are as glassy as they are miserable. She's past buzzed and well into drunk.

Of course she's drunk. It was two years ago that her

brother... That was the day her heart broke, the day she locked me out. Took a few months to make it official, but it was two years ago I lost her.

Two years ago exactly.

I turn back to the woman. "Sorry, sweetheart, I'll have to take a rain check. I'll see you around."

She pouts.

Violet takes another step backwards. Then she turns and hightails it out of the alley.

There's nowhere for her to run. The parking lot is around the corner. She's far too drunk to drive.

I run after her. Even in her heels, she's fast. I have to sprint to catch her.

Damn, those heels do things to her already long legs. Her crimson and black dress is tight around her curves.

Every fucking inch of my body wakes up at the thought of pinning her to the wall. Of her lips on my skin. Of her hands on my hips.

It's not like with the groupie. It's not like with any other woman.

Fuck knows I've tried finding another woman who feels like Violet. There's no one.

I grab her wrist. She stumbles, so I pull her body against mine and hold her steady.

My voice is dripping with frustration. "Vi, where the hell are you going?" No matter how badly she hurt me, I'm not letting her hurt herself.

"Not planning on watching you screw a... I guess she's a 'groupie' now that you're a rock star and not a guy playing at Chain Reaction."

"You upset about me being a rock star now?"

"Don't really care what you do, Ethan. Fuck as many *sweethearts* as you want. I hope you enjoy it."

"I do."

"Good. You have something to say to me or you here to brag?"

"You're drunk."

"I'm aware of that." She pulls her arms free and spins on her heels.

"I'm not letting you drive anywhere."

Her eyes find mine. "I haven't heard a word from you in almost two years. You don't get a say in what I do or don't do."

"You planning on driving drunk?"

She folds her arms, unwilling to admit I'm right.

"Didn't think so."

"Okay. You win. I'm calling a cab. You've done your civic duty and warned the inebriated woman she shouldn't drive drunk. Public sex aside, you're an upstanding citizen." She digs her cell phone from her purse.

"I'm not leaving you alone," I say. "Not with that hurt look on your face."

"Maybe I'm hurt because I'm not over you breaking my heart."

What the hell? She's the one who left. She got on a plane and moved three thousand miles away. But we both know that's not why she's hurt. Not right now. "I'm sorry about Asher."

"Thank you." Her eyes fill with pain. She opens her mouth to speak then she shuts it and shakes her head. "I thought you were on tour."

"You follow Dangerous Noise?"

"I hear things."

"We're on a break. Tour starts up in two days." I take a step closer. I let my fingers brush against her wrists. It feels impossible but this really is Violet.

She pulls her arms around her chest and rubs her bare arms.

"Here." I slide my leather jacket off my shoulders and offer it to her.

She shakes her head.

"We can stand here arguing all night. I'm not letting you drive anywhere and I'm not leaving you alone. Not today."

She blinks and a tear catches on her lashes. Despite the *I hate you, Ethan* stare, she takes my jacket.

"I thought you were in school," I say.

"It's spring break."

She looks small in my leather jacket, but she's not small. She's three or four inches shorter than I am. In her heels, Violet is eye to eye with me.

Damn those long legs of hers...

My cock begs me to take over. She's got that look in her eyes. That *please fuck me out of my misery* look.

Her eyes go to the ground. "Thanks for the jacket. I'll drop it off tomorrow. You staying at your parents' place?"

"Yeah. With Piper."

"I'm going to call a cab." She tugs at her short dress but it does nothing to cover her long legs.

Damn, it's getting hard saying no to the look in her eyes. *Come home with me, Vi. I'll wipe every bit of your pain away. I'll make you forget everything but your body for the rest of the night.*

That shit can't happen.

I shake my head. "I'll drive you home."

"You're sober?"

"Had one drink."

"Too busy sucking face to down a few shots?"

"Don't do shots anymore." Or suck face for that matter.

Her eyes flares with anger. She takes another step back-wards. "Go back to your groupie, Ethan. I can get around on my own."

Not like this, she can't. I grab her wrist a little harder than I should. But I'm not letting her leave drunk. "You have two choices. You can stand around with me until you're sober enough I believe you're gonna be okay or you can come with me."

She looks at me like she's looking into my soul. "I don't want to go home."

"Then you can come back to my place. Piper will be jazzed to see you." My little sister adores Violet. I can't remember the last time she went a day without reminding me I made a mistake letting her walk away.

Violet stares at me for a long time. Finally, she nods. "Fine. But I'm not going to make polite conversation."

"How is that different than how things used to be?"

Her lips curl into the world's tiniest smile. It only stays for a moment but it's still the best thing I've felt since that last time I stepped on stage.

Get Dangerous Kiss Now

Acknowledgments

Athena Wright, yes, you are the first person I am naming in my acknowledgements! Not only are you the best critique partner of all time, you're also the best chat buddy ever. I can't believe my luck that I have a good friend who laughs at my jokes, appreciates my song-title puns, and takes debates about whether or not she'd sleep with famous musicians seriously. Thank you so much for your notes on *Sinful Ever After* (and on *Play Your Heart Out*). Now get back to writing! I need Moriss's book already!

Kevin, thank you not only for your love and support, but also for picking up my slack when I get lost in book-land. You will always be the Hawkeye to my Mustang.

Thanks to: Skyla at Indigo Chick Designs, for her fantastic cover designs, my editor Tonya, Giselle at Xpresso for organizing many Sinful Serenade blog tours, my beta reading team for their amazing insights and encouragements, my ARC team for their many timely and glowing reviews, and to all the writer friends who encourage me, laugh with me, cry with me, especially Kathryn and Eitan.

A special thanks to Jesse Lacey and Pete Wentz, for

convincing my 17 year old self that someone out there under-stood, and for stoking the fires of my fixation on broken boys with tattoos and guitars, bass or otherwise.

Of course, my biggest thanks goes to the readers! Thank you for joining me on this five-book Sinful Serenade journey. I hope you'll stick with me for the spin-off series, Dangerous Noise. Book one, *Dangerous Kiss*, is available now.

This is a work of fiction. Similarities to real people, places, or events are entirely coincidental.

Also by Crystal Kaswell

Sinful Serenade
Sing Your Heart Out - Miles
Strum Your Heart Out - Drew
Rock Your Heart Out - Tom
Play Your Heart Out - Pete
Sinful Ever After – series sequel

Dangerous Noise
Dangerous Kiss - Ethan
Dangerous Crush – Kit
Dangerous Rock – Joel
Dangerous Fling – Mal
Dangerous Encore - series sequel

Inked Hearts
Tempting - Brendon
Playing - Walker
Pretend You're Mine - Ryan
Hating You, Loving You - Dean - coming summer 2018
Breaking the Rules - Hunter - coming fall 2018

88001565R00287

Made in the USA
San Bernardino, CA
09 September 2018